John Crowne

The Dramatic Works of John Crowne

Volume the Third

John Crowne

The Dramatic Works of John Crowne
Volume the Third

ISBN/EAN: 9783337268190

Printed in Europe, USA, Canada, Australia, Japan

Cover: Foto ©Andreas Hilbeck / pixelio.de

More available books at **www.hansebooks.com**

THE DRAMATIC
WORKS OF JOHN CROWNE.

WITH PREFATORY MEMOIR AND NOTES.

VOLUME THE THIRD.

MDCCCLXXIV.

EDINBURGH: WILLIAM PATERSON.
LONDON: H. SOTHERAN & CO.

CONTENTS.

THE COUNTRY WIT.

The Countrey Wit. A Comedy, acted at the Duke's Theatre. Written by Mr Crown. London, Printed for Thomas Chapman, at the Golden-Key, near Charing-Cross, 1693. 4to.

" This Play," say the Editors of the Biographia Dramatica, " contains a good deal of low humour, and was a
great favourite with King Charles II."

Langbaine observes, " this Comedy is of that kind
which the French call *Basse Comedie*, or Low Comedy,
one degree removed from Farce." Having been approved of by his Majesty, it was equally approved of by
the public, although a faction had arrayed itself to oppose its success. A large portion of the plot as well as
of the language, has been taken from Molière's Comedy,
" Le Sicilien ; ou L'amour peintre." Sir Richard Steele
has drawn from the same source for incidents and scenes
in his " Tender Husband." A translation of Molière's
Comedy not intended for the stage, by J. Ozell, appeared
in 1714 under the title of " The Sicilian ; or, Love makes
a Painter." It consists of twenty scenes, not divided into
acts ; and the general scene is in Italy.

Oldys in his MS. notes to Langbaine, in the British
Museum, queries as to Sir Mannerly : " Is not this Beau
Hewitt?—Sir George, in 1689, was made by William III.
an Irish Peer, as Baron of Jamestown in the County
of Longford, and Viscount Gowran, in the County of
Kilkenny, in Ireland. He was son of Sir Thomas Hewitt,
of Pishionbury in Hertfordshire, Baronet," and died in
the year in which he was ennobled.

Geneste remarks :—" On the whole it is a good play
—it was printed without the performers' names—Nokes
and Underhill probably acted Sir Mannerly and his
man Booby." This was in 1675, when the play was
first produced. When performed on 6th February
1708, at Drury Lane, the cast was as follows :—
Ramble, Booth ; Sir Mannerly Shallow, Pack ; Sir
Thomas Rash, Norris ; Merry, Mills ; Lord Drybone,
Fairbank ; Booby, Bullock ; Porter, Johnson ; Betty
Frisque, Mrs Birknell ; Lady Faddle, Mrs Powell ; Isabella, Mrs Saunders ; Christina, Mrs Bradshaw ; Porter's
Wife, Mrs Willis."

Nokes was a famous comedian, and from his perform-
ances on the stage acquired, and left to a nephew at his
death, an estate of £400 a-year, at Totteridge near Bar-
net. He was originally a toyman in Cornhill. Upon his
commencing Player, King Charles II. first discovered his
merit while he was acting the Duke of Norfolk in Henry
VIII. In compliment to him, Dryden wrote the character of Gomez in the Spanish Fryar. Cibber thus de-
scribes him : " This celebrated comedian was of the
middle size, his voice clear and audible, his natural
countenance grave and sober; but the moment he spoke,
the settled seriousness of his features was utterly discharged, and a dry, drolling, or laughing levity took
such full possession of him, that I can only refer the idea
of him to your imagination. In some of his low characters, that became it, he had a shuffling shamble in his
gait [such as is in these times indulged in by clowns, and
by Mr Sothern as Lord Dundreary] with so contented
an ignorance in his aspect, and an awkward absurdity in
his gesture, that, had you not known him, you could not
have believed that naturally he could have a grain of
common sense." Dryden, in his tenth epistle addressed
" to Mr Southerne, on his comedy called the Wives' Excuse, acted in 1692," insinuates that the audience had
been so accustomed to the presence of this facetious
actor, that they could not tolerate a play where his low
humour was excluded :—

> "The hearers may for want of Nokes repine ;
> But rest secure, the readers will be thine."

Underhill, a low comedian, was before the public
for a long period. The Tatler, on the occasion of
"the benefit of Cave Underhill, the old comedian," at
Drury Lane, on 3d June 1709, when he was announced
for the character of the first gravedigger in Hamlet, in
which he had formerly gained great notoriety, thus
recommends him to the favour of the town,—" I wish
to recommend to my friends honest Cave Underhill,
who has been on the stage for three generations; my
father admired him exceedingly when he was a boy—
there is certainly nature excellently represented in his
manner of action, in which he ever avoided the gene-

ral fault in players of doing too much—it must be con-
fessed, he has not the merit of some ingenious persons
now on the stage of adding to his authors ; for the actors
were so dull in the last age, that many of them have
gone out of the world, *without ever having spoken one
word of their own in the theatre.*

"Poor Cave is so mortified that he quibbles, and tells
you that he pretends only to act a part fit for a man
with one foot in the grave—that is, a gravedigger—all
admirers of true comedy, it is hoped, will have the gratitude to be present on the last day of his acting, when, if
he does not happen to please them, he will have it even
then to say, that it was his first offence."—*May* 30.

His last appearance on any stage was at the Green-
wich Theatre, Aug. 26, 1710, for the benefit of Pinketh-
man who leased the theatre for a short summer season.
For further information respecting him, see introduction
to " The Man's the Master," D'avenant's works, vol. v. p.
5, in the present series.

The patron to whom Crowne dedicated his " Country
Wit " was fully qualified to judge of its merits, and his
acceptance of the dedication goes far to prove that a
nobleman so distinguished for his wit and taste must
have held the author in considerable estimation ere he
permitted it to appear under his patronage. " He was,"
says Lord Orford, " the finest gentleman in the voluptu-
ous court of Charles the Second, and in the very gloomy
one of King William. He had as much wit as his first
master, or his cotemporaries Buckingham or Rochester,
without the Royal want of feeling, the Duke's want of
principle, or the Earl's want of thought. The latter
said with astonishment, that he did not know how it was,
but his lordship might do anything, and yet was never
to blame." *

As Earl of Middlesex, his lordship is not generally re-
cognized, and his being the direct male descendant and
representative of the author of Gorboduc, the oldest
classical English tragedy existing, is entirely forgotten.
As he enjoyed the honours of Middlesex only from the

* Lord Orford's Royal and Noble Authors, by Park—London,
1806, vol. iv., p. 13.

4th of April 1675 until the 27th of August 1677, it creates little surprise that the Middlesex peerage was lost sight of, and as the Court of the second Charles was much too frivolous to appreciate the excellences of Gorboduc, which his ancestor,* the author, had caused to be performed before Queen Elizabeth, to her Majesty's great delectation, Crowne, even if aware of the existence of such a drama, might fear that he might displease his patron by referring to it, and thus exposing it to the ridicule of Buckingham and Rochester.

Charles, Earl of Middlesex, was the eldest son of Richard, second Earl of Dorset, whom he succeeded, 27th August 1677, by Lady Frances Cranfield,† eldest daughter of Lionel, first Earl of Middlesex, who was, says Sir Anthony Weldon, " a fellow of so meane a condition, as none but a poore spirited nobility would have endured his perching on that high tree of honour, to the dishonour of the nobility, the disgrace of the gentry, and not long after to his owne dishonour."‡

When George Villiers, Duke of Buckingham, was providing for his female relatives and connections by marriage, Lionel Cranfield, a London merchant, a widower, a person of mean extraction, who, having excellent business habits, and being a man of very good acquirements,

---

* It is asserted that in the composition of this Drama, Thomas Sackville, afterwards Lord Buckhurst, received the assistance of Thomas Norton, who, it is alleged, on very imperfect evidence, wrote the three first acts, and Lord Buckhurst wrote the two last. Warton doubts whether Norton had by any means so great a share in it. It is reprinted in Dodsley's old plays, under its original name of Ferrex and Porrex. It had previously been reprinted in 1736 as Gorboduc. Lord Buckhurst's induction to the "Mirror for Magistrates" has been admired by all genuine lovers of poetry, and was reprinted by Capell in his prolusions in 1759. He was related to Queen Elizabeth through the Boleyn family. He received from her, his Barony of Buckhurst in 1567, and the Garter in 1588. On the accession of James, he was created Earl of Dorset. He died suddenly of apoplexy whilst sitting at the Council Board in 1608.

† The Countess survived, and had, as her second husband, Henry Powle, Esquire, Master of the Rolls. She lived to a good old age, and died on the 20th November 1692.

‡ Secret History of Court of King James the First. Edited by Sir Walter Scott, Bart. Edinburgh: Ballantyne & Co. Edin. 1811, 8vo. p. 452.

was fortunate enough to take as his second wife, Anne, daughter of James Brett, of Houby, in the county of Leicester, by Anne, sister to Mary, Countess of Buckingham, the mother of the Duke his Grace thought so much of him that he made him Master of Requests—next, Master of the Great Wardrobe—and, lastly, Master of the Wards and a Privy Councillor. He was created Lord Cranfield in Bedfordshire, and next year Earl of Middlesex. Having thus ennobled him, he finished by constituting him Lord High Treasurer of England.

The fall of Middlesex was as rapid as his rise. Incurring the ill-will of his patron,—generally hated for his insolence of office, and despised for his low origin by the old nobility, his fall was easily accomplished. He was deprived of all his offices and declared incapable of holding place, or employment in the State. He was imprisoned in the Tower of London during pleasure, and, according to Weldon, fined £20,000,* excluded from parliament, and interdicted to come within the verge of the court.

As a fitting sequel a bill was passed to render his estate liable for the fine and other accounts, and to make restitution to all such, whom he had wronged as should be allowed by the discretion of the house.†

This was a somewhat severe penalty for opposing the great favourite, who, aware that his tenure of power was somewhat precarious, in order to strike terror into his enemies, poured out his vial of wrath upon Middlesex, who had found out how much James now detested the man once so beloved and cherished, and who was only saved from falling by his majesty's opportune death, hastened by the unauthorized acting of Buckingham, which would have led to an enquiry only prevented by the dissolution of parliament, and the misplaced confidence reposed in him by Charles I.

Lord Middlesex saved his honours by the intervention, it is said, of the bishops. It is evident that he preserved the greater part of his fortune. He died in 1645, aged

---

* Banks, in his Dormant and Extinct Peerage, says the sum was £50,000—vol. iii., p. 514.
† Banks, vol. iii. p. 515.

seventy, and, notwithstanding his disgrace, was buried in
Westminster Abbey, where a monument was erected to
his memory.*

There was a pretty general belief that the death of
James was hastened by Buckingham dispensing with
the services of the Royal Physicians, and sending an em-
pirick, who applied "a black plaster," and administered
"a powdir." †

Lord Dorset was born on the 24th of January 1637,
and, being a minor during the great civil war, escaped
being involved in that unhappy contest which de-
luged England with blood. Upon the restoration he
was returned as one of the members for East Grinsted,
being then styled Lord Buckhurst. In the first Dutch
war he volunteered to serve under the Duke of York,
and, on the 3d of June 1665, when the Dutch Admiral
Opdam was blown up, and above thirty vessels captured
or destroyed, on the evening preceding the engagement,
it is said, he composed the celebrated song commencing :—

> "To all ye ladies now at land
>   We men at sea indite,
> But first wou'd have you understand
>   How hard it is to write.
> The Muses now, and Neptune too,
> We must implore to write to you,
>   With a Fa, la, la, la, la!" &c.

It has been questioned, on the authority of the Earl of
Orrery, whether these verses were actually composed on
the evening stated. Prior had the means of ascertaining
the fact just as well as the Irish Earl, and we may rest
assured when he stated it to be so, in the dedication of

* See Secret History, vol. i., p. 49.

† The Earl was twice married—by his first wife, Elizabeth
Shepherd, daughter of a London tradesman, he had three
daughters, two of whom married noblemen, and the youngest,
Mary, died unmarried. By his second wife, he had four sons,
two of whom successively succeeded to his honours and estates,
the last, Earl Lionel, died in 1674, sine prole, and was interred
in Westminster Abbey beside his father. The Peerage became
extinct, but was revived in the person of his nephew, Charles
Sackville in 1675, the eldest son of Lady Frances, and continued
in his male descendants, who failed about the middle of the present century.

his poems to Lord Dorset's son Lionel, afterwards the first Duke, that he was quite satisfied it was true. Orrery was not a particularly impartial evidence, as he had rather a taste for detraction.

It is but fair to quote the following passage from the diary of Pepys, 2d February 1665-6,—"To my Lord Brounker's, by appointment in the Piazza in Covent Garden, where I occasioned much mirth with a ballet I brought with me, made by the sailors at sea to their ladies in town, saying Sir W. Penn, Sir G. Ascue, and Sir J. Lawson made them." Lord Braybrooke, the editor of Pepys, supposes this to have been the song written by Lord Dorset; but that does not follow, for Pepys, who is so minute in his diary, assuredly would have given the true name of the author in his curious record, and the first lines do not correspond with those of the song admitted to be composed by Dorset, as the one is addressed by the seamen to "their ladies in town," and the other to "all ye ladies now at land."

Pepys was a great collector of ballads and penny histories. His collections are carefully preserved in the Library of the Magdalene College, Cambridge, to which he bequeathed them; and, being secretary to the Admiralty, many naval ballads might naturally have come his way. Relishing a joke, he thought upon the ballad falling into his hands, how much Lord Brounker would be amused at his dinner by a song from the sea, written by three of the first Admirals of the Navy, and he was right, for it "occasioned much mirth." As the story would circulate pretty generally, it would probably reach the ears of Buckhurst, and suggest the idea that such a poetical address from the sea, not to the "Ladies in the Town" but to the "Ladies in the Land" might not be unacceptable.

Of his humour Lord Orford has preserved the following instance :—"Lord Craven was a proverb for officious whispers to men in power. On Lord Dorset's promotion, King Charles, having seen Lord Craven pay his usual tribute to him, asked the former what the latter had been saying. The Earl replied gravely, 'Sir, my Lord Craven did me the honour to whisper, but I did not think it good manners to listen.'"

His Lordship and Waller are said, on the same authority, to have assisted the matchless Orinda in her translation of Corneille's "Pompey." His poems, chiefly of a fugitive nature, will be found in the same volume with those of the Earls of Roscommon and Rochester, printed at the commencement of last century.* He also, with Henry Saville, ridiculed Sir Robert Howard's Duel of the Stags in a satire called the Duel of the Crabs.†

He was twice married, and, by his second wife, Lady Mary Compton, had one son, named Lionel, his successor, seventh Earl and fourth Duke of Dorset. The Earl, declining in health, went to Bath, where he died on the 29th of January 1705-6, and was buried with his ancestors at Witham, on the 17th of February following.

* 8vo, Lond. 1716.
† State Poems, vol. I. p. 201, in which, however, the name of Henry Saville does not appear.

PROLOGUE.

Oh, Sirs, this is a monstrous witty age,
Wit, grown a drug, has quite undone the stage.
The mighty wits now come to a new play,
Only to taste the scraps they flung away.
Poets now treat you at your own expense,
All, but the poets now, abound in sense ;
City and country is with wit o'erflown,
Weeds grow not faster there, than wits in Town :
New wits and poets every day are bred,
Each hour, some budding critique shews his head.
Plays are so common, they are little priz'd,
And to be but a poet, is despis'd.
The saucy tongue much boldness wou'd display,
That durst in spight of all this plenty, say
Poets and critiques too, are very rare,
Yes, sirs, we to our sorrow find they are ;
More to the making of a wit there goes,
Than niggard nature commonly bestows.
A writer at the least, 'tis not a grain,
Only to season, and preserve the brain
From sav'ring of the fool, nor at the best,
To spice discourse with an insipid jest.
Writing, like Roman gloves, should scent a room,
Each thought shou'd have in it a strong perfume ;
But oh, few smell of wit, so very rank,
Nature of late is turn'd a mountebank,
A winter,* or a daffy,† and puts off

* One who requires to come twice over the same ground.
Also, an implement to hang in a grate, and for warming any-
thing on.
† One who speaks not in time, or roughly.

For wit and sense, some foolish chymick stuff.
A quintessence, but not of wit, Heaven knows,
Which she to all most liberally throws.
Noise in the cit, and noise upon the stage,
Who wou'd not think it were a witty age ?
Never more noise and talk of wit was known,
The triflingst wretch himself a judge will own,
And, on his bench of judgement, frowning sit,
And dub the poet which he likes, a wit.
Oh, wou'd these quacking tricks but nature leave,
And not the poor unhappy world deceive
With heat which seems like wit, but is not so,
Then real wit into esteem wou'd grow ;
Men wou'd not foolishly then take in hand,
To judge, or write, but first wou'd understand ;
Then he, who has but little wit, wou'd know it,
And not presume to be a judge, or poet.

TO

THE RIGHT HONOURABLE

CHARLES, EARL OF MIDDLESEX.

One of the gentlemen of His Majesty's bed-chamber.

My Lord,—It is a bold expedition which a writer undertakes, when he sends his forces abroad into the world ; he is to encounter enemies of all kinds ; not only vast populous provinces of effeminate understanding, who often defeat with their numbers ; but, bold, barbarous, hardy, and invincible fools, who will die upon the turf, rather than yield : nay, and his friends too often break their league, and send secret supplies to his enemies. All reputations look on themselves as invaded, and every one pretends to reputation. Fame is a great common, where every cottager thinks he has a right, and will rather suffer it all to lye waste than any part to be enclosed. Every man thinks himself by birth a wit, as every Spaniard thinks himself a gentleman ; he has as good blood in his veins as persons of the greatest dignities, only wants their titles ; that is to say, every man wou'd be a wit, if he had it. Yet as much value as they have for it in themselves, they hate no man more than he who abounds in that, for which they wou'd have themselves esteemed. But the enmity of poor vulgar heads were nothing, if men of the first rank of wit had not feuds among themselves. 'Tis a strange lunacy that possesses 'em : a man that has

the largest habitation in fame will yet think all
his windows darkened, if another soars over him.
Men have not the same phrenzies in other things.
The greatest lover of music in the world does not
think he shares one note less of it for a crowd of
list'ners; what ever quarrels there have been among
trading nations, about ingrossing commerce, none
ever sought to ingross the winds, because no ship
had the less for another having his sails full: and
yet wit-adventurers perpetually contend for the
breath of the multitude, and think themselves be-
calm'd, if any one has a gale. In short, a writer is
look'd upon as an invader of the world; and all
mankind are in arms against him. In such a desperate condition he must implore of some potent
person either his conduct, or at least leave to awe
the world with his name; and I know no greater
name, nor more able to afford me protection, than
your lordship's. It is but pretending your lordship favours this play, and that shall give it safe
conduct through understandings of every degree
and climate; it can pass through no region where
your lordship has not an absolute command. The
traders to the hot Southern climes of wit, find, in
your lordship, the golden coast; vast heaps of that
wit which passes current in the world, and bears
the images of others, are known to be coined out
of your lordship's ore; but nothing can be richer
than that of your own refining. More temperate
heads, which ake under the oppression of that heat,
delight themselves in your lordship's courtesy,
generosity, integrity, honour, and all the more
familiar virtues: no part of mankind but may find
some particular excellence or other in your lordship to please them. The virtues of this age,
methinks, converse with one another, like the wits
of it, in parties and factions; seldom uniting to-

gether; every virtue takes a house by it self, and
there debauches with a thousand vices. How often·
do we see wit inseparably associating with that
rascal, ill nature; and those fops, conceits and
selfishness, and not one virtue in his company?
as often do we find courage blust'ring by it self,
and wit not daring to come near him. Integrity,
friendship, and honesty, are so miserably under
the hatches, one knows not where to find those
poor creatures; they never in any age lived in
much height, they are not born to great fortune,
and seldom acquire one; knavery has the only
Dutch genius to get an estate, but yet they never
were so down as now, they now scarce at all
appear, or, if they do, we find wit not often in their
company. And thus I might discourse should I
go round to all the moral virtues; but they are
not all so unsociable as never to meet, they can
come together when they like the place, and they
are so fond of your lordship's soul, not one of 'em
fails of resorting thither. And, as people use to
dress themselves well when they are to appear in
great assemblies, so those excellent qualities,
which we often find slovenly habited in private
lodgings, by themselves, do now in so much good
company shine in your lordship's breast, in their
richest equipage: That, repairing to your lordship's
protection, I march not so much under the conduct
of one, as of many great men, united in one. But
far be it from me to sacrifice such a hecatomb to
the multitude; no, rather let me offer this, and all
their applause to your lordship; for, after all, that
is my real design. It is true, my lord, I have not
much of it to lay at your feet. The play I present
you cannot boast of extraordinary merit; it is not
of the first kind of plays. A thing may be good in
its kind, and yet an ill thing because the kind is

ill; those who do not like low comedy will not be
pleased with this, because a great part of it consists of comedy, almost sunk into farce; yet, if
they will allow it well in its kind, I shall desire no
. more favour from 'em; any may perceive I never
intended to build high, by the poor foundation I
laid, and yet, as it happened, the building stood
firmer than I expected, and withstood the battery
of a whole party, who did me the honour to profess themselves my enemies, and made me appear
more considerable than ever I thought my self, by
shewing, that no less than a confederacy was
necessary to ruin my reputation. Had they over-
turn'd this they cou'd not have hurt me, since I
had long before parted from it, as a trifle, where I
never intended to repose; but, as it happened, I
had the diversion to see the play stand, and them
choak'd with the dust they made about it: if they
wou'd have done me the favour to have taken me
into their society, I wou'd have join'd with them
in damning a great part of it; for I design'd it for
damnation; but if they had done so, I fear we
shou'd not have agreed in what part: for as if we
were design'd for enmity, with all that I loath'd
they seem'd extremely diverted. All this, I say,
my lord, only to offer your lordship my present
as clean as I can make it, which I take the more
pains about, because I offer it not as a bribe, but
purely a present. The common declared design of
dedication, like the concealed one of devotion, is
in other terms bribery; men do not pray to serve
heaven, but pray that heaven may serve them; so
dedicators, who trouble great men only to gain
their protection, sacrifice not to their patrons, but
sacrifice their patrons to themselves. I declare, I
beg not your lordship's protection, but acceptance
of this play, and then let it perish if it will. Vic-

tims ought to die, nor does it come to your altars without a crown, and one received from a royal hand ; a fortune more glorious than I could expect. I designed it, as any one may see by the low characters only to serve an apprenticeship to the city, but, being honour'd with the King's favour, I thought I ought to treat it with respect, and I cou'd not do it greater honour than to put it in your lordship's service ; and so I discharged my self of a double debt, and paid all under one : the duty I owed to what the king favour'd, and the much greater duty and honour I owe to a person, whom Heaven has favour'd with qualities admir'd by all the world, but by none more than,

My Lord,

Your Lordship's most humble,

And obedient Servant,

John Crown.

●

ACTORS' NAMES.

MEN.

SIR THOMAS RASH, *father to Christina.*

RAMBLE, *a wild young gentleman of the town, in love with Christina.*

MERRY, *his man.*

SIR MANNERLY SHALLOW, *a foolish country knight.*

BOOBY, *a dull country clown, servant to Sir Mannerly.*

LORD DRYBONE, *an old debauched lord, that keeps a wench, and is abused and jilted by her.*

RASH, *a porter.*

WOMEN.

LADY FADDLE, *aunt to Sir Mannerly.*

CHRISTINA, *daughter to Sir Thomas Rash, in love with Ramble.*

BETTY FRISQUE, *a young jilting wench, kept by Lord Drybone.*

SISS, *her maid.*

GOODY RASH, *an herb woman, the porter's wife.*

WINNIFRED RASH, *her daughter.*

ISABELLA, *Christina's maid.*

Constable, Watch, fiddles, servants' attendants.

Scene : THE PALL MALL.—*In the year,* 1675.

THE COUNTRY WIT.

ACT I.

SCENE. SIR THOMAS RASH'S *house.*

Enter SIR THOMAS RASH, CHRISTINA, *and* ISABELLA.

Chris. Marry to-morrow, sir ?

Sir Tho. Ay, to-morrow, sir ! why not to-morrow, sir ? what great affairs have you to do that you cannot marry to-morrow, as well as to-morrow come twelve-month ?

Isab. What a rash giddy old man is this ! he will compel my lady to marry one she never saw, and to a marriage he has not thought on above these ten days. [*Aside.*

Chris. If I must marry, sir, I think marriage is a great affair ; and so great a one, that I ought to consider of it more weeks and months than there are hours betwixt this and to-morrow.

Sir Tho. O, pray do you throw considering-caps aside, they are not for your wear. No considering-cap was ever made fit for a woman's head yet.

Isab. How ? No considering-cap fit a woman's—

Sir Tho. Why, hussey, who bid you prate ?—— I say the marrying, loving, embracing part is yours ; the considering part is mine : I have considered enough of it. [*Turning to Chris.*

Chris. I doubt not, sir, but you have prudently consider'd of it : but whether enough or no, perhaps may be a question : for please to remember, sir, but few days are past since you first

thought of it : and almost the same hour you first
thought of it, you resolv'd of it : and tho' I doubt
not but you consider'd of it as well as possible for
so short a time, yet certainly you did not allow
yourself time enough for so weighty an affair.

Sir Tho. Not time enough ! Why what had I to
consider of that requir'd time? Here's my daughter
Christina, and £5000 portion ; there's Sir Mannerly Shallow, a young baronet, and £2000 a year.
In short, I'll have no more considering. The affair
is concluded, articles are drawn up betwixt the
Lady Faddle and me, by the consent of her
nephew, Sir Mannerly Shallow, and Sir Mannerly
will be in town to-morrow, and to-morrow he shall
marry you before he sleeps, nay, before his boots
are off, nay, before he lights off his horse; he shall
marry you a horse-back but he shall marry you
to-morrow.

Isab. And he shall bed her a horse-back too,
shall he ?

Sir Tho. Why, hussey, will you be interrupting
still ?——Get you out of doors !

Isab. I ha' done, sir.

Sir Tho. I say, get you out of doors !

Chris. Prithee, Isabella, let him alone.

Isab. What flesh and blood can endure to see
such a fool's match ?——By a fool, to a fool, if
reports be true.

Sir Tho. Your flesh and blood, sauce-box,—or
I'll set you out of the room.

Chris. Give o'er, Isabella, when I forbid you.
Well, sir, but suppose Sir Mannerly upon his
arrival should not like me.

Sir Tho. Not like you? he shall like you, or I'l
try it out at law with him : I have it under black
and white, and my black and white shall make
him like your red and white, in spight on's teeth.

No, no, there's no such clause in our articles, there's no such proviso, he's to marry you absolutely, *bona fide*, and with a notwithstanding.

Isab. Marry her with a *bona fide*, and a notwithstanding! what stuff's this? what's his *bona fide?*

Sir Tho. What's that to you, hussey? will you ne'er ha' done? If I lay my cane o'er your *bona fide*, I'll make you repent your prating.

Chris. Have you no respect, Isabella, to my commands? Don't you see that your talking does but enrage him?

Isab. Who can endure to have you thus rashly thrown away on a fool, as all the world says Sir Mannerly is?

Chris. Let me alone with the management of my own affairs.

Well, sir, but supposing fortune should flatter me with inclinations to Sir Mannerly.

Isab. A worthy piece of flattery!

[Sir Tho. looks angrily.

I ha' done.

Chris. If I should be so unfortunate not to have the same inclinations for him, I hope, sir, you will not compel me to marry one I cannot love, and consequently to be the most miserable of women?

Sir Tho. One you cannot love, maid! you shall love him, I'll make you love him. What cannot you love £2000 a year, and a fair mansion house, and all conveniences, as fine as any in all Cumberland?

Chris. No doubt, sir, but I shall like his estate, and his house, and his moveables well enough.

Isab. But the main moveable, the man! there's the question?

Sir Tho. Well, Sauciness! you talk very boldly, pretty box,* of a baronet of £2000 a year, to call

---

* Buxom.

him a moveable :—but I will make her love the main moveable.——

Isab. Ay, there's the thing :—if she will like the main moveable; if the main moveable will please her.

Sir Tho. Well, well, it shall please her ; I'll make it please her.

Isab. Pray, sir, lay aside passion, and let us reason the case a little.

Chris. Isabella, don't you see that you provoke my father ?

Sir Tho. How would you reason ? Come then, have at you. Let her alone, I'll give her free leave to plead what she can. Since she would reason, I will reason with her. Come !

Isab. You will own, sir, that Sir Mannerly Shallow is a country gentleman.

Sir Tho. And so I would have him.

Isab. One that never so much as saw London.

Sir Tho. As I would have him.

Isab. One that never had anything but country breeding.

Sir Tho. As I would have him.

Isab. One that knows nothing but what belongs to dogs and horses ; that never saw a better assembly than what meet at fairs, cockfights, and horse-races.

Sir Tho. Just as I would have him.

Isab. Well then, is it possible for a lady, such a one as my lady, that has never breath'd out of the air of the town :

Sir Tho. And by consequence never in wholesome air.

Isab. Who has always liv'd to the height and gallantry of it ;

Sir Tho. To the height of the foppery of it.

Isab. And conversed with the most refin'd wits of the times ;

Sir Tho. With the most debauch'd rascals of the times.

Isab. Should ever endure a dull country clown, and a melancholy country life?

Sir Tho. Ay, hussey, better than a lewd, fantastical, debauch'd town fop, and a scandalous town-life.

Isab. You are scandaliz'd at debauchery, sir? I will prove the country gentlemen are full as debauch'd as the very lewdest men of the town : Nay, their debaucheries are the more rude and brutish of the two, and are only thought innocent because they are insipid.

Sir Tho. How! more debauch'd than the town rascals? the very rake-hells and scum of iniquity, that run up and down from tavern to tavern, and from bawdy-house to bawdy-house, and get so many poxes and claps, that half their estate scarce pays for the cure of them?

Isab. And is that worse than running from ale-house to ale-house, and farm to farm, and getting so many bastards, that half their estates will scarce pay for the maintaining of them?

Sir Tho. Men that are always quarrelling, and fighting, and duelling.

Isab. Men that are always quarrelling, and never fighting nor duelling.

Sir Tho. Men that turn away their wives, and keep whores in their houses.

Isab. Men that beat their wives, and keep whores in their houses to boot.

Sir Tho. Do country gentlemen keep whores in their houses?

Isab. Yes, what are their house-keepers, and nurses, and servants, I'd fain know?——

Sir Tho. Are they their whores? You lie, hussey, you lie!

Isab. You lie!

Chris. Pray, Father!

[*Sir Thomas with his cane runs after Isabella, to beat her, but is held by Christina.*

Isab. Sir Thomas——

Oh, Sir Thomas, I do but argue; did you not give me free leave to say what I could in argument?

Sir Tho. Is giving the lie an argument? Hussey, you saucy——

Isab. I ha' done, I ha' done, sir: I'll dispute no more.

Sir Tho. You had best not, hussey.——And for you, madam, who began the argument, that are at your likes and your not likes; and your inclinations, and your compulsions, and I know not what; know that I expect an entire submission to my commands, prepare, without more logic, and syllogism, to marry Sir Mannerly the minute he comes to town, or in plain terms to get out of my doors. If you refuse him for your husband, know I will disown you for my daughter; and see how you'll live to the height and gallantry of the town then: see if the refin'd wits will maintain you. Go to the refin'd wits, go!——refin'd wits? with a pox; unrefin'd, lewd, debauch'd fops, that scarce ever read a book in their lives, except it were a play; that understand nothing but writing lampoons upon civil people, breaking of jests on all things, turning all things civil and sacred into ridicule, as they call it; ridicule, there's a pretty bastard word; a son of a whore of the times, ridicule! No more ado, but prepare to marry Sir Mannerly, or I'll turn you into ridicule.

Chris. Good sir, what need all this tempest of passion? I do not refuse your commands.

Sir Tho. Tempest of passion! Oh, you are at your metaphors are you? Tempest of passion!——
Virgin! my tempest of passion is to drive you

aground upon the shallows ; there's a trope for your
trope. To shew you a broad Jacobus, or a Carolus
wit of the last age, is, I take it, of as much value,
as a little Guiney wit of this. But you, forsooth,
and your refin'd wits, think there were never any
wits but your selves ; that your fathers were all a
pack of honest marrying fools, that had no more wit
than to bestow all their love upon their wives, and
all their estates upon their children, to starve themselves of all pleasure in a conjugal pond, that so
the young filleys may wince and neigh amongst the
mares in the fat meadows. I must confess we
were all fools in the event : for, had we known we
should have gotten such an age of rake-shames as
we have, we should rather have conspir'd together
to have unpeopled the land ; we have a great deal to
answer for lying with our wives. But though we
were wits, we were no prophets, we could not fore-
see what the age would prove ; for if we had,
i'faith we had mump'd * your refin'd wits : they
should ne'er have known what lampoon and ridicule
was.

Chris. Dear sir, what need you continue in this
anger, and discompose your self? I shall endeavour
to submit to your commands. But pray, sir, give
me leave to say one thing, and be not angry.

Sir Tho. Well, come, come !

Chris. Nay, but promise me not to be angry.

Sir Tho. Well, come, come !

Chris. Have you forgot already, sir, you have as
good as engag'd me to Mr. Ramble ; that all his
friends daily expect when the match shall be concluded ?

Sir Tho. Oh, are you thereabout ? I thought it
would break out at last. I have pump'd you now,
i'faith.—And have you so little wit or honour in

* Cheated.

you, so little of the pride of the house of Rash, to
love a wild, lewd, debauch'd fellow, who never
sought any thing but to abuse you : who pretended
honourable articles, on no design but to get within
your sconces and halfmoons, and then seize on
your garrison, and deceive you?

Chris. How do you know, sir, his purposes were
ill? Did he ever reveal 'em to you? I am sure he
never did, nor durst to me.

Sir Tho. How do I know? Do not I see how he
behaves himself to all women? He has not been
come from France above three months, and here
he has debauch'd four women, and fought five
duels : not a keeper in the town can preserve his
doe from him. And does not he come every night
here in the Pall Mall, under our own noses, serenad-
ing with his fiddles and fools, and at every bush
where he thinks there is a hare for his game, setting up a hollow?

Isab. Nay, indeed, madam, there is too much
truth in this. I must needs say, I do not think
him a man worthy of you : and though I would
not have you married to a fool you cannot love,
neither would I have you married to a false man
that does not love you, at least not half so much
as you merit.

Chris. Dost thou conspire with my father too to
make me wretched?

Isab. I cannot but join with in him the truth.

Sir Tho. O ho! are you convinc'd? then I perceive, hussey, you disputed only for the sake of
disputing.

Chris. All is not truth that is reported. He may
love the conversation of women, out of the airyness and gaiety of his temper, and yet have no ill
design.

Sir Tho. Airyness and gaiety of his temper?

Lewdness and debauchery of his temper! and, maid, I know what you mean by your pleading for him; you mean to run away with him, do you?

Chris. I scorn the thought, sir.

Sir Tho. I shall not trust your scorn; I will have better security : I will make you fast enough to Sir Mannerly as soon as ever he comes, I assure you : and for Ramble, if ever he approaches my doors, I will fight him; nay, I'll fight him where'er I meet him : and so get you to your chamber, and prepare all things for to-morrow. A light here, a light! who waits there?—nobody? where are my people?

[*Sir Tho. goes out.*

Isab. I see Sir Thomas is resolv'd—— There's no avoiding, madam.

Chris. What shall I do? I am almost distracted.

Isab. There is nothing to be done, but to call in your heart as soon as you can; you see it is in a public banker's hands, that deals with so many, that is impossible but he must break with some. Some will scarce ever get their interest, and few the principal.

Chris. Ah, Isabella, what would I give to be assur'd of that? Oh, how much ease it would afford my heart; I then could with as much delight and pleasure hate him, as now I love him.

Isab. Heaven!—assurance?—what assurance, madam, do you expect? would you fain see him abed with some woman? will no assurance serve you but that? To be plain, he's false to you; and I dare sware you make but one of the fifty in the catalogue of women he makes love to. To satisfy your self do but enquire.

Chris. Enquire? was I till now never inform'd of this? have I not oft been vex'd with these reports? and have I not as oft accus'd him too? and has he not deny'd 'em still with oaths? such oaths,

that if he thinks he has a soul, he must believe it
damn'd if he be false. Do you not know that all I
say is truth?

Isab. I do! and do you not as well remember I
told you all was falsehood he affirm'd? He thinks
he has a soul! alas, good man, he seldom sets his
thoughts on those affairs; he loves his soul but
as he loves his bawd, only to pimp for pleasures for
the body, and then, bawd like, it may be damn'd,
he cares not.

Chris. He is beholding to you for this character.

Isab. The scurvy picture is too like the life.

Chris. He gives me too much cause to fear it is.
Heaven! for the future comforts of my life,
Grant me but one, but one discovery;
If after that bless'd hour I do not hate him,   .
Hate him with perfect hatred; nay, contemn him,
Contemn him, as the abject'st thing in nature,
Let me be doom'd t' eternal infamy;
To live the scorn and scandal of my sex;
And die for love of him consum'd to ashes,
By some new, flaming, pestilential fever:
And let those ashes serve to dry the billet doux
He writes to common and abandon'd wenches.

Isab. What an unheard of curse have you
      invented!
And may he flay off all my skin for paper,
If I employ not all my wit to trace him:
And women's wits have always edge and point
In these affairs. I'll to his lodgings presently,
And hunt him dry-foot thence. Would odds were
      laid me
I did not rouze my wild, out-lying buck
This hour, and catch him browsing on some
   ·   common,
Where he, perhaps, little suspects a hunter.
But,—Sir Thomas——

Enter SIR THOMAS *with two servants with lights.*

Sir Tho. Come, come, to your chamber, maiden
And fit your accoutrements against to-morrow.

Enter a Servant.

Ser. Sir, my Lady Faddle is coming to speak
with you !

Sir Tho. My Lady Faddle ? news I warrant from
her nephew, Sir Mannerly : her ladyship is welcome.   Where is she ? wait on her in ! [*Exit Serv.*

Isab. Now we shall have a mess of fine stuff,
bragging and praising her self and her nephew, in
conceited fantastical language ; making court to
her self, in such an absurd manner, that it would
make pride humble to see it self appear so ridiculous.

Chris. Ay, and still railing against the bad women
of the town, only because they get all the men from
her.   Because she can get no lovers, she would fain
have love out of fashion.

Isab. Ay, and still most severely censuring all
that are young and handsome to be naught ;* though
she, at the same time, does all she can to seem
handsome, that she may be naught.

Chris. That is like her railing against painted
women, at the same minute she is painting herself.
But—'st, she's a coming !

Enter LADY FADDLE *and* BRIDGET, LADY FADDLE
with a letter.

Sir Tho. My Lady Faddle ! your ladyship's very
humble servant.   What kind occasion gives me the
honour of your ladyship's visit thus late ?

L. Fad. Sir Thomas, how dost thou do ? Dear
Sir Thomas, I have receiv'd a letter this instant,
which tells me news, which I am persuaded will
not be undelightful.   Chritty ! how dost thou do,

* Naughty.

sweet Chritty? Thou hast a very passionate adorer posting to thy altars : Thy lover is flying to thee on the wings of love and honour, as the poets say in their plays.

Chris. What stuff's here?

Sir Tho. News, I warrant, from your nephew, Sir Mannerly.

L. Fad. Exactly conjectur'd. I'll assure thee, Sir Thomas, he writes me word he intends, out of a piece of gallantry, to ride post all night, that he may visit his mistress by break of day. He's unwilling the sun should see her before him.

Sir Tho. A very fine expression! I'll give him a thousand pound more with her for that expression. He's unwilling the sun should see her before him! I protest I have not heard a wittier and finer passage.

Chris. Oh, most delicate! here's one glimpse of the fool's picture I am to marry already; I shall see it more at large presently.   [*Aside to Isab.*

L. Fad. Nay, I assure you, sirs, you'll find him a notable youth. Chritty, thou must look over thy academy of compliments* to-night, Chritty, against he comes, or on my honour he will be too hard for thee; he'll run thee down. He puts the country gentlemen to such non-plusses, that they do not know what to say to him. He is call'd the very wit and spark of Cumberland ; and is indeed the very flower and ornament of the North.

Chris. I'll warrant you his wit and sparkship lies in being an infinite babbler, and a most expert fool at questions and commands, carrying of counsel, cross purposes, and some such ingenious sports.

                                                      [*Aside to Isab.*

* A popular hand-book of the day. "A new Academy of Complements ; or, the Lover's Secretary. Being wit and mirth improv'd, by the most elegant expressions us'd in the art of courtship, in divers examples of writing or inditing letters, relating either to love or business, &c. &c. The fourth edition with additions, Lond. 1715," 12mo.

Isab. Ay, and, I warrant, writes anagrams and acrosticks.   [*Aside.*

Sir Tho. Is it possible that one can be so finely bred in Cumberland ?

L. Fad. Oh, you will wonder at it when you see him, to see how finely bred he is, how juntee and complaisant.

Sir Tho. Marvel !——what, and has never seen the town ?

L. Fad. Never seen any town, almost. You must know, his father, the old baronet, was a man that had mortal enmities to the town, and to all sorts of town-vanity ; and would never suffer him to wear a genteel suit, to read any book, except a law-book, nor to stir from home but in his company ; and that was seldom any whether but to his farms, and tenants, to see his grounds and woods, or overlook his quarries and coal-mines. And then his mother, my sister Shallow, on the other side, was the fondest creature of him, and would never suffer him to be out of sight, except when he was with his father: and both these having not been dead above a twelvemonth, and the affairs of his estate employing him much at home, I am persuaded the bounds of his land have been the utmost extents of his travel ; except since his parent's death, he has given himself a swinge* to some race, or fair.

Chris. He is like to be a most accomplish'd person.   [*Aside.*

Sir Tho. Your ladyship puts me in admiration ! Good madam, which way could he come by this fine breeding ?

L. Fad. Oh, Sir Thomas, you will put me on a piece of vanity.

---

* *i.e*, Swing. "If they will needs follow their lustes, their pleasures, and their own swinge, yet in the end, he will bring them to judgement."—*Dent's Pathway.*

Isab. And that needs not on my word.　　[*Aside.*

Sir Tho. Oh, your ladyship's humble servant.

L. Fad. If I must answer you the truth, Sir Thomas, I must say, in spight of my modesty, he is indebted to me for the most of his accomplishments.

Chris. Then they are most accomplish'd accomplishments.　　　　　　　　　　　　　　　[*Aside.*

Sir Tho. Oh, I beg your ladyship's pardon, I did not conceive that before.

L. Fad. Oh, good Sir Thomas, it is easily granted; you must know I accustomed myself, in my sister's life-time, to bestow my company on her every summer.

Chris. Indeed, if I had been she I would never have thanked you for the gift. I would rather you had bestow'd your absence on me.　　　[*Aside.*

L. Fad. And you may imagine, for the honour of my family, I neglected no occasion of instructing my nephew in all things that was pertinent to a well-bred gentlemen; and truly I found him a very docible scholar.

Sir Tho. Nay, if your ladyship had the forming of him, he is the most perfect of gentlemen, the pattern of breeding and virtue; for no common excellencies could be deriv'd from such a noble instructress.

L. Fad. Oh, Sir Thomas, you over-run me with too great a flood of language.

Sir Tho. Oh, 'tis your ladyship only is the governess of that province.

L. Fad. Oh, Sir Thomas, it is you are the inheritor; 'tis you have the learning, and the parts.

Sir Tho. Oh, 'tis your ladyship has the phrase, and the mine.

L. Fad. Oh, Sir Thomas, it is you have all.

Sir Tho. Oh, the sovereignty is your ladyship's.

L. Fad. Oh, Sir Thomas, you depose yourself from your rights.

Sir Tho. Oh, 'tis your ladyship dethrones yourself.

L. Fad. Oh, Sir Thomas !

Sir Tho. Oh, madam !

L. Fad. Intolerable presumption it were——

Sir Tho. I beseech your ladyship.

L. Fad. I protest, Sir Thomas—[*Falls a coughing.*

Chris. Oh, how seasonably this cough comes to deliver my poor father. [*Aside.*

L. Fad. Fie upon this tickling rheum !

Sir Tho. Oh, your ladyship strains yourself too much, to be obliging.

L. Fad. Oh, Sir Thomas !

Sir Tho. Oh, no more, I beseech your ladyship. I will not presume to enter any more into the lists and tournaments of the tongue with your ladyship : I yield the laurel to your ladyship. But to return to the discourse from which we wandered, of Sir Mannerly : I am infinitely glad to hear of his accomplishments and perfections ; for now I hope I shall convince my daughter, when he appears, that there grow finer things in the country than pinks and daisies. The country is able also to produce a fine gentleman ; yes, daughter, and, I hope, as fine a man as your ador'd Ramble too. She thinks him, madam, the very top of the creation, the flower and quintessence of gallantry, the wit of nature, a mere poem.

L. Fad. Oh, fie upon thee, Chritty ! dost thou debauch thy affections with that lewd fellow still ?

Sir Tho. Ay, madam, pray chide her !

L. Fad. Strange ! did I never tell you how he courts a young wench that lives over against my lodging in the Pall Mall, one Betty Frisque ?

Isab. This is the wench I told you of.
[*Aside to Chris.*

Chris. I give never the more credit to the story
from her authority. [*Aside to Isab.*

L. Fad. This wench, you must know, is kept by
that filthy old fellow, my Lord Drybone, an old
harass'd fellow of the town ; one that has been an
eminent sinner these thirty years; was a great
comrade of Prince Griffin's in the beginning of the
war.

Sir Tho. I am more happy than to know him.

Chris. If the truth were known, he was some
quondam gallant of her ladyship's. [*Aside.*

L. Fad. And she being exceeding pretty, as I
must needs say she is, some say she bears some
little of resemblance of me. I think indeed she has
a little of the air of my face.

Sir Tho. Then she wants for no beauty.

L. Fad. Oh, Sir Thomas, I did not lay a plot for
that compliment !

Sir Tho. Oh, madam !

Chris. Ridiculous ! [*Aside.*

L. Fad. She being, as I said, wonderful pretty,
he is fond of her to distraction ; and so jealous,
that he locks her up closer than a nun, will scarce
let her stir so far as the balcony, will not let her
see any man, though but through the casement.

Sir Tho. And to be brief, this wild fellow, Ramble,
plays tricks to deceive the Lord Drybone of his
beloved prize ?

L. Fad. Most certain !

Sir Tho. And your ladyship has seen these
passages ?

L. Fad. Not I ! I know not the fellow when I
see him : I hate fellows that run after such creatures.—I know such fellows ?—Foh !—I have
'em from the wench's own mouth. You must know,
out of pity to her, because I know her friends, I
give myself the trouble to sit with her sometimes,

to endeavour to draw her from that vile course of
life, and return to virtue, of which she has yet some
few sparks remaining.

Sir Tho. Well, I heartily thank your ladyship
for this story ! now I am confirm'd what a fellow
this Ramble is. And does he rank my daughter
with his Betty Frisques, and his trulls ? let him
but come near my doors if he dares. Now, maid,
you will importune me for Ramble again, will you ?
yes, Betty Frisque and you shall try a frisquin for
him,—you shall duel it, you shall. Well, madam,
Sir Mannerly will be in town to-morrow, you
say ?

L. Fad. Before the sun is up.

Sir Tho. My money is ready, madam. We must
not delay this business, lest any inconveniency
should arise if Ramble comes to have any intelligence of it.

L. Fad. They shall marry on sight.

Sir Tho. I could wish Sir Mannerly had kept to
the letter of the articles, and been in town as he
was oblig'd, four days ago.

L. Fad. You know I gave you the reason, and
two or three days can break no square. I know,
Sir Thomas, you are a person of that honour as
not to take any advantage.

Sir Tho. Not in case no damage arises by delay.

L. Fad. There shall none, I warrant thee, Sir
Thomas.

Sir Tho. Well, it grows late ! I am your ladyship's most humble servant.—I beseech you let me
wait on your ladyship to your chair.

L. Fad. It needs not, Sir Thomas.

Chris. I love my father for this;—he very civilly
and complimentally turns her out of doors. [*Aside.*

Sir Tho. Oh, madam, what do you take me to be ?
Do you think I will be so rude ? Take lights here !

Christina, pay your duty to your lady-aunt that
must be,—and see her in her chair !
  [*Sir Thomas ushers Lady Faddle out, Isabella
    carries lights.*
  Chris. Oh now I am alone, my heart would
    break,   [*Music plays.*
But that I scorn to let so false a man
Plant trophies on my grave.   [*Music without.*

Enter ISABELLA *running.*

  Isab. Oh, madam, madam ! Mr Ramble's fiddles
are just now going by the door; your father in a rage
calls for his sword, and will go fight him. If you
please I will dog him, and discover his intrigue.
  Chris. Where are they ? Which way went they ?
My scarf, and my vizard masque, quickly !
                                    [*Exeunt running.*

  SCENE.   *The Pall-Mall.*

MERRY *goes over the stage, followed by music.*

Enter LADY FADDLE *holding* SIR THOMAS RASH,
    followed by a Chair and flambeaux.

  Sir Tho. Fear not, madam ! there shall no mis-
chief come of it.
  L. Fad. At my request, Sir Thomas.
  Sir Tho. Your authority over me is so absolute,
I will pawn my honour to your ladyship there
shall no mischief be done. I will only send him
further from my door.
  Foot. The music goes near your ladyship's door.
  L. Fad. Near my door ? He will not have the
impudence to serenade me, sure ? [*Goes into the chair.*
I am afraid the fellow will pester me with his
amours :——
Go home quickly !   [*To the Chair-men*
Sir Thomas, good-night !   [*Exit.*

Sir Tho. Boy, my buff-coat and my tuck !* [*Exit.*

The music goes over the stage. Enter CHRISTINA *and*
ISABELLA *vizarded, following it.*

Chris. Now I shall discover my gentleman ;—
I thank Heaven for the ease this will give me.
But oh how wretched is a lover's fate,
When those we love we study arts to hate. [*Exeunt.*

ACT II.

SCENE. *The Street.*

Enter MERRY *and the fiddles, followed by* CHRISTINA
and ISABELLA.

LADY FADDLE *and* BRIDGET *in the balcony.*

Mer. Go, stand here ! This is the place; it will
not be long ere my master comes.

Isab. This is, as my Lady Faddle said, my Lord
Drybone's house.

Chris. That foolish woman was in the right I see.

Isab. Oh, I will believe her intelligence about
these matters, as soon as any one's. She, that plies
in all places so diligently as she does, to get the
reversion of some intrigue, never fails of true intelligence in these affairs.

Chris. And yet railing against love is the perpetual subject of her eternal tongue.

Isab. Oh she has reason, for love uses her very
scurvily, considering how much she courts it.

Chris. Heark !—I think I hear babbling in her
balcony.

Isab. I warrant she's lending her foolish ear to
the music.

L. Fad. Not Ramble's fiddles ?

* Rapier.

Bridg. No, madam!—I saw the gentleman's face as a link pass'd by.

L. Fad. Then the serenade is to me ; and I will know who dares be so bold.

Bridg. To your ladyship ? why should you think 'tis to you, Madam ? 'tis over at my Lord Drybone's house.

L. Fad. What if it be ? Why may it not be directed to me ? Is my person secure from the trouble of amours ? Thou speak'st this out of contempt to me ; I take it for an affront.

Bridg. I beseech your ladyship think not so.

L. Fad. I do not think so; my person is not yet—

Bridg. I do not talk of your person, madam.— Lord what diligent watching and scouting have we to get a forlorn lover into our weak ambush, and cannot ! (*Aside.*) Madam, I only say 'tis over the way at my Lord Drybone's.

L. Fad. Still continue in contradiction to me ? Dispute no more, but go and command the person from me, whoe'er he is, to come over to me ; and if he has a passion, let him express it in a decent manner : in such a manner as I may with honour receive it.

Bridg. If he has a passion ?——that is the thing she would be at. [*Aside.*

L. Fad. And let all my servants appear, that he may know of what quality she is whom he pretends to serenade.

Bridg. That he may know what a kind coming lady she is who would fain be serenaded. [*Aside.*

[*Ex. Lady Faddle and Bridget.*

Chris. It was her voice !

Isab. She was standing there I warrant in a fit of envy ; repining at the plenteous feasts of other beauties, whilst she would be glad of the crumbs that fall from their table. .

Chris. What's the reason Ramble's fiddles are so long silent? I am resolv'd I'll stay here till I see the event: whether the thing he serenades will come to him or no.

Mer. 'Tis a very dark night! there's not light enough to shew me the end of my nose. What stays this master of mine so long? some new love-adventure, I'll lay my life on't; for nothing else could stay him, I'm sure. Oh, 'tis a brave universal lover! What pity 'tis such a large spacious soul, that holds such vast prodigious quantities of love, should have but one body to vent it at: the vent is too narrow: all the convenience is, that it is never empty.—— But see! here's a pretty woman coming out of that house.

Enter BRIDGET.

Isab. Here's my Lady Faddle's woman coming!

Mer. Like master, like man. My master is a leviathan in love, and I am a very grampois; all but my master are porpusses* to me. Some neighbouring she-vessel, afraid of me, has thrown this vessel over-board for me to play withal, and see she swims towards me.

Chris. They meet!

Isab. 'Tis Merry, Mr Ramble's man!

Chris. What design should they have together?

Mer. To me, madam?

Bridg. Yes, sir! a lady of quality over the way has something of concern to discourse with you, and desires you will oblige her so far as to come over.

Mer. A lady of quality have concerns with me?

* " Wallowing porpice."—*Drayton.*
" Porpoises have the warm blood and entrails of a hog."— *Locke.*
    " Parched with unextinguished thirst,
    Small beer I guzzle till I burst,
    And then I drag a bloated corpus
    Swell'd with a dropsy like a porpus."—*Swift.*

[*aside*] Some blessing thrown on me from love, I hope, to reward my diligent labours in his service. No adventure with a woman can be ill : I'll hazard my person.—Wait you at that corner!——(*to the fiddles*). That way my master will come : if he ask for me, tell him I am call'd out in the service.

[*Ex. Merry and Bridg.*

Chris. Gone in with my Lady Faddle's woman ? Does Ramble hold secret correspondence with his public enemy my Lady Faddle ? Is he come to that piece of treachery ?

Isab. Only secret love-correspondence between Merry and Bridget. My Lady Faddle cannot be guilty of so cunning a plot : you honour her understanding too much, to accuse her of it.

Chris. Well, why do I submit to such baseness, to creep after a false fellow who deserves not my meanest thought ?——

Mr Ramble, farewell ! your fiddles have cur'd me of the tarantula of love, and the paltry animal shall set his little venomous teeth in me no more, I warrant it.

Isab. Come, come, hang it ! forgive a little extravagance for once. He loves you well in the main, I think in my conscience ; besides, all men are as bad ; the whole nation is infected with the same disease. There is not a sound-hearted wholesome lover in it, except it be such a one as your country fool ; and a thousand to one but he brings to town some country itch too ; a passion for a dairy-maid : Oh, the invincible charms of a sillibub !

Chris. Dispute not ! I hate him, and the hour when first I saw him, and myself that ever I lov'd him. Nay, I hate the passion of love for his sake, and with this blast of rage goes out that flame which his false fires enkindled. And now I will never spend one thought more of him : all my vexation is, that I must suffer for his crimes. Because he has been false, I must be condemn'd to pine away my life in the embraces of a clown. A reasonable piece of justice!

Isab. Come, madam, never conspire to your own unhappiness. Hearken not to pride; pride is a huffing, vapouring ass, pretends to conquer love, and do greater matters than he is able: love is not to be hector'd by such a coxcomb. Hearken to love, and make yourself as happy as you can, if you cannot be as happy as you would, or as you deserve.

Chris. Leave thy politiques and thy idle discourse, or leave me! my resolution is fix'd. I know, when I do examine Ramble about it, he will have the impudence to deny it all: but I will circumvent him. Have you borrow'd my cousin's lodgings for our plot?

Isab. Yes, madam! the whole house is at your service.

Chris. I'll go thither with speed. Do thou watch thy opportunity to speak to Ramble.   [*Exit.*

Enter BRIDGET *laughing.*

Brid. What sport have I had!—Now the amorous star, whom my lady has so long courted, has shed his influence. She has gained a lover, now her heart will be at rest; and her tongue too will have many a minute's repose, which was before continually railing against intrigues, and wanton women, and lewd men, and I know not what. But the way of gaining him was pleasant; she plainly frighted the man into love, fac'd him down, he serenaded her,· and she would right her honour, that the poor man is forc'd to pretend an extraordinary passion for fear of being cudgel'd.

But see, he was coming away already! I believe he suspects a beating still.

Enter LADY FADDLE *and* MERRY.

Mer. Oh, madam, what do you mean to give your sweet beauteous self this trouble ?

La. Fad. What should I mean, sir, but to express my civilities ?

Mer. The air is damp, madam, and you may catch one of these scurvy reigning colds, that possess almost all the lungs and noses of the town ; and you are now in more danger than any, because a cold will be ambitious to inhabit your fair person.

La. Fad. Oh, sir ! you are very ingenious. I may well endure a mighty cold air for you, who have sigh'd so many cold evenings, as you say you have, under my window.

Mer. That I have indeed, madam.

La. Fad. Well, sir, to tell you truth, I dare not be unkind to you : for as some men have unlucky hands, where they strike they kill, so I have unlucky eyes, where I wound I swear I very often kill. I swear so many have died for me, that I begin to have a little regret in my mind, and resolve to bring no more innocent blood on my head.

Mer. O, blest be that pious resolution ! but for this comfort my fate had been the same : my soul might have gone to the music of the spheres, but never to the fiddles that wait for me in the street.

Enter a FIDDLER *running.*

Fid. Where is he ?—Jack ! Jack Merry, your master is come ! come away quickly !

Mer. You saucy rascal, whither do you press ?
[*strikes him.*

Fid. How now, you puppy, what's this for ? I'll make your master cudgel you. [*Exit Fiddler.*

Mer. Dog, I'll run him through !

La. Fad. Hold, hold, sir ! what's the meaning of this ?

Mer. A rude fellow to press into a lady's presence; because we jest with one another in the streets, he must come and play his horse play here.

La. Fad. What does the fellow mean, sir?

Mer. You must know there is a gentleman in this town, one Mr. Ramble, that is a great comrade of mine; we live together, and are sworn brothers, and call one another out of raillery master and man; sometimes I am his man, and sometimes he is my man: and indeed we are inseparable; join hearts, join secrets, join fiddles together; he knows of my love, and I know of his love; and both our mistresses living so directly opposite one to the other, we bring our fiddles and serenade both under one: and this wild fellow you saw is a gentleman that we admit in our company, because he plays his part on the violin: and he has no more manners than to press after me into a lady of Quality's presence, like an ill-bred scraper as he is.—I swear I'll ——

La. Fad. Oh sir, let there be no quarrels!

Mer. No, no, madam, I'll warrant you.

La. Fad. Nay, but promise me; it will make me public, and dishonour me.

Mer. I will engage my honour there shall not. Well, most dear, dear madam, we are now each other's for ever; to-morrow the formalities of the church shall conclude what is so happily begun.

La. Fad. Farewell, dear sir!

Mer. Farewell! most dear madam. Oh happy night! O happy hour! Oh happy me!

La. Fad. Well, I swear this was unexpected.

[*Exit.*

Enter RAMBLE *and music at one door:* RAMBLE *meets* MERRY.

Ramb. Who's there? Merry?

Mer. Who should it be else? who walks the streets o' this time of nights but you or I, sir?

Ramb. I have been staid by the bravest adventure.

Mer. I have not been idle, sir; I dare compare adventures with you for what you please.

Ramb. I'll tell thee mine anon.

Mer. And I'll tell you mine, when you have a mind to laugh. Well, sir, my comfort is, you nor I shall not have much to answer for, for neglecting the talents Nature has given us; we have no loss of time lies on our consciences. While other lazy people sleep and take their ease, we are conscientiously labouring in the cause; and yet these wicked people censure us, and say we turn day into night, and night into day, and invert the order of Nature.

Ramb. The order of Nature? the order of coxcombs! the order of Nature is to follow my appetite: am I to eat at noon, because it is noon, or because I am a hungry? To eat because a clock strikes, were to feed a clock, or the sun, and not myself. Let dull grave rogues observe distinction of seasons, eat because the sun shines, and when he departs lie drown'd some nine hours in their own flegm; I will pay no such homage to the sun, and time, which are things below me; I am a superior being to them, and will make 'em attend my pleasure.

Mer. Most nobly resolv'd! how proud shall I be to have the sun my fellow-servant.

Ramb. The world is Nature's house of entertainment, where men of wit and pleasure are her free guests, tied to no rules and orders. Fools indeed are her household-stuff, which she locks up, and brings forth at seasons; handsome fools are her pictures; studious, plotting, engineering fools are

her mechanic implements ; strong laborious fools
are her common utensils; valiant bold fools are
her armoury ; and dull insignificant fools are her
lumber, which, by wars, plagues, and other conveniences, she often throws and sweeps out of the
world.

Mer. Very well, sir. And pray what fool am I ?

Ramb. An amphibious creature, that livest in
both elements of wit and fool ; the major part
of thee is fool; but that part of thee that is wit
is true wit; and so thou art a nobler animal than
many of those poor creatures that thou seest swim
after men of wit and sense, for the scraps and orts
of wit that fall from them ; they leap and play out
of the water, as high as they can, but they are
but fish still; folly is their element, and there
they must stay. I pity the poor poets ; these
creatures do but spoil our mirth, but they ruin
the poets' labours. They are to them as the fox is to
the badger ; when the badger has with great pains
scratch'd himself a hole, the fox comes and stinks
him out of it. But enough of this.—Come, to the
business in hand ! however 'tis in other affairs I
am for reducing love to the state of nature ; I am
for no propriety, but every man get what he can :
however invasion in this case I am sure is lawful.
When a pretty young woman lies in the possession
of an old fellow, like a fair fertile province under
the dominion of the Turk, uncultivated and unen-
joy'd, no good Christian but ought to make war
upon him :—that mine is a kind of holy war, and
I deserve a benediction. And so my musical pil-
grims to your arms.

Mer. Sir, you will make the jealous old lord
cut the pretty creature's throat.

Ramb. Oh, sir, he loves his divertisement too
well for that. Like an old cat that has been a

good mouser in his time, he loves his prey, though
it be but to mew over it.—But look, I see a light !

Mer. I hear her voice too. I am sure 'tis hers.

Ramb. She's coming to the window !

Rogues, run and light your flambeaux, or call a
link that she may see me !   [*To his Footmen.*

Mer. Up so late ?

Ramb. Ay, poor creature, she, like the rest of
her sex can have no rest in this world, neither
with a man, nor without a man ; not with a man,
for if he be young he lets her have no rest ; if he
be old she lets him have no rest ; and without a
man, to rest is impossible : so, poor souls, they
have no rest in this life.—Hcark, they are loud !
let's listen.

Lord Drybone, Betty Frisque, *and* Cis, *come to
the window.*

Lord Dry. What do you come to the window
for ? Come to bed, I say !

Betty. I will not come to bed.

Lord Dry. Will you still be thus humorsome ?

Betty. Yes, that I will.

Lord Dry. Come, you are a proud, silly, whimsical, inconsiderable, fantastical jilt.

Betty. Come, you are a weak, trifling, old no
man.

Ramb. Oh admirable ! this is a serenade to me.

Lord Dry. How dare you talk thus to a man of
my quality ?

Betty. What care I for your quality ? do you
think I am in love with a patent ? 'tis a man, and
not a piece of parchment that I value.

Ramb. A very wit, as I live.

Cis. Pray, madam, do not anger my lord so.

Lord Dry. Do you know who I am, that you
dare say this ?

Betty. Yes, I know you to be a thing with a title ; or rather nothing with a title : your lordship is titular, your manhood is titular, and every thing titular but your money ; and your substantial money compounds for your titular person.

Lord Dry. Do you twit me i'th' teeth with my bounty to you ? Forgive the fault, Mrs Elizabeth Frisque, I shall be penitent and reform.

Betty. I doubt not your penitence and reformation. I shall have some ambassadors from Guinea to-morrow, to treat of a peace ; the King's image in gold must make satisfaction for the faults committed by the image of a subject.

Ramb. The most admirable tongue-fencer I have heard ! he cannot get a hit of her.

Lord Dry. You are very civil, Mrs Elizabeth. To shew how damnably I shall frustrate your expectations, I this night put an end to your reign. Your way of livelihood is much after the mode of the Tartars ; when you have graz'd all you can in one province you seek out a new one. And so prepare to-morrow for fresh forage.

Betty. My way of living with you has been much after the mode of the Tartars, for I have tasted since I came nothing but horse-flesh ; and fresh forage I will seek to-morrow,

Lord Dry. And so you shall. [*Exit Lord Drybone.*

Mer. Do you hear, sir ? the fair faulcon will have her hood and her bells pull'd off to-morrow, and set to fly at liberty.

Ramb. I hear. I want but a light to lure her down on my fist. Where stay my loitering rogues ?

Mer. I am afraid 'tis so late there's not a light to be got.

Betty. Come, Cis, I'll go lie with thee !

Cis. Why do you vex my lord so, madam ?

Betty. This is the discipline I keep him under.

Not a syllable he speaks to-night but shall cost him dearer than printing a book in folio. He shall be glad to-morrow to tie me and all my things in my chamber with point de Venice, and barricado me with stones as rich as the philosopher's stone, and mortar of amber grease.

Cis. Well, I swear 'tis a rare thing to be an absolute Prince, and have rich subjects. Oh how one may pill 'em and poll 'em.* [*Exeunt.*

Ram. Oh dull rogue that I am! I have staid till she's gone; gone as I live! the window is shut and all dark. Strike up, you rogues, and retrieve her! never stay for tuning. She does not come yet. Scrape as loud as you can, make your catsguts squeak as loud as a concert of catterwaulers would at the roasting of one. She's gone to bed! I am ruin'd. Sing! join all your throats and bawl, beat a travalley on the drums of their ears. I hear somebody at the window; 'tis she I hope.

[*Lord Drybone peeps out of the window.*

Now be more melodious, lest you fright her hence.

Lord Dry. Music at my door at this time o' night? now I shall discover my gentlewoman's intrigues. 'Twas for this she came to the window? I'll listen to try if I can find out any mystery by their song, and then steal to the door, and see who they are.

Song.

A pox of impertinent age,
The pleasures of youth to invade;
The cheat who has long been broke,
Has impudence still to trade.

* A common phraze, meaning to rob and to cheat. "Thou sal noght be tyrant till thaim to pille thaim and spoyle thaim, als the wicked princes dus."—*M.S. Coll. Eton* 10. *f.*
"And have wynked at the pollying and extorcion of hys immeasurable officiers."—*Hall's Union* 1548.

Awaken fair Celia betimes,
    Before thy sweet youth's undone;
Come sow thy delights in a breast
    Will yield thee a hundred for one.

I bring thee hot youth and love,
    Come mingle thy fires with mine;
We'll serve to the night for stars,
    And make 'em ashamed to shine.·
Come down to my plentiful feast,
    Lye picking o' bones no more,
The scraps of a dish ill dress'd,
    And the leavings of many a whore.

As they have done singing, Enter SIR THOMAS RASH
    in a buff coat, with a long sword by his side,
    followed by two or three Footmen with long swords.

Sir Tho. Where is this Ramble and his fiddles?
1 *Foot.* I heard 'em, an't like your worship, but
just now hereabouts.

Sir Tho. How shall I know they are his?—A
company of rogues, to lay my buff-coat out of the
way, that I have lost Ramble while I have been
looking for my coat. And you, sirrah, to let your
torch go out!   [*To one of the Footmen.*

Ramb. What an unlucky puppy am I! She does
not look out yet.

1 *Foot.* Sir, sir, an't like your worship, I see a
heap of men at yonder door. I believe they are
they.

Sir Tho. How shall I know that, sirrah? come
along! I'll listen, and hear what they talk of. If it
be Ramble I'll Ramble him; I'll teach him to come
rambling and rumbling after my daughter.

2 *Foot.* O' my conscience, 'tis he, sir; for I
heard the fiddles hereabout.

Sir Tho. Hold your tongue, you puppy! [*listens.*

Enter LORD DRYBONE *in his night-gown, with a sword in his hand.*

Lord Dry. So, they are here still? I was afraid they were gone. Now shall I discover who they are. [*Goes behind them and peeps.*

Mer. She's gone to bed, sir! she will not come out any more to-night.

Ramb. How unlucky was this!

Sir Tho. I have found him, i' faith; that's Ramble's voice, and that's my daughter they talk of : she has promised to come out to him, it seems. Here's brave doings! I'll make somebody smart. Rogues, be ready when I give the word. Let me peep whereabouts he is. [*Sir Tho. peeps.*

Lord Dry. So, so, they expect to steal her out? Oh, brave whore! Who can this be? let me peep! [*Peeps about Sir Tho. and Sir Tho. about Lord Dry.*] A fellow in a buff-coat! and by what I can perceive, an old fellow too. What, has she intrigues with Hectors, and old Hectors? methinks an old rich lord should be as good as an old poor Hector.

Sir Tho. Ha! in his night-gown? just ready to chop to bed to her when she comes. They have made a match to lie together here to-night. Oh sweet virtuous Madam Christina, I have bred you up to fine purpose! I'll stay till you come, to give my blessing on you both together.

Mer. Come, sir, you had as good go to your repose; the jealous old coxcomb does so watch her water, that she cannot get out.

Lord Dry. The jealous old coxcomb? Oh brave! what rogue is this?

Sir Tho. The jealous old coxcomb? sirrah, your throat shall be cut for this.

Ramb. Pox on him for me! he has made me lose a night fatigue.

Lord Dry. Pox on him!

Sir Tho. Pox on him! yes, I'll give you five thousand pound with my daughter to bid a pox on me,—I will.

Mer. Sir, sir, whate'er the business is, the door is open. If you will, I'll enter softly, and see what it means.

Ramb. Do, oh do, prithee dear Merry! Oh, heav'n grant—

Lord Dry. Stealing to the door!

[*Lord Drybone gets betwixt Merry and the door.*
Who's there?   [*He gives Merry a box o'th' ear.*

Mer. A friend!   [*Merry strikes him again.*

Lord Dry. Ho, Peter, George, ho! my people, ho!

Sir Tho. Are you quarrelling amongst yourselves? I'll make one among you.—Ramble! where are you Ramble? I'll Ramble you. Fall on!

Ramb. Sir Thomas Rash's voice? I'm ruin'd! retreat, retreat!

[*Ramble and Merry retreat, followed by Sir Tho. Rash's men, the fiddlers run several ways.*

Sir Tho. Ramble is my man: and here he is! Are you running into your castle, sir?·

[*Lays hold on Lord Dry.*

Lord Dry. George, Peter, George!

Sir Tho. Oh, you change your voice, sir, now I am come, do you? 'tis not George, nor St. George shall help you now, sir. I'll teach you to make a whore of my daughter, sir.

Lord Dry. How! her father here? is this old Hector her father?—Make a whore of your daughter, sir? your daughter was a whore before I had anything to do with her.

Sir Tho. Oh horrid, she's common! However I will have my pennyworths out of you.

Lord Dry. Murder, murder! George, Peter, Thomas, rogues, come help me!

Enter LORD DRYBONE'S *men.*

2 Foot. My lord assaulted ?

Sir Tho. Murder, murder! Andrew, Nicholas, Will, rogues, come help me !

Enter RAMBLE *and* MERRY *fighting with* SIR THO.'s *men.*

Ramb. Sir Thomas calls out murder.

Sir Tho. Foot. My master thereabouts !

    [*Sir Tho.'s men run away from Ramble,*
     and fall on Lord Drybone.

Lord Dr. Ho, the watch ! a constable, a constable !   [*Lord Drybone runs in calling constable,*
    whilst all the rest fight helter skelter.

   Enter CONSTABLE *and* WATCH.

Const. Knock 'em down, knock 'em down !

    [*The Watch knock the servants down.*
Seize that man, and that man, and bring 'em before me !   [*Watch seizes Sir Tho. and Ramble.*
Who are you ? what are you ? come before me ! Sir Thomas Rash ! and Squire Ramble ! I know you both. What's the meaning of this, gentlemen ? a man of your worship, Sir Thomas, to be a fighting in the streets o' this time o' night ! fie upon it. And Squire, you use to be more civil.

Ramb. Sir Thomas, I am glad to see you so well : I hope you have got no hurt. Who was it quarrell'd with you ?

Sir Tho. Oh fine fellow ! he has got his cloaths on already to put a cheat upon me ; and the better to promote it, pretends he knows nothing of the quarrel. No, sir, no, I have got no hurt.

Ramb. I am glad of it with all my heart.

Sir Tho. To make a whore of my daughter is no hurt to me.   [*aside.*

Ramb. I was very fortunate to pass by.

Sir Tho. And so was I to discover this roguery.
                                        [*aside.*
Const. This is like gentlemen; now I commend
you. Come, gentlemen, you are both my friends; I
will convey you safe home with my fleet of lanthorns,
and let's be merry as we go. The man in the moon
and I are dukes of midnight. Give a spill * to my
Watch, and my grace shall drink your health in
claret.
Sir Tho. Less of your wit, and more of your office,
Mr. Constable! I will have revenge, though I put
my daughter in Bridewell. Seize that gentleman,
Mr. Constable!
Ramb. Me, sir, for what? you are in some mis-
take. I came to your assistance.
Sir Tho. Seize him, I say!
Ramb. What's the meaning of this?
Sir Tho. You shall know the meaning presently.
Const. Come, come, gentlemen! pray let us make
you friends.
Ramb. Sir, there was never any enmity betwixt
us. There is no man in the world that I am more
servant to than Sir Thomas Rash.
Sir Tho. Yes, sir, I know what service you do
me, and you shall have your wages. Seize us both,
I say, and carry us before the next justice of peace!
Const. I am sorry for this, I' faith, gentlemen.
Ramb. Sir Thomas, there need be no seizing, I'll
wait upon you. Mr Constable, if you please you
may let me walk at liberty, I will engage my
honour to you I will wait on Sir Thomas Rash
wherever he pleases to command me.
Sir Tho. No thanks to you, sir, I'll make you do
it. I'll try if there be law against such lewd doings
as these are. Bring him along here!
                              [*walks before in haste.*
* A douceur.

Const. What have you done, Squire, to Sir
Thomas ? he is a hasty choleric man.

Ramb. I have only hindred him from having his
throat cut. If he be angry at that, I cannot help it.

Mer. What devil brought this old follow hither ?
and what ails him ?

*A noise within of drunken Bullies, who enter with their
swords drawn, roaring.*

Om. Bul. Hay, hay, scour ! scour !

1 *Bul.* An honest gentleman going to prison ?

Om. Bul. Rogues, rogues !

[*The Bullies fight, and beat the Watch.
All go off scuffling and roaring.*

ACT III.   SCENE, *The Street.*

Enter RAMBLE.

Ramb. I am beholden to the honest drunken
bullies, that procur'd my liberty from these night-
corsairs and Algerines call'd the Watch, that picka-
roon* up and down in the streets, and will not let
an honest Christian vessel, laden with burgundy,
sail by.   But I was little beholden to Fortune, to
stand in need of their help. I do not like the adventure with this choleric old father-in-law of mine ;
a pox of the formal coxcombs for me, that invented
the rules of manners and civility, and foolery. I
must endure the humours of this old fellow, only
because he club'd to the production of the fair
Christina ; as if a man were bound in civility to
stand under the droppings of a conduit all days
on's life, because once at a coronation it ran claret,
and he was drunk with it.

* Pickeer :—Skirmish.

Enter MERRY *and* ISABELLA *vizarded.*

Mer. Sir, sir, I have the most glorious news for you!

Ramb. Ha! quick, quick; thou fir'st me !—What is it?

Mer. A most delicate young lady, wife to a person of very great quality, has been sick for you these six months; and her husband happening this night to be out of town, she has sent her woman for you.

Isab. O, why did you say so, sir? I told you I stole out o' my own head, out of pity to her. She knows nothing of it.

Ramb. No, no, she knows nothing of it to my knowledge.

Isab. I know when I bring him she will kill me : but I had rather she should kill me than love should kill her.

Ramb. I will save both your lives, dear creature ! lead me quickly to her before her disease grows desperate.

Isab. Well sir, you must send your man away; nor must you know whither you go.——Dear, what am I a going to do?

Ramb. Come along, sweet rogue !——Merry, to your own affairs. [*Exeunt Ramble and Isabella.*

Mer. I have a cursed itch to be following 'em, and see whither they go.——They are gotten into chairs, and the rogues are in their trot : Now they have turn'd the corner.—Let 'em go, I'll to my own honest conscientious matrimonial affairs. [*Exit.*

Enter two chairs : The scene a room : The chairs are set down, and Ramble and Isabella vizarded come out of them.

Isab. I have brought you thus far, sir; but

Heaven knows how to lead you any further; my wit is here at an end. I dare not for my life introduce you.—Cannot you pretend some mistake or other?

Ramb. A thousand, a thousand!—I will pretend some mistress of mine had newly chang'd her lodging, and I mistook this for it.

Isab. That will be excellent: I see you want no wit upon these occasions! But will you be faithful to my lady's honour, sir, and not trust your man, nor any friend you have, with a secret of such importance?

Ramb. I will cut out my tongue if I talk of it but in a dream.

Isab. Dear sir, do! Well, stay but a little bit of a minute, whilst I run in and see in what humour my lady is, and I will come back and shew her chamber. [*Exit Isab.*

Ramb. Ten thousand thanks, my dear, dear providore. Sent for by a young handsome lady, so her instrument says she is, to supply not only the absence, but defects of a husband. Let me see! what ready love have I about me? I should come off bluely now if I should not have enough, but be forc'd to cheat her of one half of the reckoning. No matter, she is rightly serv'd to surprize me so; she ought to have given me fair warning, and not have drawn so great a bill as this on me, to be paid at sight: she might well think, I that am such a constant trader cannot have much money in bank. Ay, but she is in love, and love is blind; one may put a false piece of coin on him now and then, especially after I have paid him a great sum; he will not be so scrupulous. Well, I am a Catholick man of strange universal use, I ought to have a pension for the public service I do the State; but though I am an excellent subject, I am a trai-

terous lover. How like a barbarous villain do I use
that divine creature Mrs Christina! if I were fifty
Rambles bound together, I had not merit enough
for her love; and I, though I am but one, yet parcel my self out every minute to fifty women : yet
'tis not for want of love to her, for the enjoyment
of other women gives me not so much delight as a
smile from her : and yet, I'gad, the enjoyment of
her would not keep me from the chase of other
women. Here I am raving mad after a woman,
only tickled with an image in my own fancy, of a
young, pretty, melting, twining, burning creature,
who, for aught I know, may be only an old, ugly,
lecherous Succuba, like a burning hill, with snow
on her top, and fire in her guts; and has enchanted
me to her embraces with a delicate young amorous
picture, put in my head. No, no, it cannot be ; if
she were ugly, she would not have the impudence
ʻo send for me ; nay, she would not have the impudence to love. No, no, she must be handsome,
ay, and extremely handsome too. Let me see ! what
kind of woman may she be ? she has a large, roul-
ing, smiling, black eye, full of fire ; a round, sweet,
juicy, melting lip, full of blood ; even, small ivory
teeth ; full, round, white, hard breasts ; a small,
strait, delicate shape ; a white little hand, inclining
to be moist ; a little, neat foot ; her stature mid-
dling. Ay, this is she, I know her as well as if I
were married to her : I am sure 'tis she. I'gad I
am passionately in love with her. Oh, my dear
envoy, come back quickly with full commission
from thy lady, or I shall fall into a fever. Come,
come, come ! Here she is ; here she is !—my dear,
let's go, let's go, let's go ! shew me the way, shew
me the way, my dear scout, for my forces are all up
in arms, and they will charge in spight of my teeth.
I cannot hold 'em in.

Enter ISABELLA.

Isab. Ah, sir, begone, begone, or I shall be ruin'd,
be kill'd! I gave my lady, to try what she would
say, but a little hint, not of your being here, but
only said, What if I could bring you hither, or
so? and she ran distracted. I thought she would
have died; I never saw one in such a passion in
my life. Oh, sir, there is no hope; she is so tender
of her honour, that it is impossible to come at
her.

Ramb. What dost thou say? thou tortur'st me!
wrack'st me! kill'st me!—'tis impossible to come
at her?——'tis impossible not to come at her.—I
am all o' fire, and I must go, will go!

Isab. Oh, sir, what do you mean? do you bear
me malice? have you a mind I should be kill'd?

[*Holds him.*

Ramb. I love thee, next thy lady, above all the
creatures in the world. I will take all upon my
self, and pretend I came in by mistake; and no
creature shall know anything.

Isab. Oh, sir, she will know it all to be a mere
invented story, a flam, for I have the keys of all
the doors, and no body can come in but by my
consent.

Ramb. Oh, but you left open the door to-night
by accident.

Isab. Oh, no, no, sir, I shut 'em, and told her I
shut 'em! and was more careful than ord'nary to-
night, because of his lordship's being abroad and
few servants in the house.

Ramb. A pox o' the doors, I must go in!—I will
go in, I cannot but go in!

Isab. Have you a mind I should be kill'd—do
you thirst after my blood?

Ramb. I will protect both thy life and honour.

Isab. But, sir, you cannot. My lady will call up all the footmen in the house.

Ramb. Then I will call up one of my feet, and kick 'em all down stairs.

Isab. Oh, I beseech you !—I entreat you !
[*Falls down and holds his leg.*

Ramb. Dear creature, I cannot forbear. I am a certain steed that am us'd to leap into other men's grounds ; and I must leap though with a clog at my foot. [*He drags her.*

Isab. Oh, sir, let me but go in and settle my countenance, that I may appear as if I knew nothing of the plot ; do but do that for me.

Ramb. Ay, with all my heart, dear rogue : I will do anything that's reason. [*Isabella runs in.* In what a heat am I ! this looks like a trick in this slut, to make me so fierce and ravenous, that, like a hungry lion, I shall prey at last on her.

Enter ISABELLA.

Now, my dear !

Isab. Oh, sir, ruin'd, ruin'd ! my lady has overheard all our talk, and is ready to fall into fits. I am undone, undone !

Ramb. Is she in fits ? I am the only man at fits in the world.

Isab. Oh, sir, you cannot get to her, she has lock'd herself in her chamber; and if you offer any violence she will call out to the neighbours.

Ramb. A pox on her for falling in love with me, and o' thee for telling me ! find out some way of making an interview betwixt us, or open wars will break out, and I will march to her frontiers.

Isab. I cannot find out one, though I should break my brain with study.

Ramb. Then keep thy brain whole, and I will break the door.

Isab. Hold, sir, hold sir ! since it must be so, I
have thought of one. Say after me as loud as she
may hear you, for her chamber is but hard by,
and we will see what that will do :
Excuse me, Mrs Andrews, for forcing myself so
rudely into your lady's house.   [*She speaks softly.*

Ramb. Excuse me, Mrs Andrews, for forcing
myself so rudely into your lady's house.

[*He speaks loud.*

Isab. It is an invincible passion which I have
for your lady.

Ramb. It is an invincible passion which I have
for your lady.

Isab. I must speak with her now my lord's
abroad.

Ramb. I must speak with her now my lord's
abroad.

Isab. If she will ruin her reputation and be
obstinate she may.

Ramb. If she will ruin her reputation and be
obstinate she may.

Isab. For I die if I do not see her.

Ramb. For I die if I do not see her.

Isab. Now let me run and see how this has
wrought. I must call to her through the key-hole.

[*Exit Isabella, and calls within, madam.*

Ramb. This jade has heated me till I am all in
a foam.

Enter ISABELLA.

Isab. This has done good. Since her honour
would be wholly ruined if there should be any
hubbub made to preserve her honour, my lady
consents to admit you.

Ramb. Oh sweet rogue !

Isab. Not so fast, sir ! you must swear not to
divulge anything.

Ramb. Ay, ay, I swear! what else ?

Isab. I must run and tell her.

        [She goes out, and comes in immediately.
And you must swear not to see her, or call for a
light, or draw the windows or curtains.

Ramb. I swear, I swear !

Isab. I'll run and tell her.

        [Exit, and enter immediately.
And you must swear not to talk to her, or at least
compel her to talk, to guess who she is by her
voice !

Ramb. I swear I will not give her leisure to
talk, I will employ her tongue otherwise.

        [Exit Isabella, and enters.

Isab. And you must swear not to touch her.

Ramb. Nay then I shall be articled out of all.
I will keep my past articles, I will not make one
article more.

Isab. Well then, since it must be so, follow me—
follow me ! Softly, that none of the servants may
hear. Hold, sir ! to let you see what an extraordinary esteem my lady has of you, she will trust
you with her honour, and discover the beautiful
empire which your victorious charms have conquer'd. See, sir, this is the wounded lady !

The scene is drawn, and discovers CHRISTINA.

Ramb. Christina ! am I betray'd ? Oh, for an
art to walk away invisible !

Chris. Whither, whither, cruel sir, are you con-
veying my felicity away now I have taken such
pains to attain it ? Oh ! use not that empire nature
has given you over poor women's hearts too tyr-
annically. Consider we are poor, soft, loving
things, and a little cruelty will kill us. Have pity
on a poor lady that dies for you, and is forc'd to
descend from the modesty of her sex, to court you

to a minute's conversation, at an hour when the rest of the happy world enjoy, some their loves, some their repose, and all are at ease but poor me.

Ramb. Jade, you will pay for this! [*To Isab.* Nothing can help me now but impudence. So, madam, you think you have put a fine trick on me now, you think you have catch'd me?

Chris. I warrant you knew of the plot.

Ramb. I warrant you think I did not.

Chris. Why did you?

Ramb. Did I? a likely matter that I should not know Isabella's voice!

Chris. Why, thou prodigy of impudence, dar'st thou impose such a falsehood as this on me? I believ'd thee against the reports of the whole world, which long since assur'd me of thy baseness; but dost thou think I will believe thee against the testimony of my eyes too? know I this minute tear thee out o' my heart, and after this never see me more.

Ramb. Ha, ha! What, shall we jest till we quarrel?

Enter a SERVANT, *running.*

Serv. Madam, madam, here's your father a-coming! it seems he miss'd you out of your lodging, and is coming in a great rage to see if you be here.

Ramb. Ah, what will he say if he catch me here? Let me be gone! make room, make room!

[*Ramble creeps away at one door.*

Enter at another SIR THOMAS RASH.

Sir Tho. So, maid, have I found you out o' doors? Go!

Chris. Who do you speak to, sir?

Sir Tho. To the corruption of my blood, to the

disease of my soul, to the filth of my house, to the putrefaction of my honour; a blot which my sword should this instant scrape out of being, if the rent could be hid from the eyes of the world, or all the dust of the grave conceal thee.

Chris. Oh, heaven!

Sir Tho. Speak not, thy voice is more horrid to me than the groans of a mandrake; thy sight more odious than a monster. No sense of mine will endure to hold communication with thee.

Isab. Hey, hey! all this for an innocent frolic.

Sir Tho. For a frolic, and an innocent frolic! Oh the incomprehensible impudence of the age! lewdness is a frolic! and abomination innocence! Oh sweet world, how art thou set with thy heels upwards since I knew thee! virtue and honesty were innocence, when I first came into thee; but now filthiness is innocence, and hell and the devil a frolic! Oh that the gout, or a Greenland frost had seiz'd the fingers of the destinies ere they had spun out my thread to such a frolicsome age.

Chris. Good sir, why do you disorder yourself, and afflict me, with these causeless transports? I know not the sense of your discourse; your language has to me no meaning; they are words never enter'd into my ears before; 'tis all distraction to me.

Sir Tho. Oh, you are for the substance, and not the picture in words and phrases. I'll tell you my meaning more plainly. Then know, Mrs Innocence, you are naught, you have been naught with Ramble, he own'd it, confess'd it, boasted it to me, to my face, to my throat, with his tongue, with his sword. He said you had been lewd with him, and that you had been lewd before ever he touch'd you.

Chris. Oh!—   [*She swoons.*

Isab. She swoons, she swoons ! help, help !

Sir . Tho. Let her die ! would she had died in
the cradle, in the womb, that she might never
have brought this shame and vexation to me. :

Isab. She has not, she did not, none can say it,
none did say it, none dare say it, or if they did,
they lie ! Ramble lies, and you lie, and you are
all liars ! and shou'd an angel from heaven say it,
I would say he were a liar, and that she has more
innocence than he.

Sir Tho. You are her procurer, and now will be
her maintainer, will you ?—Out o' doors !

Isab. In this condition ?—You are a natural
father !

Sir Tho. She's none of my daughter ! her whole
mass o' blood, her whole body, her whole soul is
chang'd.

Isab. She is thy honour, thy glory.

Sir Tho. Then infamy follow me henceforward !
Go, 1 say !

Isab. She shall not go. I will defend her whilst
I have a nail or a tooth.

Sir Tho. Nay, then, drag them hence ! he that
refuses I'll drag to the devil. (*To his Footmen, they
thrust them out*) Go, to Ramble with her ! and after
six months' iniquity, when his beastly appetite
is gallop'd to his journey's end, and is tired with
whipping and spurring so long in the dirt, then to
the bawdy-houses and common shops of lewdness
with her, and so to the pox and beggary, and so
to rottenness and the grave, and so to the devil:—
an admirable journey,—go ! Now will I with all
speed to the writ-office, and take a writ to arrest
my Lady Faddle in an action of a thousand pound,
for breach of articles. Sir Mannerly was by
covenant to be in town, and the marriage to be
completed, four days ago ; he is not come, my

daughter is debauch'd, my family dishonoured. and all by means of their breach of articles. It is not a thousand pound can make me reparation ; I will not abate one farthing of what the law will give me. And I will also have a pluck with that worthy gentleman, Mr Ramble ; I will try if there be no law against inveigling young women to lewdness and naughtiness. 'Tis more than break of day ; I'll go get the writ and bailiffs, and see it serv'd myself in person. Before she is up, my bummers shall have her in bed.   [*Exit.*

SCENE, LORD DRYBONE'S *house.*

Enter the LORD DRYBONE.

Lord Dry. Get my coach ready, quickly !
                                    [*Speaks within.*
How now, what rumbling's that ?—Ciss !
                                    [*A noise within.*

Enter CISS.

Ciss. My lord ?
Lord Dry. What's the rumbling within ?
Ciss. Nothing, my lord ! but my lady's packing up her things to be gone, as you warn'd her last night.
Lord Dry. I had forgot it ; is she so capricious with me ? I'll stay her, if it be but to cross her.
[*Goes out and re-enters immediately, pulling in* BETTY FRISQUE, *followed by a porter with a trunk.*
Sirrah, set down the trunk !   [*To the Porter.*
Betty. Sirrah, carry down the trunk !
Lord Dry. Sirrah, set it down, or I'll kick you down stairs!
Betty. Sirrah, carry it down, or I'll break your neck down stairs ! .

Lord Dry. Sirrah, stay a while, or I'll run my sword into you! Since you are so humoursome, gentlewoman, take your choice; your trunks shall go and you shall stay, or you shall go and your trunks shall stay. If I have not paid dear enough for you to have you be mine, I am sure I have bought and paid enough for all that is in the trunks to dispose of them.

Betty. Well, and I think I have paid dear enough for those things, in enduring all your cross jealous peevish humours.

Lord Dry. What jealous humours? I love you too well, that's my fault.

Betty. Yes, indeed, you love me very well, not to let me breathe so much as a mouthful of fresh air once in a month, and at home not to enjoy an hour of quiet.

Lord Dry. Yes, indeed, I shou'd do wisely to let you take the fresh air, as you call it. You never go to a play, but you fall in love with some young fellow; you never go to Hyde Park, but you are enamour'd with some rich gilt coach; you never go to the Exchange, but you have a violent passion for some rich point of forty or fifty pounds value; [so] that the air is a dear element to me. Your fresh air costs me all my earth almost.

Betty. I fall in love with some young fellow? I deny your words; I defy you or any one in England to prove the least falsehood in me to you, since I have known you: and for the gilt coaches and points, I have no more than what is convenient and necessary. I am sure other women cost other men twice as much as I cost you: here are some, that I can name, come to visit me in a morning sometimes with the richest points, and the gloriousest petticoats, would dazzle one's eyes to see 'em. I am sure the faces of some of 'em had need of 'em ; their beauties are like those of a peacock, all in their shining tails.

Lord Dry. Well, there's none of 'em all should outshine you, if you would be good-humour'd.

Betty. I do not know what you call good-humour'd ; if I had not the patience of a saint, I am sure I could not bear with your humours.

Lord Dry. ·Well, well, say no more ! I hate this wrangling. Have you any business at the Exchange this morning ? I am sending George thither.

Betty. No, not I.

Lord Dry. Prithee, give over these frumps, and fooleries ! Now I think on't that point you was offer'd for forty pound was a good pennyworth; I'll send for it.

Betty. You may an you will, but I'll ha' none on't.

Lord Dry. Shall he call at the jeweller's, as he goes by, for the locket you had a mind to ?

Betty. What you will ; not for me.

Lord Dry. And, well remembered, I will make him bring Mr. Drawwell the limner along with him. I take it ill of him ; he has promis'd me to come any time this fortnight, and put me off from time to time, and yesterday he promis'd to be here this morning. I will make him come and draw thee in these frumpish humours, that thou mayst see how ill they become thee.

Betty. He may come if he will, but I won't sit.

Lord Dry. Nor have any occasion for the point, or the jewels ?

Betty. No.

Lord Dry. Then George may spare his labour. Well, goodmorrow !

Betty. Goodmorrow !

[*He offers to go, and she stops him, she claps him on the cheek.*

Well, the deuce take you ! What ails me to be so

fond of nine and fifty? What have you done to bewitch me?

Lord Dry. Ah, Cokes!*

Betty. You have given me some love potion, I'm sure.

Lord Dry. Yes, yes, assafœtida—and garlick.

Betty. Confess, confess! I could never be thus fond, thus——

Lord Dry. Ah——

Betty. Blind! I am perfectly blind. I don't see a wrinkle; you appear a very boy to me, a very Cupid!

Lord Dry. Oh, thou notorious wheedling slut! Shall I still put up [with] such impudent abuses as these?

Betty. Yes, and be glad of 'em too.

Lord Dry. Well, age is an abominable thing! it makes one pay dearer for the lees, the dregs, the vinegar of love, than youth does for the sweetest, briskest juice of the grape. Well, hussey, George shall go: I will pay the tax you lay upon me; but 'tis hard a man should pay such devilish high chimney-money, and never have any fire.

Betty. That's none of my fault. I am sure I blow often enough.   [*Exeunt.*

SCENE, *The Street.*

Enter SIR MANNERLY SHALLOW *and* BOOBY.

Sir Man. Well, did one ever see the like? What a brave place is this London! It is, as the song says, the finest city town that ever I saw in my life.

Boo. Oh 'tis a brave place! 'tis not a city, 'tis a great country all o' houses.

Sir Man. It is, as the poet says, the habitation of the Gods: Hominumque Deumque.

* Fool; or, rather, a person easily imposed upon.

Boo. What is that Numque Umque, ant' like your worship?

Sir Man. Hominumque Deumque, Deumque for Deorumque, that is of gods and men.

Boo. I never heard London call'd Numque Dumque before? 'tis a brave thing to be a schollard. How chance your worship never came to Numque Dumque till now, but live in the country all this while?

Sir Man. Thou talk'st like an ignoramus; but I shall not trouble my self to instruct thee. Well, if I had known what a gentle, what a gallant place London was, my honourable father should not have stay'd me in the country, though he would have married me to the finest gentlewoman all round about, given me his manor house, his park, his fox-dogs, and the best hunting-nags in the stable : neither dogs nor nags, no nor my lady mother, should have persuaded me to stay.

Boo. Both his and her worship were to blame, an't like your worship, for staying your worship.

Sir Man. For that trick, as soon as ever I have married the fine gentlewoman I come to town to marry, for she is but a gentlewoman till I have married her, and then she is a lady. I say, as soon as ever I have married her, I'll stay here as long as I live, and never go into the country again.

Boo. I thought your worship said you would go into the country to fell Lubbertown woods.

Sir Man. Yes, I do intend to go into the country for that ; but I'll stay here as long as I live.

Boo. What a brave life shall we live here in this brave place, where all the houses are as big as your worship's manor, and all over nothing but folks.

Sir Man. Ay, and all gentlefolks ! and the civil'st gentlefolks that ever I saw in my life. I no sooner came into town, and ask'd for an inn, but an

ancient grave gentleman, that I am sure must be
an officer in the militia, mayor of some town, or a
knight, for he had a long great linen scarf tied over
cross his shoulder, by that I thought him a major,
or a colonel in the Militia ; but he had over that
a great silver chain, like our mayor's chain, by that
he should be the mayor of some town.

Boo. May be he is mayor of a part of this city,
an't like your worship, for this is too big to have
but one mayor.

Sir Man. Ay, but then he had on his breast a
great round silver thing, as big as the bottom of
our great silver sugar-dish, with his coat of arms
upon it, by that he should be some London knight.
But one of these three I am sure he must be ; and
of his own accord he came to my very horse side,
shew'd me an inn, and held my stirrup in spight of
my teeth whilst I lighted ; I never saw such a civil
person since I was born. He made me so asham'd,
that all I could say was to entreat him to do me
the honour to accept of a poor supper with me at
my inn. And, Anthony Booby, do you see to find
him.

Boo. I spoke to his worship, and he promis'd he
would come without fail.

Sir Man. See that the mutton broath have white
bread sippets in it, and all things be order'd handsome, as our cook maid us'd.

Boo. I shall, an't like your worship.

Sir Man. But this was not all : I had no sooner
taken my leave of the ancient gentleman, and gone
to the street gate, but a coachman of his own accord came and civilly tender'd me a coach to
carry me.

Boo. The horses were something lean, an't like
your worship.

Sir Man. I suppose 'tis some complimenting

coach kept o' purpose to compliment strangers; and abundance of strangers coming to town, the horses might be worn out with much complimenting; for I perceive it is the custom here to compliment strangers so; for I had no sooner thank'd the coachman, giving him something for his civility, and presented my service to his master, but at least half a dozen more complimenting coaches came up to me, as hard as they could drive, to proffer their services.

Boo. I believe the gentry has been told how ready your worship is at any time to lend your best team to any neighbour.

Sir Man. No, no, I saw 'em do the same to twenty more as well as myself. Well, 'tis the civil'st place that ever I came in days of my birth: for I'll tell thee more, Booby, after I had gone a little way in a great broad street, I turn'd into a tavern, hard by a place they call a park; and just as our park is all trees, that park is all houses, you cannot see so far as you can spit: and I ask'd if they had any deer in it; and they told me, yes, but not half so many as they us'd to have; they us'd to have the best deer in all the town, and scarce a venison pasty was formerly made, that had not the venison out of their park. But they said the park was now quite spoil'd, and the best deer were all gone to the other end of the town, and those that stay'd were poor rascal deer, not worth baking.

Boo. I don't wonder they are poor, an't like your worship, for I did not see a bit of grass, except some sprinklings among the stones, and a little mouthful here and there on the tops of houses.

Sir Man. I warrant the deer here a kind of goats, and climb on houses to brouse. I had a

great mind to taste 'em, and spoke for a pasty,
and they told me the strangest thing; they said
their rooms were full of cold pasties, so big two
people might sleep in one; and that if I had a
mind to a doe, they would put me in a pasty, and
put a doe to me.

Boo. Oh strange! and did your worship go into
a pasty?

Sir Man. No, I'll tell you what happen'd.
Just as I ask'd for the doe, in comes a couple of
young gentlewomen, the handsomest, finest gentlewomen that ever I beheld,—Mrs Anne Lackwit,
the great beauty of Lubbertown, is nothing to 'em;
—and they were all over lace, and had the finest,
reddest cheeks and lips that ever I saw, no ripe
cherry is so red; they were so red, that the blood
came off the very outside of their lips, and as I
kiss'd 'em left a redness on mine.

Boo. Is't possible? I warrant your worship
kiss'd 'em too hard; you made their teeth bleed,
and that was the business.

Sir Man. No, no, it was the very blood of their
lips, that was dried on.

Boo. Well, I never saw the like!

Sir Man. No, nor I neither; for I had no sooner
saluted 'em to shew my breeding, but they of their
own accord took me about the neck, and kiss'd
me as if they had been my sisters, or as if they
had known me these twenty years, that I fell so
in love with them, that, i' my conscience if I had
not been engag'd already, I had married the handsomest of 'em before I came away.

Boo. Is't possible? but did not your worship
ask for the great pasty?

Sir Man. I should ask for victuals before gentlewomen, should I? That were fine breeding! no,
but they of their own accord were so civil as to

invite me up stairs to a pasty : and just as I was going up with them, I chanc'd to put my hands in my pocket, and, as if the devil had been there, my money was all flown out of my pocket, I know not how, nor whither.

Bco. Flown out of your worship's pocket ?

Sir Man. Ay, flown out o' my pocket.

Boo. What, of itself !

Sir Man. Ay, of itself ?

Boo. And nobody to help it ?

Sir Man. There was nobody near to help it.

Boo. What, all ?

Sir Man. All but one sixpence, that was in a corner of my pocket.

Boo. There must be witchcraft in this, and if I was your worship I would make that sixpence find out all the rest.

Sir Man. How like a fool thou talk'st ! how can that sixpence find it out, when I could not find it myself, tho' I look'd up and down in every corner o'th house ? nay, the gentlewomen were so very civil as to help me, nay would have come out to help me look it in the streets, if I would have let them.

Boo. Well, this was old Goody Wrinklenose's doings, that lives on the side of your worship's woods by Lubbertown. If I were your worship I would write down into the country and have her hang'd.

Sir Man. Nay, I am sure it was the devil, for, I remember as the gentlewomen were kissing me, I felt a thing scratch in my pocket just like a rat.

Boo. Nay, then it was Goody Wrinklenose, and the devil has brought her to town before us. If I were your worship I would make her an example.

Sir Man. Nay, I do intend to trounce her, for . this is demonstration. Well, but now what shall

I do to find my aunt, my Lady Faddle, for I have lost my directions? all I can remember is, that she lives in a place they call the Pall Mall, and the Pall Mall I find but cannot find my aunt's house. And she is to help me to find out my baronet father-in-law, Sir Thomas Rash, where I shall find his daughter, Mrs Christina, whom I am bound in a bond of a thousand pounds, with my aunt, my Lady Faddle, to marry four days ago, and my lady aunt writ me word, that my baronet father-in-law was very angry for my not coming; and if I did not marry Mrs Christina, and come up to-day, he would take the forfeiture of the bond.

Enter to them A PORTER.

Boo. See, an't like your worship, here comes the ancient gentleman that you invited to supper, that held your horse! if he be mayor of any part of the town, as he looks to be, it may be he can tell whereabout your lady aunt lives.

Por. Bud, here are the complimenting people! let me get away from them.

Sir Man. Hold, worthy sir, noble sir! I do not know how to return the great favours and honours you were pleas'd confer on me, who am but a peregrine. I commanded my man Booby to entreat you to accept of a small supper with me, not as a return, for I know you have a better supper at home, but as it were to shew how much I am oblig'd for all your noble favours. Now, worthy sir, I make bold to request you to add one favour more to all your past favours; to acquaint me if you have any acquaintance with a lady and aunt of mine, by name Lady Faddle.

Por. Well, I have ply'd here these forty years, and never met with such an odd sort of a blade in my life.—Who is it you ask for?

Boo. An aunt of his worship's, one Lady Faddle.

Por. I do not know her, master. I cannot direct you.

Sir Man. This is strange, that no body can tell where my lady aunt should be.

Boo. I think in my conscience, an't like your worship, I have asked above a hundred folks for her, and not one knows where she should be ; no not so much as knows her worship. Nay, I ask'd all about the neighbourhood, and the very neighbourhood did not so much as know her worship.

Por. You must not think you are in the country ; people do not know one another here that live in the same street, nay in the same house, nay sometimes that lie in the same bed together.

Sir Man. Hey day ! why I know all the gentry round me in the country for above twenty miles.

Por. Ay, but 'tis not so here.

Boo. How do they do not to know one another ? do they do it on purpose ?

Por. People never mind one another here, unless they have business together ; but let them go as they come, and come as they go.

Sir Man. Hey day ! why I know all the dogs and horses in the country that are eminent, whether I have business with them or no.

Por. Ay, but you may be a dog, or a horse, or a man here, no body will mind you unless they have some concern or other with you.

Sir Man. Hey day, I never heard the like !

Boo. Nor I in my life.

Sir Man. Then if I ask a thousand people for my lady aunt, there's nobody knows her.

Por. You may ask ten thousand before you meet with one that knows her.

Sir Man. Hey day ! then I shall forfeit my

bond, for I shall not find her to help me to find Mrs
Christina before the sun is set. What shall I do ?

Boo. Your worship can prove you were come
to town, and so, if you cannot find 'em, the fault
is none of your worship's.

Sir Man. Ay, but I did not think I could not
find 'em, and so there is no such clause in the bond ;
for I am bound to marry Mrs Christina whether I
can find her or no.

Boo. Then I'll tell you what your worship shall
do ; send for a vicar, and say over your worship's
part, and then you can prove you have done all
that belongs to your worship.

Sir Man. I swear that's very well thought of ;
for now I think on't, I seal'd and deliver'd the
bond in the country to my baronet father-in-law's
use, without his being present, or ever seeing of
him in my life : so I will send for a parson, and
marry myself to one of you two, for Mrs Christina's
use, and this will be as good in law as if she were
present.

Boo. Right ! for if the marriage be not good,
then how is the bond, since they are both made
after the same manner ?

Sir Man. Right !

Por. Do these men jest, or are they as errant
fools as they seem ? I believe they are fools ; for I
never heard such a deal of simple stuff and complimenting, as I have had with them to-day, since
I was born.

Sir Man. I swear this was the best thing that
ever was thought on. Now do not I care whether
I find my aunt or no.

Boo. This old gentleman's worship having been
with you ever since your coming to town, your
worship had best ask his worship to be a witness,
and see you married to me.

Sir Man. I can have no better witness, for he— he can prove all. Noble and obliging sir—

Por. Now he falls a complimenting again ; I wonder he stayed so long from it. I would the devil had his compliments, he has made my head ake.—Hold, hold, master, spare me for heaven's sake ! I remember my Lady Faddle, she once sent me of an errand ; your compliments buzzled me and put it out of my head. I know where she lives ; I'll lead you to her house !

Sir Man. Oh, sir, what favours do you confer upon me !—But, sir, you shall not go a foot ; Booby, fetch my horses !

Por. Horses ? my feet are my pad-nags.

Sir Man. Oh, sir, you will swell your high obligations to such a——

Por. Swell my thighs with hobbling ? no, no, hobbling is my trade.

Sir Man. Well to Cumberland commend me for gentility,

But to London for good breeding and civility.

[*Exeunt.*

ACT IV. SCENE I. *The Street.*

Enter SIR MANNERLY, BOOBY, *and* PORTER.

Por. Look you, sir ! you are now at the door.

[*He knocks.*

Sir Man. Oh, sir, why do you condescend to give yourself the trouble of knocking ?

Enter a SERVANT.

Por. Is my Lady Faddle within ?

Ser. Who would speak with her?

Boo. Her nephew's worship, Sir Mannerly Shallow, and I are come to town; tell her!

Sir Man. Presume to speak before me? where's your manners? Sir, I am her humble servant, nephew, and baronet, Sir Mannerly Shallow.

Ser. Oh dear, sir! are you Sir Mannerly Shallow? my lady expected you this morning early; she will be mighty glad you are come. She is within; please to walk in, sir! whilst I run in and acquaint her of your coming.   [*Exit Servant.*

Sir Man. This is good luck! noble sir, I beseech you honour me so far as to walk in with me.

Por. Oh, master! what do you mean?

Sir Man. I beseech you, sir.

Boo. Come, pray your worship walk in.

Por. What do these people mean?

Sir Man. Nay, but, sir, I am to be married to-night, and I swear I will not marry if you will not grace my nuptials with your presence; therefore, sir, if your affairs call you away, yet promise me, on your honour, that the joys of my marriage shall be encreased with the happiness of your company. Your presence will be the principal dish at my feast.

Por. He means to dish me up. Well, master, if you want anybody to wait, and go of errands, I'll promise you I'll come.

Sir Man. Your most humble servant! I will not rest, till I requite your civilities.

Por. What odd kind of contriv'd men are these?
[*Exit Por.*

Sir Man. Booby, do you carry yourself well now before my lady aunt, and do not disparage me. Observe what I do, and then you'll do finely.
[*Exeunt.*

SCENE, *The* LADY FADDLE's *house.*

Enter LADY FADDLE, BRIDGET, *and* SERVANT.

La. Fad. My nephew come? this is good news,
where is he? Introduce him speedily!   [*Exit Ser.*

Enter SIR MANNERLY *and* BOOBY.

Sweet nephew!
　　[*She runs forward to salute him, he still goes back-*
　　　ward, and compliments.

Sir Man. Honourable aunt! The extreme joys
and felicities of your society, which a long paren-
thesis of time has interrupted, but now time, as
it were penitent—　　　　　　　[*Still runs back.*

La. Fad. Why, dost not salute me, nephew?

Sir Man. Yes, madam, as soon as ever I have
done my compliments.

La. Fad. Oh, thou should'st salute the first
thing thou dost.

Sir Man. Yes, madam, but a salute being a kind
of a present, or rather tribute to a lady, and as
one would not present an empty purse for tribute
to a princess, so neither an empty mouth to a lady,
but as full of rich and golden compliments as it
could hold.

La. Fad. This is witty to extremity, I swear.
Salute me! that I may be at leisure to praise'thee.

Sir Man. Your most humble servant, aunt!
　　　　　　　　　　　　　　　[*He salutes her.*

Boo. Your worship's most humble servant!
　　　　　　　　　　　　[*Offers to salute La. Fad.*

Sir Man. How now, saucebox, kiss my aunt?

Boo. Did not your worship bid me observe what
you did?

Sir Man. Did I bid you kiss ladies of quality?

La. Fad. What rude fellow's this?

Sir Man. Forgive him aunt, 'tis his want of breeding.

La. Fad. Well.   Bridget !

Bridg. Madam ?

La. Fad. Bid John run with all speed to Sir Thomas Rash, and acquaint him my nephew is come, and run to my milliner's for my gloves and essences, and run to the Exchange, and run to my coach-maker's for my new harness, and run for my new towre,* and run—

Bridg. I shall run, madam, to bid him run, or otherwise the poor fellow will be made to run all over the town.   [*Exit Bridg.*

La. Fad. Well, nephew, thou wilt enjoy to-night a delicate lady. I have so exalted thee to her with exuberant praises, that it will require a great expense of wit and breeding to maintain the glorious character I have given thee. Come, give me an account how thou hast spent thy time ; how hast thou improv'd those documents, and rudiments of good breeding, which I instill'd into thee ?

Sir Man. Oh madam, I have improv'd every document, not a slip of rudiment your ladyship set but is grown up to a flower. Indeed, my father did all he could to spoil me ; he would let me read nothing in his lifetime but law-books, Cook upon Littleton, and books of reports, and judges' reports, and I read reports and reports so long till it was reported I was a fool.

Boo. Ay, but your worship now reads comedy books, and prodigy books.

Sir Man. Tragedy books thou meanest ; ay, and songs, and verses, and drolleries : Covent Garden

---

* A curled frontlet. Also about 1710, used to signify a high head-dress.

drollery, Westminster drollery, and Windsor drollery.

La. Fad. Very well, this is as to the accomplishment of the mind ; but now to the external ornaments of the body, as dancing, singing.

Sir Man. Oh, I have had dancing-masters, fencing-masters, and singing-masters.

La. Fad. Ay, those masters must make thee fit to be a servant to ladies.

Sir Man. I can dance corantoes, and jigs, and sarabands.

Boo. And hornpipes.

La. Fad. Canst thou rise well ?

Sir Man. In a morning, madam ?

Boo. His worship gets up by break of day.

La. Fad. No, rise high in dancing. If you will rise high in ladies' favours here you must rise high in dancing, that is to say, dance loftily.

Sir Man. Oh, I can dance very loftily.

Boo. The country says, his Worship carries himself too loftily.

La. Fad. Make an essay of a lofty dance.

[*Sir Mannerly sings and jumps.*
Very graceful, I swear, and very lofty !

Boo. Oh, his Worship will jump like any jackdaw, that has but one wing cut.

Sir Man. Jackdaw, sirrah ? don't you make such saucy comparisons.

La. Fad. Well, nephew, thou wilt kill a great many ladies this winter ; those heels will advance thee, thou wilt jump into preferment. I see a witty man is good for anything ; one would wonder thou should'st jump so high, with such a weighty brain in thy head.

Boo. As heavy as a pail of milk.

La. Fad. Thou art ingenious at both ends, both thy head and thy heels ; it's rare for one to be witty,

more than at one end. Well, nephew, thou wilt
dance away all thy country flesh this winter; thy
heels will be invited to shew their parts to dance,
in every fine entry, in the masques and plays,
and—

Sir Man. Why, do they dance in entries here ?
We dance in the country in our halls and dining-
rooms, because the entries are too narrow.

La. Fad. Oh fie, thou dost not understand the
terms of thy own art yet ! to dance in an entry,
that is to say, in an entry, an entry of any thing.

Sir Man. Of freestone or brick ?

Boo. Your Worship's are all freestone.

La. Fad. No, no, fie, fie ! expert in the science,
and ignorant in the terms, in an entry of shep-
herds, or gods and goddesses.

Sir Man. I can dance in any entry in England.

La. Fad. Strange, that thou shouldst not appre-
hend me ; but to let that pass—Well, but how is
thy singing ?

Boo. Oh, his Worship out-sings all our parish.
At church the clerk is asham'd to set the psalm
before him.

Sir Man. Sing a psalm, I have sung my part in
recitativo, as they call it. I had a recitativo acted
at my own house, and I acted in it, and sung ; I
was London, or Augusta, and I had a high-crown'd
hat, to signify Paul's steeple, and I had one acted
the River Thames, I had a great nose made on
purpose to signify London Bridge, and the River
Thames swam under my nose. I have my nose in
my portmantua ; if I had it on, you should see
Booby and I would act.

La. Fad. Then thou canst act, nephew ?

Boo. And so can I too.

Sir Man. Oh, I have all the new comedy books,
and tragedy books, sent me, as fast as ever they are

made. Oh, I love them that huff the gods, they make no more of a god than we do of a constable.

Boo. Your Worship and I acted a tragedy book, you know.

Sir Man. Yes, and I was an hero, and I remember two of the bravest lines.

> If saucy Jove my enemy appears,
> I'll pull him out o' heaven by the ears.

There's ramping for you.*

La. Fad. Saucy Jove, that's very great ! that took mightily here.

Boo. Oh, that rumm-dumm,derry-dumm ! oh, but the two knocking verses, an't like your worship.

Sir Man. Oh, ay, you must know, my part, aunt, was to beat an army, and so when I had beaten an army, and two armies more that came to their relief, and won four kingdoms in three hours, I cried,—let me see, it's a little out of my head ; I cried, I'll, I'll,—Booby, thou canst think of it ?

Boo. O yes, an't like your worship, I can remember it perfectly, I'll, I'll,—mackings, I ha' forgot it, I ha' dropt it upon the road somewhere.

Sir Man. What a noddle hast thou ! thou actedst with me.

Boo. Ay, but your worship kill'd me before you spoke the speech. The butler, the ploughman, and I, was the army.

Sir Man. I did not kill thee in earnest, did I ? let me see ! I'll.—

Boo. Oh, now I remember, single, it begins with single.

Sir Man. Oh single, single,—it begins with single,

> My single sword both men and gods shall maul !

Oh, but the next is the bravest.

---

* Hall, in describing Joan of Arc, says, she was "a rompe of such boldnesse, that she would course horses and ride them to water and do thynges that other young maidens bothe bhorred und wer ashamed to do."

I will kill all the world, nay more than all.

Boo. There's your rowzers !

Sir Man. There's your thumpers !

La Fad. Oh, they have a brave ingenious way of writing now.

Sir Man. Oh, but then the fine tender things that would make one cry. You must know, aunt, my part, was to be in love with my dairy-maid, and her name was Celemena, and mine was Philaster, and I cried

How does my fairest Celemena do ?

And she cried

Thank you my dear Philaster, how do you ?

La. Fad. Very natural and soft.

Boo. Oh, the dairy-maid is very soft.

Sir Man. Oh, but then the two next are tender. I cried,

Does my sweetheart me any kindness bear ?

And she cried

I love you dearly, now, I vow and swear.

La. Fad. Very tender !

Boo. Oh, Mary is a very tender good natur'd maid.

Sir Man. Tender as an over-boil'd chick.

La. Fad. Very wittily comparison'd, the sense is ready to drop in pieces ! 'tis very fit for women's weak stomachs.

Sir Man. Oh, but when my maid and I came to die, I don't know why we were to die, but we died mighty mournfully, and then I having learnt to sing, I groan'd so musically, I died in effaut flat, oh, cried I !

La. Fad. Oh, that was sweet.

Sir Man. Oh, but then the similes—I love the similes dearly ! to see two heroes, or two armies go to it as formerly, with sword and buckler, so now with sword and simile, simile and sword ; hack-slash, slash-hack, for you must know a simile serves instead of a buckler, for if a man be ready to strike another, if t' other up's with a simile he can't strike till the simile's gone.

La. Fad. Oh, they have a fine way.

Sir Man. Ay, and then they have such plenty of similes, you shall have a play stuck as full of similes as a country garden of flowers, you may gather posies o' similes.

La. Fad. Wittily said again, stuck full o' similes, and posies of similes. I swear, thy head is as full of similes as the plays are.

Sir Man. Oh, sir, a witty man's head is a simile-bed, and breeds similes as fast as an oysterbed breeds oysters.

La. Fad. Witty again ! he has strange parts.

Sir Man. And then they have the finest odd out of the way of similes, similes that are most commonly no similes at all, as now, speaking of a lady's bright eyes, says one

How do the nimble glories of her eye,

Frisk, and curvett, and swiftly gallop by ?

There's a fine comparison, to compare a lady's eye to a horse.

La. Fad. Ay, and nimble is a fine odd, out of the way epithet for glories, nimble glories. Well, dear chuck, how camest thou by all this admirable and, as I may say, nimble knowledge ?

Sir Man. You must know I had a couple of gallant gentle blades lay at my house, that were great men in London ! here they are called critwiques, and they taught me the finest things.

La. Fad. Oh, the critiques are great men indeed, they make poets as 'fraid of them as a lion is of a cock.

Sir Man. Some say that is not at all.

La. Fad. An old lion, it may be, is not, nor an

old poet, of a critique, but your new poets are so afraid of them, that if a critique crows they are ready to faint away.

Sir Man. Is't possible! could not one buy a critick's place?

Boo. Pray your worship do, and let me be your clerk.

La. Fad. Buy? alas thou may'st judge and critick for thy half-crown, as much as thou wilt.

Sir Man. That's a pitiful place, if one can buy it for half a crown.

Boo. Oh, but the clerk may get money though.

La. Fad. 'Tis not money but Wit makes a man a critick.

Sir Man. Then I am a critick already.

Boo. Oh, brave! then I am a clerk.

La Fad. Well, dear flesh and blood o' mine, let me embrace thee, that I may say I have my arm full of wit. Thou art a bridegroom for a princess; how wilt thou honour my education? Well, hast thou brought up any clothes to be married in?

Sir Man. My portmantle full.

La. Fad. Go and adorn thyself with all speed, whilst I prepare for the same affair, for I am to be married as well as thyself.

Sir Man. Is't possible?

Enter BRIDGET.

Bridg. Andrew, madam, has been at Sir Thomas Rash's, and can hear no tidings, neither of Sir Thomas, nor madam Christina. Madam Christina lay out all night, and is not come home since; Sir Thomas is gone somewhere in a great combustion, and the servants can give no account of either of 'em.

La. Fad. That's strange! Oh, I'll warrant you, they'll be heard on, nephew. Go and dress thyself,

meanwhile I'll step to the Exchange for some
things I want, and after that I'll go over and invite Betty Frisque to my wedding. I have much
kindness for that poor creature.

Sir Man. So you see, madam,
    I bring to town a mind and wit in fashion,
    And doubt not but to grace your education.

The SCENE *changes to the Street.*

Enter RAMBLE.

Ramb. Into what a villanous trap am I fall'n !
dull rogue that I was, not to know Isabella's voice.
Where were my ears, my senses ? they were all in
my pocket. I was tickled with my ravishing expectations, into a perfect numbness into death ; now am
I discovered in all my rogueries and intrigues, and
falsehoods ; and must never hope to enjoy the
sweet pleasure of lying and foreswearing any more ;
I must now either repent, and become a downright
plodding lover to Christina, or in plain terms lose
her. I must either forsake all the world for, or her
for all the world. Well, if I do forsake her, she
has this to boast, I do not forsake her for any one
woman, I forsake her for ten thousand. But what
do I talk of forsaking her ? will not she forsake me
after this discovery ? and besides her own anger,
will not Sir Thomas compel her ? for he is horribly
provoked against me, whatever the matter is.
Well, I cannot bear the loss of Mrs Christina ! I had
rather endure marriage with her, than enjoy any
other woman at pleasure.—I must and will repent
and reform ; and now should an angel appear in
female shape, he should not tempt me to revolt any
more.

Enter MERRY.

Oh, Merry, I am ruin'd !

Mer. Oh, sir, you are a happy man! I have not time to ask you the success of your last adventure, I am so transported with the pleasure of the present. Cannot you limn, sir?

Ramb. Limn, what dost thou mean?

Mer. Why limn, sir; draw pictures in little.

Ramb. I draw pictures?

Mer. Yes, sir, you can, sir.

Ramb. But I cannot, sir.

Mer. But you can, sir, you can limn, and you must limn, and you shall limn, sir. Coming along by Charing Cross, who should it be my fortune to meet with but Mr Drawell, the limner, going in all haste to my Lord Drybone's, to draw Mrs Frisque's picture—and what comes into my head, sir, but to beg of him to write an apology for not coming, and send you with it to perform the work in his stead; and to prevail with him I promis'd him the gain of the picture, without the trouble.

Ramb. Thou hast undone me, seduced me from the ways of virtue and constancy, just as I was entering into 'em; I am not able to resist the temptation of this plot. But how shall I manage it? for I can no more make the picture of a face, than I can make a face; I have not so much skill as a man may learn out of the Complete Gentleman, and other elaborate pieces that teach that faculty.

Mer. No, sir? did I not hear you the other day in a mercer's shop promise his wife her picture, in the presence of several ladies, and the good man scrap'd you many legs, to express his extraordinary sense of so great a favour, and said he would wait upon you, with his wife, at your chamber?

Ramb. Thou say'st right! glowing with extreme appetite to her, my tongue and brain overheated with motion, in the stream and whirlpool of thought and babble, I very impudently invited her to sit to me for her picture, and the foolish cuckold her husband did accordingly bring her, and leave her with me; where, when I had squeez'd his orange, I gave him the rind again; and requited him with the shadow of it, drawn by one that could perform it.

Mer. Can you not draw then, sir? what shall we do? our plot is spoil'd.

Ramb. Not at all, sir; I can draw well enough for my purpose. By this plot I may draw her as I did the mercer's wife; that is I may draw her to my chamber, that's enough.

Mer. That's very well thought on, and, to continue the quibble, this plot will give you a colour to visit her.

Ramb. Well quibbled again! where's the apology? is that as witty?

Mer. A good, honest, plain, country apology.

[Gives him a letter.

Ramb. Come along, Merry! thou must help in this business. Well, I must turn thee away before thy wicked counsels have undone me.

Mer. Indeed, sir, it is ill done of me, but it is done out of pure pity, like a good natur'd nurse, that cannot forbear giving a feverish creature, that is ready to die of thirst, what drink they crave. I cannot for my life hear you groan after a wench night and day so pitifully, and not help you.

[Exeunt.

Enter LORD DRYBONE *and* BETTY FRISQUE.

The SCENE, *a Chamber.*

Lord Dry. Go, go, hussy! you are an unkind naughty girl, to make me pay thus dear for every smile and smirk I get from you. I dare safely say not a dimple you make when you smile, that does not cost me, one with another, forty pound a dimple.

Bet. 'Tis your own fault, my dear lord! you will be chiding o' one, and quarrelling with one.

Lord Dry. Chiding o' one, and quarrelling with one? ay, and I had better quarrel on. I am a fool to buy peace so dear, considering what a poor trade I have and how little I get by it.

Betty. People that cannot barter commodity for commodity, must send money in specie. You know they do it all the world over.

Lord Dry. But that's a very ruinous trade. One had better war with such a country, and forbid all traffic with it, my dear Frisky.

Betty. Ay, if one can live without it, my dear lord, you.

Lord Dry. Come, no more of this, prepare to sit! Mr Drawell's a coming. I am glad you like your point and jewel, it puts you in good humour, and makes you the fitter to sit.

Enter CISS.

Ciss. There's one below from Mr Drawell desires to speak with your lordship.

Lord Dry. How! has he fail'd me again? what an unworthy fellow it is, he shall never draw it now though he will do it for nothing.

Betty. May be he has not fail'd you, my lord. Send for the man up, and know his message.

Lord Dry. Let the man come up :   [*Exit Cis.* These sort of fellows, if they grow anything famous, they grow so saucy with it that they are not to be endured.

Enter RAMBLE, *disguised.*

Ramb. I come from Mr Drawell, my lord! he sends this letter by me to your lordship.

[*Gives him a letter.*

[Lord Drybone opens the letter and reads.
My noble Lord—Fortune maliciously, just as I was
upon the way a-coming,—I have, by much im-
portunacy, obtain'd the extraordinary kindness of this gentleman, to come in my room,
one of the first men in the world, formerly my
scholar ; have a care, I beseech your lordship,
not to speak to him of any recompense, for he
is a gentleman of quality, and draws only for
his own divertisement,

Your Lordship's humble servant.

DRAWELL.

Betty. This gentleman come to draw my picture ?
I know him. I love him for this piece of ingenuity,
I swear. *[Aside.*
Lord Dry. Sir, this is a great favour ! indeed, I
will assure you, sir, I take it for a great honour.
See, sir, this is the person whom I recommend to
your skill. *[Ramble salutes her.*
Betty. I receive this favour with a great deal of
satisfaction ; this is an honour beyond expectation.
I could not hope for such an illustrious limner.
Ramb. If I had no skill at all, so beautiful a
person would inspire me.
Betty. Oh ! sir, I rather need all the favour your
pencil can afford ; your excellent skill must hide
the faults and defects of nature.
Ramb. Nature, madam, has not committed one
the pencil must for ever despair of.
Lord Dry. Come, enough of this, if you please,
sir, let alone these compliments, and to your
business ; this is not at all to the purpose.
Betty. If your pencil, sir, flatters as much as
your tongue, the picture you will draw will not at
all resemble me.

Ramb. Heaven that made the original has taken away all means of flattery.

Betty. Heaven that made!—

Lord Dry. I say I will have no more compliments. Come, sir, if you please, begin your work.

Ramb. I am ready !

          [Pulls out his pencils, colours, and palate.

Betty. Where shall I place myself, sir ?

Ramb. Here, madam! this place receives the light best of any we shall find.

Betty. Do I sit right ?   *[She sits.*

Ramb. Indifferent, madam; a little more upright, if you please, a little more this way, your body turn'd thus ; lift up your head, that the beauty of your neck may appear, your breast bare, thus,— (*Goes and feels her breasts*) very well, a little more, —more yet—

Lord Dry. What a pudder is here ! I do not like all this ; cannot you sit as you should ?

Betty. This is all new to me, I never sat before. 'Tis the gentleman's business to place me, let him set me how he will.

Ramb. You sit admirable well, madam ! keep yourself thus.

Lord Dry. So, sir, pray to your seat.

Ramb. A little more towards me, madam, your eyes always on me. I beseech you, madam, your looks fix'd to me.

Betty. Now, sir, pray do not flatter me ! I am none of those women, who, if pictures be but handsome, they care not whether they be like or no ; one fine handsome picture might serve 'em all ; for all demand the same things, fine features, and delicate complexion. For my part I desire no charity at all, let my picture be but like and I desire no more.

Ramb. You are so rich in beauty, that the

pencil can add nothing to you ; it may possibly detract, it cannot flatter. Ah, what sweetness is
there ! what charms! I undertake a bold work
to represent those perfections. [*Talks and paints.*
I remember a story of Apelles : Apelles once
drew the picture of a mistress of Alexander the
Great ; and, as he was painting her, fell so passionately in love with her, that he was ready to die.
Alexander, out of pure generosity, bestowed her
upon him. I could do as Apelles did ; but my
lord, I am afraid your lordship will not prove an
Alexander the Great.

Lord Dry. Come, sir, I pray proceed in your
painting ! we have neither of us any business with
Alexander the Great that I know of.

Ramb. If Alexander the Great were by, he
should not hinder me from saying, I never saw
anything so charming, so—

Lord Dry. Sir, in plain terms, you talk too
much in my opinion, and do not at all mind your
pencil.

Ramb. My lord, on the contrary, I discourse
out of regard to my pencil ; to quicken the spirits,
and put a briskness and gaiety in the face.

Enter MERRY, *running dressed like an Attorney,
with a green bag under his arm.*

Lord Dry. How now, what would this fellow
have ? Who let him in without my acquaintance ?

Mer. I beg your lordship's pardon for my rude
pressing in, I am unknown to your lordship, but I
have business of extraordinary concern to your
lordship, which I must acquaint you of with all
speed.

Lord Dry. Business of extraordinary concern to
me ? what is it ?

Mer. I must impart it to your lordship in private.

Lord Dry. We are private enough here. I won't go out of the room, for I don't like this picture drawer. [*Aside*

Mer. Look you, my lord; ay, this is it; no, [*Draws him aside, and whispers, and produces several long scrolls.* this is not it; ay, this is it! no, no, ay, now I come to it.

[*Ramble starts from his feet, and falls on his knees before Betty, watching Lord Drybone still.*

Lord Dry. I would thou wert come to it at once.

Ramb. Oh, charming creature! if you have any pity in your soul, save the life of a poor languishing lover, that has been dying for you these two months. I have expressed my love to you by signs, and you have regarded them, and now I have studied this way, to tell you in more intelligible manner how much I love, admire, adore you, above all the creatures of the world, above all I can express, and shall, as long as I live; but that life will not exceed this minute, if you put me not instantly out of despair.

Betty. I know you, sir, I have observ'd you, I confess, and do further acknowledge, your love is not unpleasing to me, but it is impossible for me to give you any satisfaction.

Ramb. If you say the word, it is, and shall be possible, nay, it shall be impossible to hinder it.

Betty. But, sir, I am a close prisoner, and cannot stir out to save my own life, and much less yours.

Ramb. Now you speak unkindly, for I have seen you abroad.

Betty. It may be so, but, like a prisoner in the king's bench, never without my keeper.

Ramb. You can shake off your keeper, if you please.

Betty. My lord and I now are upon pretty good terms ; where do you lodge ?

Ramb. At the brazier's in the Mall.

Betty. Be within about two in the afternoon.

Ramb. Divine creature !

Betty. But hope for nothing but a visit, for there will be more words to a bargain than these. I will have a farther trial of love, and I will have a better love than perhaps you intend.

Ramb. Oh, heavenly creature ! you shall have as much as you can hold.

Lord Dry. How now, Mr Painter, what are you doing there ?

Ramb. Is this a mole, madam, or a little speck of dirt ?

Lord Dry. A mole, madam ! I' Gad, this same picture drawer—

Mer. Now, my lord, if the conveyances be drawn thus.

Lord Dry. Prithee, ha' done with thy conveyances, for I do not understand one word thou say'st.

Mer. No, my lord ? look you, I'll make it plain.

Lord Dry. Well, if thou mak'st it never so plain, what is all this to me ?

Mer. Not to you, my lord ? why are not you my Lord Buck's ?

Lord Dry. No, nor my Lord Doe neither.

Mer. What a rascal was the porter to tell me this was the Lord Buck's !

Lord Dry. What a rascal was you, sirrah, to come to trouble me !

Betty. Begone ! my lord's jealous, and grows into
                                          [*Exit Merry.*

choller. If he grows out of humour, our plot's spoil'd.   [*To Ramble.*

Ramb. Well, madam! enough for once.

Lord Dry. Yes, sir, and too much.

Ramb. To-morrow I will wait on you again.

Lord Dry. I shall desire your pardon, you have done enough; too much at this time to come here any more.

Betty. How, no more? what, shall he not finish my picture?

Lord Dry. You mean my picture. Tis you that sit, but 'tis my picture that must be drawn, and in an ugly shape too.

Enter LADY FADDLE.

La. Fad. How now, what is this noise? fie, my Lord Drybone, out upon thee! wilt thou never let this poor creature have any rest? I swear, I wonder she will live with thee. What's the matter, Frisky?

Betty. Here's a noble gentleman has done me the honour to begin my picture, and my lord turns him away uncivilly, and won't let him complete his work.

Lord Dry. I know what work you would have him complete. Stay, let me see! I will make an experiment. Shew me your work before you go, let me see how I like it.

Ramb. Alas, my lord, at present it is but rude; you can see nothing. Four days hence something will appear.

Lord Dry. Let me see it as it is, sir! what a devil of a face is this?   [*Ramble gives him the picture.*

Ramb. Alas, it is but—but—a pox on me for not looking on some book, to get the terms. (*Aside.*) It is but departed colours.

Lord Dry. Departed colours, what are those? dead colours, you would say, I believe.

Ramb. Ay, dead colours! the other is a term gentlemen use.

Lord Dry. Ay, such a gentleman as you are; but, sir, can this ever be a face?

Ramb. A most beautiful one when my pencil has lickt it.

Lord Dry. Lickt it? ay, indeed, it is more like a bear's cub than a face.

Ramb. It is a way of drawing I have.

Lord Dry. Is it, sir? pray, if you please, let that door be your way at present, and pray let my house be never in your way of drawing more. Come in, Betty! I'll talk with Drawell for this trick.

[*Exeunt L. Dryb. and Betty.*

La. Fad. This gentleman a picture-drawer? I swear he is the handsomest picture-drawer that ever I saw. Hold, sir! pray, a word with you.

Ramb. Madam, I am commanded hence.

La Fad. Sir, I have empire enough here to reprieve you, at least for a moment, and you shall stay! Sir, I understand, you draw pictures, and so handsome a picture-drawer must needs draw very handsome pictures, whatever my Lord Drybone says.

Ramb. When I draw yours, madam, I cannot do otherwise.

La. Fad. I swear, an incomparable well-bred man! Noble sir, you have drawn your own portraiture, in most gentle colours, that I am extremely ambitious to have mine drawn by so delicate a hand.

Ramb. Madam, my hand is unworthy of that honour. Your picture deserves rather to be drawn in a coach and six horses, in triumph round the town.

La. Fad. I swear that is very witty and sur-

3   7

prizing! Sir, you now more and more inflame me
with an ardent desire to taste of your skill; I will
not rest till I obtain the felicity.

Ramb. My pencil will be proud of the glory.
How shall I be rid of this impertinent woman?

[*Aside.*

Enter CISS, *whispers* RAMBLE.

Ciss. Sir, my lady is extremely troubled and
asham'd, my lord has treated you thus uncivilly;
by good luck, my lord is just now call'd out about
an extraordinary affair, and will not be back these
three hours. She so extremely desires to have her
picture drawn by you, that, if you will step down,
she will meet you at the door, and go and sit for
an hour in any place you shall think convenient.

Ramb. Most excellent creature, I adore thee for
thy message! were I on a precipice, I would leap
down to such an invitation. I will disentangle
myself from Madam Impertinence, that hooks herself to me, and be at the door in an instant.
Madam, an affair of consequence calls me away,
(*Exit Ciss*), my pencils, my oystershells, my brightest
colours, the exactest motion of my hand, and the
best of my skill, shall always attend your fair
physiognomy. Your ladyship's most humble servant, and picture-drawer. [*Exit Ramb.*

La. Fad. The top, the cream, the flower, the
quintessence of wit and ingenuity; his harmonious
tongue has left a tang, a relish of a passion behind
it! I swear I feel a little palpitation, I shall not
be at repose till I commence my intrigue; and, oh
my brutish and obtuse memory, I have forgot to
ask him what happy place he honours with his
abode. But now I think on't, Frisky can lend me
the knowledge; I will run with speed, and borrow
it of her. [*Exit La. Fad.*

The scene, the Street, before RAMBLE'S *lodging.*

Enter RAMBLE *and* BETTY FRISQUE, *vizarded.*

Ramb. Heaven be prais'd, we are safe at the place of battle ! This is my lodging ! in, in, my dear —my sweet—

Betty. Hold, sir ! I have honourably walk'd with you into the field, but now I'll article with you.

Ramb. I abhor the word ! it has been lately mischievous to me, and I will not hear it.

Enter a Woman vizarded, as out of RAMBLE'S *lodgings.*

Woman. Oh, Mr Ramble, are you come ? I have been waiting for my picture this hour.

Ramb. Oh, curse on my memory, I forgot this assignation ! I have such bundles of billets-doux that I must keep a clerk to enter them in a journal. Dear madam, I beg your pardon, I was pre-engag'd to a person of honour, and I quite forgot. Come an hour hence, and I will not fail you. [*Exit Woman.*

Enter to them a second Woman.

2 *Wom.* So, Mr Ramble, you serve me finely ! I have been staying for my picture these two hours, and here you promise 'em to flirts. Here is a flirt newly gone out has kept me a prisoner in a closet this hour, I was so afraid to be seen, for fear of my honour.

Ramb. Oh, dear madam !

2 *Wom.* No, sir, I scorn to sit, if you draw the pictures of every flirt.

Betty. So, sir,—but oh, I am ruin'd ! my Lady Faddle's coming ! whither shall I run ? she will know me by my clothes.

Ramb. In, in, dear madam ! this disease is

fastened on me; how shall I be cur'd of her?
What an unlucky rogue am I in my amours!

*[Betty and Ramble strive to run in, Betty gets in,
but Lady Faddle catches Ramble.*

La. Fad. Have I found you, sir? this is fortunate! I will not part with you till I obtain the
glory to be deciphered by your ingenious hand.

Ramb. Oh, madam, what Appelles is fit for so
great a work? You are so admirably painted.

La. Fad. Not at all, sir, you are misinformed, I
only use a little red. Foh, painted? I swear I hate
a painted woman in my heart, I suspect their
virtue; besides, 'tis nasty! Painted? foh!

Ramb. I mean, by nature's hand.

La. Fad. I beg your pardon, I misunderstood
you.

Ramb. That art were saucy to contend.

La. Fad. Oh, sir, you put me in a longing expectation! I beseech you let us to some convenient
place, where you may begin your work. Put me
in any posture you please, sweet sir, and let me
taste plentifully of your skill.

Ramb. Madam, I want some poet to assist my
fancy. You shall be drawn in a triumphant posture,
with all the gods and goddesses attending; Venus
crying for not being so handsome; Juno scolding
for jealousy of you; blind Cupid borrowing glass
eyes to stare on you; Jupiter transforming himself into a lap-dog, to kiss you; Mars lying naked
under your feet, in the shape of a back-sword.

La. Fad. Oh, admirable! when shall this most
rare piece be begun?

Ramb. That, madam, I do not know.

La. Fad. Not know, sir? why, sir, is it not
your noble hand that performs it?

Ramb. My hand will not have the glory.

La. Fad. Whose then, sir?

Ramb. I do not know, madam,

La. Fad. Fie, fie, sir! this is superlative modesty. Come, come, sir!   [*She pulls him.*

Enter MERRY.

Mer. Master! sir—How? my wife that must be, here?

La. Fad. Oh, dear, my servant here? I shall be dishonoured. This is unfortunate!

Mer. Does my master deal with stale flesh too? and is he making me a cuckold before I am married? I do not much care: he cannot cuckold me of her money; how shall I do to outface him now? —how now, Jack Ramble, engross all the ladies?

                    [*Winks and nods on Ramble.*

La. Fad. What shall I reply? what shall I invent? This is infernal!   [*Aside.*

Ramb. How now, sirrah, how came you and I so familiar? What is this thy rogue's plot?

                    [*Merry winks and nods on Ramble.*

Mer. So, madam, this is fine!

La. Fad. I swear, sir,—I swear!—I don't know what to swear, I am in such confusion.

Mer. Very well, madam, this is a good beginning!

Ramb. This rogue is intimate with her.—This is some plot, that I cannot discover. But, ha! here is Sir Thomas coming this way in haste.

La. Fad. Sir Thomas Rash catch me here? this is dishonour upon dishonour.

Enter SIR THOMAS RASH *and four* BAILIFFS.

Sir Tho. So, have I found you! That is the lady! I command you, take her!

1 Ba. Lady Faddle, I arrest you in the King's name, in an action of a thousand pounds at the suit of Sir Thomas Rash, here present.

Sir Tho. Come, put in substantial bail, or go to jail!

Ramb. An arrest at my lodging?

Mer. My wife that must be, arrested?

La. Fad. Arrested!

[*Ramble and Merry offer to draw, and the Bailiffs step in and disarm them.*

Sir Tho. Hold, sir, be not too forward! Your turn will come soon enough.

La. Fad. Is this done, Sir Thomas, like a civil person, and a person of honour?

Mer. What is the business, madam?

La. Fad. I will declare before all these gentlemen. Know then, that a nephew of mine, a baronet in the country, was bound in a bond of a thousand pounds to come up to town, and marry Mrs Christina, Sir Thomas's daughter, four days ago, and I was bound in the same bond.

Ramb. What's this?

La. Fad. And, my nephew failing to come up, Sir Thomas, like an uncivil person, takes the forfeiture of the bond.

Ramb. How, Sir Thomas, have you engaged your daughter to any one, after you have promis'd her to me?

Sir Tho. I promis'd her to you to be your strumpet, did I?

Ramb. My strumpet? Sure, Sir Thomas, you are craz'd, I know not what you mean, nor do you know your own meaning.

Sir Tho. That shall be tried.

Mer. Is this all the business?

Sir Tho. Come, Bailiffs, with your prisoner to the jail!

Mer. Hold, hold, sir, I'll release her! Madam, we will have a trick for his trick; say you are my wife, and plead covert-bearn.

Ramb. Was this the rogue's plot ? He has gull'd this simple lady into matrimony.　　　[*Aside.*

Mer. Yes, sir, she is the wife of me, John Merry Esq., of Merry Hall. Now meddle with her, sir, if you dare.

Sir Tho. Say you so, sir, are you come over me so ? Very well ! then I shall speedily take out a writ to arrest John Merry, Esq., in an action of a thousand pounds, and he shall pay it me every farthing, if all the estate the said John Merry and his wife, the late Dame Faddle, have in the world can pay it.

La Fad. Sir Thomas, I would have you to know that, do your worst, my estate is able to pay twice that sum, yet I have enough remaining.

Mer. I am glad to hear of that ! three or four thousand pounds will be good sauce to make the old goose go down.　　　[*Aside.*

Enter CHRISTINA *and* ISABELLA *vizarded.*

Chris. Hold ! before this noble company part, I have something of great importance to say to Mr Ramble, in the presence of you all. Sir, do you know me ?

Ramb. Madam ? [*Discovers herself to be Christina.*

Chris. Sir, I am your unfortunate daughter, (*Kneels to Sir Tho.*) who, in obedience to your commands am going to remove so great a misfortune as myself for ever from your family; but ere I depart, I beg you, by all your past fatherly love, by the secret remains of it still in your breast, by the remembrance of my dear mother in heaven, to give me leave to vindicate my self, and challenge this base villain in the presence of heaven, who knows my innocence, in your own presence, to whom he has wrong'd me, in the presence of all these, to affirm, if he dares, if there be any truth, or shadow of truth, in any word or tittle of what he spoke, in prejudice of my honour.

Ramb. Hey, what mystery? what riddle? what dream is this?

Sir Tho. Yes, sir! now affirm to her face what you said of her last night; that she had been naught with you before, that she had made an appointment then to be naught with you, and that she had been naught before ever you touch'd her.

Ramb. O, horrid! What devil has forg'd such an abominable falsehood of me? May heaven strike me dead with thunder; may the earth sink and swallow me; may all the curses of injured innocence pursue me, if ever such an impious thought came into my soul!

Sir Tho. Oh, impudence! impudence!

Ramb. And to shew my words and thoughts are the same, I here declare her as pure and spotless as a soul in heaven. I desire no greater happiness in the world than to possess her with all those misfortunes which I am accus'd to have brought upon her.

Sir Tho. Was ever the like impudence heard? He said all this I charge him with to my face, and fought with me to maintain his words.

La. Fad. Very well, I shall have nothing to do with you, or your disputes; know, my nephew is come to town; but he shall go back again, and break off the match; and so take your course.

Sir Tho. Sir Mannerly come? Hold, madam, one word more with your ladyship, and I'll end all controversies. Well, Mr Ramble, you declare in the presence of my Lady Faddle, and us all, that you never meant the word you said.

Ramb. That I never said or thought anything of this lady, but what a votary might say of the saint he prays to.

Sir Tho. That you acknowledge her entirely innocent of—

Ramb. That her innocence is equal with her beauty; and that her beauty can be equall'd by nothing, but her own innocence : and that she can be compar'd with none but herself.

Sir Tho. And that you will marry her, whenever I please, and leave her fortune to my discretion.

Ramb. That I will marry her, without any consideration of a fortune, rather than any other woman in the world with a Kingdom.

Sir Tho. Very well, then take notice, I will marry her to Sir Mannerly Shallow; and so, my Lady Faddle, I release your ladyship; and now our contest is ended.

Ramb. What's that?

Chris. Hold, Mr Ramble, do not dare to interpose! my father has declar'd his pleasure, and I declare my ready obedience; however, I will never have you of all men.

Ramb. Oh my torment!

La. Fad. Well, Sir Thomas, you have dealt, let me tell you, ungentilely with me; but however, to put an end to controversies, I forgive you; and so let the match proceed.

[*Exeunt Sir Tho. Rash, La. Fad., Chris., and Isab.*

Ramb. Merry, a word! is this lady your wife?

Mer. Yes, in earnest, sir.

Ramb. Then, sirrah, make her break off this match, or I'll cut your throat, how dear soever I pay for it.

Mer. Well, sir, a word to the wise is enough. You may be sure I'll do what lies in my power.

[*Exit Merry.*

Enter BETTY FRISQUE.

Betty. So, so Mr Ramble, you are a very fine
man! some women come to you for their pictures,
and others for promise of marriage; I have heard
all passages. This is you that lov'd, admir'd, ador'd
me above all creatures in the world; above all
you could express; that you could have no rest
day nor night, for thinking and sighing after me?
Poor loving man! I had been sweetly serv'd if I
had been such a fool as to have believ'd you, and
fall'n a loving you as hard as ever I could drive.
Well, I thank you, you have done me a kindness;
I shall endure my confinement a little better after
this, nay, I shall thank my old lord for keeping
me out of the temptations of such false, dissembling, insinuating men.   [*Exit.*

Ramb. So, so, forsaken and hated by every one?
all afflictions come together; I am justly serv'd
for my liquorish, greedy, insatiable, ridiculous
temper; that, like Adam, could not be contented
in Paradise, but must be tasting all sorts of fruit,
lawful, or unlawful, though I had pleasures enow
in Christina's love to satisfy a demi-god, and more
than any mere creature could merit. Well, despair
shall be damn'd before he shall have the fing'ring
of me, yet. Opportunity has not so turn'd his
bald crown on me, but I can have hold enough of
his ears yet; at least I will have hold of my
rival's ears, whoe'er he be. This shall give him to
understand (*shows his sword*), what portion he shall
have with his lady; nay, what lady he shall have,
for this fair, slender creature shall enjoy his body,
and speedily.   [*Exit.*

ACT IV. SCENE I., *The Street.*

Enter SIR MANNERLY SHALLOW, *and* BOOBY.
Sir Mannerly drest in a fine country-fashion'd suit.

Sir Man. How do my clothes become me, Booby?

Boo. Bravely, an't like your worship.

Sir Man. And am I pretty handsome ?

Boo. I never see a handsomer man peep out of a suit of clothes.

Sir Man. Well, I long for my bride! oh how gentilely I could salute her now ! madam, what a spring, a source, a fountain, a river of love and beauty flows from your eyes ; a Nilus of beauty overflows the Egypt of your face.

Enter a Servant.

Ser. Sir Thomas Rash, nor Madam Christina, are nowhere to be found, sir.

Sir Man. Hey, not to be found? Well, then, there is knavery in this, they do it on purpose to make me forfeit my bond. Oh dear, here comes the person of quality I invited to my wedding! what shall I say to excuse myself to him ?

Enter the Porter.

Noble sir, I swear I am so out of aspect, I know not how to demean myself. I was so bold as to crave the honour of your company at my wedding-supper to-night, and I swear, sir, I cannot find my bride.

Por. Not find your bride, sir? that's strange! it's a common thing here in London for women to run away from their husbands after they're married, but I never knew a woman run from her husband before she was married till now. Well, sir, there's no hurt done.

Sir Man. Hold, noble sir ! I have received an

many noble favours from you to-day, that I will
not let you stir till I know to whom I am so much
oblig'd, that I may know to whom to repay. I
beseech you, sir, to let me know your honourable
name, for I am sure you are of noble quality.

Por. Ay, sir, I am a knight! I was dubbed last
Lord Mayor's show.

Sir Man. Look you there, Booby, did not I say
he was a knight? I beseech you, sir, of what
order? for by your silver chain, and noble silver
plate, you must be of some order that I have not
read of in heraldry.

Por. I am of a very old order, sir; of the order
of Issachar. I stoop under my burden, and my
crest is an ass couchant.

Sir Man. Look you there, Booby! I beseech
you, sir, your name?

Por. My name is Rash, sir, at your service.

Sir Man. What—not Sir Thomas Rash?

Por. Old Tom Rash!—Sir Thomas, if you will
have it so.

Sir Man. O strange, Booby!

Boob. Sir Thomas Rash's worship?

Sir Man. Did one ever see the like? Here have
I been angling and trowling for my father-in-law,
and have had him at my hook all day.

Boob. This is just as your worship and I look'd
up and down for your boots one day, and you had
'em on your legs.

Sir Man. Just so, for all the world.

Por. What have I done now? I am afraid I have
brought more compliments on my head. They
come, they come full swing! oh, what will become
of me? oh, sir, have mercy on me!

Sir Man. Noble father-in-law!

Boob. His worship's father-in-law's worship!

[*Sir Man. and Booby run and embrace him.*

Por. What! do they call me father-in-law?

Boob. Your worship, Sir Thomas, I believe, does not know my master's worship; my master's worship is Sir Mannerly Shallow, that is come to town, according to his bond, to marry your daughter.

Por. Come to town to marry my daughter? I begin to think 'em merry men again. Let me be hang'd if I can guess whether they be fools, or no, for my life; I 'facks, I rather think they make a fool of me.

Sir Man. I am the same Mannerly Shallow, on my honour, sir.

Por. Sir Mannerly Shallow! ha, ha! what comes in my head? (*laughs*). I heard my master, and name-sake, Sir Thomas Rash, talk of one Sir Mannerly Shallow that is to marry my young lady, and, I warrant, this simple gentleman is he; and he hearing my name to be Thomas Rash, and calling myself in waggery, Sir Thomas, he takes me to be my master: ha, ha, ha! (*laughs*). Hark you, master, are not you Sir Mannerly Shallow?

Sir Man. I am, on my honour, Sir Thomas!

Por. Ha, ha, ha!   [*Laughs.*

Sir Man. Ay, the same; ha, ha, ha!   [*Laughs.*

Boo. It is his worship!   [*Laughs.*

[*They all three laugh, and the Porter laughs the more, to see them laugh.*

Por. I have laugh'd my heart sore. What a knavish prank could I play now, to pass for Sir Thomas Rash, and pop my daughter on this silly knight. Well, sir, I will not cheat you, I am honest Tom Rash, a poor porter, and servant to that very Sir Thomas Rash you want; and come along, I'll lead you to him!

Sir Man. Come, father-in-law, this is not gentle, now you have owned yourself, to deny yourself

again; you do it, now you see who I am, to make
me forfeit my bond--but what have I discovered?
Let me compare the very same coat of arms. (*Pulls
out a letter, and compares the seal with the arms of
the porter's badge,*) I swear this was well thought
on, I'll take my oath; now if you deny yourself,
I'll go to law with you, for I know you by your
arms.

Por. This is better and better, ha, ha, ha!
[*Laughs.*

Sir Man. My father-in-law I see is a merry man!
[*Laughs.*

Boo. Sir Thomas, his worship did but jest, ha-
ha! [*Laughs.*

Por. Well, I'll own myself to be Sir Thomas
Rash, carry him to my cellar, and there let my
wife look to him, whilst I call my master. Come,
son-in-law, I am your father-in-law, and I am
heartily glad to see you; I'll conduct you to my
off-spring, and your bed-mate that must be.
What sport is here!

Sir Man. Did not I say 'twas he? [*Exit Porter.*

Boo. What luck was this to find him, just as
your bond was forfeited.

Sir Man. Ay, and by the coat of arms; you must
know, I am very well skill'd in coats of arms. I
can tell all our own coats, and all the quarterings,
ever since King Cadwallader. Oh, but Booby,
was it not pretty, that I should invite my father-
in-law to his own daughter's wedding?

Boo. I warrant, that made his worship laugh so
heartily.

Sir Man. Well thought on, I swear! now run to
my cloak-bag and fetch my bag of money to pay
for my wedding-dinner. [*Exit.*

Boo. I shall, an't like your worship! [*Exit.*

Enter RAMBLE *and* MERRY.

Mer. Sir, am not I a loving servant, that forsake the wife of my bosom, now love has cook'd
and dish'd her up; and leave her piping hot, to
run after your appetite?

Ramb. Thou art an honest fellow, Merry; but
all things consider'd, the kindness is as great to
thyself as me; however, I accept it. But hast thou
hunted out my rival?

Mer. I saw him hereabout not a quarter of an
hour ago.

Ramb. What a kind of fellow is he?

Mer. Oh, 'tis such a Cumberland piece, he is
much farther from understanding, than his country
is from London; and has such a living log follows
him, as you never saw: many a wiser block has
suffered martyrdom for Christmas, in his master's
hall chimney.

Ramb. Prithee let's inquire hereabout for them.
By thy description they are so remarkable, everybody that has seen 'em, will inform us of them.

[*Exeunt.*

THE SCENE, *An apple-shop.*

Enter RASH *and his* WIFE.

Wife. How, are you mad, Thomas? lose such a
fortune for my daughter?

Rash. What, shall I play the knave o' that
fashion?

Wife. Is it knavery to own your christendom?
is not your name Rash? and were not you
christened Thomas?

Rash. But I was not christened Sir Thomas,
was I?

Wife. Well, if the knight will christen you Sir
Thomas, what's that to any one?

Rash. What ? I shall ha' my Master Sir Thomas, ha' me up, coram nobis, for forgery.

Wife. Well, let him coram nobis you as much as he dares; there's no law against owning one's own name. Let him take his silver badge again, and he will; we can live without his chain, we shall be as good as he now.

Rash. I tell you, I won't do it!

Wife. Won't you ? then let my goods rot and they will, I'll ne'er sell pennyworth of apples or gingerbread more whilst I live.

Rash. These women will rule the roast! well, I'll be Sir Thomas then, but if I look through a Scotch casement for this, that is to say, a pillory, I'll lodge a cudgel in your middle story backward.

Wife. Let them do what they dare, they shall find a mess of hot codlings o' me, I warrant them. Give me my clean kercher, and my hat, and run quickly, and fetch Winny from school!

Rash. There, there! don 'em quickly! our son-in-law comes.

Enter SIR MANNERLY *and* BOOBY, *with a bag of money under his arm; a beggar-woman with a child begging of* SIR MANNERLY.

Sir Man. Well, I never saw such a fine street in my life!

Beg. Wo. Pray your worship, give a poor woman something.

Sir Man. Begone, beggar-woman!

Rash. Son-in-law, you are heartily welcome! See, this is your mother-in-law.

Wife. For want of a better, sir.

Sir Man. Madam, your most humble servant.

Rash. Well, son, I'll run and fetch your bride! she is but two doors off at a boarding-school, where I kept her for good breeding. You wonder to see

so many apples here? my wife and I, you must
know, are great lovers of apples, and we are laying
in our winter store into our cellar; that's my
cellar, but that great house is my habitation.

Sir Man. Oh stately! that's like the palace of Sol-
sublimibus, Alta Columnis: and gold on the
top too! clara micante auro.

Rash. Ay, to show I love apples, I have a golden
apple, a golden pippin on the top. Well, I'll leave
you with my wife; I'll be back presently.

[*Exit Rash.*

Sir Man. Is your ladyship so great a lover of
apples? I shall agree with you then mightily in
diet, for I love apples as well as ever Adam did,
and here are as many fine apples as ever I saw in
all my life.

Boo. Curious apples indeed.

Wife. Pray, son-in-law, be pleas'd to eat one!
there's a pippin, as good a one as ever tooth was
put in, and as sound as myself.

Boo. A pure pippin!

Sir Man. Your ladyship's most humble servant!
My lady's a plain woman, Booby.

Boo. She seems a very hearty woman, an't like
your worship.

Enter RASH *and* WINNIFRIDE.

Rash. See, son! here's your young yoke-fellow,
that must into the noose with you.

Sir Man. A most transcendent beauty!

Rash. A plain girl.

Sir Man. Not at all, she's the epitome of perfection; I am enamour'd above the capacity of expression! I deserve to forfeit a thousand bonds of
a thousand pound, for staying the thousandth part
of a minute from her embraces. I will pay the for-

feiture of my bond in love and kisses ;—I will number up.

Beg. Wo. Pray, good your worship !

Sir Man. What a troublesome woman art thou ! dost not see I am busy a complimenting ? I say, I will number up by art arithmetical.

Beg. Wo. Pray, your worship !

Sir Man. Did one ever see the like ?

Boo. Woman, do not trouble his worship.

Wife. Begone, or I'll send for the beadle !

Sir Man. I say, I will number up, I will number up. This scurvy beggar-woman has broke off my speech, that, I vow and swear, I do not know what I was going to say. I had better ha' given her a shilling, than have lost such a speech.

Boo. I could find in my heart, beggar-woman, to kick you, for spoiling his worship's speech ; no matter, your worship has twenty more as good.

Rash. No matter for compliments. Come, son-in-law, to church, if you please, and there let the parson compliment you both into man and wife, and that's the compliment of compliments.

Sir Man. With all my heart ! and may a thousand cupids hover over every pew, to fill your heart as full of love, as mine is of love and admiration.

Boo. Did you ever hear such pure compliment ?

Rash. Never in all my days ! *As they are going off,*

Enter RAMBLE and MERRY.

Mer. That's he !

Ramb. Is that he ? 'Tis so ridiculous a fellow, I cannot be angry with him.

Mer. Go, sir! manage him, whilst I handle Log, the second King of frogs, that follows him.

[*Ramble takes Sir Mannerly, and Merry Booby, aside.*

Ramb. Sir, one word with you in private.

[*To Sir Man.*

Mer. Sir, one word with you in private.

[*To Booby.*

Sir Man. With me, sir?

Boo. With me, forsooth?

Ramb. Ay, sir, it must be very private.

Mer. Ay, sir.

Ramb. Is not your name Sir Mannerly Shallow?

Sir Man. It is, sir! what then, sir?

Ramb. Are not you come to town to marry Sir Thomas Rash's daughter?

Sir Man. I am, sir! what then, sir?

Boo. Four oxen to run for a wager, sir, do you say?

Mer. From Tweed to Newcastle.

Ramb. Then you must not have her, sir.

Sir Man. How! not have her, sir?

Ramb. No stirring, sir! If you do, this runs into your guts.

Sir Man. Into my guts, sir?

Ramb. Ay, into your guts, sir!

Boo. My master's pied ox to be one!

Mer. For a wager of fourscore load of hay.

Sir Man. Booby!

Ramb. No Booby, sir.

Sir Man. No Booby, sir?

Ramb. No Booby, sir.

Boo. To be eat all with mustard.

Mer. All with mustard.

Boo. An ox eat mustard?

Mer. All with mustard.

Ramb. I shall be very brief with you. I shall propound but two things to you; take your choice, either to go out immediately and fight me, and he of us two that comes alive out of the field shall have the lady, or else this minute to take post for

Cumberland, and not to come up till I am married to her.

Sir Man. To go and fight with you, sir ?

Ramb. Ay, sir ! till one of us fall dead, or ride post for Cumberland. Take your choice!

Sir Man. Ride post for Cumberland, sir ?

Ramb. Ay, sir ! chuse instantly, or this goes into your guts, sir.

Sir Man. My guts, sir ?

Ramb. Ay, sir.

Sir Man. Booby !

Ramb. No Booby, sir ! Speak quickly, what you'll do !

Boo. And the ox that wins to be knighted ?

Mer. To be knighted !

Boo. I never heard the like ; let me tell his worship—

Mer. Presently, when I ha' done : I have not half done.

Ramb. Say what you'll do, and that instantly !

Sir Man. Sir, I'll——

Ramb. What will you do, sir ?

Sir Man. Sir, I'll——

Ramb. Dispatch, sir !

Sir Man. Sir, I'll—sir, I will not, sir ! What ha' you to do to make me fight, or ride post either, whether I will or no, sir ?

Ramb. No questioning my authority. Speak instantly, I say instantly !

Sir Man. I never met with such a fellow in my life.

Ramb. You will not speak, sir ?

Sir Man. Sir, I'll——

Ramb. What, sir ?

Sir Man. Sir, I'll ride post, sir !

Ramb. Then come along, sir ! I'll see you mounted, and attend you, or one shall for me, one forty or fifty miles on the way, no looking o'er your shoulder, sir.   [*Drags him out, Sir Mannerly looks back and offers to speak, Ramble stops his mouth.*

Wife. Mr Booby, Mr Booby! there's a gentleman runs away with your master. Call a constable! Thomas, a constable! Come along with me, Winny, to call a constable.

Rash. Is the woman mad to make a hubbub?— Hold your tongue!

Wife. I will not! He carries away our son-in-law by force.   [*Exit. Rash follows her.*

Boo. One steal my master?

Mer. No stirring, sir,

Boo. No stirring? What! you help to steal him, do you? Here, beggar-woman, hold my bag of money a little! (*Gives the Beggar-woman the bag of money to hold*) and I'll try a friskin with him. Thou shalt not come at thy sword.   [*Merry and Booby fight off the stage.*

[*A noise of a hubbub within, and meanwhile the Beggar-woman watches her opportunity, lays down the child, and runs away with the money.*

Enter RAMBLE *and* MERRY.

Ramb. This is good! the constable and the rabble have seiz'd our foes ; and we, the aggressors, have escap'd, whilst the two clowns stick fast in the mud of the dirty crowd. Let's pursue our fortunes, overtake Sir Thomas and the company, be very impudent and obstinate, and see what that will do.

Mer. With all my heart, sir, for I do not care for coming within the reach of that heavy fisted fool any more.   [*Exeunt.*

Enter CONSTABLE, SIR MANNERLY, BOOBY, RASH,
WIFE, *and* WINNIFREDE.

Sir Man. You have let go the thieves that would
have stolen me, and here you hold my man and me.

Con. Stolen you, sir? I found this man in actual
battery.

Boo. He batter'd me as much.

Rash. Come, come, son-in-law, never make a
bustle on your wedding-day! give the constable a
spill.*

Sir Man. There's a spill! but I take my oath he
would have stolen me.

Con. No more words on't! Come! there, go about
your business!

Sir Man. Come, madam, as the poet says—*per
varios casus per tot discrimina rerum.*

[*Exeunt Sir Man., Rash, Wife, and Win.*

Boo. I think I plough'd his chaps for him; an'
he had cuff'd a little longer, I would ha' pull'd up
his nose by the roots—but where's the beggar-
woman with my bag of money? Look, if she has
not laid it in the street, like a baggage! a thousand to one but it might have been stolen—hey,
my bag of money is alive! a bastard, a bastard!
—(*Takes up the child*) Stop thief, stop thief! a beggar-woman has run away with a bag of money, and
has left a bastard in the room! Stop thief, thief!

[*Lays down the child, and offers to run away.*

Wat. Mr Constable, Mr Constable, here's a fellow has lain a child in the street!

Con. Stop him, stop him, knock him down!
how now, sirrah, lay a bastard in the street?

Boo. Is it my bastard? Is it not the beggar-
woman's bastard that was a begging here, and has
run away with all my money?

* The bishops, who consecrated this ground, were wont to
have a spill or sportule from the credulous laity.—*Ayliffe.*

Con. She was your whore, was she, sirrah ? Here's a fine plot of a rogue, neighbours, to make a bustle in the streets, that his whore might have an opportunity to lay a bastard to the parish. Yes, sirrah ! the parish shall maintain such a lusty rogue as you in lechery ?—Come, sirrah, to the house of correction.

Wat. Ay, Mr Constable, whip him, whip him ! this way the parish money goes ; I have been sess'd above fifteen shillings this year, for such rogues' unlawful lecheries.

Boo. Whip me ? I never saw the woman before in my life.

Con. Then you lay with her in the dark, did you, sirrah ?

Boo. I am but newly come to town.

Con. Then you shall be whipt as soon as you come ; a whipping-post shall be your welcome.

Boo. Whip me if you dare, since you go to that, for I belong to a critic.

Con. A critic ! what's that ?

Boo. A great judge ! that was he that was here just now.

Con. He a judge ? he looks like a man fit to hold the scale of justice, indeed ; he is more fit to hold a grocer's scale, and weigh plums and comfits than causes.

Con. Come, sirrah, I'll let out your hot blood ! I'll plant a grove o' birch in your arse-o'-peak.

Boo. Oh, Mr Constable, my master is a northern judge indeed, and a baronet. I can prove it.

Con. I care not what he is, sirrah ! Will he put in security to keep the child, and buy off your whipping ?

Boo. Why must he ? Or must I be whipt ?

Con. That time shall try.

Boo. Oh, Mr Constable, come along ! my master's

worship shall be bound, and give you any content.

Con. Well, let's see what he will do!   [*Exeunt.*

Enter SIR THO. RASH, MERRY, CHRISTINA, LADY
    FADDLE, ISABELLA, BRIDGET, *and* RAMBLE.

La. Fad. Where have you been, Mr Merry ?

Mer. Only settling some things about my estate.

Sir Tho. Do not follow and tantany us, Mr
Ramble, for, I declare positively, thou shalt never
have my daughter.

Chris. Mr Ramble, my father is engag'd to
another ; but whether he was or no, the words
you said are never to be forgiven. Neither extravagance, raillery, drink, nor nothing can excuse 'em ;
they have fix'd you in my eternal hatred ; and
you are the only thing of all Heaven's creatures I
abhor.

Ramb. Then I am the only wretched thing of
the whole creation, and the more wretched, since
I suffer innocently : for whatever have been my
other sins, from that unpardonable one of blas-
pheming your honour, I am wholly innocent.
Consider why I should say it, what should move
me to it ? what did provoke me ? and what
should I gain by it when said ?

Chris. That foppish vain-glory which possesses
all your sex, of defaming those women whose
honours you cannot otherwise abuse.

Sir Tho. Why, sir, what should move me ? what
provoke me ? and what should I gain by telling a
lie, sir ?

Isab. I swear, madam, I begin to pity him, and
think there's some mistake.

La. Fad. I dare not interpose, for fear of dis-
covering the affair about my picture.

Mer. Come, sweet-heart ! you are the chief

person concern'd; you must resign your claim to this lady, for Jack Ramble is my friend, and though I know nothing of the business, I know he is innocent, because I know him to be an honest fellow. But whether innocent or no, I will have matters made up; for, in plain terms, if my friend may not bed the woman he loves, I will not bed the woman I love; I will never be happy while my friend is miserable.

La. Fad. How, Mr Merry?

Sir Tho. Let me alone with him, madam. Sir, what have you to do to intermeddle in my affairs? bed who you will, sir, and what you will, sir, but if you say he did not say these words I give you the lie; and there's my glove.

Mer. Take your glove, sir! your hand is old, and will catch cold.

Ramb. Some devil has appear'd to him in my shape, and said this.

Enter BETTY FRISQUE, *and* CIS.

Betty. Oh, dear! have I met with your ladyship? (*To Lady Fad.*) this is lucky! if ever you will be kind to me in your life, madam, take me into your company. I have been abroad but two hours, and my lord has been to seek me in such a rage, that if you do not excuse me, it will be a parting quarrel.

Ramb. Betty Frisque here! how do my sins follow me? what shall I do? now I think on't, she dares no more own the knowledge of me than I dare of her: my standing virtue, impudence, must aid me.

La. Fad. Why dost thou do this, Betty?

Enter LORD DRYBONE.

Lord Dry. So, gentlewoman, are you herded?

Ha! what do I see here! her father? That's he I
saw last night, I'm sure on't; I remember his face
again, though I saw him in the dark. Very well,
sir, take your daughter again! I am very glad 'tis
you she runs to, I thought to have found her in
worse company. There, sir, take her, take her,
and make the best of her!   [*To Sir Thomas.*

Sir Tho. My daughter, sir? To whom do you
speak, sir?

Ramb. What! more mistakes?

Lord Dry. To you, sir.

Sir Tho. To me, sir? I am as good a man as yourself, sir.

Lord Dry. As good a man, sir?

Mer. Hold, hold, gentlemen!

Lord Dry. Sir, I am a person of honour, sir.

Sir Tho. And I am a person of quality, sir.

Lord Dry. Well, sir, be of what quality you
will, sir, you came last night to my door with
fiddles, and challeng'd me for debauching your
daughter, sir; then you could own her in the dark,
for your own pleasure, sir, and now I will make
you own her for mine. And, as I told you last
night, she had been debauch'd before I touch'd her,
so I tell you again, if she had not, perhaps I would
have consider'd her.

Ramb. The mistake comes out.

Sir Tho. Hold, my lord! was not you in your
night-gown and drawers?

Lord Dry. Yes, sir, and you was in a buff-coat.

Sir Tho. Mr Ramble, where art thou? Wilt thou
forgive me? Canst thou forgive me? honest Mr
Ramble, forgive me!

Ramb. Now, Madam.

Sir Tho. My lord I thank you heartily for this
discovery: you have clear'd up a mistake in which
I persisted, to the injury of an honest gentleman;

but now I will do myself and him right. Know then, this gentleman is a servant to my daughter, and this is my daughter I challeng'd you about; and, finding him something airy and wild, was desirous to hinder the match; and, he passing by my door with fiddles last night, I in a rage pursu'd him to your lordship's and mistaking your lordship for him, in the dark, I challeng'd you with intentions of debauching my daughter, and your reply intangled us in difficulties, which now are vanish'd.

L. Dry. Then this is the lady it seems was serenaded. [*To Christina.*

Ramb. The same, my Lord! the playing at your door was but a blind——

Bet. No, no, 'twas to me!

Chris. He brings himself off wittily.

L. Dry. But hold, sir! now I remember, you came to draw her picture to-day.

Chris. Has he that trick too?

Ramb. I did so!

Bet. Ay, ay! I have an intrigue with him.

Ramb. But it was only for divertisement. I never saw her before in my life.

Bet. Why do you say so? 'Twas an appointment. Well, my lord, you and I must part! you see how false I am.

L. Dry. Dear Betty, forgive me! I see thou hast more virtue and goodness than I have estate to reward. Live with me again, and I will become a new creature.

Bet. That must be by some very strange miracle indeed, that an old man should become a new creature—but, however, mend as much as you will, I shall never mend; I shall continue my intrigues with picture-drawers, and pages, and hackney-coachmen—and every man I can come near.

L. Dry. Oh, do not treat me thus severely! I have

injur'd thy virtue, but I will make thee recompence for my life, and all the pleasure of it lies in thy favour.

Bet. No, no, this keeping of old women, by you old sinners, is but done out of a scurvy custom, not any need you have. Like old snuff rakers, that cannot live without snuff, though it never makes them sneeze, do but break your self off the custom for one month, and you will find no want. But come, since you are humbled, I make a proposal! promise, before all this noble company, to make a settlement of £500 a-year on me for life, that, if we ever quarrel, I may have something to trust to, and I will return to my dominion again, and govern you as formerly.

L. Dry. I engage it! and you shall have it drawn by what lawyers you please.

Bet. Then I am yours in the new-fashion'd matrimony for ever.

L. Dry. I am, as formerly, your most obsequious keeper.

Sir Tho. Oh, these are fine doings! but I say nothing.

Ramb. Now, madam! it is my turn to quarrel, and be unkind.

Chris. Yes, indeed, you had need boast of your innocence; witness the importunate temptations of a young lady, which you manfully resisted last night, and could by no means be brought to her embraces! witness this creature, whose picture it seems you drew, an excellence I never knew you had till now.

Ramb. Oh, forgive me! I acknowledge my faults with grief and penitence. I am amazed, how it was possible for me to think of anything but you; but hopes of love are like the prospect of a fair street a great way off, and you cannot blame a poor

thirsty traveller, if he takes a sip here and there
by the way—— .·   [*Kneels.*

Sir Tho. How! on thy knees, Mr Ramble? I
swear, we rather ought to kneel to thee. Rise,
rise, man! were I not to forfeit a thousand pound
bond thou shouldst have my daughter before any
man.

Ramb. Say you so, sir! dirt shall never be laid
in the scale with beauty. I will pay the forfeiture.

Isab. This is brave, I swear! Now, madam, you
are bound in honour and gratitude to forgive him.

Sir Tho. Mr Ramble, this is so generous a proposi-
tion, that I will pay the forfeiture of the bond, give
thee my daughter and a thousand pound more
with her, than ever I design'd for her portion,
with any man. Take her, she's thine!

Chris. Well, sir, I hope you will give over your
picture-drawing?

Ramb. Now I am in heaven, and all my sins
forgiven, upbraid me not with them. I will draw
no pictures but my own, and those never without
your help.

L. Fad. How, Sir Thomas, will you use my
nephew thus scurvily?

Mer. How! will you oppose my desire? Resist
my virgin authority?

La. Fad. Mr Merry, I will not have my nephew
thus abus'd.

Enter SIR MANNERLY, WYNNIFRIDE, PORTER, *and*
WIFE.

See, he has found us!

Sir Man. My lady aunt, wish me joy!

La. Fad. Wish thee joy, sweet-heart, for what?
for losing thy bride? Here is Sir Thomas Rash,
after all our articles, is going unworthily to bestow
his daughter upon another.

Sir Man. How, aunt? you do not know Sir
Thomas Rash when you see him, nor his daughter
neither. Sure I have her fast enough, I am married
to her already, and here she is!

Chris. This the creature that was design'd for
me? Bless me! what a deliverance have I had.

Sir Man. This, Sir Mannerly.

La. Fad. What dost thou say, art thou married
to that girl?

Sir Tho. Married to my porter's daughter? This
fellow is my porter, madam, and his wife is my
apple-woman.

Sir Man. Your porter! what's that?

La. Fad. He goes of errands for groats and
testers and pence. This is Sir Thomas Rash, and
this is his daughter!

Sir Man. How! am I cozen'd so? Is this Sir
Thomas Rash? and is this his daughter?—Are you
no Sir Thomas? and you no my lady? And do
you go of errands for groats, and pence? And do
you sell apples?

Por. Faith, son, 'tis a folly to disown it, now
all is done. These are our occupations! I am no
knight, but of your dubbing. You would dub me
a knight whether I would or no; I was not ambitious of the honour.

Wife. Well, though we are poor folks, we are
honest and true.

Sir Man. Honest and true? sirrah! come back
and unmarry me again.

[*Beats the porter.*

Sir Tho. Hold, hold, Sir Mannerly! now 'tis too
late. How came this mistake, Tom?

Por. My being your worship's namesake caus'd
it. He would needs bear me down I was your
honour, and marry my daughter in spite of my
teeth.

La. Fad. Oh, how hast thou dishonour'd our family !

Sir Man. Fear not, aunt, I'll feague 'em !* Porter, I'll make it a scurvy errand to you ; and, apple woman, your daughter shall be a costly pippin to you.

Wife. Do your worst !

Enter CONSTABLE *and* BOOBY, *with a child in his arms.*

Boo. Here's his worship ! Oh, an't like your worship, if you won't be bound to maintain this child for me, I shall go to prison, and be whipt presently.

Sir Man. Maintain that child ? What, ha' you got a bastard since you came to town already ?

Boo. 'Tis a beggar-woman's bastard, I never saw in my days before.

Sir Man. Get a bastard off a beggar-woman in a day's time ? Do they breed so fast in London ? that's faster than our tame coneys do ; no wonder London is so full of people.

Boo. An't like your worship, I never saw or touch'd the woman, or any woman, I never lay with any woman in my life ; give me a book, I'll kiss it upon it.

Sir Man. How could you come by this bastard, then ?

Boo. I did not come by it, it came by me. I gave a beggar-woman the bag of money to hold, whilst I cufft with the thief's man, that would have stole you, and she lays down the bastard, and runs away with the bag of money.

Sir Man. How ! lost my bag o' money ? then be whipt, I'll keep none o' the bastard.

Con. Then come along, sir.

Sir Tho. Have pity on the poor fellow !

* Perplex them.

Sir Man. No, since he would not keep my bag o' money, I won't keep his bastard.

Boo. Oh, an't like your worship, be but bound for me, I'll keep it myself,—I'll serve it out.

Sir Man. Well then, apple-woman, since I am married, do you keep my man Booby's bastard for nothing; that shall be for a portion with your daughter.

Wife. I don't care if I do; the child is a fine likely child.

Sir Man. Well, I scorn to be beholden to you, I will pay for the keeping of it. But Booby, I will send you down quickly into the country, if you get bastards thus fast.

Sir Tho. Mr Constable, discharge the man! I'll see that the gentleman, his master, performs his word.

Con. Well then, o' your word, Sir Thomas, I release him.

Sir Man. So, I have come up to London to a very fine purpose; I ha' lost my mistress, lost my money, am married to an apple-woman's daughter, and must keep a beggar-woman's bastard; whereas, I thought to have liv'd in London, and never seen the country more. I will now go down into the country, and spend all my time in railing against London. I will never see London more, so much as in a map; I will burn my map of London that hangs in my parlour.

Sir Tho. A very honest, and as the times are, pious and wholesome resolution, Sir Mannerly. Better live in the country, and burn your map of London, than live in London, and spoil your map of humanity with drinking and wenching.

Por. Ay, son-in-law, better go into the country, and live lovingly with my daughter, than stay in town, and turn her away, and keep a wench in her stead, as gentry do that marry, and live here.

Sir Man. Why! do they?

Wife. Ay, the more shame for 'em.

Sir Man. Then I'm resolv'd I'll stay in London! and Booby, you can find bastards, do you find a wench for me.

Wife. Keep a wench under my Winny's nose? I'll tear her eyes out.

Sir Tho. I will dissuade him. Well, Sir Mannerly, I am very sorry for the misfortune you have met with in coming to town for my alliance; I will cancel the bond to make you some recompence. And, since my daughter is not so happy to enjoy you, let my house have the honour to entertain you; whither I also invite the rest of this noble company. My Lady Faddle and her husband, my Lord Drybone, and his settlement, and Tom Rash, and thy wife, be of our society now: this noble alliance has advanced thee; be a knight to-day, and prince of porters for ever, and thy wife, lady of apple-women. I will have both your statues made in ginger-bread, and set up in Costermongers, Hall, and noble brides and bridegrooms all walk in,

And love apace, as fast as you can drive!

And may the trade of love for ever thrive.

[*Exeunt.*

EPILOGUE.

Spoken by SIR MANNERLY SHALLOW, *the Country Wit.*

Brothers, I'm newly come to town from Cumber-
Land, to be one of your ingenious number.
I am afraid I shall disgrace you all,
But I'm resolv'd I will a damning fall;
Since you have ten ill plays for one good play,
I think to damn 'em all the safest way.
But I in all things, sirs, shall copy you,
And save or damn, as you great judges do.
As for the poet who is try'd to-day,
I know him not, and so can little say;
If all in his petition here be true,
He did not write this play, great wits, for you.
He says, long since, you mighty judges swore
That you would never ride this circuit more;
That you have ta'ne the malefactor napping,
He writ for wits of London Bridge and Wapping,
Who hate to see a muse in buskins strut,
As much as in gilt coach a gaudy slut.
That his defence he's unprepar'd to make,
Yet for an honour does your presence take,
And says, he does it more renown esteem
To die by you, than to be sav'd by them.
Sirs, for my sake, let all his faults be wav'd,
He's not the first damn'd poet I have sav'd.

THE

AMBITIOUS STATESMAN,

OR THE

LOYAL FAVOURITE.

The Ambitious Statesman, or the Loyal Favourite. As it was acted at the Theatre Royal, by His Majesties Servants. Written by Mr Crowne. London, Printed for William Abington, at the Black-spread-Eagle at the West end of St Pauls, 1679.

This drama, in the opinion of its author, was the most vigorous of all his labours, " but born in a time so unhealthy to poetry, that it met not with the applause which some people thought it deserved." That it is superior to most of the tragedies of the reign of Charles the Second is obvious. The language is vigorous, the interest never flags, and the versification is highly poetical. Passages of extreme beauty may without difficulty be pointed out,* and there is, moreover, an entire absence of that immodesty with which Otway and Dryden were accustomed to flavour their dramatic pieces. Yet with all these excellences the plot was not calculated, from the more than ordinary villany of the " Ambitious Statesman," the principal character, to please the public.

Geneste observes,† " The plot of this tragedy may have some slight foundation in history, but it seems to have been invented by Crowne." The authors of the " Biographia Dramatica" refer to Mezerai and De Serres. Langbaine gives a list of authors who have written on the history of Charles VI., and ascribes the character of the " Ambitious Statesman " to Bernard D'Armanac, Constable of France, who received the sword of Charles D'Albret, the previous Grand Constable, slain with half the French nobles at the battle of Agincourt in 1415.

---

* The following may be taken as an example :—

> " Wars are good physic when the world is sick,
> But he who cuts the throats of men for glory
> Is a vain savage fool. He strives to build
> Immortal honours upon man's mortality,
> And glory on the shame of human nature,
> To prove himself a man by inhumanity.
> He puts whole kingdoms in a blaze of war
> Only to still mankind into a vapour ;
> Empties the world to fill an idle story.
> In short, I know not why he should be honoured
> And those that murder men for money hang'd."

† Vol. I., p. 259.

A brief reference to the history of France at the time
will show the fallacy of the supposition that the tragedy
bears upon real fact.

Charles the Sixth succeeded to the throne of France in
1380, at the early age of twelve years and nine months.
He was a mere boy, consequently, when he was crowned
at Rheims, on the 4th of November of that year.   He
had the misfortune to take as his wife Isabel of Bavaria,
one of the most depraved of her sex, in the year 1383.
By her he had many children.   One of the daughters
became wife of Henry V.   Shakespeare, in his " Chronicle
History " of that monarch, introduces Isabel, who bestows
her blessing upon nuptials which brought misery on
France as well as England.   President Henault says,
quoting Brantome, " That she was detested by all true
Frenchmen."*   The two eldest sons, both named Charles,
died young before 1400.   Then Lewis became Dauphin,
but died 18th December 1415, without any issue by his
wife Margaret of Burgundy.   John, the next Dauphin,
was poisoned on the 5th of April, 1416, and was
succeeded by Charles, afterwards the seventh of France,
who ascended the throne in 1422, at the age of twenty,
so that he was only fourteen years of age when he became Dauphin.

Henry the Fifth fought the battle of Agincourt upon
the 25th of October 1415, when the Constable's sword was
transferred to Bernard D'Armanac, who, with his friends
and allies, was murdered in May 1418,† and Paris was
pillaged after the fashion usual in that capital.   Bernard
was the faithful adherent of the unhappy king and his
son the Dauphin.   This was the result of the machina-
tions of Queen Isabella, who hated her husband for
causing Boisbourbon, one of her gallants, to be drowned,
and her own son, the Dauphin, and the Constable, for
making her refund the treasure of which she had plun-
dered the State.   In revenge she surrendered Paris to
their enemies, when the King was captured, but the
Dauphin was enabled to escape.   " The Constable of
Armanac having been captured, was, with his family and

* " History of France," translated by Nugent, vol. I., p. 271.
† " De Serres," translated by Grymestone.   London, 1624
folio, p. 261.

friends, cruelly murdered." " The bodies of the Constable and Chancellor lying naked upon the stones are carried to the marble table in the Palace Hall. To note the Constable by his accustom'd scarfe, they flea a bend of his skinne and tye it about his body. This spectacle is drawne about the city three daies together, and then carried out in a dung cart to a place where they cast all their carrion and filth, without any burial. Men of the highest and lowest are alike slaughtered. Not only are the Armanacs murder'd, but all people that are suspected of aiding them. The rascals fall upon the rich and killing them as Armanacs, they spoile their houses, as a lawful prey of their conquest. The eye of this furious multitude spares neither sexe, age, nor quality. The Duke of Bourgogne's followers are lookers on of this spectacle, and watch that none escape." *

The preceding reference to facts, names, and dates, proves that Crowne was not indebted to history for any portion of the plot of his play, and that it is altogether his own creation. Bernard D'Armanac was the faithful subject both of King Charles and the Dauphin. The latter was scarcely fifteen when his mother endeavoured to place him in the hands of his enemies, from which fate he escaped by the assistance of a faithful servant, when the Constable was betrayed into their hands by a faithless one. It is hardly necessary to add that Louise de Guise and her deceived lover, the gallant and high-minded Vendosme, are myths.

So much was the infamous Queen disliked by the Parisians, that, upon her death in the year 1435, her body was removed from her hotel, and put in a small boat, without any other ceremony or pomp, and carried in that manner to her tomb at St Denis, like the body of a common person.

The noble lady to whom Crowne dedicated his tragedy was the eldest daughter of Henry Cavendish, second Duke of Newcastle, who, dying in 1691 without male issue, became, with her four sisters, his co-heirs. Her first husband was Christopher, only son of George Monk, Duke of Albemarle, through whose instrumentality the restoration of the Stewarts was chiefly accomplished.

* P. 261.

A remarkable account of the legitimacy of Christopher will be found in the "Dormant and Extinct Baronage of England."[*] His father, then a colonel in the Republican army, had in his service a farrier named Clarges, whose daughter Anne married, in the year 1632, in the church of St Laurence Pountny, one Thomas Rutford, son of another farrier resident in the Mews, by whom she had a daughter, born in 1634, who died four years afterwards. She lived with her husband at the Three Spanish Gipsies in the New Exchange, and sold wash-balls, powder for the hair, gloves, and such things, and taught girls plain work. In addition to all this she was a sempstress, and about the year 1647 was employed in that character by Monk. The following year both her father and mother appear to have died, and in 1649 she fell out with her husband, and a separation ensued,—perhaps in consequence of Monk having taken her under his protection.

In 1657 she married, in the church of St George, Southwark, General George Monk, and in the following year was delivered of an only son, christened Christopher, "who was suckled by Honour Mills, who sold apples, herbs, oysters, &c."

There is certainly no evidence that the first husband was dead when Anne became the wife of Monk; but, as Christopher was recognised as legitimate when his father died, and not only allowed the Dukedom, but created a Knight of the Garter and made a Privy Councillor, it would be rather a strong measure to bastardize him now. His father was descended, through a female, from the Plantagenets; and when he married Anne Clarges, was a military officer of great weight and power, and might have been a dangerous opponent to Cromwell.

These startling facts transpired in an action for trespass brought by William Sherwin, Esq., as heir and representative of Thomas Monk, Esquire, the elder brother of George, Duke of Albemarle, against Sir William Clarges, Bart., and others, for recovery of the manor of Sutton and others, in the county of York, and tried at the King's Bench on 15th November 1700.

The defendant was Walter, the only son of the brother of Duchess Anne, to whom Christopher had devised these

* By T. C. Banks, Esq., Lond., 1809, 4to, p. 37.

lands, and who died October 4, 1695, at his house in Piccadilly.* After this legal exposure of origin, it is amusing to be told by genealogists that "this family is descended from Declarges, in the province of Hainault, of which was Thomas de Clarges, who had issue John de Clarges, who came into England in the reign of King Edward IV." What brought the French worthy to England is not mentioned, but, if the information is scanty in this earlier portion of the genealogy, the deficiency is supplied at a more recent period, for we learn that the brother-in-law of Monk and the son of the farrier, who is himself understood to have been a blacksmith, was one of the chief instruments in the restoration of Charles II., for which meritorious service he was made a Baronet upon the 30th October 1674. His Majesty took a long time in considering what reward he should bestow upon him for his service, as he did not receive it until four years after his brother-in-law's death, and fourteen years after the Restoration.

Christopher succeeded his father, was a K.G. and Privy Councillor. He allied himself to the literary Cavendishes of Newcastle, and in 1687 received the appointment of Governor of Jamaica, which he did not enjoy for more than a year. Short as was his reign, he—or rather his executors—were greatly enriched, as we learn from Evelyn. "6th June 1677. There was about this time brought into the Downs a vast treasure, which was sunk in a Spanish galeon forty-five years ago, somewhere near Hispaniola or the Bahama Islands." The Duke of Albemarle's share, as Governor of Jamaica, came to £30,000. In a note on the text, it is stated to have been about £50,000.

The estate which had been left by Duke Christopher was very considerable, and was claimed by John Granville, Earl of Bath, who, with Monk, had been a great promoter of the Restoration, for which, and in consequence of his being a son of Sir Bevil Grenville, who fell at the battle of Lansdowne in the cause of Charles I., he received the Earldom and subordinate Viscounty of Granville. Banks states that in 1661 the King "passed a

* Kimber and Johnson's Baronetage, Lond. 1771, 8vo, vol. ii p. 384.

warrant under the privy seal, whereby he obliged himself, and recommended it to his successors, that in case of failure of issue male to General Monk, the title of Duke of Albemarle should descend to him and be continued in his family." * He was said to have been a kinsman of the Monks, but in what degree, if at all, is not explained.

It does not appear that, prior to the marriage of the Duchess Henrietta to Lord Montague any claim had been made by Lord Bath to the Albemarle heritage; but subsequently the two noble earls went to law, and the following account of the issue is given by Evelyn :— " June 18th, 1696. The famous trial between my Lord Bath and Lord Montague for an estate of £11,000 a-year left by the Duke of Albemarle, wherein on several trials had been spent £20,000 between them. The Earl of Bath was cast on evident forgery."†

On the 2d September 1702—" Died the Earl of Bath, whose contest with Lord Montague about the Duke of Albemarle's estate—he claiming under a will supposed to be forged—is said to have been worth £10,000 to the lawyers. His eldest son shot himself a few days after his father's death; for what cause is not clear. He was a most hopeful young man, and had behaved himself so bravely against the Turks at the siege of Vienna that the Count had made him a Count of the Empire."‡

The Duchess remained a widow for about two years before she became the wife of Ralph, Lord Montague, who had been raised to the dignity of Earl of Montague on the 9th of April 1689. His Lordship had previously espoused the Lady Elizabeth Wriothesly, daughter of Thomas, Earl of Southampton, and widow of Joceline Percy, the 11th Earl of Northumberland, by whom he had a large family. This lady dying in 1690, he paid his addresses to, and was accepted by the Duchess

---

* Dormant and Extinct Peerages, vol. ii. p. 59.

† Diary, vol. ii., p. 343, Lond. 1854. Forgery seems to have been fashionable about this time, as the third entry that follows the preceding, states a similar attempt was made by a Mr Temple, endeavouring to defraud Lady Purbeck Temple by a deed "proved to be forged."

‡ Ibid., p. 366.

of Albemarle, who brought him a vast fortune, which enabled him to maintain his position as Duke of Montague, to which dignity he had been elevated by Queen Anne, with splendour and magnificence. "As he had a refined taste of wit and good sense, so was he a great encourager of learning and of liberal arts and sciences, and a noble patron of men of merit." His Grace departed this life on the 9th of March 1708-9.*

His second Duchess, by whom he had no family, died at a very advanced age at Newcastle House, in Clerkenwell, on the 28th of August 1734, and was buried, 11th of September following, near her first consort, Christopher, Duke of Albemarle, in King Henry VIII.'s chapel, in Westminster, where his father, the first Duke, had also been interred.

* Collins' Peerage, vol. i., second edition, p. 340, London, 1741, 8vo.

THE DUCHESS OF ALBEMARLE.

POETRY seems on earth, madam, in the condition of the philosopher's music in the heavens, placed in a vast solitude, where there is nothing to hear it but some few angels that move those heavens.

The earth wants no inhabitants; but whilst those inhabitants want sense 'tis as solitary as the heavens; and a poet sings like a bird in the desert. Yet there are some angels and excellent spirits below, and in the first rank of 'em is your Grace.

What angels are, we know not; but, when we wou'd make 'em visible to our thoughts, we dress 'em up in such qualities as nature and fortune have bestowed on your Grace; excellent wisdom, great power, boundless generosity, and profound humility; and they, to requite our good thoughts of 'em, when they make themselves visible to our eyes, assume such beauty as yours. Then since we bestow on them all the excellencies of your mind, and they borrow all the beauties of your body, we may very well lend your Grace their name.

And in this, madam, I do not flatter you, but myself; I do not advance you above what you are, but I raise myself among those who were honoured to be the entertainers of angels, but with this difference: they knew not their guests, and so

were to be pardoned their unleavened bread, and
their fatted calves; else a foolish beast had been
an absurd treat for a creature, who was all mind,
and that mind all wisdom.

But all the world knows your Grace's delicate
spirit, and therefore my hospitality becomes my
crime. I set before your Grace unpleasant fruit,
that blossom'd in a stormy time, and so had much
ado to grow, and never cou'd be ripe.

The sun seldom shines on a poet's orchard. We
talk much of shades, and we always live in 'em.
If we soar, 'tis but to sing like larks; and, though
our notes are heard, our selves are invisible, and
our nests are always on the ground. Our wit, like
the pine tree, affects desolate places, barren rocks,
and steep mountains, and to shoot high in the air,
and meet those winds which shake its fruit to the
earth, where toads creep over it, and beasts devour
it. That a poet at no time, but especially at
this miserable time, is fit to entertain any but
himself.

We cannot think our soft songs should be heard,
when church music grumbles with loud and unpleasant discords, and the whole State seems out of
tune.

But, madam, I have for my excuse, I design not
so much an entertainment, as a sacrifice. And I
am very safe, since I agree with the noble Kingdom in faith and worship. I think there are no
dissenters that will not fully join with me in pay-
ing all manner of honours to the Duchess of
Albemarle; a Princess whose excellencies of mind
are as great and eminent as her quality

Many tests are made to try men's faith. I
think the honour men have for your Grace is the
best test to prove their understandings. This is
an ill time to erect images for worship, and the

porch of a trifling play an ill place for so glorious a thing as the image of your Grace.

'Tis true, I have very often seen great persons lye in such porches, begging the charity of well disposed passengers to give their names a poor subsistence. 'Tis a sad sight to see persons of honour in so wretched a condition, that they have no dwelling for their names, but are forced to lodge 'em in the hovels of miserable scribblers, and on the straw of a little flattery. I shall not presume to place the worst statue of your Grace among such poor company. I only beg leave to be my own porter, and stand at the gate of my work in your Grace's livery, that, if any enter, they may not dare to sully the apartments that belong to your Grace, and where you may sometimes be pleased to walk.

And that your Grace may be encouraged sometimes to walk in 'em, they are adorn'd with an image of a virtue, to which your Grace is nearly allied both by blood and marriage.

Loyalty, a virtue of which the Duke of Newcastle, your grandfather, and the Duke of Albemarle, the father of your illustrious lord, were the most glorious examples that ever were, or ever shall be in the world. They were the two Hercules pillars of honour and loyalty, beyond which none can travel. Beyond them, all is sky, air, and sea ; bright notion, empty imagination, and fluctuating fancy.

The Duke of Newcastle was a pillar, like that of Seth, erected before the great flood of Rebellion, withstood all the fury of it, and, when it cou'd no longer support the throne, it supported itself, and lifted up its head above the waves, when the waves covered the highest mountains, and our palaces far under water were become the habitations of monsters. This pillar out-lasted the flood, and on it were engraven all that cou'd be done by arms, and all that cou'd be written by wit. And to that eternal monument of wit, valour, and loyalty, the Muses and the Heroes of all ages shall repair, to pay their grateful devotions, to read their instructions, and consecrate their wreaths.

The Duke of Albemarle was a pillar, which nature and fortune erected by wonderful art under the waters, when there seemed not the least foundation for such a work, and the work impossible. Few saw it, till it was finished; then it appeared to all, and the throne was established upon it. Then did the waters sink to their proper places, the infernal lakes and springs whence they came : then men began to plant vineyards and to rejoice in the increase of the earth, and the fruit of their labours.

On these two columns, shining with gold, but more excellent in the glorious works engraven on 'em, stood the palace of the British Sun.

And now, madam, it cannot be displeasing to your Grace to look sometimes on the image of that virtue to which you are so nearly allied, and from which you derive such a vast inheritance of glory. And truly at this time both image and substance seem to need protection, when some are endeavouring to reduce again the substance to an image.

But that is too sad a note to dwell upon. I shall leave it, and humbly beg that poetry, though here poorly clad, may have leave to lye at your gates, because 'tis of the same nation and kindred with that fair quality which the Duke of Newcastle took into his bosom and crown'd.

Then, when the world shall see how your Grace

delights to honour it, that destruction shall never reach it, now and always intended it, by the mighty empire of fools.

Then shall my Muse, though often sleeping, as often stumbling, and always in the dark, be secure under the roof of your Grace's favour, and walk boldly and pleasantly with such a light shining round it, as the title I beg of,

Madam,

Your Grace's most obedient

humble servant,

JOHN CROWNE.

THIS play, which I think the most vigorous of all my foolish labours, was born in a time so unhealthy to poetry that I dare not venture it abroad without as many cloaths as I can give it to keep it warm. Let this excuse then serve to cover some of the nakednesses and deformities of it, that they are not so much mine as the faults of the troublesome times. I always expected to be assaulted by enemies, but, I did not expect they should drop out of the clouds. I had heaped together all the fancy I had to place myself out of the reach of my enemies, but as I was building my Babel, those things which disordered greater matters than these confounded my language, and made me give over my work, that in the end of the play you will find me descended into the plains, and lain down weary and fainting. But where I shew least wit I shew most wisdom, for there I take my ease, and elsewhere I take pains to none, or very little purpose. To please friends is hard, to please myself more difficult, but to please my enemies impossible. How foolish, then, is my toil? Few friends are made by poetry, but many enemies, and amongst 'em a most powerful one, Fortune.

Fools damn good plays, and fortune good poets. He may not be the best, but I am sure he is the wisest poet who writes so that he can scarce be discovered to be a poet; then Fortune will be afraid to shoot at him, lest she wound one of her own party, the fools. Much is lost by poetry—time, pains, and often friends. Nothing is gotten but a little reputation, and that some envious enemies of ours will rather fling to the dogs than let us have it. Witness the silly malice of some adversaries of mine, who, because my Epilogue had great success, would let anything rather than me be the author, though I had succeeded as well in the same kind in my Epilogues to both my " Jerusalems." Since my enemies are such little creeping creatures as not to dare to look in the face of a good play, but to bite at the tail, 'tis a shame to oppose 'em.

To those who, perhaps thinking themselves wiser than others, will not accept of my excuse of laziness and discouragement for the inequalities of the play, but ascribe 'em to my want of judgement, I shall only say :—supposing their charge were true, I know no poet that, like a bird of paradise, lives always in the air, and never lights, or, if he does, he must sleep there sometimes. Did a man take eternity to write in—though there be perfection in eternity, there is none in man— and he would be giddy and fall in going that vast round, especially if he always looked upwards.

THE PROLOGUE.

How? a new play? is this a time for plays?
Wit was a wretched thing in its best days,
A fair poor wife, which only had a white
And tempting skin, which vermin love to bite.
But now the nation in a tempest rowles,
And old St Peters justles with St Pauls,
And whilst these two great ladies fight and brawl,
Pickpocket Conventicle whore gets all.
Ungrateful jade! from Rome it is most clear
She had the stinking fish she sells so dear,
And in this broil no shelter can be found
In our poor play-house, fallen to the ground.
The time's neglect, and maladies have thrown
The two great pillars of our play-house down;
The two tall cedars of the vocal grove,
That vented oracles of wit and love,
Where many a nightingale has sweetly sung,
Whose boughs with shrieks of owls too oft has rung;
But such strange charms did in their echoes lie,
They gave the very owls a harmony.
But in our shrubs no such sweet echoes dwell,
Here wit will find but rods to switch her well.
What makes her then appear? what makes a kind
Young wench go meet her friend in rain and wind,
And rather than the assignation fail,
Daggle at once her honour and her tail?
Nature who did dispose her to the trade,
So soon, that she was scarcely born a maid.
Perhaps she'll blame her stars, but she would fall
To sinning, if there were no stars at all.

Nature to writing such delight has join'd
To propagate man's wit as well as kind,
This poet draws his lust to write from thence.
Did malice blast him like a pestilence,
Like the blind piper he'd the plague out-brave,
And tune his pipe though carried to the grave.

ACTORS' NAMES.

CHARLES, *King of France.*

THE DAUPHIN.

THE CONSTABLE OF FRANCE.

THE DUKE OF VENDOSME, *his son, Favourite of the King.*

COUNT BRISAC, *the Dauphin's Favourite.*

COUNT LA FORCE, *a great Commander, a malcontent.*

LA MARRE, *a foolish villanous courtier.*

The Women.

MADAMOISELLE DE GUISE, *a beautiful young Lady, beloved by the Duke of Vendosme, and contracted to him, and by the ill arts of the Constable wrought to be secretly married to the Dauphin.*

LA GUARD, *her Woman and Confidante, but false to her, and is the Constable's instrument.*

Conspirators, Courtiers, Officers.

The Scene: PARIS.

THE AMBITIOUS STATESMAN;

OR,

THE LOYAL FAVOURITE.

ACTUS PRIMUS.

Enter GREAT CONSTABLE *alone.*

SCENE, *His Apartment in the Louvre.*

Constable. Yesterday charged to come no more
  to Council !
Last night depriv'd of all my great employments !
A soft dismission, stuft with downy words
Sent me to sleep upon ! and sleep I may ;
My doors are quiet, and my rooms are empty,
No courtiers ruffle in my anti-chamber ;
Waiting my rising ; no petitioners
Attending in the hall my coming down :
All full of melancholy death-like silence.
Have I rul'd France ten flourishing years and more,
Under, or rather far above the King,
And shall I now be ruin'd by the Dauphin,
A proud rash boy ? Let the young Polypheme
Devour the calves of court, I will outdo
Ulysses : I will kindle such a fire
Shall burn the giant and his den together.
Ho ! there.

Enter SECRETARY.

Secret. My lord ?

Const. Are the dispatches gone,
To Gascoin, Normandy, and Aquitain ?

Secret. They went above an hour ago.

Const. That's well !

Those Provinces are ready for Rebellion.   [*Aside.*
And I have spurr'd 'em on ; there shall be shortly
Such a strange thing as liberty in France.
I hope, ere it be long, to hear in France
The English drums beat Freedom, Freedom !
I've sent a secret invitation
To their brave fiery young King, Henry the fifth,
And I've enrag'd the Duke of Burgundy,
That he is enter'd into league with him.
And I'm preparing a Rebellion ;
A noble fire to warm him at his landing,
From the cold moist sea-air.

   Secret. He's strangely troubled !   [*Aside.*

   Const. No messenger this morning from my
     son ?

   Secret. Not any yet, my Lord.

   Const. Where's the gentleman
Who came last night ?

   Secret. I do not know, my Lord.

   Const. What did he say ? When will my son
     be here ?

   Secret. He said, my Lord, his Excellence was
     resolv'd
To be at Court this afternoon at farthest.

   Const. His Excellence ? his Excellence is an
     ass ;   [*Aside.*
A fellow full of honesty, morality,
Of loyalty, philosophy, and foolery :
But I have laid a bait to try his morals.
Ha ! knocking ?

Enter a SERVANT.

Serv. Count La Force, my Lord, desires
Admission to your Lordship.
    Const. Bring him in!

Enter LA FORCE.

Const. Friend, you astonish me! How dare you
    approach
The unhealthy shade of an old blasted tree?
None come to me but he who wants a gibbet,
And fain would hang himself the decent'st way.
    La For. I was your friend, my Lord, when you
        were honest,
No sordid flatterer of tyranny,
Before you climb'd the mountains of advancement
To feed on winds, as Spanish horses do.
    Const. My Lord, you love those winds as much
        as I do;
And hate the fogs that haunt the dirty vales.
    La For. That dirt is bred by tempests from
        above,
From clouds of tyranny, where you have liv'd, ·
And torn the Kingdom by the thund'ring power
Of Constable of France.
    Const. You wou'd ha' mounted
To the same clouds, and made a Marshal's staff
A witch's staff, to carry you aloft,
Cou'd you ha' got one: but you were denied it.
The King might cheaper have burnt all his
    forests   .
Than sav'd that staff: for you, and your good
    friends
Set, in revenge, the Kingdom in a flame.
    La For. I made that fire to melt down all our
        chains.
I hate to see my countrymen abus'd.

Const. Hence with dissembling! we know one
   another.
You and I wou'd not care our countrymen   .
Were all to horses turn'd, so we might ride 'em?
   La For. I do deny't; I hate to ride my country.
   Const. But 1 hate more my country should be
      ridden
By cowards in the army, fools in council.
Who can endure to see the honest industries
Of many scores of men plunder'd by law,
To feed a fool, who is not half a man?
   La For. Well, is Brisac, the Dauphin's Favourite,
To have your offices?
   Const. So 'tis design'd.
   La For. Cannot your son, the King's great
      Favourite,
Whom he created lately Duke of Vendosme,
Assist you?
   Const. He?—A studious, moral fool!
A moth, who has so long been fed on books
His skin is paper, and his blood is ink;
Insensible of all delights of man.
   La For. Of all?
   Const. Almost of all.
   La For. What does he love?
   Const. Only his book, his friend, his honesty,
And, when the King, and Kingdom have occasion,
He loves his sword; else it might rust for ever:
He would not draw it to procure himself
The empire of the world; he says, he needs it not.
And he calls him a miserable wretch,
Who needs the universe to make him happy.
   La For. His temper differs much from yours.
   Const. From mine?
He walks directly backwards from my steps.
I wonder in what posture I begot him,
Or in what humour: surely I was thinking

Of something else ; and, if I was, I cannot
Imagine how he should creep through my loins,
Like Alpheus through the sea, and never season
Himself with any relish of my nature.

    La For. Sure he rush'd from you in a mighty
    torrent.

    Const. Rather I threw him from me with abhor-
    rence.

    La For. Then you can hope for little aid from him.

    Const. Oh, yes ! I have observ'd in my philosophy,
Nature, an enemy to tyranny,
Does always leave some tender place unguarded
About unmatchable vast harnest animals,
Where death may give the world revenge and
    freedom ;
So this proud fellow's spirit, more invincible
Than whales, than crocodiles, or elephants,
Has a soft place, his heart, which has been
    wounded
By the small needles of a woman's eye.

    La For. Then does he love ?

    Const. He does !

    La For. Whom, for Heaven's sake ?

    Const. She whom all love, that wonder of the
    world—
Madamoiselle de Guise.

    La For. That beauteous creature ?
And what success has he ?

    Const. They are contracted.

    La For. And no one hear of it ?

    Const. He keeps it secret,
I know not why, but such has been his humour.

    La For. And what of this ?

    Const. The Dauphin is his rival.

    La For. Ha ! Then is she the talk't of hidden
    beauty
The Dauphin makes secret addresses to ?

Const. The same.

La For. Good heaven ! What does the Dauphin
    mean ?
Is not the match with Burgundy concluded ?

Const. It is, and therefore is this kept so secret
By the King's strict commands; who strove to
    break it
But could not.

La For. How came you to find it out ?

Const. A servant of my own happen'd to love
Madamoiselle's chief woman, and sole confidante ;
Whom I, perceiving always vext and thoughtful
With a face full of guilt, strictly examin'd,
And got it out of him ; and how his mistress
And he design'd to ruin my son's interest,
And raise their fortunes by this greater marriage.

La For. Here was a mine cut to your hand
    already !

Const. It was ! I pardon'd him, bid him proceed,
Because he serv'd in it his Prince, the Dauphin,
And I would join with 'em.   Whilst I was plotting ;
Fortune, which always takes into her favour
A hundred villains for one honest man,
Gave my design a noble rise : brought news
To Court, that, whilst my son quartered at Metz,
He and the fair young Princess of Lorrain
Had charm'd each other.

La For. This inconstancy
Wou'd enrage Madamoiselle de Guise to madness,
For she is the haughtiest young woman living.

Const. Yes, had you seen her letters you wou'd
    say so.
My instrument, her woman, always brought 'em
    to me ;
I'd see if they were fit to go ; at opening 'em
I thought I had untied a witch's knot,
And let a tempest out.

La For. And you I warrant
Answer'd these letters, in your son's hand counter-
    feited.
    Const. Exactly guess'd. I stopt the good fool's
    letters,
Wherein the wretch prov'd himself very innocent ;
And, in their room, I sent my forged ones to her ;
Wherein I made my son own the inconstancy,
Desire a mutual release of vows.
He wou'd give her the glories of the Dauphin,
If she'd give him the beauties of his Princess.
    La For. Did she not tear the letters, and her
    hair ?
    Const. Yes, and her flesh, and, to complete her
    madness,
I brib'd some cowardly officers, my son
Had thrown out of his army, to attest
All my false letters said ; and more, how he
Spoke of her openly with much contempt.
    La For. Was ever a design manag'd like this ?
The Dauphin, after this, sure had small difficulty
To press her to accept his love and glory.
    Const. That you may guess.
    La For. What ? Are they married then ?
    Const. They were the other night, in such great
    privacy,
The King scarce knows it yet.
    La For. But can the Dauphin's
Amour be wholly hidden from your son ?
    Const. No, but he ne'er distrusts his mistress
    falsehood ;
He only thinks her jealous, and sent messengers
T' appease her anger, whom she wou'd not see.
    La For. Most excellent !
    Const. Now, when my son returns,
I will charge all my tricks upon the Dauphin ;
Nay, more, perhaps I'll say, he whores the lady.

And then the Dauphin envies him, and hates him,
For saucily outshining him in arms.
Fortune has had so very little manners
To slight the Dauphin, and attend my son.

    La For. Here are most gallant hopes of a
      Rebellion.

    Const. Brave hopes !
For I have spread such lies against the Government,
Have frighted all the people from their wits,
I doubt not but in little time to beg
The Kingdom for a fool, and be its guardian.

    La For. I have a mind to be a doing again,
Though I've estate enough.

    Const. Oh ! damn estate !
'Tis useless, without power, to a great mind.
What ? I may keep a table, and be popular ?
That is, feed fools and knaves, and have no thanks.
If I cou'd cram an ox in a rogue's jaws,
It would not gag him from detracting from me.
But I may compass women ; what o' that ?
If they be newly shell'd from hanging sleeves
They are so tender that they have no taste :
So ignorant, they know not what to do with you.
If ripe, they know too well then what to do with
    you.
In short, power is my pleasure.
Five hundred thousand livres yearly flow
Into my coffers ; I have palaces
Exceed the King's ; yet now, thrown out of power,
I think myself a miserable wretch.
Come, bear me company an hour or two,
And see how I will flounder in my shallows
Like a great whale ! I'll make 'em glad to give me
Sea-room enough, or I'll o'erset the Kingdom.
I'll seem religious to be damn'dly wicked,
I'll act all villany by holy shows,
And that for piety on fools impose,

Set up all faiths, that so there may be none,
And make religion throw religion down.
I will seem loyal, the more rogue to be,
And ruin the King by his own authority :
Pretending men from Tyranny to save,
I will the foolish credulous world enslave.　　[*Exit.*

SCENE, *a Bed-Chamber.*

Enter the DAUPHIN *and* LOUIZE.

Dau. What is the reason of this great unkind-
　　ness ?

Louiz. Unkindness ?

Dau. Yes, you are unkind to me,
You forc'd yourself last night out o' my arms,
And, when I thought it was to sleep, you sigh'd,
Nay, more, you wept, wept bitterly; I heard
　　you,
Though I pretended sleeping ; but the damn'd
As soon might slumber in their pains as I.
When we were arm in arm lockt close together,
Cou'd any sorrow ere have got between us
Had not your hollow bosom let it in ?
Out of what corner of the heavens blew
The wind that did compose so many sighs,
And made such stormy weather in my bed ?

Lou. I will not tell you. I'll in nothing gratify
Him who can think so very meanly of me,
To doubt my kindness to a Prince I've married.

Daup. I do not only doubt, but am assur'd
You love some secret miserable wretch ;
For I will make him so, and in your sufferings,
If him I cannot find.

Lou. Oh ! in what chains——　　　　[*Aside.*
Have I myself in my distraction bound,
For Vendosme's falsehood has destroy'd my wits ;
The fall of heaven could not have broke me more.

Vendosme, and falsehood? I thought heaven and
    hell
Wou'd sooner have been join'd than those two
    words.

    Daup. Ha! are you weeping lest my fury find
Your hidden lover out? I'll find him out!
This morn you early rose, and from your cabinet
You fetch'd his picture out.

    Lou. Oh! I'm discover'd!——   [*Aside.*

    Daup. Then to the window went and gaz'd
    upon it.
Debauch'd the morning in its infancy,
To light you whilst your eyes enjoy'd the picture;
They mingled wantonly with every line in't,
They shot themselves quite through and through
    the shadow.
The modest morning was asham'd to open
Her blushing eye-lids to behold your wantonness;
Whilst you, contented not alone with looks,
Did scorch the picture with your burning kisses,
As if you fain wou'd kiss it into life.
I lay expecting when th' enlivened shadow
Would start into a man, and cuckold me.

    Lou. Oh! you have spoken largely in the praise
Of your great wisdom, kindness, generosity.

    Daup. I think I shew'd myself generous enough
I did not rise and tear th' adulterer's picture,
Your body, soul, and reputation,
Into a thousand pieces!

    Lou. Wou'd you had!
Then death had freed me from your tyranny.

    Daup. Then you love death it seems better
    than me.
You reward well my slighting, for your sake,
The sister of the Duke of Burgundy:
And, by that scorn, for hauling on my head
The wrath of Burgundy, a war from England,
The curses of all France, and of my father.

Lou. Did you not draw all these upon your self,
Threat'ning destruction to my family,
And death to me, if I refus'd your love ?
  Daup. Oh ! You do well to call to my remem-
    brance
Those hateful things ; as if you was afraid
Lest I should love you.
  Lou. I am weary of this,
I'll hear no more of it ! Good morning to you.
  Daup. What ? Will you leave me then ?
  Lou. Shou'd I stay here,
To hold my hand up like a criminal
Before your jealousy ? a base born passion,
That has not one brave thought of all its race.
I'll leave you till your soul gets better company.
                                                    [*Exit.*

Enter LA MARRE.

  Daup. She makes me mad ! Ha ! Sirrah, are
    you here ?
  La Mar. Oh ! here's the Prince in one of his
    mad fits,
There's no scaping him ; what shall I do ?
  Daup. You are a rogue !
  La Ma. I am, sir, if you say so.
  Daup. Sirrah, you are, whether I say it or no.
  La Ma. Yes, sir, I am !
  Daup. You are a flattering rogue !
  La Ma. Yes, sir.
  Daup. A double-tongu'd, dissembling rogue !
  La Ma. Yes, sir.
  Daup. Who serve your King for your own ends.
  La Ma. Most certain, sir.
  Daup. And do not care how odious
Your knavery renders him, so you can get by it.
  La Ma. Most true, sir, it has been my constant
    practice.

Daup. And when you have gotten all you can
   by him,
For new advantages will turn his enemy.
La Ma. With all my heart, sir.
Daup. A seditious rogue !
And think there lye no obligations on you
Of loyalty, of gratitude, or honesty;
But you will rather side with factious rogues,
With such a rogue as the great Constable,—
Because he did prefer you to the Court,—
Than to the King, who made you what you are ?
La Ma. That, sir, I've always done.
Daup. And don't you merit
Hanging, sir ?
La Ma. Ay, sir ! that's not to be question'd.
Daup. Ho ! Take this fellow here, and use him
   severely !

Enter GENTLEMEN.

La Ma. With all my heart, and take it for an
   honour.
Daup. I'm sick of choler still! this narrow soul'd—
This shallow slave cannot contain the half—
      [*The Gentlemen thrust out La Marre.*

Enter BRISAC.

Daup. Oh ! my Brisac, give me thy speedy
   counsel
Or else I shall run mad.   I've been abus'd——
Bris. By whom, sir ?
Daup. By that beauteous thing I've married.
I know not what she is, woman or devil;
She's both, I think.   To me she's a devil :
When ever I embrace her, from my arms
She vanishes in lightning, and in thunder;
But there's a slave, I know not who he is,
A hidden slave, who finds her flesh and blood.

Bris. Oh! say not so, sir.

Daup. I have proofs of it!
But I'll have more: I'll rifle all her cabinets,
I'll rack her servants, nay perhaps rack her!
Why shou'd I not? She has tormented me.
Along with me!   [*Exit.*

Bris. This Prince, though young and brave,
And heir of France, how wretched is he: hated
By his lov'd wife, his father, and all France.
Our envy never wou'd great men pursue,
If their great plagues, and passions too we knew.
                                         [*Exit.*

Finis Actus Primi.

ACTUS SECUNDUS.

Enter LOUIZE, *and* LA GUARD.

La Gua. Would I had never meddled in this
     business!   [*Aside.*

Lou. Comes he to Court to-day?

La Gua. The Duke of Vendosme—

Lou. You might have answer'd me, without im-
     pertinently
Naming a name so very unpleasing to me.

La Gua. Ah! that's not true; that name, if she
     were dead,
Call'd o'er her tomb, would raise her up to life.—
                                         [*Aside.*
Yes, madam, he does come!

Lou. Oh! then will be——   [*Aside.*
The mighty parting pang. Does he come married?
Not that I care, I ask for curiosity.

La Gua. Ah! pride; her heart is breaking,
     though she hides it.   [*Aside.*
I know not madam.

Lou. Go, and ask your friend!

La Gua. I was now talking with him.
Lou. Call him hither!

LA GUARD *brings in the* CONSTABLE'S
SECRETARY.

Well, do you hear yet if the Duke of Vendosme
Be married to the Princess of Lorraine?
 Sec. 'Tis thought so, madam.
 Lou. Did you ever see her?
 Sec. Oft! I have oft describ'd her to you, madam.
 Lou. It may be so, I never think of her.
What! is she handsome?
 Sec. Judg'd by all, the greatest
Beauty in the whole world, next your Highness.
 Lou. How tall is she?
 Sec. She is——
 Lou. Well—'tis no matter!
Did you ever see the Duke and her together?
 Sec. Who rather ever saw 'm asunder, madam,
Since their acquaintance?
 Lou. And did you ever hear him
Make me the subject of his camp-discourse?
 Sec. Only in wond'ring how he came deceiv'd
Into the opinion that you were fair.
'Tis true, he said, the Princess of Lorraine
Was so extravagantly beautiful;
After the sight of her, no other woman
Could be endur'd. His cashier'd officers
Can tell you more at large.
 Lou. Yes, they have told me.
Leave me! Here was the excellent man pretended
Such virtue! How wou'd the dissembler talk;
Talk like an angel!
 La Gu. Yes, and look like an angel.
He is the loveliest man mine eyes ere saw.
 Lou. Go, burn his picture! Ha! the Dauphin
  here?

Enter the DAUPHIN.

Daup. Ha! Have I catch'd you again at your
    devotion
To your soul's idol? Quickly give it me!
Lou. Oh! You delight to shew the giant strength
Of your young conjugal authority,
What will the monster do when grown?
Daup. This Hercules
Shall strangle biggest serpents in its cradle.
The picture, come!
Lou. What picture wou'd you have?
A map of jealous Italy or Spain?
Look in your bosom, there's a most exact one.
Daup. Give over! it's dangerous trifling with me.
Lou. Nay, if you threaten, threaten those that
    fear:
Your threats are lost on me.
Daup. Then I entreat!
Lou. Then I do grant. There, take the pic-
    ture, sir!
La Gu. Oh! she has given it him! Now all
    will out.   [*Aside.*
Daup. What's this, the sister of the Duke of
    Burgundy?
Lou. I hate myself for this deceit, but more
                                                 [*Aside.*
The man that makes me such an odious creature.
Daup. Was this the cause of all your secret
    sorrows?
Lou. Death wou'd be easier to me than lying,
                                                 [*Aside.*
If I cou'd bear a mortal wound in honour.
Yes, there's the Princess, sir, that has your love;
In me you married but your haughty will,
Which madly drove, because it was oppos'd.
And now the brittle corner of your heart

Which kept some love for me is broke, and all
The vapour fled ! and now you see your error,

 La Gu. Rarely come off !—   [*Aside.*

 Daup. And have I wrong'd thee so ?
I am a brute, and thou art a bright angel :
No wonder heaven has blasted the unnatural
And horrid mixture of a brute and angel,
Yet there is manhood in the ruins of me.
I was a Prince, before that dog, my jealousy,
Fast'ned upon me, and tore me into this shape.

 Lou. Oh ! you wou'd hide your kindness for that
  Princess,
Under the veil of jealousy ?

 Daup. I hide
My kindness for her ? I'll proclaim my hate to
 her !
I'll pave the streets of Paris with her pictures
The day I make my happy nuptials public :
Nor will I dart the thunder of my vengeance
On a thin shadow only, and so lose it.
I will make Burgundy the seat of misery,
That malefactors shall be banisht thither,
When they deserve worse punishment than death.

 Lou. Oh ! what a change is here ! your head
  will grow
Giddy, I fear, with turning round so fast,
And you will fall again from this high love.

 Daup. Oh ! never ! never !

 Lou. Yes, in little time
I shall be call'd the Helena of France,
Fatal incendiary, enchanting mischief,
That brings your father's curses on your head,
The curses of all France.

 Daup. Thou art all blessing !
And Heaven rain thee down upon my head,
Soft as a flake of snow, and full as cold ;
But yet thy coldness sets my blood a burning.

Lou. This is a present humour put in motion.
Weak was the philtre from my eyes you drunk ;
It only works when some wild passion shakes you.
  Daup. No more ! I love ! and bow my knee for
    pardon.
  Lou. Rise, sir, and be assur'd, I will not, cannot
Make myself more unworthy of your love,
Than by a subject's birth I am already.
  Daup. Excellent creature ! Thou wert never born,
But cam'st immediately from Heaven's hands.
Perfection cannot come from imperfection.
  Lou. Wretch that I am ! to hate a Prince who
    loves me,   [*Aside.*
And love a base false subject who contemns me.
                                                [*Exit.*

          Enter the KING, *attended.*

  A Gent. The King, sir !
  King. In posture of devotion
To your fair mistress ?
  Daup. Sir, I love her well.
  K. Yes, I believe you do ; you love her better
Than your obedience to your King and father,
Or than the peace and welfare of your country.
  Dauph. My country's welfare ? why shou'd Princes
    marry
To make their country happy ? give themselves
Most cursed nights, that slaves may have good
    days ?
Will any subject marry a damn'd wife
Only for wealth, and give his King the portion !
That match with Burgundy was the advice
Of some old cowardly covetous counsellors ;
Who fear the soldier, in few months, shou'd spend
What they have all their lives been cozening for :
Or that their paltry issue shou'd be kill'd,
And ne'er enjoy their father's knavery.

For 'tis the constant creed of most old fools,
That they enjoy their wealth when they are dead,
In the damn'd silly persons of their sons,
When the young fools themselves do not enjoy it.
From all these knaves I will defend your honour.

    K. Win your self honour! you have now occasion.
I know you hear the King of England's landed.

    Dauph. I am glad of it! 'tis summer now in
    France.
Fear sinks the blood in your old councellors' veins,
As a cold hand does water in a weather-glass;
You cannot guess the weather then by them.
Now frosty peace is gone, the weather's hot:
So hot 't shall scorch the English troops, and
    make 'em
Sweat all their souls away in bloody baths.

    K. I doubt it, for I know 'em a brave nation:
If we e'er get the better it must be
By fasting longer, and by hiding better
Behind thick woods, and by broad lakes and rivers,
By trusting to our trees, not to our men:
To our cold rivers, not to our hot blood:
For if they ever come to blows they beat us.

    Dauph. These are your Vendosme's cold imagin-
    ations.

    K. He has a cooler head, but hotter heart,
Than thou hast; that brave youth thou enviest.

    Dauph. I envy him? I scorn him, he's a Dutch-
    man!
He has no spark of the French fire in 's nature,
No more true conduct than his father honesty;
I'll drive 'em both out of the Court and army.

    K. I'll part with thee before the Duke of Ven-
    dosme.

    Dauph. Value the son of a traitor above me?
I'll humble the proud slave when e'er I see him.

                         [Exit.

K. 'Tis very well: you King it, sir, betimes!

Enter a GENTLEMAN.

Gent. Sir, the Great Constable attends without!
K. Let him attend, he has offended me. .
Did not his son's great merits plead for him
I'd ruin him; howe'er I'll let him know
I understand his actions, and resent 'em. [*Exeunt.*

Enter the GREAT CONSTABLE. LA MARRE, *and other*
COURTIERS, *pass by, and look scornfully upon him.*

Const. How many ages will they make me wait?
Ha! Is it so indeed? And am I fallen
Into these wretches' scorn? Nay, then I know
How the wind blows. You sir, who like a fly
　　　　　　　　　　　　[*to La Marre.*
Are blind in autumn, when the cold approaches
And the tall trees begin to shed their leaves.
And is it autumn with me then indeed?
Do you not see me, sir? Must I for ever
Attend here? ha!
La Ma. My lord, I cannot mind
All men's affairs and businesses, not I.
Const. All men's affairs, sir? do you level me
With all men?
La Ma. I must wait on the King's business,
And the King's business must be done, my Lord.
Const. I prithee, what's that business thou
　　attendest on?
To carry charcoal in to air his shirt?
I know thee, thou wert once my menial servant,
And I preferr'd thee to the place thou holdest.
La Ma. 'Tis true, my Lord, you laid an obliga-
　　tion on me,
But what then? I am now his Majesty's,
And his Majesty's business must be done.
Const. His Majesty's business ——

La Ma. Nay, my Lord, I fear you not ;
I know what the King said of you just now,
And what the Dauphin said to me this morning.
You'll never come in play again, I'm sure :
And so your Lordship's servant. [*Exit.*

Const. Villain and fool!
How such a slave, like dirt, flies in his teeth
And dirties him who raises it from the earth !

Enter LA FORCE.

La For. My Lord, the King has gotten informa-
tion
Of all your plots ; give 'em o'er, they will ruin you ;
Like vipers, they will tear their mother's bowels
That gave 'em being.

Const. Ha ! got information ?
Then, like a whorish woman, once discovered,
I will grow impudent ; lye in in public
Of my designs ; I'll fling 'em in the world
As carelessly as nature does all monsters,
Never appointing certain times of birth ;
My monsters shall be borne with teeth and fangs too.

La For. You will undo yourself ! take good
advice,
And live at ease.

Const. I cannot in disgrace.

La For. You have a vast estate.

Const. I am a beggar,
When I want all the wealth I value, power !

La For. You have great palaces.

Const. Great gaols, great dungeons,
Dark horrid dungeons ! now the light of all
My honour is gone out.

Enter the KING *attended.*

La For. See ! see ! the King !
Take good advice before you ruin all.

Const. Ha ! he regards me not.   Oh ! torment !
torment !
Sir, with your pardon ; I must speak with you.
Are you resolved, sir, on your own destruction ?
For let me tell you, sir, I am your eyes ;
And you let traitors tear me from your head,
And then conduct you blindfold to destruction.
You find it not, but, sir, I do, with sorrow.

   K. Hence with thy tears ! they fall upon the
ground ;
And there discover thy dissembling face.
There is no hell to thee like a low fortune ;
And when thou art in hell thou art a devil :
Tormenting both thyself and all the world.
Rebellion first did light thee to the Court.
I have permitted so many to light
Themselves to greatness by that filthy flambeau,
That all the Louvre's black'ned with the smoke,
And all my councils strongly smell of knaves.
But I'll chace them, and that ill practice, from
me !
In short, for thy son's sake, I fully pardon
All thy past faults, and give thee thy estate.
Go home, and live in ease and honesty !
Be wise ! accept this favour whilst 'tis offer'd.

   La For. Do, do accept it !   ⌊*Aside.*

   Const. Peace ! I will be damn'd first.
Sir, can I either live in ease or honesty
When by retiring I resign you up
To those who seek your life ?

   K. Ha !

   Const. Sir ; 'Tis true.

   K. And who are those ?

   Const. They are such whose impious hands
The ties of nature, one would think, should hold
From deeds so horrid !

   K. Who dost thou mean ?   My son ?

La. For. Oh ! have a care, retreat !
You're on a precipice.   [*Aside.*
    Const. Let me alone !   [*Aside.*]   We are told by
   . philosophers
The principles of death spring from our natures ;
He who intends your death sprung from your loins.
    La For. He will undo himself. ——   [*Aside.*
    Const. Sir, it is truth !
And his beloved Brisac is his chief counsellor.
    K. Know if each word thou say'st swell not with
    truth,.
The breath of plagues should be less fatal to thee
Than that that form'd and vented this foul charge.
    Const. So ! so ; an honest man has great en-
    couragement
To serve his Prince ? 'tis well I have a conscience.

Enter the DAUPHIN and BRISAC.

    K. Here they are both ! come answer for your-
    selves !
The Constable accuses both of you
Of blackest treasons.
    Daup. How ! accuses me ?
    Const. Yes, you, sir ! take my head for speaking
    truth,
I'll proudly suffer martyrdom for loyalty.
What dost thou charge me with ?
    Const. With close designs ;
To get Brisac my offices, that he
May assist you to get the King's great office.
    Daup. Oh ! Villain ! villain !
    Const. I can prove it, sir.
    Bris. Oh ! sir, I kneel and call Heaven to my
    witness.
    Const. You may call long enough before he'll come.
Sir, to oppose this impious design
Was that that made me bear th' uneasy Court

When it was grown such an unpleasant clime.
I saw not in a year one summer's day ;
My enemies were a perpetual storm,
And you permitted 'em to blow upon me :
Yet, for your safety I endur'd it all,
Not for the love of greatness, Heaven knows !
 Daup. No, no ! not you.
 Const. Sir, I was born with greatness ;
I've honours, title, power, here within,
All vain external greatness I contemn.
Am I the higher for supporting mountains ?
The taller for a flatterer's humble bowing ?
Have I more room for being throng'd with followers?
The larger soul for having all my thoughts
Filled with the lumber of the State affairs ?
Honours and riches are all splendid vanities ;
They are of chiefest use to fools and knaves.
A fool indeed, has great need of a title ;
It teaches men to call him Count and Duke,
And to forget his proper name of fool.
Gold is of use to every sort of knave ;
It helps the ambitious knave to offices,
Th' unjust contentious knave to other's right,
The lustful knave to other's wives and daughters ;
Then, strow'd on all the blots of a man's life,
It does not only cover 'em, but gild 'em.
But what's all this to a wise innocent man?
 Daup. Ay ! such another as yourself, good man.
 Bris. Sir, cou'd an actor make himself a god
By flying o'er a stage on golden wires,
Then might he make himself an honest man
By mounting high on rich and golden words.
But dares he boast thus of his innocence,
Whose treasons are most visible to all ?
Has he not fill'd all France with factions ?
O'erspread the Kingdom, like an Indian tree,
With mighty forests sprung out of himself?

Const. Why shou'd I do this, sir? I wou'd not
 break
My sleep to get your crown; what shou'd I do
 with 't ?   .
Palsies wou'd shortly shake it from my head.
Nor wou'd I care to leave it to my son;
'Twill be all one to me when I am dead,
If he be crown'd or victim'd on my tomb.
If he be crown'd, his glory will not shine
Into my grave and warm my dust to see it:
If he be victim'd there, I shall not feel it.
'Twill be no more than if they pluck'd
Some pretty flower that grew out o' my dust.
 Daup. Oh! pretty words! fine phrases!
 K. Well, Brisac,
Accusing him proves not you innocent;
You first shall come to trial.
 Bris. Sir, I beg it.
 Const. Yes! and I beg, sir, he may be secur'd.
 Bris. Load me with fetters, keep me in a dun-
 geon !
 Const. Yes! you shall be secur'd, whilst they
 suspect you
Honest, but when you shall appear
That useful thing, a knave, Court witchcraft then
Shall mount you o'er all scaffolds, and all gibbets,
Out of the reach of justice.
 Daup. There's no trick
So base, I will not play in thy opinion !
 Bris. Then to prevent all hopes of my escape,
I humbly beg, that I may be his prisoner.
 Daup. His prisoner ?
 K. You are too concern'd to speak.
It shall be so.
 Daup. Come, then, I give him to thee.
But hark! I'll have him weigh'd, and if thou dost
Return him to me lighter by one grain,

Thy flesh shall fiftyfold repay the loss;
If he shall lose one hair, I'll have thy head.

   Const. Oh! these are equal doings; but no **matter**!
I shall return him heavier than I had him,
For I have weighty witnesses,——here's one!——
   La For. Who, I?——   [*Aside.*
   Const. You must be one!——   [*Aside.*
I will draw in
This wary fool. ——   [*Aside.*
   Daup. How! thou a witness, villain?
   La For. Villain?——
Nay, then, I'll own myself a witness.   [*Aside.*
Yes, I'm a witness, sir!
   Daup. Oh! lying slave!
   K. Begone! I'll bear no more outrageous car-
    riage.
   Daup. I will obey you, sir. Remember, Con-
    stable!   [*Exit.*
   K. Now I'll this minute seize on both your
    fortunes,
I'll leave you no materials for bribes.   [*Exit.*
   La For. How's this?——
   Const. Am I thus served?
   La For. You have engag'd me
In a fine business.
   Const. I will make thy bowels
Sew up this breach.
   Bris. Wilt thou abuse me then?
   Const. Away with him!

       A Guard carry out Brisac.

I'll make him own all I have charged him with,
Or I will let the sun behold his entrails.
I scorn their threats! my son returns to-day
With a brave army.
   La For. And a troop of virtues.
   Const. I'll thrust my principles or **dagger** in him!

I love my power and honour above him;
I got him in one night, I did not get
Honour so fast : I toil'd for that some years.
  La For. Hence with your damn'd designs! if
  they succeed
You will be call'd a false ungrateful villain,
To seek the ruin of that King from whom
You have received so many Royal favours.
  Const. Old favours are old almanacks, ne'er lookt
  on;
Who minds what weather 'twas a year ago?
The last year's sun ripens not this year's fruit.
Nor am I a false man, in being wise,
For as the money's false that's mixt with brass,
So he is a false man, who is an ass. *[Exeunt.*

Trumpets. Enter at one door, the KING *and Train,*
  LA MARRE *among the Train. At the other, the*
  DUKE OF VENDOSME, *followed by* OFFICERS.

  King. The Duke of Vendosme come? Welcome,
  my friend!
More welcome than the victories thou bring'st.
  Duke. You owe 'em to your cause and gallant
  army.
  K. Thou art to all men just, but to thyself.
  D. 1 do not love, sir, like too many generals,
To steal renown out of the public baggage.
  K. Instead of that thou givest away thy own;
Praise is the only thing thou runn'st away from.
  D. I'm not ambitious much of any Kingdom,
But least of all to have one in the air;
Where, let a man have ne'er such large dominion,
A hurricane will be a greater Prince.
The force of that can tear up trees and rocks:
But all the stormy praise, that all the heroes
Can by their blust'ring swords collect together,
Cannot pull up one stoic by the roots,

Who stands in full defiance of their madness.
How fond* is it to toil in the world's forest,
In hewing down mankind, only to hear
Some hollow hearts echo our mighty blows!
But 'tis more foolish to toil all one's life
That fame may toss our ashes when we're dead.
So we have no repose living or dead.
They who are gone to rest in marble beds,
Sleep fast enough, and need no wind to rock 'em.
   K. I ne'er thought fame a lawful cause of war.
   D. Wars are good physic when the world is sick.
But he who cuts the throats of men for glory,
Is a vain savage fool; he strives to build
Immortal honours upon man's mortality,
And glory on the shame of human nature,
To prove himself a man by inhumanity.
He puts whole Kingdoms in a blaze of war,
Only to still mankind into a vapour;
Empties the world to fill an idle story.
In short, I know not why he shou'd be honour'd,
And they that murder men for money hang'd.
   K. Thy sentiments are great, and worthy of thee.
   D. I hate these potent madmen, who keep all
Mankind awake, whilst they by their great deeds
Are drumming hard upon this hollow world,
Only to make a sound to last for ages.
Yet flatterers call these mighty madmen, heroes!
   K. Yes! and they honour 'em with public
     triumphs.
   D. They shame 'em rather; for to me a triumph
Appears a public sacrifice to insolence;
Adoring pride as they did plagues and fevers.
If ever I had seen a Roman triumph,

* Foolish, impudent.—
        " Tell these sad women
      'Tis fond to wail inevitable strokes,
      As 'tis to laugh at them."—*Shakespeare's Coriolanus.*

I shou'd ha' pitied the poor conqueror,
To see the tender man fallen so sick,
By the ill favours of a field of slaughter,
That he came home with his head bound with
    laurel,
Gasping in chariots for the people's breath.
    K. For ever cou'd I hear thee thus discourse;
But I have business must divert our talk.
    D. Yes, sir! I hear the King of England's
    landed.
    K. He is!
    D. He leads a very gallant nation :
I've tried 'em oft in battles and in sieges.
They despise walls and trenches, they are so us'd
To cross the ocean they laugh at trenches.
    K. My son despises 'em.
    D. He's too brave !
His too hot martial fires burn out the eyes
Of his clear understanding.
    K. His too hot
Amorous fires have kindled this ill war.
    D. Now dare not I enquire into this story, [*Aside.*
For I've been thunder-stricken with report.
    K. If he be married, as I fear he is,
A war is like to be his fair wife's portion ;
And a rich portion too in the esteem
Of him, and his licentious followers.
    D. War is the harvest, sir, of all ill men ;
In war they may be brutes with reputation.
    K. Now let me whisper thee about thy father.
    La Ma. This Duke here keeps a-talking with
    the King,
He hopes to hold himself up with his wit.
Pshaw! wit's a thing will never do at Court.
    K. Now, sirs, I charge you all, do not report
Or think the Duke is shaken in my favour,
Because his father's fallen; his father, like

A heavy lumb'ring beam in a house-top,
Did rather press him down than hold him up;
To honour the Duke's merit then shall be
Esteem'd by me as merit; and so, sirs, embrace
   him !
   La Mar. Oh! I am in a very fine condition,
Who have affronted and oppos'd his father.
I thought their damn'd great family was ruin'd!
Pox o' these Court intrigues! a man is trapt
And snapt, he knows not how to turn himself.
Why is the King so fond of this same Vendosme?
He is no dresser; do but see how awkwardly
His damn'd crevat is tied! Were I a King
I'd hang a man shou'd come into my presence
With such a damn'd crevat, and tied so slovenly.
Then he is no dancer neither. What's he good
   for?
Oh! he is a wit, forsooth! Hang all these wits!
They are good for nothing but to jeer and scribble.
This Vendosme must be lov'd because his tongue
Hangs well; I would his neck were hung as well.
But 'tis in vain to mutter, I must flatter him.
My noble Lord! your Grace's humble servant.
   D. Honest La Marre, how dost?
   La Mar. Ever in health,
And in good fortune when your Grace is so.
   D. I thank thee, good La Marre !
   La Mar. My Lord, I'm tied
By most particular strong obligations
To your Grace's family. I owe my fortunes
To your most noble father's love and bounty.
   D. I will succeed him in his love to thee.
   La Mar. So now my interest which was off the
   hinges
Is nailed on fast again; but I will go
Shortly behind the door, and clinch the nail;
I'll make him a particular address

At his own lodgings, and then all is done.
Then I'll not fail to make my court to him
Almost at all his levyes and his couchees.*
    K. Come in with me, my Lord!
I must talk more with you.   [*Exeunt.*
    D. I will attend you, sir.   My soul is troubled.
Where e'er I go, I meet a wand'ring rumour :
Louize is the Dauphin's secret mistress.
I heard it in the army, but the sound
Was then as feeble as the distant murmurs
Of a great river mingling with the sea.
But now I am come near this river's fall,
'Tis louder than the Cataracts of Nile.
If this be true——
Doomsday is near, and all the heavens are falling.
I know not what to think of it, for every where
I meet a choking dust, such as is made
After removing all a palace furniture;
If she be gone, the world, in my esteem,
Is all bare walls; nothing remains in it
But dust and feathers; like a Turkish Inn,
And the foul steps where plunderers have been.
                    [*Exit.*

ACTUS TERTIUS.

Enter GREAT CONSTABLE *alone.*

SCENE, *His apartment in the Court.*

    Const. All seiz'd at once! Is this the good effect
Of my wise plots? Oh! my unquiet spirit!
Sure some men's souls are given 'em for plagues;
My soul to me is all the plagues of Egypt.

---

* The time of visiting late at night.
   "None of her sylvan subjects made their court :
   Levees and couchees pass'd without resort."—*Dryden.*

My thoughts are frogs, and flies, and lice, and
  locusts.
When honours are rain'd down on any other,
A plague of hail is rain'd down upon me.
When men's prosperity shines hot upon me,
My poisonous nature breaks out all in boils.
Oh! come, my Lord! let's meditate revenge.

Enter LA FORCE.

La For. Had we been wise we ne'er had needed
  it.
Const. Were the King wise we ne'er had liv'd to
  plot it.
The King's unskill'd in gallant wicked men;
Undo us, and not send us to the devil?
The devil for that shall send us to the King.
No man so brave as he who dares be wicked;
Ill has no friend to trust to but its own
Bastard, success; the offspring of its strength.
La For. Know you your son's arriv'd?
Const. Is he?
La For. He is!
Const. So, that's good news! I am prepar'd to
  cheat him.
In pious dress I'll steal into his bosom,
As knaves, they say do, in St. Francis' habit,
Cheat Heaven, and creep into old Abraham's bosom.
La For. I doubt he will not be deceiv'd so easily.
Const. Oh! he, who has foolish good nature in
  him,
Has a soft girl the portress of his breast,
Who will be easily mov'd to ope the door.

Enter a SERVANT.

Ser. The Duke, my Lord, is come!
Const. Oh! bring him.   [*Exit Serv.*
La For. I'll leave you for a while.

Const. Do, good, my Lord.   [*Exit La Force.*

Enter Duke of Vendosme.

My son! and have I liv'd to see thy face?
I thank my enemies they leave me thee,
A greater joy, than all they have taken from me.
     D. Now is my father falling to his arts: [*Aside.*
To strive to work me to his practices.
     Const. Son, I despair'd to see thee any more.
     D. Why so, my Lord?
     Const. My heart is almost broken.
     D. What breaks your heart?
     Const. Disgraces! I am thrust
To my grave's brink by injuries and dishonours.
     D. I hear you have fallen into the King's dis-
       pleasure.
     Const. Into the Dauphin's rage.
     D. For what desert?
     Const. Do any rise or fall in Courts by merit?
A want of faults is often a great fault.
How fond are some great men of fools and dwarfs,
Because they are good foils! but tall desert
Does often saucily o'erlook a Prince.
I am no dwarf to let great fools stride o'er me
To the King's breast.
     D. And shall that break your heart?
If I disdain'd to be my Prince's dwarf
I wou'd scorn more to be his marble statue;
To weep when ever the Court weather's damp.
     Const. Damp? it is stormy! one tempestuous
       blast
Tore from me all my shining robes at once.
     D. They were too heavy for your years to carry,
For all the envy of the Kingdom hung on 'em.
     Const. But they have drest up fools and blocks
       in 'em;
Such blockish fools are rais'd, one wou'd imagine.

The Court is rather pitching of the bar,*
Than raising men to honour; I can name
Some counsellors who cannot speak good sense;
The wretches have no other use of tongues
Than dogs of tails, to wag 'em when they fawn.
The shining tongue of their chief leading orator
Has neither edge nor point; but finely scabbarded
In velvet words : is like a sword of State
Borne before public business for a show.
 D. Why shou'd this grieve you ?
 Const. I abhor that fools
Shou'd go before me in command and power.
 D. He is not honour'd most who goes before ;
Mace and sword bearers go before a King.
Methinks when e'er I see Authority
Lugger a heavy fool upon her shoulders
Before me, I have State bestowed upon me,
And have a leaden mace carried before me.
 Const. Come ! 'tis unnatural, fools should be up-
  permost.
 D. 'Tis very natural vain things shou'd be upper-
  most,
In such a world of vanity as this;
Where massy substances of things sink down,
And nothing stays but colours, sounds, and shadows.
What mighty things derive their power from
  colours :
Courts owe their majesty to pomp, and show:
Altars their adoration, to their ornaments:
Women their lovers, to their paint and washes;
Fools their esteem to periwigs and ribbons.
How many trades are there that live by tones ?
The cheating beggar whines our money from us;
The player by his tone will make us weep,
When men's substantial sorrows cannot do it.
An orator will set the world a-dancing

  * Casting forward ;—throwing headlong.

After his pipe, when reason cannot stir it.
Fanatick canting priests will o'erturn Kingdoms
Only by tones, and thumping upon pulpits.
And silly human herds, as soon as e'er
They hear the wooden thunder, prick up ears,
And tails, and frighted run they know not whither.

Const. Go, angle not for me with rotten hairs,
The combings of philosophers' old pates ;
We have all our several passions that command us.
I am a slave to honour and ambition,
And thou to fair Madamoiselle de Guise.

Du. Ha ! ——   [*Starts.*

Const. Have I touch'd you, sir ? Now sir,
    suppose
This beauteous parcel of your soul, this parcel,
This soul of yours were torn out of your body,
Wou'd you not feel it ? ha !

Du. He stabs me   [*Aside.*
In my old wound !

Const. Oh ! Are you startled, sir ?
Say she were whor'd, sir ?

Du. Oh ! I am abus'd,——   [*Aside.*
All, all agree about this cursed story.

Const. What now, you are awake ? I have rous'd you
Out of your dream of stoical philosophy,
And you have blood and passions stirring in you ?
I thought your veins were only veins in marble.

Du. No, no, my lord ! I am a man, no statue,
No Pasquin only to hang libels on.

Const. Then since thou art a man, and hast some
    feeling,
I will not say she's whor'd, but I will say
A married man enjoys her.

Du. Do not say it, my lord.

Const. 'Tis true ! I have seen 'em folded in em-
    braces,
Have seen their souls skip from their eyes and dance

On wanton looks, like tumblers upon ropes.
Have seen their tilting lips meet close, and grapple,
As they wou'd tug each other from their faces ;
Then, with what breath their pleasant strife had
    left 'em,
They'd fling with scorn out of their laughing mouths
The name of Vendosme ; more they scarce cou'd say,
But when they had breath they'd cry, Phi-lo-so-pher.

    Du. Who does she play this modest game withall ?
    Const. With one whose sport you dare not spoil,
The Dauphin.
    Du. Oh ! It is so ? This woman has been false,
To get a crown :—— Oh !——
    Const. Are you pain'd ? Be comforted !
You quickly shall have ease, for, know, your death
Is plotted by 'em both.
    Du. My death ?
    Const. Your death !
I'm ruin'd cause I know all their designs :
For now Court secrets are like fairies' revels,
Or witches' conventicles ; men are spoiled
With sudden blasts that either tell or see 'em.
They do not spare their Favourites and Creatures.
Brissac, once lov'd both by the King and Dauphin,
Because he honestly oppos'd your murder,
Is falsely charg'd with treason, and tormented
To make him own it, and name you a party.
    Du. Can there be wickedness enough in Hell
To furnish out with truth this horrid story ?
    Const. I know thy thoughts are calling me a liar.
Ho ! there.

              Enter a SERVANT.

    Ser. My lord ?
    Const. Open those folding doors.

The Scene is drawn, and Brissac is shown bloody and
                    asleep.

Sleeps he ?

Ser. He's fallen into so deep a sleep,
His sense is sunk out of the loudest call.

Const. I gave him opium to ease his pains :
I cou'd not bear to hear his piercing groans.
Now, sir, I hope you will believe your eyes.

Du. This horrid barb'rous fight confounds my soul.

Const. Oh! now it works him, I shall fool him
  finely.   [*Aside.*

Du. I'll search the depth of this, though it reach
  Hell.   [*Aside.*
Wake him!

Ser. We cannot.

Du. Cannot you?

Ser. We cannot.

Du. Then shut the door! I cannot see him longer.
I'm strangely mov'd.

Const. What if we went to prayers,
And recommend to Heaven the King and Dauphin?

D. To prayers? To arms! fit weapons to re-
  venge us.
But I am justly serv'd for having th' impudence
To put on virtue in this dirty world,
And drag the robes of angels on a dunghill.

Const. Indeed those robes starve every man that
  wears 'em.

Du. But I did only put 'em on to act in.

Const. To act in?

Du. Yes, and wrapt my self so cunningly,
The Devil with all his flambeaux cou'd not see me.

Const. How? Art thou not what thou pretend'st
  to be,
A man of virtue, loyalty, and honour?

Du. The pretty jingling of the chains of fools.

Const. Ha! Is it so? this is most wonderful!
I always thought thee a poor mountaineer,
That liv'd on virtue's cold and barren hill,
Till all thy blood was froze, and sense benumb'd.

Du. No, no! my blood is hot, and my pulse beats
As strong as any man's, rings all the changes
Of love, ambition, fury and revenge;
I'll give myself revenge, my country freedom,
I will transform my enslav'd nation
From mules, and burthen-bearing beasts, to men.
No beast is half so wretched as a Frenchman:
He always has a bridle in his mouth,
And he has nothing but his bit to champ on.
    Const. Right! He is forc'd to give his meat for
      salt.
    Du. He's flead and salted.
    Const. He's a pickled mandrake!
An Englishman will eat him for a salad,
And pluck him by the roots out of his trenches.
When e'er he has a mind, in spite of all
The pretty gard'ning way, you now have got,
Of keeping your muskmellons from the weather.
No wonder the stout English always beat us,
We squeeze the heart and soul out of our peasants,
Then flap the enemy with the empty bags.
    Du. But now I'll stuff the peasants' skins with
      manhood,
And break the chain that links to the King's
      throne
The Nobles, as the globe is to Jove's chair.
I hate dependence on another's will,
Which changes with the breath of every whisper,
Just as the sky and weather with the winds.
Nay, with the winds, as they blow east or west,
To make his temper pleasant or unpleasant:
So are our wholesome or unwholesome days.
    Const. Nay with his diet, if his cook but gives
      him
A melancholy dish; or, if his doctor
Give him a pill shall stir up choler in him,
We may perhaps be purg'd out o'th' Court.

And then we boast of destinies and stars,
When we are made or spoil'd by quacks and
   cooks.
   Du. Nothing more true! nay, we are finely rul'd
Between a wild young Prince, and dull old King.
   Const. A Royal image, and brave fiery spirits
Do only burn like waxen tapers round him,
As if it was the funeral of the Kingdom ;
Rather like lamps i'th' urn of a dead Kingdom.
   Du. 'Tis dead ! for it has long been deadly sick.
   Const. Oh ! surfeited with fulsome ease and
   wealth,
Our luscious hours are candied up for women,
Whilst our men lose their appetite to glory ;
Our pilots all their skill, for want o' storms.
   Du. The Kingdom's dead, or in a lethargy !
I'll try and lance it now about the head.
   Const. The King ?
   Du. The King !
   Const. Thou art a wicked fellow,
Where didst thou get this wickedness, and when ?
   Du. I got it that brave night when you got me,
You made me wicked in my mother's womb,
And I have trebly improv'd your nat'ral stock.
I set my foot firm on the present world,
Nor, like a boy skipping between two ships,
Slip down between 'em and so lose 'em both ;
But here I stow my fortunes, and I cast
All goodness over-board as so much lumber.
All virtue's as a bunch of useless keys,
That will unlock no doors but those of Heaven,
Where neither you nor I have any business.
   Const. Who cou'd believe an image of a Saint
Shou'd lodge within it such a nest of spiders ?
Let me embrace thee, son, for now I own thee !
Thou wert not stole from me when thou wert
   young

By priests and schools, those common thieves in
    children,
Who spirit 'em away, and in their rooms
Send us home idiots mop'd with piety,
Pinch'd hourly by that fairy call'd a Conscience,
And blasted by that lightning call'd Religion.
Now I will own to thee, I have materials
For a great change ; and, now thou shew'st am-
    bition,
I dare confide in thee.
    Du. I'd as soon be
An eunuch, as a man without ambition.
The lust of ruling men does far excel
The brutish lust of getting 'em ; a beast
Can get his kind, but cannot govern it.
Ambition is a spirit in the world,
That causes all the ebbs and flows of nations,
Keeps mankind sweet by action ; without that
The world wou'd be a filthy settled mud.
    Const. Most excellent !
    Du. Have you no friends, my lord,
You cou'd engage ?
    Const. Thousands of all degrees :
Rebellious lords denied the rule of provinces,
Damn'd knavish Statesmen fool'd of promis'd
    offices,
Mutinous officers denied commands,
Proud clergymen who cannot get promotion
So much as for their money ; wealthy fools,
Who wou'd be knights or lords, and are refused.
And all the discontented laymen's wives,
And all the discontented churchmen's wenches,
And all the women who fain would be mistresses
And lose their reputations to no purpose :
All who have yielded to old gouty Statesmen,
With hope of pensions and were fool'd of them.
    Du. Most rare tools all !

Const. Most excellent ! With thy aid
We shall not need th' assistance of an angel.

 Du. An angel? What assistance can he give us,
Who spends his time in idleness and songs?

 Const. He's good for nothing but t' inspire a
  fiddler.

 Du. Your's are the tools : cou'd you not bring
'em to me?

 Const. At an hour's warning.

 Du. Pray, my lord.

 Const. I will.

 Du. And I will bring a guard and seize 'em all.
            [*Aside.*

So, now I've opened all the filthy vault,
And let out such foul air has made me sick.
But yet within this vault I find a lamp
Of joyful hope, Louize is not false,
But wrong'd by flying rumours, which, like birds
Soaring at random, mute* on any head.
'Tis plain, my father turns the stream of rumour
Tow'rds her, to carry me along to treason.
I'll beg my father's life, but I'll secure him
From hurting of the King.—   [*Aside.*
Farewell, my lord !

 Const. Farewell, dear son !   [*Exit Duke.*

Enter LA FORCE.

 La For. What news? What good success?

 Const. I've fool'd him admirably.
Oh ! I have put such crabbed stuff into him
Has curdled the milk-sop. Well, I have promis'd
 him,
That you and all our friends shall talk with him.

 La For. We will !

 Const. I'll call you suddenly.

---

 * " I could not fright the crows
  Or the least bird from muting on my head."—*Ben Jonson.*

La For. I'll wait you.——   [*Exeunt.*

Enter LOUIZE.

Lou. I've seen the wicked, perjur'd, charming
     Vendosme ;
Have view'd him o'er and o'er, and heard him talk.
Heaven has not blasted one of all his graces ;
His tongue has all the harmony it had,
When ears, and hearts, and all the gates of souls
Flew open at the sound ; still, still, his words
Resemble, as they did, the heavenly manna,
Feasting all ears with what they most delighted.

Enter LA GUARD.

La Gu. Madam, I've spied the Duke watching
     the Dauphin !
They are both coming hither.
     Lou. Then draws near
The time of our most terrible encounter.
Come to my aid my honour, give me vigour !
If love approach me, let me throw it off
With all the strength a woman in convulsions
Will do an infant. Let me dash its brains out !
And, to begin the battle, I'll receive
The Dauphin in his sight with doting fondness.

Enter the DAUPHIN, *followed at a distance by the*
     DUKE OF VENDOSME.

Du. I've followed him with trembling steps
     unseen,
Fearing he leads me to the fair enchantress.
My fears deceive me, or I heard him name her.
Oh ! If he leads me to her, Heaven govern me !
'Tis so ! 'Tis she ! They meet, embrace, and kiss.
Devil loose my hand, thrust it not to my sword !
     Daup. Love, I must tell thee news, Vendosme is
     come ;

That fortunate proud slave ; but I am going
To take his pride from him, and tumble him
With that great knave, his father, in the dirt.

[*Exit.*

   Du. Hark ! hark ! My death is plotted by 'em
    both.
All true my father told me !——Nay, your lover
May take my pride from me, for he has taken
My shame from me, the falsest woman living.
   Lou. You here ?
   Du. Yes, I am here !
   Lou. Dare you approach me ?
   Du. Yes, but with fear, for sure you are not a
    woman.
A comet glitter'd in the air of late,
And kept some weeks the frighted Kingdom
    waking,
Long hair it had, like you,—a shining aspect ;
Its beauty pleas'd at the same time it fright'ned,
And every horror in it had a grace.
It has not now appear'd these several months.
Are you that comet ? Some astrologers
Say sun, and moon, and stars, are living creatures
That feed on vapours ; are you come below
To feast upon the reek of smoking hearts,
Burnt by yourself in that inflaming shape ?
   Lou. I understand you not.
   Du. Sure some ill spirit
Assumes the shape of the divine Louize ;
And yet methinks a demon us'd to darkness
Should not be able to approach such light.
May I have leave to touch that beauteous hand,
Only to know if it be flesh and blood ?
   Lou. If you wou'd know, go ask your Prince, the
    Dauphin.
   Du. What ! are you asham'd to shew it ? it has
    lost

Its native pureness, and is forc'd to borrow
Whiteness from Royal ermine and Crown lillies.
   Lou. All this is dark.
   Du. I'll bring you to the light.
This pack o' hounds, we call our passions,
Shall hunt your falsehood, and, where e'er it earths
    · itself,
I'll dig it out, and bring it to the day.
But if you'll take it in your arms and kiss it,
And say 'tis your's, 'tis like you, I am satisfied.
   Lou. My lord, I lov'd you once, still love your
    merit ;
But I, like heaven, save none for human excel-
    lence.
Were you the greatest man that e'er was born,
Yet if you fondly worship gaudy idols,
And will have no belief in me, away with you
To your suppos'd Elizium's idle dreams !
   Du. What do you call adoring gaudy idols ?
To gaze on 'em ?
   Lou. To gaze on 'em with pleasure.
Who worships me must speak, and look, and think,
According to my rules ; and, if they seem
Too hard to practise, let him take his course,
I will not give my heaven to libertines.
   Du. But what if she I gaz'd on was your image ?
Is it idolatry t' adore your image ?
   Lou. Yes, without leave. But you adore
    another
Only as my image, and blaspheme th' original.
   Du. I blaspheme you ?
   Lou. You know what you have done.
   Du. Yes, I once vow'd my heart to you for ever.
   Lou. That is not all.
   Du. What else ?
   Lou. I scorn to think of it.
   Du. You blush !
    VOL. 3.   13

Lou. Nay, you would have me die, no doubt.
You are enraged, after your cruel usage,
To find me living; living gloriously.
    Du. If you were in your grave, you were more
        glorious
Than in your guilt.   There is no shame in death.
    Lou. Yes, but there is much shame in death for
        love ;
A woman die for love ? Oh ! infamous !
I hate to see't it so much as in a play,
And think such plays are libels to our sex.
I laugh when I see ladies weeping at 'em ;
Weep till they quite disorder their *doux yeux* ;
Weep till their tears wash away all their paint.
I wou'd not have that woman sav'd should shame
Our sex by dying so immodestly.
Indeed 'tis never done, or, if it be,
'Tis never own'd ; the very waiting-women,
When their hearts break, do scorn to have it
    known ;
And their friends never put it in the bill.
What thinks your Grace ? Am I in any danger ?
Do I look pale at all ?
    Du. No, heaven be thanked !
Your Highness, madam, looks exceeding well.
Alas ! you are in th' climate which agrees with you,
The scorching clime of glory ; but, methinks,
The heat might put some blushes in your cheeks.
    Lou. No, Heaven forbid !
I wou'd by no means have it.
Did secret love devour me I'd no more
Disclose my torment than the Spartan boy
Did, whilst the hidden fox gnaw'd all his entrails.
But love's a fire, and if it burns within
'Twill smoke without ; do you see any smoke ?
Or in my looks one sign of inward torment ?
    Du. Not the least, madam.

Lou. I am very glad of it !
My looks are honest then, and tell no falsehoods.
 Du. I wish your heart were but as faultless,
  madam,
As your looks are.
 Lou. My heart will serve my turn.
 Du. Yes, it has served your turn, for it has
  turn'd,
And turn'd, and turn'd, but always to the sun.
 Lou. Think and report it too, rather I had
A thousand times be thought ambitious, perjur'd,
Than such a wretch as a forsaken woman.
 Du. Madam, I'll do you right.
 Lou. You will oblige me,
And yourself too, never to see me more ;
For I shall ever vex your haughty heart.
 Du. Well, madam, I will make a shift to bear it.
But you, by this, give me to understand
I am a storm that trouble your delights ;
You cannot sing your songs to your new lover,
With such a thorn as I am at your breast.
 Lou. Oh ! you conjecture wrong, my lord.
 Du. No, madam:
Well, I will leave you ; my tempestuous breath
Shall not ruffle your bridal curtains.
 Lou. Oh ! you cannot ;
Nor blow but one loose feather from my pillow.
 Du. Oh ! Yes ! yes ! I will go ! but wou'd it
  not
Be for your ease to send your conscience with me ?
 Lou. Your own is heavier than you well can carry.
 Du. But yours, I fear, is murder'd ; if it be,
Its ghost will make your glories burn as dim
As lamps that faint when an ill spirit appears.
 Lou. Well, stay or go, I'll not talk with you, of
  you,
Look on you, think upon you, any more.----

Enter a GENTLEMAN.

Gent. Madam, the Dauphin's asking for your
    Highness!

Lou. Oh! ere I see him, I must pour my grief
    out,   *[Aside.*

For my heart's full, and it is running over. *[Exit.*

La Gu. So, now the worst is past!   *[Exit.*

Du. Was ever falsehood

Drest in such gorgeous swelling robes of arrogance?
It is so big, no slender robes can fit it.
Now sorrow thou hast found a passage to me,
All other ways my soul was inaccessible.
Fame I contemn! her temple is a brothel,   •
Where good and bad lie mingled all together.
Victory I scorn, I am not proud! mankind
Is capable of cowardice, and death.
Titles I scorn! they are often fixt to pamphlets.
Beauty is the only thing that conquers me,
I am disarm'd by a white brittle wand,
Vanquish't and robb'd of all, and then forsaken.
Still there's some chink made in us, sons of sin,
For misery and death to enter in.   *[Exit.*

FINIS ACTUS TERTII.

ACTUS QUARTUS.

Enter the Duke of VENDOSME.

Duke. Farewell, oh, world! thou school of
    bearded boys!

Here empty fools are honour'd for full bags,
And well-fill'd minds despis'd for empty pockets;
Men's eyes are dim, but women's blind to excel-
    lence.
This beauteous woman look'd upon my head

And saw no Crown on it, and look'd no deeper.
Thus are our sex by women oft deceiv'd ;
The gallant thinks his mistress sees his qualities,
She only sees his equipage and garniture.
Th' old wooden lord sees a young beauty glance
He thinks on him ; alas ! 'tis on a toy,
More wooden than himself, his coronet.
The Statesman thinks his great parts charm his
    mistress,
She only looks on's great house, his great train.
The brave young hero thinks his mistress values
    him,
Because his courage can support her honour ;
'Tis for his pages to hold up her tail.

Enter a SERVANT.

   Ser. All things, my lord, are ready for your
    journey.
   Du. I'm ready then. [*Exit Serv.*] Now will I seek
    some place
Where I may never more see any thing
Like man or woman ; specially like woman.
In some dark forest will I live, whose shades
May guard my eyes securely from the moon,
Because 'tis bright, and changing like a woman ;
Therefore I'll never see't but in eclipse.
Barren shall be the earth, and so benumb'd
And mortifi'd with shade, not all the courtship
Nor golden proffers of the sun shall woo it,
Or bribe it to one smile ; because if flattery,
Riches and pomp, can gain it, 'tis a woman !
I will want breath ere let the winds approach me,
Because they're like th' inconstant sighs of woman.
I never will see summer's vanishing dew,
Nor winter's shining ice, 'cause both, like woman.
The dew turns air when once the sun has kiss'd it,
And woman in enjoyment proves delusion,

Something less real than the dreams of fancy.
The ice dissolves under the sun's bright smiles,
And woman always yields when glory tempts,
And then whate'er is built upon her sinks.

Enter a SERVANT.

Ser. Monsieur La Marre, my lord, attends without.
Du. La Marre? What has that fool to do with me?
Ser. He says he has a message from the King.
Du. He lies! the King would send a wiser
    messenger;
But, since he uses the King's name, admit him!

Servant goes out and introduces LA MARRE.

La Ma. Now I'll establish a firm interest in
    him.   [*Aside.*
Your Grace's most obedient humble servant,
I am extremely joyful for your Grace's
Glorious success; your Grace has done strange
    marvels;
His Majesty has a very vast esteem for you,
He and I have talk't of you a thousand times.
    Du. I thank you, sir! well, to be short, good
    sir,
Have you any business with me?
    La Ma. To be short,
There is no person in the world, my lord,
More in esteem both with the King and Dauphin,
And, for my own part—
    Du. For your part, I mean, sir,
Have you any business with me?
    La Ma. Business, my lord?
Only that I'm your Grace's humble servant,
And so forth, and to pay my high respects,
And so forth, and so forth—I know your Grace
Has heard the great Court news; the Dauphin's
    marriage

With Madamoiselle de Guise is now made public.
Truth is, she is a very curious creature;
Devil take me if she be not.
    Du. Now I find it.
This senseless rogue is put on to abuse me. [*Aside.*
    La Ma. What thinks your Grace ?
Would not so sweet a creature
Refresh you finely after a campagne ?
In short, there will be a great ball to-night,
The King, the Dauphin, and his beauteous bride,
Do all expect your Grace to be a dancer.
    Du. Plain, plain abuse! Sir, when was I a
    dancer ?
My foot shall dance upon no earth but this.
                        [*Kicks him.*
    La Ma. How ? Kick, my lord ?
What do you mean by this ?
    Du. You are put on by some to abuse me,
    sirrah.
    La Ma. You are put on by some to abuse me
    rather :
My lord, I do not understand the meaning of it ;
I shall not put up this,——   [*Offers to draw.*
    Du. Shall you not, sir ?
        [*The Duke offers to draw. La Marre puts up.*
    La Ma. I shall at present, but the King shall
    know this.
I am more considerable with the King
Than you believe.
    Du. Indeed there are in Court
Too many such soft heads as yours, embroider'd
And made State cushions, for great men to lean on ;
And fortune often jumps from Heaven upon 'em.
    La Ma. Soft heads and cushions ?
Come, my lord, be it known to you
His Majesty's servants are not to be call'd
Fools and soft-heads, by e'er a peer of you all.

The King shall know this ! he'll not take it well.
All this is, 'cause I did affront his father ;
I'll do his father's business for this trick.— [*Exit.*
   Du. I find all Courts are apt, like all great
     mountains,
To breed such little cattle ; and these runts *
Do often draw weighty affairs along.
But oh ! the insolence of this vile woman,
To set her fools upon me, to abuse me !
Oh ! there is thunder forming in my soul,
Now, should I meet my father and his firebrands,
Off shou'd I go, and rend the Court in pieces.
He said he'd bring me hither his conspirators.
I'll run for fear the strong temptation seize me.

The SCENE *is drawn, the* DAUPHIN *and* LOUIZE *are sat*
   in State, and entertain'd with music and dancing.
   The Entertainment ended,

   Enter the DUKE ; *he sees the* DAUPHIN *caressing*
     LOUIZE.

A SONG.

1.

Long, long had great Amintor lain
At Celia's feet and wept in vain ;
Not all his youth, his love, or glory,
But once cou'd make her hear his story.
One smile she to that youth deny'd,
For whom a thousand beauties died.
   Chor. Yet all the while fair Celia prov'd,
     So haughty, so cruel, she secretly lov'd.

2.

Still, still he bravely bore his pain,
With patience took her proud disdain,
Though all her looks with wounds did fill him,
And every word did almost kill him,

   * A contemptuous expression for small cattle.

To see her, or to hear her speak,
He was content his heart shou'd break.
 Chor. Yet all the while fair Celia prov'd,
  So haughty, so cruel, she secretly lov'd.

3.

But beautiful Celia now fearing
His heart should grow hard with long bearing ;
  Not willing to lose him,
  Does gentlier use him,
And drives away all his despairing.
 Oh now, brave Amintor, no pity afford,
 Thou hast got her by storm, now put all to th'
  sword ;
 To the altar of modesty, if she would fly,
 It is but an image, and there let her die.

4.

Now Celia for pity is crying ;
But oh ! the delight of that dying !
  Her soul cannot shew it,
  Her soul does not know it,
Her soul in a rapture is flying.
 Love, like the great Turk, in his pleasures does
  sport,
 With mutes, in the innermost parts of his
  Court ;
 He drives the dull counsellor, *thinking*, away,
 And himself and his mutes out o' breath he
  does play.

 Du. Oh ! What infernal spirit brought me
  hither ?
I am decreed for wickedness ; I shall
Destroy that Prince, in spite of all that poor
Court household-stuff, that imagery about him.
 Daup. Ha ! Vendosme there ? Leave me a
  while, my love !

Lou. I will, but I will watch you do not hurt
    him.   [*Aside.*
For still I love him, spight of all his falsehood.
                           · [*Exit.*
   Du. He's coming! My heart swells, that my
    ribs bend
Like bowes of steel, ready to shoot my soul at him.
   Daup. Sir, you have long soar'd o'er my head,
    but now
I'll bring you down! Where is your commission?
   Du. How? My commission? Where it shall
    remain
Till the King takes it; sir, in my own keeping.
   Daup. How? Shall? [*Puts his hand to his sword.*

Enter LOUIZE.

   Lou. Oh! hold, my lord!
   Daup. What dost thou mean?
   Lou. Oh! to hurt him will pierce your father's
    heart;
I beg you then, upon my knees, be calm.
   Daup. What storm so rude, which such a beaute-
    ous halcyon
Cannot soon calm? Traitor! this angel here
Has given thee life; but know, thou art preserv'd
To perish with thy father on a scaffold.   [*Exit.*
   Lou. I'll save him too from that, or perish with
    him.   [*Aside. Exit.*
   Du. Now a brave fool, that had more blood
    than brains,
Whose soul lay in his arm, not in his head,
And had my wrongs, and my power to revenge
    them,
Would thrust his foolish arm to reach revenge,
Though he pulled all the kingdom on his head.
He would accept the match the devil offers me
Instead of my lost mistress, his own daughter,

The heiress of all Hell, Rebellion.
I the next minute could confound the town
Into a temple o' death, and marry her in it;
And, with her, get the riches of all France.
And Hell has sent to treat about the match
His kindred, cursed passions to my heart.
Here come his agents on the same affair,
Mountain on mountain pil'd, to scale my honesty.

Enter the GREAT CONSTABLE, LA FORCE, *and*
CONSPIRATORS.

Const. Son! here are all our friends.
Du. Away with you!
You scare my loyalty out of its wits.
Const. Thy loyalty? thou art afraid, I see;
These are the honest friends I told thee of.
Du. You mean the traitors.
Const. How?
Du. Yes, such as you promised me,
And I give men and things their proper names.
Scuffle for the world then how you will, you traitors,
There was but one sweet spot in it I valued,
And it is sunk beneath me; all the rest
Take he that will, and how, I do not care.
Go turn the globe about then how you will,
There shall be in this wide world one honest man,
Though he has much ado to keep his honesty.
Const. Hold, sir! come back again.
Du. No, I have said.
Const. Thy thoughts?
Du. My thoughts!
Const. And art thou such a fool?
What dost thou in a Court, or in the world?
Go be a monk, in hope of being sainted,
Give friars all thy gold, in the rich hopes
When thou art dead, they'll tip thy skull with
      silver;

Stink all thy life, to be ador'd when dead,
And have thy rotten bones to cure lame legs.

   Du. Do you go join your plotting heads and
     lose them !   *[Ex.*

   La For. Is this your fooling him so admirably ?
How chance we let him go, and did not kill him ?
Graves have no echoes, skulls want coverings
Of flesh and blood, but hide a secret better.

   Const. I'll kill him with more pleasure than I got
     him.
I got him ? I ne'er got him, he's a bastard !
No honesty could ever spring from me.

   1 *Consp.* Curse on his piety !

   Const. Some priest begot him,
Lay with his mother when she slept at prayers;
That makes the world appear a dream to him.

   La For. The mother is the chief ingredient in
     him.

   Const. I ought not to get children of a woman,
I ought to mix with nothing but a chaos,
And get confusion to the universe,
And then the children would be like the father.

   La For. I ne'er approved trusting so rank a secret
To such a tender mind ; I knew 't would gripe him.
His conscience would have qualms.

   Const. Ay, there's the thing !
We breed our children's minds as tenderly
And womanish as their bodies ; he, who means
To have a gallant son, must plunge his soul
O'er head and ears betimes in wickedness,
Then when he is a man 'twill be his element.
He must not let him go wrapped warm in silk
Spun from the silly worms in a priest's head,
But go stark naked, then he'll feel no cold,
For conscience is but the soul's outward skin :
Use it to nakedness, it feels no weather,
Use it to labour, and it never blisters.

If I had used this fool to sin, I might
Have lodged my treason in his brawny head .
As safe as poison in an ass's hoof.
 La For. But now it cracks his chrystal wit, and
  spills.
I hate these chrystal wits! they are good for nothing
But to make flattering looking-glasses for ladies.
 Const. He says he'll keep his honesty; damn'd
  sot !
What will he do with it? Go beg with it?
For in this age 'tis of no other use,
But, like a beggar's child, to move compassion, .
Yet never gains the half it cost in keeping,
For all men will suspect it for a bastard.

   Enter an OFFICER *with a* GUARD.

 Off. and the Gua. Resign yourselves, my lords!
You are my prisoners.
 Const. How, sir? your prisoners?
 Off. Your own son, my lord,
Charges you with high treason against the King,
And bloody cruelties to Count Brisac.
 Const. Oh ! cursed villain !
 La For. Villains both of you !
 1 *Consp.* You are ; you have betray'd us all!
All betray'd !
 2 *Consp.* A trick to ruin us, and beg our fortunes.
 Const. Ha ! ha ! ha !   [*Laughs.*
 La For. How ! are you laughing at us ?
 Const. Yes ; I am !
 1 *Consp.* You did design we should be seiz'd
  then ?
 Const. Yes !
And I laugh heartily to see you all sigh,
As you were bottling up air in your bellies
To serve you when your wind-pipes are cork'd up.
But come, poor men, be comforted ! all's well !

I ramm'd this fool up to the mouth with treason,
Not to hurt us, but to break him in pieces.

Enter the KING, DUKE, GUARD.

K. So sir, your son informs me ex'lent things of
    you.
Const. Art thou, unnatural monster, my accuser ?
Du. I am ! the secret's tore out of my breast
And broke all bars of nature.
Const. Oh ! vile wretch !
Seek to destroy his being, who gave thee thine ?
Du. What greater curse than being could you
    give me,
With all the plagues your sins entail upon it ?
You spent your own and all my sins beforehand,
And mortgag'd me to Hell before you got me,
For more than I was worth.
Const. Thou mak'st me mad !
Du. Ambition makes you so.
If I had that disease, I'd have my head
Trepan'd, to let out all the windy vapours,
Rather than swell so big till my brains crack.

Enter the DAUPHIN, LA MARRE, *and Train.*

Dauph. Where's the Constable ? Bold daring
    traitor !
And hast thou dared to wrack the man I loved,
For whose least hair I took thy head in pawn ?
Know I will have thee broken on the wheel,
If thou hast dared only to break his sleep.
Const. I am contented.
K. Why ! Is he not hurt ?
Const. Not that I know of.
K. Did not you inform me
You saw him newly taken from the wrack ?
Du. I did !
Const. You did ? Then it was you that wrackt him.

If so, sir, you have served me a fine trick,
To torture him and put it upon me.
 K. But, sir, he says you put it upon me,
And sought by that to tempt him into treason.
 Const. I never tempted him nor talked with him.
I scarce have seen him since he came to Court.
 K. I am amaz'd !
 Dauph. What juggling's here between you ?
 D. I'm half afraid he has put some trick upon
  me.   [*Aside.*
 Const. You see he's silent, sir ! he knows not
  what
To say, nor I to think. Well, I've observ'd
These damn'd half-witted and half-honest fellows,
Like Africa, have things of different kind
Meet and engender, and get monsters in 'em.
Their wit and folly couple, and get nonsense,
With a strange face of sense; their knavery and
  honesty
Beget a devil with an honest look,
And such a monster is this fellow's lie.
Or else perhaps he is a down-right traitor,
And is a partner in Brisac's conspiracy,
And he would make my blood the aquafortis
To eat his partner's prison bars asunder.
I believe that.
 Daup. Come, you are villains both !
 La Ma. An't please your Highness, you have hit
  upon it.
The Duke of Vendosme affronted me this morning
Only because I mention'd you with honour ;
I told him I would find a time to tell you.
 K. Who bids you meddle ? Give away that
  fellow's
Employment presently.
 La Ma. Give away my employment ?
 K. Begone, sir !

La Ma. Sir, it cost me five years' purchase.

K. Begone, sir!

La Ma. Sir, I have had no salary
Since I came in it.

1 *Courtier.* Stand prating to the King?
Out of the presence!

La Ma. Sir, I've paid for prating.

Court. Well, if you have, sir, go prate somewhere
else.

La Ma. Here's a fine business! turn'd away for
loyalty.
Well, I will be reveng'd upon the Court:
I know some malcontents that I will stick to.

Const. Now, to conclude the strife, open those
doors!

The SCENE *is drawn, and* BRISAC *is sitting drest,
awake, and well.*

Du. This sight, or th' other was a strange
delusion.

Const. Witchcraft! You know I traffic with the
devil.

Dau. I am amaz'd at this! How does Brisac?
Vendosme reported that his father wrack'd thee.

Bris. He threatened me, indeed, but durst not
do it.

Daup. Some damn'd design was forged between
'em both;
I'll trust thee to him no longer.

K. I'm convinc't:
You tampered with your son, and put some trick
on him.

Const. So, I am still judg'd guilty? though my
innocence
Has past the ordeal of the burning noon;
Has trod the light unscorch't! Oh! equal* doings.

Daup. If thou beest innocent, thy son's a cannibal,

* Impartial.

Who feeds his greatness with his father's flesh;
And to the horrid feast invites the King.
  [*Const.*] 'Tis so! 'tis so! the monster, sir, abuses
    you,
He gives you philtres in your father's skull,
And you drink down the damn'd bewitching
    draught.
Throw't up again, if you will keep your Crown!
  K. I'll keep my Crown! and therefore I will keep
Him who protects my Crown from thy ambition.
Come in! I guess the meaning of this riddle.
                    [*The King goes out leading the Duke.*
  Const. Not all this do?   [*Aside.*
  Daup. And shall this potent slave
Still rule the King, and trample upon me?
I'll make his father ruin him! [*Aside.*] My lord,
I find you were misrepresented to me.
  Const. I'm glad you find it, sir. Your noble youth
Has not yet play'd enough with the world's tennis
    ball,
To know its cursed tricks.
  Daup. I am convinc'd
Your son's the villain, that I thought you were.
  Const. I'm now convinc't of it to my great
    sorrow.
  Daup. He blackens you, to make himself seem
    bright.
  Const. And, sir, 'twas he that black'ned you to me.
  Daup. Oh! villain!
  Const. Now, I find his tricks; he secretly
Puts pirates' colours out at both our sterns,
That we might fight each other in mistake;
Then he shou'd share the ruins of us both!
  Daup. I will remove him.
  Const. Oh! by all means, sir.
  Daup. My father's old! What then? Age like a
    caterpillar

Will crawl upon the leaves of a young tree,
Till it has eaten away all its beauty ;
And I'll not waste my golden youth in bondage
To a proud slave.

Const. 'Twere better he were damn'd.
Had I more sons than would eclipse the sun,
I'd kill 'em all, if they stood in your light.

Daup. That's nobly said !

Const. I'll do as well; the King
Shall send this slave ere night to the Bastile.

Daup. Do this, and you and I will share the
Kingdom.

Const. Sir, let me share your heart! that's all I ask.

Daup. You shall have that, and all that France
can give.

The CONSTABLE *kisses the* DAUPHIN'S *hand.* The
DAUPHIN *embraces him.*

Enter COURTIERS.

1. *Court.* How's this ? He's great again ! he's
wound himself
Into the Dauphin's favour, who abhor'd him.

2. *Court.* Who ever thought this had been possible ?

3. *Court.* Nothing's impossible to this damn'd
Constable. [*Aside.*

1. *Court.* He'll be more absolute than e'er he
was. [*Aside.*
Well, I will be the first shall strike in with him.
Gentlemen, I'm glad to see this sight !
The Constable's a man of excellent parts.
Devil take his parts and him !—— [*Aside.*

2. *Court.* Oh ! most rare parts.
Pox on his parts ! He'll stick on all our skirts.
[*Aside.*

Daup. My Lord, from this time forward I'm
your friend.

Const. And I your Highness's most faithful slave.

Bris. Sir, are you in earnest with him ?

Daup. Ask no questions.　　　[*Ex Daup., Brisac.*

The COURTIERS *run all and salute the* CONSTABLE.

All. My Lord ! my Lord !

Const. Oh ! now the flies come buzzing ?

All. My Lord, your Grace's humble servant.

Const. Buzz !

All. My Lord ! my Lord !

Const. Nay, gentlemen, start fair!
Don't think you are in a progress ; carve me hand-
　　somely.

1. *Cou.* My Lord, believe me, I'm your Grace's
　　servant.

Const. I know it, sir.

1. *Cou.* I am, indeed, my Lord !

Const. I'll take my oath on't.

2. *Cou.* My Lord, I honour your Grace most
　　particularly.

Const. Particular coxcomb !　　　　　　[*Aside.*

3. *Cou.* Oh ! my Lord, I honour you,
And ever did with all my heart and soul.

Const. Sir, you and I have but one soul between
　　us.

3. *Cou.* Nay ! I beseech you.

Const. Pylades and Orestes.

1. *Cou.* Your Grace is pleasant.

Const. Oh ! your worship's jester.

2. *Cou.* Damn him, he laughs at's all !
I'll scrape no more to him.

Const. Out ! out you silly rascals, do you hope
To sell your legs, and bows, and nods to me ?
Were but your legs as rotten as your hearts,
I'd pull 'em off, and beat you about the heads
　　with 'em,
For thinking you could pawme such stuff on me.

All. What? what?

Const. Out! out! I say, you flies! you maggots!

　　　　　　　　　　　[He thrusts them out.

This greatness is a perfect Holland cheese,

Pour wine into't, and it breeds maggots presently.

The Dauphin only pour'd some smiles into me,

And see how soon the maggots crawl about me.

Well, ha'n't I brought you off?

　　All. To admiration.

　　La For. Now I shall dare to trust my fortunes
　　　with you once more.

　　Const. How, trust your fortunes? You may ven-
　　　ture

To have your heads cut off, if I advise you,

For I have tricks to put 'em on again,

And put 'em on better than e'er they were.

　　La For. I had rather keep mine on just as it is.

　　Const. Now I will tell you how I fool'd my son.

I cast Brisac into deep sleep with opium,

Then shew'd him as if taken from the wrack,

Thinking that way to fool him: if I cou'd not—

I laid a trap for him to fool himself.

So every way I rid the mule, and made him

Carry me up the Alps of my designs.

I'm now about a plot shall take effect;

You'll see th' event with speed.

　　La For. Farewell till then!

　　　　　　　[Exeunt La Force and Conspirators.

Const. Now to my work! here comes my instru-
　　ment.

Enter LA GUARD.

　　La Gua. My conscience! conscience!

　　Const. Now, what ails your conscience?

These little souls wear great long proking* con-
　　sciences,

　　　　　　* Entreating—insisting on.

That make them stumble every step they go.
Away with thy fool's bauble of a conscience !
A horn-book is not so ridiculous ;
Thy mother tied it to thee in thy childhood,
And thou art such an ass to wear it still.
Away with it ! and do me one more kindness.
 La Gua. I'll do you no more kindnesses.
 Const. You shall !
Do not refuse me, for fear I use you scurvily.
 La Gua. What dare you do ?
 Const. Do not you dare to trust.
You I have fast ; your lover is my slave,
And he shall to the gallies !
 La Gua. To the gallies ?
 Const. What to prevent me ? you'll complain
  perhaps
How ill I use persons of quality.
A noble knight and lady of the post.—
 La Gua. Of your own dubbing.
 Const. Who are very dextrous
At any knavery ; and to keep your lover
You'll have his ears nail'd to the pillory.
 La Gua. Oh ! base, base man ! Now, dare not
  I refuse him.
Well, what is this sweet business I must do ?
 Const. To bring the Princess and my son together,
And when in talk their spirits begin to mount,
And get a prospect of the treachery,
Confess it all, and lay it on the Dauphin.
 La Gua. And what if your son kills me ?
 Const. How ! He kill thee ?
Ah ! poor tame fool, he will not kill a flea.
 La Gua. Nay, he is not so bloody a man as you
  are.
 Const. Well, let him be as bloody as he will,
I'll guard thee safely. Take thy lover, then,
And fly whither you will, I'll yearly give you

A pension shall maintain you in such equipage,
That go to England, and thy Love shall pass
For a French count, thou for a French Countess.
See, my son comes! go fetch the Princess presently.
 La Gua. Well, this shall be the last foul trick
I'll play.   *[Exeunt.*

   Enter the DUKE *of* VENDOSME.

 Du. I'll go! I'll go! Farewell my fortunes,
  honours,
Successes, glories, power, gaudy rags,
Which, all together, make up one fine baby.
I'll fling the rags and tinsel to the winds,
And let chance pick 'em up, and give 'em fools.
Let pride and vanity give women's hearts
To whom they will; let destiny give Crowns,
Let England now belch fire and o'erwhelm France;
Let Old Time mix the nations in his cup
To please his palate, and then drink 'em off ;
Let tyrants pour down rivers of men's blood,
To grind the world ; all this shall never reach
My care or thoughts, and, when I once am got
Into the still and silent rooms of death,
Not all the coil and rumbling skuffling nations
Can. keep over my head, will e'er wake me.

   Enter LOUIZE *weeping.* LA GUARD.

See, here ! the beauteous cause of my destruction,
And weeping ? Oh ! I have observ'd, though pride
Endeavours to fill up her robe of glory,
It drags in sorrow, and it does not fit her.
Madam !
 Lou. He here ?
 Du. Nay, do not fly me, madam.
 Lou. Have I not told you my firm resolutions.
 Du. Madam, you have ! but you can change your
  mind.

Lou. You come with hopes to vex me with new
    upbraidings.

Du. I come to please you, with acquainting you
I'm going to free you from this wretch for ever.

Lou. Or go, or stay, I am indifferent.

Du. Pardon me, if I think you are not indiffer-
    ent.

I've peep'd on the inside of your marriage chain,
And find it gold, but slightly lin'd with love.
Yes, you have given yourself to pomp, not love :
To the King's son, not to the youthful bridegroom;
You hug not him, but Pharamond and Pippin.
You have married titles, crowds, and noise, and
    forms,
And now the lumber hurts you, makes you weep.

Lou. I am contented you believe all this.

Du. Well, madam, Heaven pardon you my
    ruin !

My life has stream'd o'er fortune's richest mines,
But ne'er did taste of any thing but love,
And that sole sweetness you make bitter to me.

Lou. Oh ! this is full of art, twisting the mind,
The wrong side outward, breaks no bones, I see.

Du. Madam, I'm well assur'd, you will not send
One poor thought after me, much less a messen-
    ger,
To know the truth; but if you do, he'll find
In some unfinisht part of the creation,
Where night and chaos never were disturb'd,—
And now grown old, are uglier than ever,
And bed-rid, lye, in some dark rocky desert,—
There will he find a thing, whether a man,
Or the collected shadows of the desert
Condenst into a shape, he'll hardly know ;
This figure he will find walking alone,
Poring one while on some sad book at noon,
By taper-light, for never day shone there.

Sometimes laid grovelling on the barren earth,
Moist with his tears, for never dew fell there.
And when night comes, not known from day by
    darkness,
But by some faithful messenger of time,
He'll find him stretch't upon a bed of stone,
Cut from the bowels of some rocky cave,
Off'ring himself either to sleep or death,
And neither will accept the dismal wretch.
At length a slumber in its infant arms
Takes up his heavy soul, but, wanting strength
To bear it, quickly lets it fall again ;
At which the wretch starts up, and walks about
All night, and all the time it shou'd be day,
Till quite forgetting, quite forgot of ev'ry thing
But sorrow, pines away, and in small time,
Of th' only man that durst inhabit there,
Becomes the only ghost that dares walk there.
For ghosts turn paler when they look that way.
Thus never ends his grief, but now ends yours.
                                [Offers to go.

    Lou. Oh ! stay, my Lord ! What do you mean
      by this ?
Must not you blame yourself for all the sorrows
Which we both suffer ? Had not you first thrown
Contempt on me, I wou'd have been your wife !
Have been your wife ? have rather been a tree
On which your name was carv'd, than Queen of
    France.
    Du. How ! I throw scorn on you ?
    Lou. Rude, public scorn ;
Your army is my witness, your own hand,—
I have it under your own hand and seal,—
You scorn'd my love, and beg'd release of vows.
    Du. Oh! now Hell yawns, and treachery ap-
      pears.
    La Gua. He'll kill me !

The CONSTABLE *appears between the Scenes, and stops*
    LA GUARD, *who is running out.*

Const. I'll protect thee !
La Gua. I'll begone !
Const. I'll kill thee, then !
La Gua. I'm in a fine condition !
Du. I write these things ? If this right arm
    were rotting,
And but to write such things wou'd charm it sound,
Ere I wou'd let it write, I'd let it rot.
You know this too, Why wou'd you credit them ?
My bosom friends said you were false, and I
Abhorr'd them all, as men that had the plague
Of lying and slandering, broke out upon them,
And I was ready with my sword, to write
Upon their bosoms, Lord have mercy on them.
    Lou. Besides a hundred witnesses, La Guard's
Acquaintance heard you. ——
    Du. Your acquaintance, mistress ?
You are the witch I find has rais'd this storm,
Assisted by some devil of your acquaintance.
    La Gu. Oh !——
    Du. Tell the treachery, or I will rip thee,
And search for it in every vein thou hast.
    La Gu. Indeed, my Lord, I'm innocent !
    Du. Thou liest !
No eyes but thine beheld our secret loves,
And none cou'd come behind us but thyself,
And give us such a deadly, deadly fall.
    La Gu. Oh ! pardon me, and I'll confess.
    Du. I will.
    La Gu. Swear !
    Du. Then I swear !
    La Gu. The Dauphin then perceiving
The Princess constant in her love to you,
Got all those letters forg'd, brib'd all those witnesses

To blast your interest, and forc'd me to help him.

Du. Enough—begone! Had I not sworn to pardon thee—

Yet I must do't, nature gives man a sacrament,
In his own blood, never to hurt a woman:
But quickly fly, lest I break both those oaths.

Const. (*To La Gu. between the scenes.*) Most ex'lent
liar!

La Gu. Ex'lent devil you are!   [*Exit.*

Du. I am decreed, I find, to kill the Dauphin.

Const. See, in what season my stars bring the
Dauphin!   [*Aside.*

Lou. Oh!

*Lou. weeps, faints, falls into the Duke's arms. At
that instant the Constable brings in the Dauphin,
and shews them to him.*

Daup. Ha!

Const. Oh! peace, sir, let us listen to them,
I left them kissing.

Daup. Kissing?

Const. Kissing close, sir.

Lou. For this I do abhor and loath the Dauphin.
I am resolv'd he ne'er shall touch me more.

Daup. Oh! whore!

Const. Pray silence, sir! for I'd fain have you
Be fully satisfied.

Lou. His love and glory
Were both to me a tasteless witch's feast;
They vanish when so e'er your name was named,
Like those delusions at the name of Heaven.

Daup. I've heard enough! I'll feast you, you
damn'd whore!

Du. The Dauphin?

*Dauphin draws, wounds Louize, she falls. The
Duke draws, fights, disarms the Dauphin.*

Daup. Villain! draw upon thy Prince?

Go, call the guard !
Const. Yes, and I'll call the King,
To let him see the virtues of his favourite.   [*Exit.*
Daup. What ! wilt thou kill me, traitor ?
Du. No, I will not !
The flowers of graves, and moss of royal skulls
Protect your head.
Daup. Bold slave ! talk thus imperiously
To a great Prince ? -
Du. To a great Prince ?   A dwarf,
Whom men wou'd never see, did you not stand
Upon your Kingly ancestors' high monuments.
Oh, Heaven ! that I must see that beauteous inno-
    cence
Roll in her blood, and let her murderer live,
'Cause a King got him.
Daup. How ! that beauteous innocence ?
That whore o' thine ! but I ha' cool'd her blood.
Du. Oh ! he will pull my sword upon his breast.

As he stands in a raging threatning posture, Enter the
KING, CONSTABLE, GUARD.

    Const. Now, you may see, sir, what a youth this is.
    Daup. Hold ! kill him not.   Take him alive, I
      charge you.
Your virtuous man here has abus'd my bed,
And, 'cause I have discover'd him, wou'd murder me.
    Du. How we are wrong'd !
    Daup. You wrong'd ?
    Du. Yes, by yourself.
    Daup. By me ?   Was ever heard such im-
      pudence ?
Away with him !   [*Exit a Guard with the Duke.*
    Const. What shall be done with her ?
    Daup. I care not what's done with her; let dogs
      eat her.
Hold ! now I think on't, search her for a picture.

Off. Sir, here's a picture newly fallen from her !
Daup. Look here ! the picture of her damn'd
    adulterer.
This have I seen !——Oh ! I'm too mad to talk.
    K. I'm carried from my reason with amazement.
In all this shame, behold, proud boy, the punishment
Of thy bold disobedience to my will.
And now for Vendosme's sake, I'll never love
Nor trust man more.   [*Exit.*
    Daup. Away with that lewd woman !

Louize is carried off.

And now your son, since he boasts innocence,
I will have wrack't, and do you see it done.
    Const. I see it done ?
    Daup. Ay, sir, if you expect
I keep my promise.
    Const. If ?
    Daup. Ay ! if.
    Const. If——
    Daup. If——
I put him upon this to make him odious,   [*Aside.*
And then I'll throw him off. I know him for
A turbulent great rogue, and I abhor him. [*Exit.*
    Const. Brought to an If already ? I am fool'd !
My fortune's hung on such a rotten twig.

Enter LA FORCE.

    La Force. Ha ! in distraction ?   What's the
    matter with you !
    Const. Oh ! if ! if ! if !
    La Force. What do you mean by If ?
    Const. I am possest, possest by fiends call'd
    tyrants,
And all my stomach's full of ropes and axes;
Oh ! for a lusty draught of lukewarm blood,
The Dauphin's blood, to make me throw them up.

La Force. I do not understand you at all.
Const. How shou'd you?
Your head and mine hang both upon an If.
La Force. What means that If?
Const. The Dauphin has deluded me,
Has made me tumble down my son, my pillar.
Now he's destroying me, and you, and all.
La Force. Me?
Const. You!
La Force. The devil's in your unlucky friendship!
I will take horse, and out o' town this minute.
Const. Take horse? take arms!
Go, mount my son's brave troops,
And ride them o'er the heads of these false tyrants.
La Force. They are not such asses to be rid so
  easily,
Upon an expedition to the moon.
Const. Oh! take a tube, and shew them all a
  world
Of glory in that moon, and golden mines there,
Plundering, and ravishing; then tell them all
They will be all cashier'd, and without pay,
Or rather in their General's coin be paid,
Be wrack'd for traitors, torn to single money.
La Force. Must he be wrack't?
Const. By me, his father.
La Force. Barbarous!
Const. That grieves me not. I'd make no more
  to kill
Such a tame fool, than to spill so much milk.
La Force. What! though your son?
Const. Were all mankind my children,
I wou'd hang half, to rule the other half.
My honours! honours! grieve me. Go, raise the
  army.
I'm trusted with my son, and I will tempt him,
Or force him out to them; either will do.

If he be with them, though in close confinement,
'Twill do; that will be judg'd a shew.   Go ! go !
He pauses ? So ! my whirlpool sucks them in. [*Aside.*
He shall be dipt in this ; I'll not come near it.
   La Force. He mingles reason so with all his
     knavery.
None can divide the ratsbane from the honey,
And I shall swallow't, though it rot my head off.
   Const. Rot head and tail, and every part o' me !
I had rather lose them all in noble strife,
Than let them moulder in a quiet life.   [*Exeunt.*

Finis actus Quarti.

ACTUS QUINTUS.

A Prison. The DUKE.

   Du. Who looks upon this world, and not be-
     yond it,
To the abodes it leads to, must believe it
The bloody slaughter-house of some ill power,
Rather than the contrivance of a good one.
Ev'ry thing here breeds misery to man :
The sea breeds storms to sink him.   If he flies
To shore for aid, the shore breeds rocks to tear
     him.
The earth breeds briars to rend him, plants to
     poison him,
Beasts of prey to devour him, trees to hang him;
Those things that seem his friends are false to him :
The air that gives him breath gives him infection.
Meat takes his health away, and drink his reason :
His reason is so great a bosom plague to him,
He never is so pleas'd as when he's rob'd on't

By drink or madness.   Reason is an arrow,
Shot in his head by nature, to torment him;
And ·he's in pleasure when wine rots the arrow,
Or the moon pulls it out.   All things conspire
The misery and death of the world's. tyrant;
His cups are mingled with sweat, tears, or poison.
Pain keeps both doors of this cursed world, and
      hands
The tyrant in, and dogs him all the way,
And never leaves him till she thrusts him out. [*Exit.*

Enter the GREAT CONSTABLE.

Const. Get the wrack ready !

A wrack, a table, light, pen and paper.

Keeper. 'Tis ready !
Const. Bring my son out !
Keeper. Here he is!

Enter the DUKE.

Const. Go, leave me with him.   So, sir, are you
      here ?
Now you'll believe my principles are true.
Whoever wou'd be virtuous, is a fool;
For he endeavours to plant virtue here
In a damn'd world, where it no more will grow
Than oranges in Lapland.   It is true,
'Twill peer sometimes a little above ground,
But never but in dung of poverty;
And then it smells so ill, people of quality
Ne'er take it in their bosoms.
      Du. Very well.
      Const. Nay, the projecting fool that aims at
      virtue,
Is a ridiculous chymist that wou'd make
A virtuous thing out of a man or woman,
Who have not a grain of honesty about them;

And they have some parts can never be made
    honest.
Nay, there is no false fellow like your fool.
Who wou'd be virtuous? for your steady villain
Who sticks at nothing is most true to everything;
But your lame fool who halts 'tween vice and virtue
Is false to both, and so is true to nothing,
And so has no friends in Heaven or Hell;
And that's the reason he never thrives.

    Du. Oh! divine maxims these!

    Const. Sir, they are true.
Perhaps there never were such things as virtues
But only in men's fancies, like the Phœnix.
Or if they once have been, they're now but names
Of natures lost, which came into the world,
But cou'd not live nor propagate their kind.
How shou'd they propagate? Your virtuous fellow
Is a hermaphrodite, he has two sexes,
Virtue and vice, and such a monster thou art:
To glory thou art a girl, but to woman
Thou art a vig'rous man! Oh! thou poor sinner!
To scorn ambition, the sin of angels,
And stoop to be a goat.

    Du. This accusation
Has no more truth than any of your maxims.

    Const. Deny it? You don't know you shall be
    wrack'd?

    Du. Be wrack'd!

    Const. Be wrack'd.

    Du. You bring a bed agreeing
To the fine lodging you have provided for me.

    Const. It is a bed the Dauphin has provided you,
Where you must lye, till you confess your crimes,
Your treason, and adultery.

    Du. Does the Dauphin
Give his fair murder'd Princess this embalming,
To wrap her up in stinking defamation?

Const. Oh ! I shall supple your stiff humour.
Du. Never !
You'll sooner carve me into a toad than liar.
　Const. Will you talk thus upon the wrack and
　　scaffold ?
　Du. On both; and more, I will affirm the
　　Dauphin
Wrong'd us, and not we him.
　Const. How ?
　Du. This is truth. ·
　Const. If this be truth, then am I finely fool'd.
　Du. I know not that, but I am deeply wrong'd.
　Const. Then so am I, wrong'd, fool'd, deluded,
　　gull'd !
To drink my own son's blood hot from his veins,
That I may smell most rank to all mankind,
And have dogs fly at me where e'er I go.
Oh ! barb'rous ! made to murder my own son ?
A valiant young man, a wise young man,
An innocent young man.
　Du. No more, my Lord !
There's always some venom in your paint,
You ne'er gilded any but in hopes to rot them,
You never stroke a head but it falls off.
　Const. Is it my heart, or all the city trembles ?
Oh ! that some earthquake now wou'd make all Paris
Roll, and o'er-lay her children· in their sleep,
Kill all of 'em but this young man and me.
What need I wish for slaughter ? there will be
Enough to-night, and let it be for me.
　Du. What does he mean now ?　There is in his
　　breast
A restless, bottomless, black sea of wickedness,
And I must dive into 't.　　　　　　　　[*Aside.*
What is you meaning ?
　Const. 'Tis this : your troops, the city, the no-
　　bility,
　　VOL. 3.　　　15

Both out of love to you, and hate to tyranny,
Demand your life, or clear proofs of your crimes,
Else they resolve to fill up with their swords
The gap your death will make for tyranny
To flow upon them.   I, who thought you guilty,
Was cheated by these tyrants to come hither,
And wrack you into a liar to save them.

Du. Why did I plunge into his breast a sea
                                    [*Aside.*
Wou'd make the devil sick if he flew over it,
And tumble like a bird that flies o'er Jordan ?
Oh ! how I am confounded !

Const. Ha ! I see
Loyalty struggling in thy noble nature
For a brave lie to save thy Prince from danger.
Do what thou wilt ! for my part, I'll not counsel
    thee.
'Tis true, you wou'd do well to save your Prince,
For it will breed strange gangreens all o'er France
To have a great man shuffled out of life,
They can't tell how, to please the Dauphin's envy ;
And yet, methinks, to save him by acknowledging
Yourself a villain, and the Princess whore !—
Oh ! out upon't ! I'd let the Kingdom perish
Ere I wou'd be a dog to lick its sores
With a foul tongue.

Du. Oh ! how does he distract me !

Const. I see that paper draws thy kind eye to-
    wards it,
Thou hast a mind to be scribbling,—take it !
                              [*Gives him paper.*
But you must write down all the circumstances,
How oft, and when, and where, you enjoyed the
    Princess.   [*The Duke tears the paper.*
Ha ! you resolve then rather to be torn,
And let the King be torn too, like this paper ?

Du. Not that.

Const. What then ?

Du. I will go head my troops !

Const. Ha ! Now thou speak'st indeed ! Thou art cast anew

Into the very mettle I wou'd have thee.

Ring out that bell, that passing bell of tyranny !

Proclaim thy innocence by trumpet's sounds,

And with thy sword and pike bore all deaf ears !

If thou must go into another world,

Go like a gallant man, not creepingly,

Like a poor rogue, into a house by night,

Through grates and holes will tear thy flesh to rags,

And make thy friends in Heaven asham'd to own thee.

Du. Which way shall I get hence ?

Const. In my own chair,

We will go both together out, unknown.

My chair !

Enter CHAIRMEN *with a chair.*

Du. Will you go with me to the army ?

Const. No ! I'll preserve a certain friend for thee

In case uncertain fortune prove thy enemy.

Go out a while !   [*To the Chairmen, who go out.*

Du. I want a sword !

Const. Take mine !

[*The Constable gives the Duke his sword, who draws it.*

Du. Now know, my lord, I've once out-witted you,

I've div'd into you, and I find your plots :

You have stir'd up my army to rebellion,

And now you fain wou'd fool me out to head them.

Const. A guard, there !

Du. Silence ! or you ne'er speak more.

1 know the reverence I owe a father ;

I'll no more violate you than an altar;
But we may wipe away dirt from an altar,
And I wou'd free you from this dirty world
In whose foul womb you labour like a mole,
And, when you're dragg'd into the light of inno-·
    cence,
You are sick, like things out of their element.
Since no persuasions then can make you honest,
Nor keep you quiet, locks and walls shall do it,
Both for my Prince's sake, and for your own.
Into the chair! so with me to the King.
 Const. Oh! slave!
 Du. Into the chair!
 Const. Priest-ridden slave!
Who all thy insipid life hast been transfusing
The sheepish thoughts of priests into thy head,
Dost know no way but what those wooden hands
Direct thee to?
 Du. Into the chair!
 Const. I heard
A lover, once in a rapture, tell his mistress
Her mother fed on roses; sure when I
Got thee I was confin'd to a milk diet.
 Du. Into the chair!
 Const. I'll not into the chair!
      [*Draws a long tuck out of a cane.*
I am provided for you, sir. A guard, there!

    Enter a GUARD.

Secure this traitor here! he has disarm'd me
To make escape. Now, sir, I'll handle you.
Bind him, and get the wrack prepar'd with speed!
   ·   [*The Guard bind the Duke.*
Oh! thou fool! fool! ridiculous, virtuous fool!
I cannot speak my mind, I shall betray myself.
Thou mightst have been King!—[*Aside to the Duke.*
 Du. A glorious villain.

Const. Crown'd on that scaffold where thy head
   shall falL

       Enter one of the GUARD.

Gu. My lord, the wounded Princess does desire
Admission to the Duke.   She says she has
Some things of consequence she wou'd reveal.

   Const. They are guilty then ? and she is a
     strumpet !
Admit her !—

 Enter LOUIZE *in a chair, her woman helps her out.*

   Lou. Oh ! my lord.

   Du. Help her, she faints !
In such fair ruins Heaven would have lain
If the ill angels had subdu'd the good.

   Lou. Oh !

   Du. Such a groan a breaking sphere wou'd give.

   Lou. My lord !

   Du. How does my love ?

   Lou. Exceeding ill ;
And yet not ill enough for one whose sins
Has brought such ills on you.

   Du. Your sins ?

   Lou. Oh yes !
My pride and jealousy did ruin both of us ;
'Twas wicked sacrilege to let hot rage
Melt down your golden image in my mind.

   Du. Your love, which never wander'd once
     from me
Where it was born, does talk of me as those
Do of their native countries who ne'er travel'd.

   [*Lou.*] I cannot talk or think too much of you ;
The thoughts you lov'd me once, will make me
     think myself
Above an angel, and this sight of you
Make me disrelish all the Heavenly visions.

I say this openly before the world;
I scorn to tarry till we meet in death
And whisper it behind the globe in private.

Du. Did e'er till now two lovers find such joys
In the cold barren space between two worlds?
How do these pleasures gild the gates of death,
Make pleasant walks to lead up to the shades!

Const. This is the innocent pair.

Lou. Unnatural tyrant!
My soul is often coming to my wound,
And, seeing you, starts back, and thinks you Hell.

Const. I find your wound has much corrupted
blood in't.

Lou. I faint!

Du. Oh! help!

Lou. Farewell, thou Paradise!
And for the sin of Eve, believing lies;
But to a better world than Eve was chas'd,—
To Heaven! There's one, no doubt; for, were there
none,
There would be one o' purpose made for you. [*Dies.*

Dú. She's going! she's gone! Whilst th' iron
hand
Of death broke this fair diamond in pieces,
What sparks flew round, each richer than a world!

Enter the DAUPHIN.

Daup. What do I see? Oh! torment! torment!
Hell!
How durst you suffer this?

Const. Sir, she desir'd
Admission on pretence she wou'd confess,
And only came to die in his embraces.

Daup. Oh! hot Egyptian lust! a lust which
burns
In damps of death, and makes the grave a brothel.
Vendosme! you till this moment, like a torrent,

Have borne me down like a small floating weed,
But here you shall run under ground for ever.
    Du. But I shall rise again in Paradise,
Where I shall mix with this pure stream for ever.
But, sir, you take his life who gave you yours.
    Daup. Thou give me life? Yes, as the crows
        and ravens
Give me my eyes; they dare not pick 'em out.
Thou buzzard durst not light on me, an eagle,
For thy last perch thou knew'st wou'd be a gibbet.
    Du. Sir, I'll boldly tell you more; in me
You fling away the fortune of the Kingdom.
    Daup. If France's fortune be so beggarly,
Then I do well to fling it on a dunghill.
    Du. The crown you hope to heir hangs on this
        arm.
    Daup. I'd scorn to wear a feather that had hung
On such a pin.
    Du. That scorn a rod shall scourge,
Cut from the cypress that shall shade my tomb.
Shortly you'll strive to make another me
Out of my dust, mingled with all my tears, ⤙
And all your souls: but my proud dust will slight
        you.
My loss is nothing but a world, which always
Appear'd to me a painted treacherous whore,
That leads to Hell the fools and knaves that love
        her,
And is a Hell to the brave men that scorn her.
    Daup. Sir, for the satisfaction of the world
You must confess your crimes.
    Du. You know us innocent.
    Daup. How dar'st thou tell me this? Do'st
        thou not see
That wrack there? Ha!
    Du. Yes, and I see 'tis wood,
A limb of some old fallen son of earth;

And I will not be made to speak a falsehood
By any sons of earth, or sons of Kings.
 Daup. Intolerable ! lead him to the wrack !

      [*Exit Duke with a guard.*

 Const. You see how faithfully I've serv'd you,
  sir.
 Daup. Against your son.——
 Const. Yes, sir, I've gone indeed
Against the stream of nature to serve you.
 Daup. Can I then think thou wilt be true to me ?
If thou could'st go so easily to mischief,
When thou wert shackled with the chains of nature,
How swiftly wilt thou run when thou art free.
Know, fool, I've made thee work thy own destruc-
  tion ;
I've thrown thee at thy son, and made you dash
Each other in pieces like two earthen vessels.
 Const. Ha ! did you mean, by favours which you
  promis'd me,
Only to make me hangman to my son ?
 Daup. Princes no more should keep their words
  with villains
Than priests with hereticks.
 Const. Oh ! horror ! horror !
I have fed your revenge with my blood's quint-
  essence,
The blood of him I got in my hot youth,
And now you break your league, and seek my life.
 Daup. I scorn thy wither'd life ! let it drop from
  thee,
Thy wickedness can do no further mischief,
Except it work confusion in the Heavens,
And make the sun with horror hide his head.
But nature now is us'd to barbarous deeds ;
They do not scare her into dire miscarriages,
Nor make her womb conceive unshapen prodigies.
Now thou may'st eat thy son ; the Prince of day

Is hardy grown, and will not faint and look
As girlish as he did.at Atreus' feast.
Perhaps that eye of day is dim with age,
Then live, but live in quiet.   [*Guard secure him.*
    Const. Oh ! ruin ! death ! I've torn my bowels out
To hoyse myself into this tyrant's favour,
And I've only made my fall more deadly.
Hoys'd did I call it ? rather, then I fell,
When I became a man, to be a great one,
Became a dog to wear a silver collar.
I am a dog, and I am running mad
With drinking the hot blood of my own young.
    Daup. Ha ! what means this ?

> *An alarm.   Enter* BRISAC.

    Brisac. The Duke of Vendosme's troops
Are by our guards let in upon us,
That, sir, you have no safety but in flight.
    Daup. Oh villains !
    Const. Oh ! most seasonable rogues !
    Daup. I'll fall on them be the event what it will.
That Prince who fears deserves not to be fear'd,
Nor to be greater than that man who dares
Do greater things than he.   Secure that traitor !
                                                      [*Exit.*
> [*The Scene changes.*]

Enter the GREAT CONSTABLE, LA FORCE, LA MARRE,
    YOUNG CAPTAINS ; *the* DAUPHIN *and* BRISAC
    prisoners.

    Const. Oh ! you brave heroes, greater each than
        Brutus,
He but repair'd, you build your country's freedom :
Till now, a Frenchman scarce deserv'd to come
Into the presence of a Roman statue.
    La Ma. I find the Constable will be the man,
                                                   [*Aside.*

I am resolved I will chop in with him.
My lord, I beg your pardon for past errors,
I find the Court has injur'd both of us :
I'll gladly serve you with my life and fortune
If you'll accept of them.
 Const. In my condition
I shall have great occasion for a rascal,
Therefore I will accept thee.
 La Ma. I will serve you.
 1 *Capt.* Where is the Duke ?
 Const. Ay ! there's the question.
Here in this slaughter-house is a torn wretch
Some say is he ; his father knows him not.
 All. How ? a torn wretch ?
 Const. Ah ! Sirs, cou'd you collect
In one dire figure all the ghastly horrors
E'er cover'd field, after the bloodiest battle,
When one vast paleness spreads the earth's green
  table,
And faces folded up in different grins,
With barbarous ornament, adorn it round,
And bodies pil'd prepare a gluttonous feast
For birds and beasts of prey, it wou'd not be
So terrible a sight as this I shew you.

  *The Scene drawn, the Duke is shew'd wrack't,
   Louize dead by him.*

 All. Oh ! horror ! Fire the Louvre !
 La For. Proclaim liberty !
Freedom is born, christen it with tyrant's blood.
 Du. Hold ! I command you, hold !
 La For. What's your will ?
 Du. My will is you refine, and turn barbarians !
What savage nation in the world retains not
In the disfigured mass of human nature
Reverence to Princes ? If it be too hard
To be as polish't as barbarians,

Be but as good and honest as tame beasts,
They're gentle and submissive to their masters ;
But if you will be men, subjects, and soldiers,
Fall at your Prince's feet, and ask him pardon,
Or throw me dead at yours ! do one of 'em,
Or in small time I'll throw you dead at mine,
For I have loyal troops that will obey me.

Const. His pains distract him.

La For. What do you mean, my lord ?
You have had great injuries.

Du. What's that to you ?
But I've had none : my present sufferings
Are what appearances gave warrant for.

1 *Capt.* You are wrong'd,
And do not rob your self of just revenge.

Du. Nor shall you all here rob me of my honour,
Though like base thieves you watch your opportu-
    nity
When I am all o' fire, and laid in ruins.

Const. He's mad ! stark raving mad ! Sirs, do not
    mind him.

Du. Ho ! guard ! Convey me to my loyal troops !
Those shall obey me, imprison me, or kill me.

All. We kneel, we kneel ! We beg your High-
    ness' pardon.

Du. Now, seize my father !———

                    [*All kneel to the Dauphin.*

Daup. Was e'er man so brave ?——

           Enter a MESSENGER.

Mess. The King is coming hither !

Du. Meet him all,
And fall at his feet !

*The Dauphin, Brisac, and the Captains go out.
Shouts within. After a pause all re-enter, following the King.*

K. The truth appears too late! Oh! thou rash
 youth!
Thou hast destroy'd the joys of both our lives,
A noble innocent pair! for they are innocent!
Bring in the traitress who destroy'd them both.

Enter some with LA GUARD.

La Gu. Oh! blood! blood follows me. I'll con-
 fess all,
And beg for death,—no Hell like a bad conscience.
The Princess was contracted to the Duke
Long ere the Dauphin lov'd her.
 Daup. How? Contracted?
 La Gu. Yes, sir; but, ere they cou'd complete
 the marriage,
You sent away the Duke, to aid the Germans
Against the Turks, in the meanwhile your passion
For her began: the Constable perceiving it, .
Hoping to draw the Duke from his allegiance,
Knowing that no temptation else cou'd do it,
Brib'd me, and others, wicked as myself,
To aid him, in obtaining her for you.
We counterfeited the Duke's hand exactly,
And wrote in it provoking letters to her,
Then we invented lies of the Duke's falsehood,
And by these arts so turn'd her haughty mind,
That she soon hated him, and loved your Highness.
When this was done, the Constable compell'd me
To lay his tricks and forgeries on you.
Then went and kindled a fierce jealousy in you,
And brought you on th' unhappy innocent pair,
When they were only mourning for their wrongs.
 Daup. O! horrid! horrid!
 Const. Oh! notorious falsehood!
 La Gu. The truth shall out, sir! the vile Con-
 stable
Lodg'd all these villainous secrets in my bosom.

K. Was ever such a villain ?

Const. Every man

Is such a villain, who is not a fool.

Had that damn'd sot been lord of half my wit,

He had this hour been lord of all the Kingdom.

To shew the difference in our understandings,

Mine wou'd have made him King, his noble wit

Has made himself a very gallant fellow.

[Pointing scornfully to the Duke.

K. No, thy unnatural villany wrought this.

Const. I own I twisted all those various cables

To drag that lump of lead up to a throne,

And he has broke them all.   Indeed there is

Too much already of that drossy metal

Over the State; the Church is always cover'd

    with it,

And I design'd to melt it down, and place

On top of Church and State rich gold, myself;

But, dragging him up with me, broke my pullies.

K. Impudent arrogance !

Const. A corpse, they say,

Carried to sea, does always breed a storm.

I wafting this dead fool o'er to a kingdom,

Have shipwreck'd all the glories I was laden with.

K. Away with him !

Du. Pray give him, sir, his life.

Const. How ? hast thou thrown me on hooks, as

    Turks do slaves,

Then would'st thou have me hang alive in tor-

    ments ?

No, I will rather have my limbs feed crows,

Than poorly live to be the scorn of fools.

For a wise man the image of a God

To creep to fools, scarce images of men,

I'll as soon worship golden calves with Jews,

Or with the Sumatrans a monkey's tooth.

My glory, that has kept me ever waking,
Is out, now send me t' eternal darkness!
And, young man, do you pray, pray heartily,
Be sure you get to heaven, for if your piety
Shou'd crack, and let you fall to Hell where I am,
I'll plague you worse than all the devils there. [*Exit.*

K. What a black demon had I near my throne!

Enter LA MARRE.

La Ma. Now will I fix myself.
The Constable a prisoner?
Daup. Seize that fellow!
You shall be hang'd, sir.
La Ma. Oh! sir.
Daup. Yes, sirrah, you are a great rogue.
La Ma. You wou'd not hang me were I a great
rogue.
Well, 'tis as foolish to play villany
As money, with a man of a great stock,
He can throw out and out and still play on,
We once throw out we are thrown to the devil,
Whither they come at last, for when all's done
The devil's box gets all.
Daup. My poor Louize!
K. Noble youth!
Hast thou had such great wrongs, yet give my son
His life, and me my crown?
Du. Princes are sacred!
Whate'er religion rebels may pretend,
Murderers of Kings are worshippers of devils;
For none but devils are worshipt by such sacri-
fices.
They who derive all power from the people,
Do basely bastardise it with that buckler
Which fell from heaven to protect innocence.
They protect villany; no sacrilege
Greater than when a rebel with his sword

Dares cut the hand of Heaven from King's com-
    missions,
To hide the devil's mark upon his own.
I lifted up my arm against the Dauphin,
It ought to have died and rotted in the air.
    Daup. I fully pardon you !
    Du. Then I die joyfully.
    K. Talk'st thou of dying ?
    Du. I received two wounds
In the last battle, sir, upon my breast,
Which now are torn far into death's dominions.
                    [The Duke shews his breast bloody.
    K. Oh ! miserable sight !
    Daup. Oh ! blasting sight !
    K. Here falls a Pharaoh's tower, Ephesian
    temple,
The cost of ages, wonder of eternity.
    Duke. You gild a vanishing shadow.——
May I have leave, sir—   *[To the Dauphin.*
To sleep in death by her who was your Princess ?
But in the grave there's no propriety,
In death's dark ruinous empire all lyes waste.
    Daup. You shall have that, and all befitting
    honours.
    Duke. Then come cold bride to my as cold em-
    brace !
The grave's our bed, and death our bridal night,
None will disturb, or envy our delight.—   *[Ex.*

THE EPILOGUE,

Spoken by Mr Haines, who acted La Marre.

Finding sad plays so good success have had;
To make this tragedy exceeding sad
The author doom'd me to be hang'd to-night;
But now I hop'd I should be hanged outright.
For I've three plagues no flesh and blood can bear,
I am a poet, married, and a player.
A wife has e'er since Eve been thought an evil,
The first that danc'd at weddings was the devil.
At the first wedding all mankind miscarried,
Old Adam ne'er was wicked 'till he married.
And poetry of curses never fail'd:
Homer his rags on all his race entail'd.
He was an old blind beggar and so poor,
He starv'd the dog that led him, and the cur,
To have revenge on poets, got in spite
Criticks, who worry all that dare to write.
But 'till of late a player was a toy
That either sex lik'd well enough, t'enjoy;
Happy the spark that cou'd a night carouse
With a whole sharer once of either house.
Nay, women once in our acquaintance crept;
You hardly will believe me,——I was kept.
But I, and all of us, are fallen so low;
Nothing will keep us but bum bailiffs now.
Now no divertisement does pleasure bring,
The Pope has set his foot in everything.
His priests and poets have conspir'd our fall,
Priests by bad plots, poets by none at all:
And poets like the Jesuits of the times,
Will hang and damn ere they will own their crimes.

Like Friar Bacon's brazen head, they'll speak
Just what they please and then in pieces break.
'Tis strange fond nature often takes great pains,
To build brass foreheads to defend no brains.
Well, sirs, damn plays and poets as you please,
But pray support a play-house for your ease.
Ladies some journeys to Hide Park may spare,
Our empty play-house has enough fresh air.
And gallants pray support us not for plays,
But to find ladies here in rainy days.

SIR COURTLY NICE;

OR,

IT CANNOT BE.

Sir Courtly Nice; or, It Cannot be. A Comedy. As it is acted by his Majesties Servants. Written by Mr Crown. London, printed by H. H., Jun., for R. Bently, in Russel Street, Covent Garden, and Jos. Hindmarsh, at the Golden Ball over against the Royal Exchange in Cornhill. 1685. 4to.

Sir Courtly Nice: or, It Cannot Be, a Comedy. As it is acted by his Majesties Servants. The Second Edition. Written by Mr Crown. London, printed by M. B. for R. Bently, in Russel Street, Covent Garden, and Jos. Hindmarsh, at the Golden Ball over against the Royal Exchange in Cornhill. 1693. 4to.

Ib. As it was acted by her Majesty's Servants. Written by Mr Crown. London, printed for G. Strahan; C. Bathurst, over against St. Dunstan's Church, in Fleet Street; and sold by Alexander Strahan, at the Golden Ball in Cornhill. 1750. 12mo.

Ib. As it is acted at the Theatres-Royal in Drury Lane and Covent Garden, by his Majesty's Servants. Written by Mr Crown. London, printed for C. Bathurst, Messrs Hawes, Clarke and Collins, T. Lowndes, T. Caslon, and C. Corbett. 1765. 12mo.

THIS comedy was produced in 1685, and Langbaine, in writing of it in 1691, remarks—"This play is accounted an excellent comedy, and has been frequently acted with good applause." So great was its popularity that it held the stage as a stock piece for upwards of a century.

Oldys, in his MS. notes to his copy of Langbaine, now in the British Museum, has this:—"Mr Oldmixon, in one of his histories, says, Crowne the poet told him that King Charles II. gave him two Spanish plays, and bade him join them together to form one, which he did, and shewed his Majesty the plan for his comedy of Sir Courtly Nice. He afterwards read the acts to him, scene by scene, as he wrote them. When he had finished the three first, which are by much the best of the play, he read those over to the King, who liked them very well, only he said, ' 'Tis not merry enough!' I do not say smutty, though worse might be said with truth. Crowne could easily have mended that fault, but, the King dying a month after, he let the three acts pass as they are, and there does not seem to be that deficiency of which the King complained."

Mr Dennis, at page 48 of vol. I. of his "Original Letters, Familiar, Moral, and Critical," has this account of the present comedy :—

" It was at the latter end of King Charles's reign that Mr Crowne, tired with the fatigue of writing, and shocked by the uncertainty of theatrical success, and desirous to shelter himself from the resentment of those numerous enemies he had made by his ' City Politiques,' made his application immediately to the King himself ; and desired his Majesty to establish him in some office that might be a security to him for life. The King had the goodness to assure him he should have an office, but added, that he would first see another comedy. Mr Crowne endeavouring to excuse himself by telling the King that he plotted slowly and awkwardly, the King replied that he would help him to a plot, and so put into his hands the Spanish comedy, called *No pued Esser*. Mr Crowne was obliged immediately to go to

work upon it; but, after he had writ three acts of it,
found to his surprise that the Spanish play had some
time before been translated and acted and damned, under
the title of 'Tarugo's Wiles, or the Coffee-house.' Yet,
supported by the King's command, he went briskly on,
and finished it; and here see the influence of a Royal
encouragement.

"Mr Crowne, who had once before oblig'd the commonwealth of learning with a very agreeable comedy in
his 'City Politiques,' yet in 'Sir Courtly Nice' went far
beyond it, and infinitely surpassed himself. For though
there is something in the part of Crack which borders
on farce, the Spanish author alone must answer for that.
For Mr Crowne could not omit the part of Crack, that
is, of Tarugo, and the Spanish farce depending upon it,
without a downright affront to the King, who had given
him that play for his groundwork. But all that is of
English growth in 'Sir Courtly Nice' is admirable; for
though we find in it neither the fine designing of Ben
Jonson, nor the general and masculine satire of Wy-
cherley, nor that grace, that delicacy, nor that courtly
air of Etherege; yet is the dialogue so lively and so
spirited, and so attractively diversified, and adapted to
the several characters. Four of these characters are so
entirely new, yet general and so important, are drawn
so truly, and so graphically, and opposed to each other,
Surly to Sir Courtly, and Hothead to Testimony, with
such a strong and entire opposition; those extremes
of behaviour, the one of which is the grievance, and
the other the plague of society and conversation; exces-
sive ceremony on one side, and on the other rudeness
and brutality, are so finely exposed in Surly and Sir
Courtly; and those divisions and animosities in the two
great parties of England, which have so long disturbed
the public quiet, and undermined the public interest,
are happily represented and ridiculed in Hothead and
Testimony, that though I have more than twenty times
read over this charming comedy, yet I have always read
it, not only with delight, but rapture; And 'tis my
opinion, that the greatest comic poet that ever lived in
any age might have been proud to have been the author
of it."

"The play was now just ready to appear to the world; and, as every one that had seen it rehearsed was highly pleased with it, every one who had heard of it was big with the expectation of it; and Mr Crowne was delighted with the flattering hope of being made happy for the rest of his life by the performance of the King's promise; when, upon the very last day of the rehearsal, he met Cave Underhill coming from the playhouse as he himself was going towards it. Upon which the poet, reprimanding the player for neglecting so considerable a part as he had in the comedy, and neglecting it on a day of so much consequence as the very last of rehearsal, 'Oh, Lord, sir,' says Underhill, 'we are all undone!' 'Wherefore?' says Mr Crowne; 'Is the playhouse on fire?' 'The whole nation,' replies the player, 'will quickly be so, for the King is dead!' At the hearing which dismal words the author was little better; for he who but the moment before was ravished with the thought of the pleasure which he was about to give to his King, and of the favours which he was afterwards to receive from him, this moment found, to his unspeakable sorrow, that his Royal patron was gone for ever, and with him all his hopes."

Downes notes that "the first new comedy after King James came to the crown, was 'Sir Courtly Nice,' wrote by Mr Crown: Sir Courtly acted by Mr Mountford; Hothead, Mr Underhill; Testimony, Mr Gillo; Lord Bellguard, Mr Kynaston; Surly, Mr Griffin; Sir Nicholas Callico [i.e., Crack] by the famous Mr Antony Leigh; Leonora, Madam Barry, &c." "This Comedy," he continues, "being justly acted, and the characters in't new, crown'd it with a general applause. Sir Courtly was so nicely perform'd, that not any succeeding, but Mr Cibber, has equalled him. Note, Mr Griffin so excelled in Surly, Sir Edward Belford, The Plain Dealer, none succeeding in the two former have equall'd him, except his predecessor, Mr Hart, in the latter."

Crowne, in his dedication, repeats the fact that "Sir Courtly Nice" was "written by the sacred command of our late most excellent King, of ever blessed and beloved memory." The Spanish play given him by the King had been adapted to the English stage by Thomas St.

Serfe, and acted at Lincoln's-Inn-Fields in 1668, under
the title of "Tarugo's Wiles," but with indifferent success, it, with others about the same time produced, not
having, according to Downes, been played beyond three
nights. Geneste observes: "Crown has however vastly
improved the original piece by adding to it the characters of Sir Courtly Nice, Hothead, Testimony, and Surly.
His play is a very good one; and, as he tells us in his
preface to Caligula, was as fortunate a Comedy as had
been written in that age."

Although the Comedy of "Tarugo's Wiles" appears to
have been unsuccessful, the Earl of Dorset thus compli-
ments Sydserf, in a poem addressed, "To Sir Thomas
St. Serfe; on his play called Tarugo's Wiles, or the
Coffee-House. A Comedy. Acted at the Duke of York's
Theatre, 1668:"—

> " Tarugo gave us wonder and delight
> When he oblig'd the world by candle-light.
> But now he's ventur'd on the face of day,
> T' oblige and serve his friends another way ;
> Make all our old men wits, Statesmen the young,
> And teach ev'n Englishmen the English tongue.
>   James, on whose reign *all peaceful stars* did smile,[*]
> Did but attempt the uniting of our isle.
> What Kings and nature only could design,
> Shall be accomplished by this work of thine.
> For who is such a *Cockneigh* in his heart,
> Proud of the plenty of the Southern part,
> To scorn that union by which he may
> Boast 'twas his countryman that writ this play ?
>   Phœbus himself, indulgent to thy muse,
> Has to thy country sent this kind excuse.
> Fair northern lass, it is not through neglect
> I court thee at a distance, but respect.
> I cannot act, my passion is so great,
> But I'll make up in light what wants in heat.
> On thee I will bestow my longest days,
> And crown thy sons with everlasting bays.
> My beams that reach thee shall employ their pow'rs
> To ripen souls of men, not fruits or flow'rs.
> Let warmer climes my fading favours boast,
> Poets and stars shine brightest in the frost."

Cibber, as well as Downes, speaks highly of Mr Wm.
Mountfort in the character of Sir Courtly Nice. Mount-

---

[*] The motto borne by King James I. was "Beati pacifici.'

fort was taken off the stage, and made one of the gentlemen to Lord Chancellor Jefferies, " who at an entertainment of the Lord Mayor and Court of Aldermen in the year 1685, called for Mr Mountfort to divert the company—as his Lordship was pleased to term it,—he being an excellent mimic. My Lord made him plead before him in a feigned cause, in which he aped all the great lawyers of the age in their tone of voice, and in their action and gesture of body, to the very great ridicule not only of the lawyers but of the law itself; which to me (says the historian) did not seem altogether prudent in a man of his lofty station in the law. Diverting it certainly was, but, prudent in the Lord High Chancellor, I shall never think it." See Sir John Reresby's Memoirs from the Restoration to the Revolution, 8vo.

Mountfort appears to have been the son of a gentleman in Staffordshire, and to have gone very early upon the stage. He married Mrs (i.e., Miss Percival), who, after his death, became Mrs Verbruggen. He is said to have sung very agreeably, and to have danced finely. He met his death by assassination at the age of thirty-three. One Captain Hill had entertained a violent passion for Mrs Bracegirdle, and, with the aid of his friend Lord Mohun and some soldiers whom he had hired, made an attempt to carry her off forcibly one night in a coach, but in this they were frustrated. As Mountfort was a handsome man, and frequently her lover on the stage, Hill imagined that he was the bar between him and success, and, attributing his defeat to Mountfort's agency, vowed vengeance against him on the occasion. Mrs Bracegirdle's friends sent to Mrs Mountfort, recommending her to warn her husband not to come home that night, but, ere her messenger could find him, he was accosted near his own door by Lord Mohun in a friendly tone, when Hill, who had been behind, struck Mountfort a blow upon the head with his left hand, and almost immediately ran him through the body with his sword, which he held ready in his right. This Mountfort declared, as a dying man, to his friend Bancroft, the surgeon who attended him. He was stabbed on the 9th December 1692, and lingered till next day, when he died. Hill made his escape, but Lord

Mohun was seized and brought to trial, 31st Jan. 1692-3, when, it not appearing that he was implicated in the assassination, he was acquitted. Fourteen Lords found him guilty, and sixty-nine not guilty.

It is remarkable that Anthony Leigh, who acted originally with him in " Sir Courtly Nice," died about a week after him.

Mrs Mountfort's maiden name was Percival. "Of this gentlewoman," say the Memoirs of Mrs Ann Oldfield, Lond. 1741, 8vo, " I am naturally led into the relation of one melancholy scene of her life, in which I believe no parallel can be found either in ancient or modern history. Her father, Mr Percival, had the misfortune to be drawn into the assassination plot against King William ; for this he lay under sentence of death, which he received on the same night that Lord Mohun killed her husband, Mr Mountfort. Under this almost insuperable affliction she was introduced to the good Queen Mary, who being, as she was pleased to say, *struck to the heart* upon receiving Mrs Mountfort's petition, immediately granted all that was in her power, a remission of her father's execution for that of transportation. But fate had so ordered it, that poor Mrs Mountfort was to lose both father and husband. For as Mr Percival was going abroad, he was so weakened by his imprisonment that he was taken sick on the road and died at Portsmouth."

Lord Mohun, so concerned in Mountfort's death, afterwards fell in a duel between him and the Duke of Hamilton, he himself having sent the challenge.

" Sir Courtly Nice is an imitation—No puede ser guardar una muger—no keeping a woman—which is itself an imitation of Lope de Vega, Mayor Imposible—the greatest impossibility." *Shack, Geschichte der dram. Literatur in Spanien*, vol. iii. p. 352.

" No pued esser," was written by Augustin Moreto.

In the 14th volume of Pen sil de apolo, en doze Comedias nvevas de los meiores ingenios de Espana. Madrid, 1661. 4to.—will be found "La Gran Comedia de no puede ser."

The Dramatis Personæ are—

Don Felix de Toledo.
Donna Ana Pacheco.

Don Pedro Pacheco.
Tarugo.
Musicos.
Don Diego de Rojas.
Alberto.
Donna Ines Pacheco.
Manuela criada.
Criados.

In the 3d vol. of Théatre Espagnol, Paris, 1770.
12mo, there are translations of three of Moreto's Plays.
Among these is No puede ser, under the title of "La
Chose Impossible." The characters are—

Dom Félix de Toledo.
Dona Ana Pacheco.
Donna Inès Pacheco.
Dom Diégo de Roxas.
Manuéla, *Suivante d'Inès*.
Tarugo, *Valet de Dom Félix*.
Alberto.
Valets.
Musicians.

It seems to be a literal translation.

Tarugo observes, in the first scene to his master,
who has imparted to him the qualities of which he supposes the rich widow, Donna Pacheco, to be possessed:—

"Monsieur, je conçois aisément qu'elle peut étre à la
fois, belle, amiable et riche ; mais qu'elle soit ensemble,
riche et Poëte ! c'est la chose impossible."

Which gives rise to the French title of the piece.

The song of "Stop Thief !" is taken out of Flecknoe's
Demoiselle à la Mode, who in turn had it from the
French of Moliere. It is a paraphrase of Mascarille's
"Au Voleur" in Les Precieuses Ridicules.

There was a farce called Sir Thomas Callico, or the
Mock Nabob; formed from Sir Courtly Nice. It was
acted at Covent Garden, July 6, 1758. The name of the
adapter has not transpired, and the piece has not been
printed.

The noble Duke to whom Crown has inscribed Sir
Courtly Nice, was deserving of the praises lavished upon
him in the dedication. He was truly a peer "sans peur

et sans reproche.". A loyal subject, he supported the
fortunes of Charles I. with heart and purse until the
death of the murdered monarch, and the ascendancy of
Cromwell compelled him and his wife to fly to foreign
lands, and suffer privations which they might have escaped
had they succumbed to the government of the Protector.
They remained in exile until the death of Cromwell,—
the increasing dislike of the Puritan rule, and the
struggle for power of the republican chiefs, created an
earnest desire throughout the kingdom for a restoration
of monarchy, and enabled General Monk, without a new
civil war, to bring back the exiled family.

Amongst the many interesting incidents in the varied
life of the Duke, those connected with his marriage are
the best known, and may on that account be acceptable
to the reader.

Thomas, tenth Earl of Ormond, K.G., died in 1614,
leaving an only daughter, Lady Elizabeth Butler, who
married in her early youth her cousin Thomas Butler,
who had been by James I. created Viscount Tullyophelim, and was the next heir male of the earldom, but
who, dying without issue, the male representation de-
volved on Walter, the eleventh earl, who died in 1632,
and was grandfather of James the twelfth earl, and first
Duke of Ormond.

The Viscountess Tullyophelim, becoming thus a widow,
enabled the King to dispose of her in marriage to one of
his favourites, Sir Richard Preston, on whom he had
conferred the dignity of Lord Dingwall in Scotland. His
Majesty insisted that a considerable portion of the
Ormond and Irish estates should be transferred to her
husband. This led to controversies and disputes, during
which her husband was created Earl of Desmond, in
Ireland, in consequence of his wife being descended from
an heiress of that unfortunate family.

But there was another and stronger reason for this
creation. Lady Dingwall had brought her husband a
daughter. Villiers, the worst of all the favourites of
James, had been busily engaged in procuring peerages
for all his relations. He cast his eyes upon the heiress,
and marked her out as an eligible wife for the second
son, then an infant, of his brother-in-law the Earl of

Denbigh. Lord Dingwall, being nothing loth, the affair was settled between them in this way. His lordship was created, by letters patent, Earl of Desmond, with a remainder, not to his daughter, but to George Fielding, her intended husband.

The infancy of the two contracted children necessarily prevented any immediate marriage, and fate destined it should never take place. Charles succeeded James in 1625; Buckingham was murdered by Felton in August 1628; The Countess of Desmond and Baroness Dingwall died in Wales before 1628; and the Earl, in returning from Ireland, perished in a shipwreck off Holyhead in the same year.

The bubble burst. The young lady was no longer fettered, and Charles, approving the choice, granted the wardship and marriage of the Lady Dingwall to Walter, eleventh Earl of Ormond, in order that she might be married to his grandson James, then Lord Thurles, and subsequently first Duke of Ormond. By this marriage, which was carried out in 1631 without further difficulty, the male and lineal representation of the Ormonds became united in the person of the Grand Duke of Ormond.

George Fielding, although he lost the heiress, got the Irish Earldom of Desmond, which is now in the person of the Earl of Denbigh.

His Grace was created a Duke of Ireland in 1661, and of England in 1682. He died in 1688, and was buried in Westminster Abbey, where the Duchess who predeceased her husband was interred upon the 24th July 1684. Their grandson James, the second Duke, succeeded to the English, Irish, and Scotch honours, but after the accession of the Hanoverian dynasty, was attainted. His death occurred in 1745. His Grace, not having been attainted in Ireland, then not united to Great Britain, the Irish honours were not affected by the British statute, and consequently the Earldom was successfully claimed in 1791, when John Butler of Killcash, the heir male of the Earls of Ormond, the ducal race being extinct in the male line, took his seat in the Irish House of Lords as Earl of Ormond.

To his Grace the Duke of Ormond, Lord Steward of his Majesty's Household, Chancellor of the University of Oxford, Knight of the Most Noble Order of the Garter, &c.

MAY IT PLEASE YOUR GRACE,—This comedy was written by the sacred command of our late most excellent King, of ever blessed and beloved memory. I had the great good fortune to please him often at his court in my masque, on the stage in tragedies and comedies, and so to advance myself in his good opinion ; an honour may render a wiser man than I vain ; for I believe he had more equals in extent of dominions, than of understanding. The greatest pleasure he had from the stage was in comedy, and he often commanded me to write it, and lately gave me a Spanish play call'd *No Puedesser, or It cannot Be ;* out of which I took part o' the name, and design o' this. I receiv'd the employment as a great honour, because it was difficult ; requiring no ordinary skill and pains to build a little shallop, fit only for the Spanish South Seas, into an English ship royal ; but I believe myself able for the work, because he thought so, who understood me and all men, better than I only knew myself ; encourag'd by a royal judgment that never was mistaken, I have attained a success I never should have met with, had I only followed my own feeble genius, which often deceives me. That I may enjoy the little fortune I have got with the better reputation, and not ramble the world like a bold outlaw, observing none but myself, I make this humble application to your Grace. I am sure all the world will approve my choice. I cannot be guilty of flattery if I would; nor slander wit (if I had any) by fulsome and wanton paintings. Here will be no trial of skill how I can praise; nature has done it to my hands, and devis'd and expos'd finer ideas, than I am able to translate. A gracefulness of person, excellence of understanding, largeness of heart, a loyalty, gallantry, integrity, humility, and many qualities above my description. Fortune also has been more wise than usual; she frequently honours and enriches others to her own disgrace, but here she shares in the praise, and commends her own wisdom, in what she bestows on your Grace. She has advanc'd honour in advancing you; titles, greatness, and command may be proud they have attained you. Wealth has a value in your hands; 'tis no vile pardon, poor flatterer, servile lackquey, wretched prisoner, but excellent minister of a just, wise, and liberal Prince. Should I mention all the qualities that have long gained you the highest honours from Prince and people, I should rather seem to describe a province than a man; for what single province can afford what are at once in your Grace, a general, a statesman, a courtier, and all in perfection; and which is rare in such company, a martyr? What has your Grace both done and suffered for our religion, laws, liberties, and honour? And not only in the former times of rebellion, but the latter of confusion? When the pretended Protestants of the times, out of their zeal against all Popish doctrines, abhor'd you for adhering to good works.

As an Englishman, I am bound in justice to pay you all the honours I can. You have been an ornament and support to the Crown and Church of England, both in your person and posterity. Many great men no doubt have sprung from your example, but none equalling those descended from your self. The late brave Earl of Ossory advanced the honour of our nation, both by sea and land. 'Tis hard to say in which element he made us most renown'd, and for which virtue. He was no more to be vanquished by falsehood than fear; loyalty, fidelity, and gallantry, are virtues inseparable from the house of Ormond; we find 'em in every branch of it, and at all seasons. The Earl of Arran attacked in the late days of confusion a bloody, popular, and formidable error in its camp, fortified and defended by all the strength of England, and for ever secur'd his own, and so much of the public reputation as was entrusted to him; managing that charge with the same wisdom, justice, and fidelity he has done the kingdom of Ireland, and many other great commands, for the honour and service of the King. In the young Earl of Ossory we have great assurances the grandfather and father shall live in him, and receive the last rewards of virtue men are capable of in this world, to have their honour and happiness extend beyond their own beings. And herein the history of your Grace seems a comment on the fifth commandment: you have always honoured the father of your country, and your days of honour continue long in the land, in your own person and your illustrious race; a useful precedent to England.

That I may approve myself an honest and grateful Englishman is one reason of my address: I have also other obligations on me. Your Grace has been a Princely patron and encourager of poetry; a pleasant but barren country where my genius and inclination has cast me. I am entangled among the inclinations of it, though it affords nothing but a good air, a little vain reputation, and we must climb for it, and shall miss it too, if envy or ill nature can hinder us. There were no living, if some great men, elevated not only in quality but understanding above the rest of the world, did not protect us from these barbarians, because they know us. I beseech your Grace then give me leave to pay my duty to you. Many and great are your revenues in honour, in the camp, the Court, the Church, and the whole commonwealth of learning. The poet may be employed as well as the historian. I have made but a small collection, but I have put it in hands that I hope will not soon embezzle it. This comedy has rais'd itself such a fortune in the world, I believe it will not soon run away. Give it leave to honour itself with your great name, and me with the title of,

May it please your Grace,

Your Grace's most humble and

Obedient Servant,

JOHN CROWN

THE PROLOGUE.

What are the charms by which these happy isles
Hence gain'd Heaven's brightest and eternal
    smiles ?
.What nation upon earth, besides our own,
But by a loss like ours had been undone ?
Ten ages scarce such royal worths display
As England lost and found in one strange day ;
One hour in sorrow and confusion hurl'd,
And yet the next the envy of the world.
Nay, we are blest, in spite of us 'tis known,
Heaven's choice for us was better than our own.
To stop the blessings that o'erflow this day,
What heaps o' rogues we pil'd up in the way !
We chose fit tools against all good to strive,
The sauciest, lewdest, Protestants alive ;
They would have form'd a blessed Church indeed
Upon a turn-coat doctor's lying creed.
To know if e'er he took degree is hard,
'Tis thought he'll have one in the Palace Yard.
Plot swallowers sure will drink no more stuff
    down
From that foul pitcher, when his ears are gone.
Let us rely on conscience, not on cheats,
On Heaven's wisdom, not on jugglers' feats.
How greatly Heaven has our great loss supplied !
'Tis no small virtue heals a wound so wide.
Nay in so little time to rear our head,
To our own wonder, and our neighbours' dread.
They see that valour crown'd with regal power,
They oft have seen with laurels crown'd before.
Verse is too narrow for so great a name,
Far sounding seas hourly repeat his fame.

Our neighbours' vanquish'd fleets oft wafted o'er
His name to theirs and many a trembling shore ;
And we may go, by his great conduct led,
As far in fame as our forefathers did.
At home he milder ways to glory chose,
God-like, by patience he subdued his foes ;
Now they and their designs are ruined all,
Beneath their fall'n, accurst, excluding wall.
These are not all the blessings of this isle,
Heaven on our nation in a Queen does smile ;
Whose virtue's grace by beauty shines so bright,
All the fair sex to virtue she'll invite ;
And all the clouds turn to a glorious day,
By that illustrious pair's united ray,
Who both reform and grace us by their sway.

THE NAMES OF THE PERSONS.

LORD BELLGUARD, { *Leonora's Brother, in love with Violante.*

SIR COURTLY NICE, { *A Fop, over-curious in his diet and dress: in love with Leonora.*

FAREWEL, . { *A young man of quality and fortune, his rival.*

SURLY, . . { *A morose, ill-natur'd, negligent fellow, in love with Violante.*

CRACK, . . *A young subtle intriguing fellow.*

HOTHEAD, . { *A choleric zealot against fanaticks.*

TESTIMONY, . *A canting hypocritical fanatick.*

VIOLANTE, . { *A lady of quality and fortune, in love with Bellguard.*

LEONORA, . . { *Bellguard's sister, in love with Farewel.*

AUNT, . . { *Leonora's Governess—an old, amorous, envious maid.*

Scene: COVENT-GARDEN.

ACT I.

Scene, LORD BELLGUARD'S HOUSE.

Enter at several doors LEONORA *and* VIOLANTE.

Leo. My dear—   [*They embrace.*

Vio. My dear, how is it with thee? What amendment in thy brother's humour, and thy condition?

Leo. None.

Vio. Oh! thou break'st my heart, for I love him extremely, and am, I think, as well belov'd by him; but whil'st he has this disease upon him so mortal to liberty, dare venture on him no more than if he had the plague, or any other distemper dangerous to life. For what is life without liberty? To be his wife is worse than to be a ghost, for that walks and enjoys a little chat sometimes, but I must be laid by a conjurer call'd a husband for my whole life. I would not be a Queen on the terms; no nor on any terms, because a Queen is confin'd to forms, so fond am I of liberty; but next to that I love your brother; I wou'd give all the world to cure him. Is there no way?

Leo. None that I know of.

Vio. Must we then be for ever unhappy, I in the loss of him, and you in eternal slavery?

Leo. I might have liberty, but on such terms—

Vio. What terms?

Leo. Marriage with such a coxcomb, you know him—Sir Courtly Nice.

Vio. A tempting man ; he has a vast estate.

Leo. But incumber'd.

Vio. With what?

Leo. A fop. 'Tis mortgag'd to a thousand expensive follies; if it were not, I wou'd not drink water for the sake of a fine bowl chain'd to the well. The youth I love has a fair and free estate.

Vio. Mr Farewel, is it not?

Leo. The same.

Vio. Ay, but he's forbidden fruit.

Leo. I know it to my sorrow.

Vio. What's the reason?

Leo. History must tell you. There has been a pique between our families since the Conquest ; none were thought truly of our blood, that had not that scurvy in it ; because mine began to sweeten, my father almost suspected my legitimacy; and left me no fortune but on condition I retain'd the ancient mark of our house.

Vio. There arises then your brother's great authority. He has the disposal of your fortune, by consequence of your person ; fortune is all men seek now. They are so cow'd from marriage, they will go volunteers into a battle but must be prest to marriage ; and 'tis the shilling does it.

Leo. Too true; but I believe Mr Farewel of a more generous temper ; he addresses still.

Vio. It may be he does not know how it is with you. You have the fame of ten thousand pound.

Leo. And the money too, if I marry with my brother's consent, not else.

Vio. That's hard, but Mr Farewel has enough for you both.

Leo. Ay, if he will venture on me ; yet if he will I know not how to come at him, I am so watch'd, not only at home but abroad. I never stir out but, as they say the devil does, with chains and torments. She that is my Hell at home, is so abroad.

Vio. A new woman.

Leo. No, an old woman, or rather an old devil; nay, worse than an old devil, an old maid.

Vio. Oh! there's no fiend so envious.

Leo. Right! she will no more let young people sin than the devil will let 'em be sav'd, out of envy to their happiness.

Vio. Who is she?

Leo. One of my own blood, an aunt.

Vio. I know her. She of thy blood? she has not had a drop of it these twenty years; the devil of envy suck'd it all out, and left verjuice in the room.

Leo. True, this aunt hangs on me like a daily ague; but I had rather endure her than be cur'd by such a nonsensical charm as Sir Courtly is. And nothing else can be applied to me; for, to assist my governing aunt, there is a whole army of spies in the house; and over them two spies-general. And there my brother thinks he shews a master-piece of policy.

Vio. Why? what are they?

Leo. Two, that will agree in nothing but one another's confusion. The one is a poor kinsman of ours, so fierce an enemy to fanatics, that he cou'd eat no other meat; and he need no other fire than himself to roast 'em, for he's always in a flame when he comes near 'em. His name is Hot-head.

Vio. And I warrant thee the other is a fanatic.

Leo. Oh! a most zealous scrupulous one; with a conscience swaddled so hard in its infancy by strict education, and now thump'd and cudgel'd so sore with daily sermons and lectures, that the weak ricketty thing can endure nothing.

Vio. Certainly these two must make you sport.

Leo. Oh! their faces, dresses, names are jests. The fanatick's name's Testimony.

[*Hot-head, within.*

Where is my lord? Where's my lord?

Leo. Oh! I hear my choleric cousin, Hot-head.

Enter HOTHEAD.

Hot. Where's my lord? Where's my lord, I say?

Leo. What wou'd you do with my lord?

Hot. Call him to an account if he were not my cousin, cut his pate, it may be cudgel him. Heaven be thank'd to cudgel a lord is no *scandalum magnatum.*

Leo. What's the reason of all this anger?

Hot. He affronts me. He invites me to live in his house, and then keeps a fanatic to make a jest o' me. He knows I sweat when I see one.

Leo. May be he has occasion for one.

Hot. What occasion? He is not in a plot, is he? Fanatics are good for nothing else that I know of.

Leo. Why not? Toads are good for something.

Hot. Ay, when they are hang'd and dried, so is no fanatic. He is such a canker'd rogue, he does mischief when he's hanged; let him spread ink upon paper and it raises blisters.——But here the rogue is.

Enter TESTIMONY.

Sirrah! Sirrah, What's your business in this house, sirrah?

Test. What authority have you to examine me, friend?

Hot. Friend, you dog! call me friend, I'll knock you down, sirrah.

Test. Poor soul——poor soul——

Hot. You are an impudent rascal to call me poor soul. Sirrah, I have a loyalty and a good conscience, and that's a better estate than any of your party have; and if you live in the house with me, I'll settle it on you, with a pox to you.

Test. Yes, Mr Hot-head, I know you well enough. I know you would hang us all if you could.

Hot. I need not, sirrah, for Heaven be prais'd now you begin to hang your selves. I knew when Tyburn was bestow'd upon the priests and Jesuits, the fanatics and republicans wou'd not long be without it, for they are very fond of all Church lands. Come, sirrah, if you live here, I'll make you turn over a new leaf, I'll make you go to Church, sirrah.

Test. That's more then you do your self, Mr Hothead; you go not often to Church.

Hot. What then? I'm for the Church, sirrah. But you are against the Church, and against the ministers, sirrah.

Test. I cannot be edified by 'em; they are formal, weak, ignorant, poor souls——Lord help 'em—— poor souls.

Hot. Ignorant? you're an impudent rascal to call men o' their learning ignorant; there's not one in a hundred of 'em but has taken all his degrees at Oxford, and is a doctor, you sot, you.

Test. What signifies Oxford? can't we be sav'd unless we go to Oxford?

Hot. Oxford don't lie out o' the road to Heaven, you ass.

Test. Pray what do they learn at Oxford? only to study heathens. They'll talk of Aristotle in the public; they may be asham'd to name Aristotle among civil people.

Hot. Oh! you sot.

Test. Our ministers are powerful men. Oh! Forsooth, I wish you [to *Leo*] were under one of our ministers; you wou'd find they wou'd pierce you, forsooth; they wou'd go to your inward parts.

Hot. This rogue is talking bawdy.

Test. They would shew you the great—great sinfulness of sin, that sin is one of the sinfullest things in the whole world.

Hot. You senseless rascal, what should be sinful but sin? what should be foolish but a fool?

Leo. Are not these a ridiculous couple?

Test. Come, this is very provoking, and very prophane. I shall have a sad time on't in this wicked family.

Hot. Wicked! Sirrah: what wickedness do you see in this family?

Leo. Ay, Mr Testimony, now we are all concern'd, what vices do you find among us?

Test. Suppose I see not many vices, morality is not the thing; the heathens had morality, and forsooth would you have your coachman or your footman to be no better men than Seneca?

Hot. A coachman is a better man than Seneca?

Leo. I wou'd have him be a better coachman than I believe Seneca was.

Test. Ay, and a better Christian too, or woe be to him. But truly I see great wantonness even in your self, forsooth,—the very cook debauches you.—

Hot. How? call the cook!——cook!——cook!

Leo. The cook debauch me, sirrah?

Test. I mean by pamp'ring you, morning, noon, and night with one wanton kickshaw or another.—

Vio. You coxcomb!

Leo. Sot!

Hot. Rascal, I thought the cook had lain with my cousin. Sirrah, you deserve to have your bones broke. Well, sirrah, since you find my lord's table is too lusty, I'll have it gelded; I'll make you keep Lent, and fast Wednesdays and Fridays.

Test. I will not, I abhor it. 'Tis Popery.

Hot. Then you shall fast Tuesdays and Thursdays.

Test. And then the family will slander me, and say I do it out o' contradiction,——I will not do it; I do not love to grieve the weak.

Hot. To grieve the strong thou mean'st,—thy own strong stomach.

Test. You are offensive.

Hot. I will be more. I will watch you, sirrah, and know why my lord feeds such rascals.

Test. I tarry not for his feeding. The family is a sad family, and I tarry out of pure bowels.

Hot. Out of empty bowels, which you have a mind to fill, and it may be you may fill other empty bellies, I mean among the wenches; some of you godly rogues play such tricks sometimes. I'll watch you, sirrah. [*Exit.*

Test. And I'll watch you. My spirit rises at this man exceedingly. [*Exit.*

Vio. These are a pleasant couple.

Leo. Is not my brother politic? These are to see no provisions for wantonness be convey'd to me from abroad, and be sure they will not agree to deceive him. And that I may have none at home, my brother will not venture a handsome servant in the house; he swears he will not be brother-in-law to e'er a butler or footman in England; and he has cull'd for his family the most choice pieces of deformity he cou'd find in the nation. I believe they are now altogether in the pantry, and my aunt among 'em distributing their breakfasts—— the monsters will be worth seeing —— open the door!——

The Scene is drawn, and a company of crooked, wither'd, ill look'd fellows are at breakfast, and AUNT *with them.*

Aunt. How now ? Who open'd the door without my leave ? Niece, this is one o' your girlish tricks! will you always be a child ? Will you never learn staidness and gravity, notwithstanding the perpetual counsel you have from me, the perpetual displeasure I shew at all sort of youthful follies ? do not you know how I hate impertinent youth ?

Leo. Or any sort o' youth to my knowledge.
                                                    [*Aside.*

Au. Do not I always tell you how fine a thing it is to be grave ; that youth with gravity is very passable, and almost esteem'd equal with years ? Very wise persons will not be ashamed to match with grave youth ; daily experience shews it, and will you never leave ? Fye——fye——fye !——I wou'd not for the world any wise sober person o' quality that has an inclination for you shou'd ha' seen this rudeness in you, to expose your aunt in this manner, in her undress ; it might ha' created in him an aversion for you.

Leo. An aversion to me, to see your ill dress?
                                                    [*Aside.*

Au. Madam, I hope you'll pardon the liberty I take in your presence.

Vio. Oh ! good madam.

Au. Oh ! madam——pardon me——I know I commit a solecism in good manners,——but you are a lady that has a great deal o' goodness, and a great deal o' worth——

Vio. Oh ! sweet madam !——

Au. Oh ! madam ! our family has found it—— you are pleas'd to honour us with your friendship. We may venture to expose our frailties be-

fore you, madam, you'll be so good to pardon——
madam——

Vio. Oh ! madam !——

Au. Well, really madam——I wonder where
my niece learns her wantonness, we are the most
reserv'd family in the world. There were fourteen
sisters of us ; and not one of us married.——

Vio. Is't possible ?

Leo. To your great grief——   [*Aside.*

Au. We were all so reserv'd. Oh ! madam !
no man durst presume to think of us ;——I never
had three love letters sent to me in my whole life.

Vio. Oh ! strange !

Au. Oh ! we were very reserv'd. Well, madam,
I am very much out o' countenance to appear thus
before you.

Vio. Oh ! madam, everything becomes you,
madam.

Au. Oh ! you are very obliging, madam.——Do
you hear, niece——learn o' this lady ?

Leo. To flatter you.   [*Aside.*

Au. Madam, I am extreme unfortunate, the
affairs o' the family call me away from your sweet
conversation.

Vio. The misfortune is mine, madam.

Au. Oh ! sweet madam, your most humble servant.   [*Exit Aunt.*

Vio. Your humbler servant, dear madam. Ha !
ha ! ha ! what ridiculous piece of antiquity is this ?
Thy brother has a great honour for his family since
he will keep such a relic of his ancestors as this.

Leo. All the house is of a piece.

Vio. Nay, if thou learnst lewdness at home, thou
hast a great genius to it.

Leo. Well, what do you think of my condition ?

Vio. I like it.

Leo. Like it ?

Vio. Ay, for I perceive your brother has put the whole force of his wit into this form of government; now, if we can baffle it, he will find it is a dream fit for nothing but Utopia; and never torment himself and his friends with it any more. Then he'll be a faultless creature, and all of us happy in our loves. Here he comes!

Enter Lord BELLGUARD.

Your servant, good my lord.

Bell. Your most humble servant, madam.

Leo. My lord! why do you call him lord? he's a doctor, and curing me o' the palpitation o' the heart, falling-sickness, convulsions in the eyes, and other such distempers.

Vio. A doctor! a quack by his false medicines; shortly we shall see him mount the stage, or stand at the Old——Exchange, and cry a cure for your horns! a cure for your horns!

Bell. I'm glad to see you so pleasant, madam.

Vio. How can I otherwise chuse, my lord, and see your family and government?

Bell. Faith, madam, he that will have a garden must enclose it, and cover tender plants. This is a very blasting age to virtue, 'twill not thrive without a covering.

Vio. Ay, but, my lord, you force your ground too much: what horns wou'd not grow in your soil? When wou'd not your forehead sprout? Were I your wife and thus kept, I shou'd spread like a vine, and all the walls in England wou'd not hold me.

Bell. I'm not o' that opinion, madam.

Vio. Why shou'd you think better o' me than your sister?

Bell. I judge very well of her, but must speak freely; I think few women may be trusted in this

life. This world is, and ever was a great brothel.
Where, or with whom may a woman be trusted ?
With ancient ladies? they are the chief beauty
merchants, vendors of fine love.

Leo. Ladies o' that profession.

Bell. Oh! the most excellent, and most in em-{
ploy. Pedling women cry Scotch cloath of a groat|
a yard, stuff only fit for footmen. But wou'd you '
have fine beauty, choice of beauty, and with ease,
security, and decency? go to your lady merchants. |
In common houses the work is manag'd as slovenly |
as religion in conventicles, enough to put one out ,
of conceit with it ; but, in brothels o' quality, iniquity is carried on with that venerable order wou'd
entice any one to devotion.

Vio. Fie! fie!

Bell. And with that security : a man may there '
enjoy a lady whilst her husband holds her cards.

Leo. And shall the lady o' the house know o'
these things?

Bell. And manage 'em too ; break the lady to
the lover's hands ; that's the advantage o' quality.
If a young lady has not a natural amble, a poor
bawd cannot have access to teach her.

Vio. What can a lady o' quality propound by
such doings?

Bell. Oh! many things. As presents, and pleasures. She has her house full of good company,
her ears full of wanton stories, her eye full of
tempting sights, and now and then her lips get a
close kiss. Oh! madam! do you think it does
not warm an elderly lady's blood, to have a brisk
young spark always by her side? he is her liquor
of life, and though she never gets a full draught, a
taste cheers her heart.

Leo. Who are these ladies? Where do they live?

Bell. Oh! you'd feign be acquainted with 'em?

no such matter; and yet I'll tell you where they live.

Leo. Where?

Bell. Almost every where; where there is an amorous aunt, or over-indulgent mother.

Leo. Mothers? will mothers corrupt their daughters?

Bell. Ay, or, if they won't, daughters will corrupt their mothers. Things are so inverted, that ladies who were honest all their youth to be like their mothers, turn lewd in their old age to be like their daughters. There never was such an open and general war made on virtue; young ones of thirteen will pickeere* at it, and by that time they are twenty, they are risen to be strumpets-general, and march in public with their baggage, with miss and mass, and nurse and maid, and a whole train of reformade† sinners, expecting the next cully that falls.

Vio. You talk of paltry hussies.

Bell. Very good gentlewomen.

Leo. Gentlewomen o' those employments?

Bell. Ay, purchase 'em. I have known a fair young lady give all her fortune to attend a man o' quality in his bed-chamber; be his chief gentlewoman.

Leo. Suppose so, what's all this to me? If they be bad must I be so?

Bell. Truly sister, a rambling woman, let her be never so good a manager, will be apt to bring her virtue as a traveller does his money, from a broad piece to a brass farthing : but say she does not, is reputation nothing? and, let me tell you, reputation will hang loose upon a galloping lady ; you may as well go among high winds and not be

---

* Skirmish.   † Disbanded.

ruffled, as among men and not have your good
name blown over your ears.

Vio. Those winds blow where they list. A
woman is not secure at home from censure.

Bell. But you must allow a jewel is not so safe
in a crowd as when lock'd up.

Leo. Lock'd up? Do you think to lock me up?

Bell. I think to secure thee, my dear Sister.

Women like china* shou'd be kept with care,
One flaw debases her to common ware. [*Exit.*

Act II.

Scene, VIOLANTE'S HOUSE.

Enter VIOLANTE *and a Servant.*

Vio. Is Mr Farewel coming?

Ser. Yes, madam, he's just at the door.

Vio. That's well! if this brisk young fellow has
but love enough to undertake this work, and wit
enough to go through with it, we shall all be happy.

Enter FAREWEL.

Fa. Where's your lady? Madam, your most
humble servant.

Vio. Your servant, Mr Farewel; you are a
happy man, young, rich, and in the ladies' favours.

Fa. I'm glad to hear that, madam. Who are
these ladies, madam? a day, an hour of youth
and good fortune is precious; and ladies, like birds,
must be aim'd at whilst they hop about us : miss
that opportunity you may lose 'em for ever.
Therefore the ladies, good madam, quick, quick!
for if you defer but half an hour, they'll be in love
with somebody else.

* Spelt " Cheney " in first edition.

Vio. No, Mr Farewel, there is one lady more
constant; you'll own it when I name her; my Lord
Bellguard's delicate young sister. What say you
to her?

Fa. I adore her.

Vio. And dare you attempt her?

Fa. Dare I?

Vio. Ay, for do not you know you are the only
man forbidden her.

Fa. Do I know of what race I am, madam?
Never was such a pack of fops as my Lord Bellguard's ancestors and mine. They lov'd wrangling
more than we do intriguing; kept lawyers instead
o' wenches, and begot upon their bodies a thousand
illegitimate lawsuits: the terms they observ'd as
duly as the river does the tides, and land was carried too and fro, as mud is in the Thames. Nor
were their quarrels so bitter about land, as place;
so big were their great hearts they cou'd not come
into one room together, for fear of losing place.
My Lord Bellguard's father, to end the difference,
most piously endeavours to be a better man than
any of his ancestors. That is to say, a lord.

Vio. And then the strife ended?

Fa. Was more enflam'd. For my lord was more
insolent, as having authority under the broad seal
to be proud, by consequence my father more
enrag'd; and both the old gentlemen contended
who shou'd have the greatest estate in malice, and
attain'd to be very considerable, and, when they
died, endeavour'd to settle it all upon us. But
truly the young lady and I most prodigally consum'd all our portions at one look, and agreed to
cut off the wicked entail.

Vio. You did well, but how will you accomplish
your desires? her brother has such guards upon
her.

Fa. Oh! 'tis decreed! nor shall thy fate, Oh brother! resist my vow; though guards were set on guards, till their confounded coxcombs reach'd the skies, I'd o'er 'em all———

Vio. You are in a rapture.

Fa. Ten thousand when ever I think of her.

Vio. But how will you do this?

Fa. I have leagu'd with a witch; at least a young fellow that has more tricks than a witch; he was a poor scholar at Oxford, but expell'd for studying the black arts.

Vio. For conjuring?

Fa. Yes, Madam, not only any man's pigs or poultry, but wife or daughter into his chamber. Nothing cou'd scape him, and he scap'd every thing. The proctors watch'd more diligently for him than a benefice, and cou'd never catch him. The grave doctors abhor'd him worse than a heresy, and studied more to keep him out of their families, but he confuted their skill, and they cou'd no more light upon him than on a jest.

Vio. I long to see him.

Fa. I order'd him to come hither to me.

Enter A SERVANT.

Ser. Here's one Mr Crack enquires for you, sir.

Fa. That's he!—bring him in!—

Enter CRACK.

Mr Crack, your servant.

Cr. Your servant, sir; your humble servant, madam.

Vio. Your servant, sir. I am told you have been an Oxford scholar.

Cr. A scholar, madam? a scholar's egg— emptied by old suck-eggs of all that nature gave

me, and crumbl'd full of essences, hypostases, and
other stuff o' their baking.

Vio. Why did not you apply yourself to
divinity ?

Cr. Leave wenches for pigs, madam ? 'tis true I
may wench then too, but it must be with fear and
reverence. I hate that.

Vio. Why wou'd not you be a physician ?

Cr. A gold-finder, madam ? look into jakes for
bits o' money ? I had a spirit above it. I had an
ambition to be of some honourable profession ; such
as people of quality undertake. As for instance,
pimping. A pimp is as much above a doctor, as a
cook is above a scullion ; when a pimp has foul'd a
dish a doctor scours it.

Vio. This is an arch blade.

Cr. Oh ! you are pleas'd to say so, madam ; 'tis
more your goodness than my desert.

Fa. Well, Mr Crack, you know what you have
undertaken.

Cr. I'll do't! The Lady's your's.—Give me
some money.

Fa. There, there !—

Cr. Gold ! thou son o' the sun, and brother o' the
stars, nutmeg o' comfort, and rose o' delight, as my
friend the King o' Persia calls himself,——what
canst thou not do great Prince, if I be thy chief
Minister ?   [*Exit.*

Vio. This is a notable fellow. Our next plot
must be to secure your rival, Sir Courtly Nice.

Fa. Hang him ! he secures himself by his fop-
peries. She despises him.

Vio. Not many ladies do so.

Fa. Oh ! no, madam, he's the general guitar o'
the town, inlay'd with every thing women fancy ;
gaytry, gallantry, delicacy, nicety, courtesy.

Vio. And pray put in gold too.

Fa. True, madam. Oh ! the ladies love to have him in their chambers, and play themselves asleep with him.

Vio. Well, I have provided one shall thrumble on him.

Fa. Who's that ?

Vio. Surly.

Fa. Oh! fire and water are not so contrary. Sir Courtly is so civil a creature, and so respectful to everything belongs to a gentleman, he stands bare to his own periwig. Surly uncovers to nothing but his own night-cap, nor to that if he be drunk, for he sleeps in his hat. Sir Courtly is so gentle a creature, he writes a challenge in the style of a billet-doux. Surly talks to his mistress, as he would to a hector that wins his money. Sir Courtly is so pleas'd with his own person, his daily contemplation, nay, his salvation is a looking-glass, for there he finds eternal happiness. Surly's Heaven, at least his priest, is his claret glass ; for to that he confesses all his sins, and from it receives absolution and comfort. But his damnation is a looking-glass, for there he finds an eternal fire in his nose. In short, if you wou'd make a posset for the devil, mingle these two, for there was never so sweet a thing as Sir Courtly, so sour as Surly. But how will you get 'em together ? for nothing has power over Surly, but claret and the devil.

Vio. Yes, I have. Heaven is pleas'd to think the devil himself has not mischief enough to plague that ill-natur'd rogue, and joins me in commission with him to torment him with love; he loves me.

Fa. Love? can he love ?

Vio. So much, he neglects his claret for me ; and comes hither hourly to perform his devotions to me, but in such a slovenly manner ; 'tis such a nonconformist to all decent ceremonies.

Surly (within) Where's your mistress ?

Vio. I hear him ! we'll ha' sport with him. He
abhors his love worse than murder or treason, for
those are mischiefs to others, but love he accounts
high treason against his own damnable person ; and
he's more asham'd of it, than he wou'd of a beast's
tail, if it grew out of him.   Therefore, I'll conceal,
and do you charge him with it ; you shall hear
how he'll renounce it, then will I appear like Conscience to a sick debauch, and you shall see what an
awkward penitent I'll make him.   [*Exit Vio.*

Enter SURLY.

Fa. Honest Surly, how do'st do ?

Sur. Prithee, look in my water !

Fa. In thy water ?

Sur. Ay, for I don't love to answer impertinent
questions.

Fa. Is it impertinent to enquire after the health
of a friend ?

Sur. A friend ! thy talk is more boyish than
thy face.   Do'st thou think there are such friends ?
thou believ'st there are mair-maids and centaurs
I warrant ; for such friends.   Monsters that grow
to some other beasts, and are the least part o'
themselves ?

Fa. Why ? hast thou no concern for any beasts
but thy self ?

Sur. Yes, bird, for many things for my own
sake ; for witty men whilst they drink with me,
handsome whores whil'st they lye with me, dogs,
horses or cattle whil'st they belong to me ; after
that, I care not if the wits be hang'd, the whores
be poxed, and all the cattle bewitch'd.

Fa. A very generous temper.

Sur. 'Tis a wise and honest temper. The pretended good nature is ill nature ; it makes a man

an ass to others, he bears their burden ; a rogue to
himself, he cheats himself of his quiet and fortune.
I am so very honest to my self, if the whole world
were hang'd it shou'd not rob me of a minute's
ease, I thank Heaven for it.

Fa. Was ever such a barbarian ?

Sur. Thou'rt an ass ! which is the barbarian, he
that eats man, or the man that's eaten ?   The rogue
that grieves away my flesh eats me, and is a barbarian ; so is he that with vexation gnaws himself ;
I am no such cannibal.

Fa. Hast thou no compassion ?

Sur. I know not what it is.

Fa. Suppose you see a man o' quality in misery

Sur. Let him be in misery and be damn'd.

Fa. Are you not concern'd for his quality ?

Sur. The less for that, because if he fancies the
whimsey he has it to please him.

Fa. To trouble him.

Sur. Then to comfort him I'll tell him he's the
son of a whore, and his grandfather rose by pimping.

Fa. Suppose you saw a man o' parts unfortunate ?

Sur. Let his parts look after him.

Fa. They'll afflict him.

Sur. Then to quiet him I'll tell him he's an ass.

Fa. Have you no charity ? do you never give
any thing to the poor ?

Sur. As much as any man.

Fa. What's that ?

Sur. Nothing.

Fa. Does no man give any thing ?

Sur. Not to the poor ; they give it to themselves.   Some fools have diseases in their natures,
they never see any one in pain, but they feel half
on't, and so they give money to ease themselves.

Fa. Ha' you no love for any thing ?

Sur. I have appetite.

Fa. Have you no love for women ?

Sur. I ha' lust.

Fa. No love ?

Sur. That's the same thing. The word love is a fig-leaf to cover the naked sense, a fashion brought up by Eve, the mother of jilts: she cuckolded her husband with the serpent, then pretended to modesty, and fell a making plackets presently. And her daughters take up the trade: you may import what lewdness you will into their common-wealth, if you will wash it over with some fine name. You may proclaim at market-cross, how great an adorer you are of such a woman's charms; how much you desire to be admitted into her service; that is, how lusty a centaur you are, that the horse in you is much the major part; and she shall receive all this without a blush, whil'st the beast trots to her under the name of a lover; when if she had any wit she'd know, a lover is a more impudent name than whoremaster; for a whoremaster throws all his bombs at a whole city, your lover wastes all his upon a single house, that when a woman desires a lover, she desires to have the whole brute to herself.

Fa. Ha! ha! ha!

Sur. What do you laugh at, sir ?

Fa. Only that your mistress has heard your learned discourses, sir. Pray appear, madam, and own you have lost your wager ! is he a lover or no ?

Enter VIOLANTE.

Sur. Here's a young treacherous rogue !

Vio. Yes !—a brutal one——are these your sentiments of love, sir ? was it this you meant when you talk'd of love; when we grow lovers do we degenerate into brutes? I thought there was a generous passion, of which a beast cou'd have no more sense, than he has of music or poetry. And to such love you pretended, sir.

Sur. I'll wheedle her. [*Aside to Fa.* So I do still, madam, but why must I let a boy catechise me? I have that musical, poetical, fantastical love, you speak of, and a pox on me for it; you'll neither be my slipper, nor my shoe, my wench to slip on and off at pleasure, nor my wife; that is, a whore buckled on.

Vio. You are charming in your expressions.

Fa. Mr Surly, Madam, is a mystical piece, to be understood like a prophecy, where rams and he-goats stand for Kings and Princes. Mr Surly's rank expressions must signify virtue and honour.

Vio. No, no, they signify his own filthy meaning: and the truth is, love has no other sense, in this corrupt age. Now, if a woman by blushes or otherwise, confesses she thinks a man a fine gentleman, he to requite her sends her presently a libel call'd a billet-doux, where he in fine words tells her to her face, he thinks her a wench, and invites her to lye with him. This ruins all conversation; men are always driving their brutal appetites to the plays, the Court, to Church, like drovers their beasts to every market; and there's no conversing with 'em, unless you'll take their cattle off their hands.

Sur. Madam, I love you in your own fashion, admire you, adore you, and the devil and all! what wou'd you have?——Now will this simple jade believe me. [*Aside to Fa.*

Fa. He calls you simple jade, madam, and says you'll believe him.

Sur. You malapert boy, why do you meddle in my business?

Fa. 'Tis my business; she's my friend, and I wont see her abus'd.

Sur. A friend to the woman that loves your enemy, Tom-Fool?

Fa. No, she hates him, and has quarrel'd with him, and I wou'd ha' had you step into his room.

Sur. Oh! oh!

Fa. Now who's the Tom-Fool?

Sur. I am! look you, madam, that rogue Despair made me talk like an ass, and I am sorry for it.

Vio. I know you are, sir. I know your base desire is, for your punishment, confin'd to my eyes, and I'll use you as you deserve.

Fa. Come, madam, let me interpose! though you will not receive Mr Surly as a half-horse, you may as a whole ass, a drudge. You know you have business most agreeable to his ill nature, pray employ him.

Vio. Well! I'll make trial of him. You pretend you love me generously?

Sur. Yes, and damnably.

Vio. Know then, my Lord Bellguard is, as I have of late perceived, sunk with the rest of the age into base opinions of love and women, that I am angry I ever had a good thought of him.

Sur. Good!

Vio. Look upon his address to me, as an affront, and will revenge it.

Sur. Better and better!

Vio. And you shall do it.

Sur. Best of all!

Vio. Do not you know Sir Courtly Nice?

Sur. That you shou'd join knowledge with such a fop? 'tis a question to be put to a boy. I may know philosophy, but to ask a man if he knows a horn-book? for such a thing is this fop; gilded

on the outside; on the inside, the criss cross* row,
and always hanging at the girdle of a girl.

Vio. You have describ'd him right. This fop
has my Lord Bellguard entic'd to accept his sister
with no fortune, but her birth and beauty. Now,
if you'll break the match, you'll be to me the most
amiable creature in the world.

Sur. Or the most damnable, if you jilt me.

Vio. In earnest of a farther favour, here's my
hand.

Sur. There's the devil in it. 'Tis transforming
my shape, I am growing a woman's ass, I feel the
ears prick out o' my skin already; and I must
hoof it away with her load of folly upon my back.
Well, I am thy ass at present, but if thou jilts me,
I will be thy devil. [*Exit.*

Vio. 'Tis the fittest office for thee; thou art so
like one already, you may pass for twins. Now,
Mr Farewel, let's go in and laugh! [*Exit.*

Scene, LORD BELLGUARD'S HOUSE.

Enter HOTHEAD *and* TESTIMONY.

Test. He shall not speak with her! I don't approve of it.

Hot. You approve, sirrah? what ha' you to do?

Test. I have authority.

Hot. You authority?

Test. Yes, from my Lord.

Hot. You had it then out of his kitchen, sirrah;
the beef o' the nation breeds all the maggots in the
people's heads. I am sometimes tempted to throw
down their porridge-pots, and spill the divine right
of Presbytery. In short, my Lord is a man of
honour, and you have belied him, sirrah.

Test. It is well known I make a conscience.

Hot. Ay, you rogues, making o' consciences is a

* CHRIST-*cross.* The Alphabet.—*Halliwell.*

great trade among your party, and you deserve to lose your ears for it.

Test. I mean, I keep a conscience.

Hot. Y'ave reason, sirrah, it keeps you ; but that an honest lord shou'd give money for a rogue's false conscience.——Oons !

Test. Well, but don't swear.

Hot. Sirrah, who swears ?

Test. De'e hear ?——don't swear, I say !

Hot. Oons ! Sirrah, don't preach to me.

Test. Don't swear then !

Hot. Sir, if you preach to me, I'll cut your pate.

Test. Had I a sword 'twere more than you cou'd do.

Hot. How now, sirrah ? [*Takes Test. by the throat.*

Test. Nay, but don't throttle me ! don't God-frey me ! *

Enter AUNT.

Au. What's the noise ? what's the rudeness ? Cousin Hot-head ? you a gentleman, and make a bear-garden of a person of honour's house ?

Hot. Better make a bear-garden of it than a con-venticle; here's a fanatick rogue ordain'd ruling elder o' th' family by my lord, as the rogue says, so he undertakes to govern and preach.

Au. And you undertake to govern and correct ? Cousin, nobody governs here but I ; if he had com-mitted faults, you should have brought him be-fore me.

Hot. Oh ! you 'd have him enter'd in your office ?

Au. What do you mean ? obscenely ? you are confident.   You are the first gentleman that offer'd to say a wanton thing to me.

---

* The murder of Sir Edmondbury Godfrey evidently gave rise to this phrase, as, in more recent times, the expression "to burke" was derived from the name of the ruffian who perpetrated so many murders in Edinburgh by strangulation.

Hot. To your great sorrow.　　　　　　[*Aside.*

Enter LEONORA.

Leo. What's the quarrel here?

Hot. There's a tailor wou'd fain speak with you.

Leo. All this noise to introduce a tailor?

Hot. He can't get through this fellow's narrow conscience, yet there is room for a whole common-wealth.

Au. Call in the tailor! there must no cloaths be made without my orders, that I may see 'em modest.

Leo. A tailor? I order'd no tailor.　　　[*Aside.*

Enter CRACK.

Au. How now, sir? what are you?

Cr. A tailor, madam!

Au. Who sent you? I know you not.

Cr. Your own tailor, Mr Stitch, madam.

Au. How chance he came not himself?

Cr. He's sick, madam.

Au. And can you work well, for we are very hard to please? There's scarce a tailor in town can make me endure to see my self.

Leo. The fault lyes in ——fifty——fifty. [*Aside.*

Cr. Indeed, madam, I must needs say my coun-trymen are not the best tailors in the world. This is a fine nation, and all spoil'd by the tailors. Heaven makes the women angels, and tailors make 'em hedge-hogs ; 'tis a sad sight to see 'em ! now I'll make an angel of a crooked pin.

Au. Ay, where did you learn your skill?

Cr. In France, madam.

Test. In France? Then, friend, I believe you are a Papist.

Hot. Sirrah, I believe you are a Presbyterian.

Test. Friend, if you be a Papist I'll ha' you before a Justice.

Hot. Sirrah, if you be a Presbyterian I'll kick you down stairs.

Test. What are you, friend?

Hot. Ay, what are you, sirrah?

Cr. What am I? why, I'm a tailor. I think the men are mad.

Au. Intolerable! Mr Testimony, pray leave us, and, cousin Hothead, I shall desire the same of you, unless you'll behave yourself like a gentleman.

Hot. I will behave myself like a gentleman, for I'll know of my lord, when he comes home, if he has given this rogue authority over me; if he has I'll demand satisfaction of him; if he be innocent woe be to your prick-ears, sirrah! [*Exit Hot.*

Test. I fear you not.

Au. Mr Testimony! I once more desire you'll give us liberty.

Test. Yes, forsooth! I dare trust the young gentlewoman with you, forsooth——you are a grave —— gentlewoman and in years——forsooth.——

Au. In years, rude clown?——

Test. And truly she's a very pretty sweet woman, and deserves to have great care taken of her.

Leo. Well, sir, we'll excuse the care at this time.

Test. Pretty woman!—   [*Aside.*

Leo. Pray leave us!—

Test. Sweet woman!—I profess she's strangely alluring; I had best retire lest I fall into frailty, and be discover'd.   [*Exit.*

Cr. Now, madam! before I take measure of you, I'll shew you some patterns. Please you to look upon some, madam; you have judgment.——

                    [*To the Aunt.*

Au. Let me see !

Cr. To you, madam, I wou'd recommend this piece.

Leo. Mr Farewel's picture ? oh ! Ay, sirrah ! now I guess thee——my dear——dear——

　　　　　　　　　　　[Kisses the picture.

Cr. Have a care o' your aunt, madam.——I have a letter too.——

Leo. Give it me !—quick——quick !—

Au. These are pretty silks.

Cr. The best in France, madam.
Where's my sister ?　　　　*[Bellguard within.*

Leo. My brother ? I hope he does not know thee.

Cr. No, if he does I'm a dead man !

Leo. Hast thou no disguise for fear he shou'd ?

Cr. Only this great pair of spectacles.

Enter Lord BELLGUARD.

Bell. What fellow's this ?

Leo. A tailor.

Bell. Not your tailor ?

Au. No ! he's sick and sent this fellow in his room.

Bell. How comes such a young fellow to wear spectacles ?

Cr. Young, my lord ? I'm above five and fifty.

Bell. Thou bear'st thy age well.

Cr. Ay, everywhere but in my eyes, I thank heaven.

Bell. This fellow may be a bawd for aught I know.　I'll watch him.　　　　　　*[Exit.*

　　*[Aunt views the patterns, Bell stands behind his
　　　　sister, and watches Cr.　Cr. meanwhile
　　　　puts his measure before, and delivers her
　　　　a letter.*

Cr. Well, madam ! I perceive your ladyship likes the pattern I shew'd you first.

Leo. I have seen the whole piece.

Cr. And your ladyship likes it ?

Leo. Oh! very well.

Cr. I'll assure you, madam, you'll like it mightily when 'tis upon you, and you have a sweet body to work for. I do not doubt, madam, but to get a great deal o' credit, and a great deal of custom by you among the ladies, as soon as ever they see my work.

Leo. Well, let's see your work ! and I'll say something.

Cr. That you shall and speedily, madam. I'll bring you home as sweet a piece o' work as ever you had in your life. You'll look upon the pattern I shew'd you last ?

Leo. Yes.

Cr. That's for the inside ; do you like much bombast, madam ?

Leo. No.

Cr. Well, madam——I ha' taken a survey o' your fine body——now you shall be pleas'd according to your own heart's desire. Your servant, madam. [*Exit.*

Bell. Well, sister, prepare to receive a visit from Sir Courtly Nice, this afternoon.

Au. Oh, dear ! then I must dress. He's a great critic. [*Exit.*

Leo. She designs him for herself. Wou'd she cou'd get him. [*Aside.*

Bell. Sir Courtly and I have agreed ; pray give him your promise.

Leo. So soon ? 'twill be fulsome, he's abstemious.

Bell. Therefore take him whil'st he has an edge.

Leo. You use to despise fools, how chance you marry among'st 'em ?

Bell. Because none but fools will marry. Wits are but few and commonly poor ; fools are numerous and rich. Fortune is as fond of those bits of men, as bigots are of reliques; wraps 'em in silver.

Leo. Better they were buried. A fool in a coach is like a knave in a pillory,—the object of public derision.

Bell. Oh! there are few to deride them, many to admire them; so many, I have oft admired how one apple
Shou'd such diseases in old Adam breed,
That from his loins not men, but worms proceed.
[*Exeunt omnes.*

ACT III.

Scene, COVENT GARDEN SQUARE.

Enter FAREWEL *and* CRACK *meeting.*

Fa. Oh! the news! the news! art thou an angel or a devil? Bring'st thou joys or torments?

Cr. Joys! joys! joys!

Fa. Angel! angel! angel!

Cr. In the first place I deliver'd your picture.

Fa. Rare.

Cr. And she kissed it.

Fa. Kissed it?

Cr. Sweetly, wantonly, lasciviously. She set me so on fire, I kiss'd all the wenches as I came along, and made their moist lips fiz again.

Fa. Oh! rogue! rogue! delicious rogue.

Cr. Then I deliver'd the letter, and before her brother's face.

Fa. Before his face? ha! ha! ha!

Cr. Prepare this night to be the happiest o' mortals. Give me some more money!

Fa. Money? I'll sell my land rather than thou shalt want. That one inheritance will purchase me two: one in love, and another in laughing at this politic brother.

Cr. No, no! inheritances? as for laughing, I believe you will have an annuity for life; but for love you'll only have a lease for three or four years.

Fa. Pleasant rogue! Here's money.

Cr. So, so, I wish you joy! I wish you joy! [*Exit.*

Fa. See Surly going to my rival; my affair thrives admirably. [*Exit.*

Enter SURLY. *Knocks, enter a* SERVANT.

Sur. Is Nice within?

Ser. Nice, sir?

Sur. Ay, Nice, sir; is not your master's name Nice.

Ser. 'Tis Sir Courtly Nice.

Sur. Well, sir, if I have a mind to clip half his name, 'tis not treason, is it, sirrah?

Ser. I believe not, sir.

Sur. Then get you in, and tell your master I'd speak with him.

Ser. What sort o' domineering man is this?

Scene, a CHAMBER—*Sir Courtly Nice dressing, Men and Women singing to him.*

A SONG

*To be Sung in Dialogue between a man and a woman in the Third Act to Sir Courtly Nice, at his first appearance.**

Man.   Oh! be kind, my dear, be kind,
      Whilst our loves and we are young.
   We shall find, we shall find
   Time will change the face or mind;
      Both will not continue long.
   Oh! be kind, my dear, be kind.

* Printed in all other editions of this Comedy, at the end of the piece.

Woman. No, I love, and fear to lose you,
  Therefore 'tis I must refuse you,
   When I've yielded you my crown
   You'll no more obedience own.
  No, I love, and fear to lose you,
  Therefore 'tis I must refuse you.

Man. The fair by kindness reign,
   By cruelty destroy.
  If you can charm with the pain
   Of love, then what can you do with the
    joy ?
  The fair by kindness reign,
   By cruelty destroy.

Woman. I fear to yield but cannot deny.
Man. If you do not I shall die.
Woman. So shall I.
Both. So shall I.
Chorus ⎱ Then come to joy——come to joy,
together. ⎰ Better love than we shou'd die.
   Come to joy, come to joy !

 Sir Co. Very fine ! extremely fine ! Gentlemen
and ladies, will you do me the favour to walk in,
and accept of a small collation ? I am in some
haste to dress upon an extraordinary occasion.
You'll pardon me ?——your very humble servant.—   *[Exit Music.*
 Ser. Very fine !
 Sir Co. You sot, 'twas very barbarous.
 Ser. Your honour said 'twas very fine.
 Sir Co. You clown, don't you know what belongs to a gentleman ? Complaisance is the very
thing of a gentleman ; the thing that shews a
gentleman. Wherever I go, all the world cries
that's a gentleman, my life on't a gentleman ; and
when y'ave said a gentleman, you have said all.

Ser. Is there nothing else, sir, belongs to a gentleman ?

Sir Co. Yes, *bon mine*, fine hands, a mouth well furnish'd——

Ser. With fine language ——

Sir Co. Fine teeth, you sot ; fine language belongs to pedants and poor fellows that live by their wits. Men of quality are above wit. 'Tis true for our diversion sometimes we write, but we ne'er regard wit. I write but I never writ any wit.

Ser. How then, sir ?

Sir Co. I write like a gentleman, soft and easy.

Ser. Does your honour write any plays ?

Sir Co. No, that's mechanic ! I bestow some garniture on plays, as a song or a prologue.

Ser. Then your honour is only a haberdasher o' small wares ?

Sir Co. A haberdasher, you saucy rascal ?

Enter a SERVANT.

2 *Ser.* Here's one, Mr Surly, to visit your honour.

Sir Co. Surly ! what the devil brings him hither?

2 *Ser.* He has been walking about the rooms this quarter of an hour, and wou'd not let me bring him in, till he had fould 'em all with his dirty shoes.

Sir Co. A nauseous, beastly, sloven, clown, fool, sot !

Enter SURLY.

Dear Mr Surly, your most humble servant.

       [*Sir Co. bows to receive him.*

Sur. What, are you unbu —— buckling my shoe ?   [*Sur. is drunk, stammers and belches.*

Sir Co. Dear Mr Surly——he stinks horribly ——   [*Aside.*

How came I to enjoy——a very polecat——

             [*Aside.*

This great happiness?——pox! foh! You and I
have been long *piquee*, and I'm amaz'd to see you
at my levee. [*Aside.*

Sur. I begin to think thou art a good honest
fellow, and have a mind we shou'd no longer be
two lo——lo——loggerheads, but one.

Sir Co. Dear sir, you are always so divertising.
Well, sir, shall I beg a favour of you?

Sur. What's that?

Sir Co. Leave to dress before you, sir. I am to
meet some fine women to-day; one presently.

Sur. Prithee dress, and be damn'd——shall we
di——dine together?

Sir Co. Yes, sir, I suppose, and sup too.——

Sur. That's kind! well, when?

Sir Co. About five o'clock, sir.

Sur. Where?

Sir Co. In the King's Box, sir.

Sur. Must you and I dine in the King's Box?

Sir Co. Oh! dearest! I beg your pardon ten
thousand times. I thought you ask'd me where I
shou'd meet the lady.

Sur. Pox o' the lady! I ask where we shall
dine?

Sir Co. Really, sir, I don't know. I can't put my
head into one o' your beastly eating houses, nor
swallow the filthy meat you eat there, if you'd give
me one hundred pound.

Sur. Filthy meat, Sir? I eat as good meat as
you do.

Sir Co. Oh! dear Mr Surly, no doubt the meat
in its own nature may be very innocent; but, when
once it has committed familiarity with the beastly
fists of cooks and butchers, 'tis to me an unpardonable sinner. My butcher cuts up all his meat
with a fork.

Sur. Does he cut up an ox with a fork?

Sir Co. Ay, and he cuts up an ox as neatly as a lady does a partridge.

Sur. Well then I'll accept o' thy dinner.

Sir Co. Dear sir, your most humble servant; pox on him! (*aside*) I wish I be capable o' the great happiness. For I came but last night from my country house, and I question whether I have all things in order or no. Who's there? are all things brought from my country house?

Ser. No, sir, your butler has forgot your salt.

Sir Co. Left my salt? careless rascal. Let him take horse immediately.

Ser. Sir, he's rid post for it.

Sur. Rid post for salt? whither?

Sir Co. To my country house.

Sur. How far's that off?

Sir Co. But a little way; not above forty miles.

Sur. Send forty miles out o' London for salt? Is there not salt enough in London for you?

Sir Co. Ay, stuff pawm'd by butlers and waiters; they take up the wench's coats, then handle the salt.

Sur. Here's a rogue! (*aside*) Well, come let's drink a glass o' wine then.

Sir Co. Oh! dear Mr Surly, if you name wine, you make me throw up my soul. I have abhor'd wine ever since I was in France, and saw what barbarous education they give that generous creature. Deuce take me, sir! if the clowns don't press all the grapes with their filthy naked feet. Oh! beastly nasty dogs! no wonder we are poison'd with their wine.

Sur. Prithee what o' that? the wine purges before it comes over.

Sir Co. Oh Lord! Mr Surly, what a phrase is there! you'll pardon my freedom, sir?——

Sur. Most civil coxcomb (*aside*). Well, what must we drink, for drink I must?

Sir Co. I have several drinks of my own composing at your service, as mead, cyder, ale.—

Sur. Ale ? there's sauce for a woodcock ! Come let's taste a bottle.

Sir Co. Fetch a bottle ! This fellow will poison me.—— [*Aside.*

Sur. Well I come to request a favour o' thee.

Sir Co. Your most humble servant, sir, how de'e like this cravat ?

Sur. What's that to my business ? I come to make a request to thee.

Sir Co. 'Tis well tied too, with a great deal o' humour.

Sur. A pox on thee ! mind me.

Sir Co. Your most humble servant, sir.

Sur. I am going to make love.

Sir Co. Before you drink, sir ?

Sur. Before I drink, sir.——

Sir Co. Well, sir, since you'll have it so, I'll wait on you down stairs.

Sur. Is the devil in the fellow ? I tell thee I'm going to make love.

Sir Co. Oh Lord ! sir, I beg your pardon a thousand times.

Sur. And I come to beg thy assistance.

Sir Co. Oh ! dear sir.

Sur. For thou hast a knack on't. Thou art the only Court card women love to play with ; the very pam at lantereloo, the knave that picks up all.

Sir Co. Oh, sir ! you are so obliging ;—and stinking—pox take him ! [*Aside*

Sur. And 'tis a very pretty woman I'm in love with ; my Lord Bellguard's sister, Leonora ; thou know'st her.

Sir Co. The rogue's my rival ; he was born for my confusion (*aside.*) Ay, sir, I have the honour of some small acquaintance there.

Sur. Prithee speak for me.

Sir Co. Oh ! dear sir, you have a great talent of your own.

Sur. But thine's a better.   One thing I am sure thou may'st do, there's an abominable fop makes love to her, and I am told is to marry her ; prithee tell him he's a son of a whore !

Sir Co. Really, sir, I'm unfortunate !   I ha' no manner o' genius to that sort o' conversation.

Sur. Say my words !   Tell him if he proceeds, I'll not only libel him, but tweag him by the nose, kick him, cudgel him, and run him through the guts.   Prithee, tell him this.   [*Hugs Sir Co.*

Sir Co. Oh ! pray, sir ! give me air.

Sur. Prithee, do !

Sir Co. Sir, I am ready to—

Sur. And thou wilt tell the puppy this ?

Sir Co. I will, upon my soul.

Enter a SERVANT *with wine and glasses.*

Sur. Then thou art an honest fellow—so, is the drink come ? fill a glass ! why two glasses ? do you think I cannot drink after your master ?

Sir Co. Pox o' your compliment.—   [*Aside*
                              [*Sur. flings away a glass.*

Sur. Here, Nice, my mistress's health.

Sir Co. What misery is this beast imposing on me ! he coughs in the glass too—   [*Aside.*

Sur. Pox on't, a whole gulp went the wrong way. Come, off with it !   'Tis my mistress's health.

Sir Co. This fellow's the devil—   [*Aside.*

Sur. Off with it, man !

Sir Co. I never was so embarass'd since I was born——

· *Sur.* Oons ! off with it.

Sir Co. I must take the beastly potion down, but I shall be most horrible sick after it.—[*Drinks.*

Sur. So, now thou are an honest fellow ! now I'll kiss thee.

Sir Co. The devil thou wilt ? more miseries ? (*aside*) nay, but Mr Surly.

Sur. I swear I will.

Sir Co. Ay, but you'll disorder me.

Sur. I swear I will.

Sir Co. But, sir, I'm going upon your occasions to your mistress.

Sur. Nay, then I'll give thee two kisses ; one for thyself and another for her.

Sir Co. Oh ! Hell ! (*aside*) Nay, but Mr Surly.

Sur. I swear I will.   [*kisses him and belches.* This bottle beer is damn'd windy !—Well, honest Nice, farewell to thee.   [*Exit.*

Sir Co. Who's there ? I'm sick to death,—to death ! —lead me in—get my bed ready—and a bath—and some perfumes—I'm sick to death,—I'm dead !   [*Exit.*

Scene, LORD BELLGUARD'S HOUSE.

Enter BELLGUARD *with Farewel's picture in his hand.*

Bell. Thou horrid vision ! wou'd I had met with the worst fiend in hell, rather than thee ; in thee there is a legion exciting me to blood—blood ! Who's there ?

Enter a SERVANT.

Ser. My lord ?

Bell. My coach !—to blood—blood !

Enter LEONORA *and* AUNT.

Leo. To blood ? what means my brother ?

Bell. Be gone !

Leo. To whom do you speak ?

Au. Bless us ! Nephew what ails you ?

Leo. Alas, my lord ! I fear you are a going to quarrel.

Bell. Yes, I am going to punish one who violates my father's, my will, and calls my mother whore.

Leo. What execrable wretch is that ?

Bell. Thyself.

Leo. Me ?

Bell. Yes, what dost thou else but proclaim our mother false when she conceiv'd a thing so opposite to all our father's race as thou art ?

Leo. In what ?

Bell. In infamy ; when was there a spot in our name, till Heaven for our sins sent thee among us ? and I am going to destroy thee in thy lewd undoer.

Leo. I know of no reproach in our family but your madness; destroy that. What are your spies and coxcombs, but so many capital letters, wherein you write over your door, my sister is a wanton woman ?

Bell. 'Tis truth, you are not only a wanton, but a wicked woman ; not only intrigue, but with the enemy of our family, Farewel.

Au. How ?

Leo. I am betray'd—   [*Aside.*

Bell. Do you blush ?

Leo. At your folly.

Bell. Dare you deny it ?

Leo. Who dare accuse me ?

Bell. This picture, which I found in your chamber.

Au. Horrid creature !—I shall swoon away.

Leo. How shall I bring off this (*aside*) ? All this noise for picture ? If you had found a little human effigies in swaddling clouts, there might ha' been some squawling.

Au. Do you laugh at your shame ?

Bell. She shall have no cause.

Leo. Do kill me, before you know whether he's guilty or no.

Bell. I'll know it from himself. If he denies it, it will be some revenge to make him stab his soul with lies. He shall swear not only that he never did, but never will send so much as an imagination to you.

Leo. Do, if you wou'd force him hither. What charm to a man of spirit, like daring?

Bell. She speaks sense in that.   *[Aside.*

Leo. If you wou'd be fighting, fight your own jealousy, which abuses you worse than Mr Farewel can do; my honour protects you from him. But neither wit nor honour can guard you from the rude insolence of your jealousy, which is now sending you of an errand a footman o' spirit wou'd scorn, to proclaim the dishonour of your own sister. Fie! fie!

Bell. And so I must sit down tamely with this abuse?

Leo. You are not abus'd. The picture was found at church.

Au. At church? Do you intrigue at church?

Bell. They do nothing else. The church is almost as bad as the porch.

Au. Nay, there's shameful doings, that's the truth on't. It provokes my flesh to see how the young men fling their eyes about.

Leo. And not upon her.———   *[Aside.*

Au. But tis no marvel; when women will encourage 'em. No fellows dare gape upon me, because I never encourage fellows.

Leo. A face of fifty is small encouragement.

Bell. Nay, no wonder the devil's cause thrives, he has a numerous clergy. Heaven has but one minister in the church, and, whilst he is preaching divinity, the devil has a thousand of both sexes, by all the oratory of looks and dresses, preaching fornication and adultery.

Au. Too true ! Well she's certainly undone. I dare not examine her breasts ; if there shou'd be any thing in 'em I should die.

Leo. In my breasts ?

Au. Ay, gentlewoman, do you think I regard your flim flam story o' the church ?

Leo. 'Tis not my story ; my woman found it in Westminster Abbey, at prayers, and I, knowing what work wou'd be made with it, commanded her to burn it, and she has dar'd to disobey me.

Wom. Indeed, madam, I thought to have presented it to a friend o' mine ; and, laying it out o' my hand unfortunately in your honour's chamber, my lord found it.

Bell. Oh ! how nimbly she takes the lie at the first rebound.

Au. Out upon you ! I'm extreme sick—lead me in—not you ! you are not fit to touch a woman o' my virtue. These things have strange impression upon me.—   [*Exit.*

Leo. That you don't share in 'em.—   [*Aside.*

Bell. Pray, sister, go out o' my sight ! you are an horror to me.

Leo. Your own dreams are. Y'are as mad as a prophet, you have always before your eyes a vision of horns and whores.

Bell. All this goes upon the score of Farewel's heart-blood if he be guilty. I'll make enquiry presently, and search at what gap this treachery entered.

Leo. Oh ! unfortunate negligence ! [*Aside—Exit.*

Enter HOTHEAD.

Bell. Who's there, cousin Hothead ? Testimony

Hot. Oh ! are you here ?

Bell. Ay, to your sorrow, if you have play'd me false.

Hot. You ha' serv'd me finely.

Bell. Do you first complain?

Hot. Coupled me with a dog!

Bell. But you ha' coupled my sister, sir.

Hot. With a fanatick rogue?

Bell. No—with a finer gentleman. Who brought this picture?

Hot. The common fire-fork of rebellion.

Bell. A fire-fork? Fork! me no forks. Who brought this picture?

Hot. The rotten rump shou'd ha' been burnt—when 'twas only roasted.

Bell. The rotten rump? Answer me, or I'll fight thee.

Hot. Answer you what?

Bell. Who brought this picture? I found it in my sister's chamber.

Hot. Then your fanatick rogue convey'd it thither to make me suspected, out of his malice to the Common-Prayer. I'll cut the rogue to pieces.

Enter TESTIMONY *with a great sword by his side.*

Bell. Testimony!

Test. I am here.

Bell. How now! sworded?

Test. To preserve my life. My life is threat'ned by that bloody Papist.

Hot. How, sirrah? dare you think of fighting me?

Test. Yes, and hope to do it, through Providence.

Bell. Drawing before me?

[*Hot. and Test. offer to draw.*

Hot. Will you protect a fanatick? I see what you are. Well, sirrah, though I may not cut your throat, I'll choak you, sirrah.

Test. De'e hear the bloody Papist ? He'll throttle me.

Hot. Sirrah, I'll cram the oaths of allegiance and supremacy into you, and they'll stick in your throat, though treason wont, and so I'll to a Justice presently. [*Ex.*

Bell. And stay with him, and never plague me more. Now, sir, do you resolve my question.

Test. I do resolve I will not take the oaths.

Bell. I do not ask you about the oaths.

Test. Why, if you ask me ten thousand times, I will not take the oaths.

Bell. Did one ever see such a coxcomb ?

Test. Call me what you please, I will not take the oaths. So, do your worst. [*Ex.*

Bell. A very fine account of my business.

Enter a SERVANT.

Ser. My lord, a gentleman desires to speak with your honour.

Bell. I'm not to be spoke with, I'm abroad— my soul is—in the heart of Farewel, ripping it up for this secret. What gentleman ?

Ser. One from th' East Indies, my lord; he brings a letter from your uncle Rich.

Bell. He comes in a storm; he will find worse weather here than any he met at sea. But I'll endeavour to compose myself. Admit him.

Enter a MAN *drest like a Merchant.*

Man. My lord, your lordship's most humble servant. I perceive your lordship has forgot me; you will know me better, when I acquaint you who I am. My father had the honour of being a retainer to your lordship's father, of honourable memory; and sent me some years since to the

East Indies, in the service of your noble uncle,
Mr Rich. My name is Waytewel.

Bell. Oh! Mr Waytewel, I am glad to see you.
Truly you are so chang'd, if you had not told me
who you was I shou'd never ha' known you.

Man. I believe so, my lord—for I'm sure you
never saw my face before, but the picture of it you
have—for Waytewel was my picture. (*Aside.*)
Time and travels will alter a man, but truly I
have lost nothing by my travels but my countenance ; and in the room have gotten what's better,
a convenient small competency of some seven or
eight thousand pound ; Heaven and your uncle's
love be prais'd. I have brought your lordship
some letters from your noble uncle, and a small
present of some threescore thousand pound.

Bell. How?

Man. Only the trouble of it, my lord. Your
uncle contracted in th' Indies an intimate friendship with Sir Nicholas Calico, President for the
East India Company. Sir Nicholas died, and left
most part of his estate, which was near a hundred
thousand pound, to his only son, Sir Thomas. But
poor Sir Thomas happen'd in his father's lifetime
to fall into a distemper, which gave him a scurvy
flaw in his brain, that Sir Nicholas left him and
all his estate to your uncle's guardianship. Now,
your noble uncle, perceiving his affairs are like to
detain him many years in th' Indies, and, fearing
if he shou'd die, poor Sir Thomas might be cheated
of all, he has, like a worthy and honest gentleman,
sent Sir Thomas and all his estate to your lordship's care, as these letters will testify. I suppose
your lordship is well acquainted with your uncle's
hand and seal?

Bell. I am, and this is his hand and seal. (*Reads*)
—um! um! um! to preserve him from being

cheated here, or beg'd in England, I take the
boldness to recommend him to the care of so
noble a person as your lordship—um ! um ! um !—
Well, sir, the letter expresses what you told me.
Where is the gentleman ?

Man. I brought him along with me; he's in the
next room, my lord. Poor gentleman, he has the
oddest phrases and ways with him. He will needs
be attended like a great Indian mandarine or lord,
and has brought with him several Siamites and
Bantammers that serve him as his slaves, in the
ridiculous dresses and modes of their own countries : we had such a gaping rabble after us as
we came along.

Bell. Pray call him in ! I long to see him.

Man. Sir Thomas, pray come to my lord.

Enter CRACK *ridiculously drest, attended by men in
the habits of Siamites and Bantammers.*

Cr. Which is the Peer ?

Man. This is my lord.

Cr. Great Peer, your extreme humble servant !

Bell. Your servant, sir; you are recommended
to me by my uncle.

Cr. I know it, my lord, and am most incom-
parably oblig'd to him. He is a person, my lord,
that as to the altitudes of friendship, and the most
glorious circumstances of a singular person, is not
to be cast up by the logarithms of oratory, nor
his latitude to be taken by the quadrangle of cir-
cumlocution.

Bell. So—I find I shall ha' store o' nonsense.

Cr. My lord, I'm a person that as to the circumstances of money am not indifferently contempt-
ible ; and, as to the circumstances of honour, I am
by profession a merchant, by generation a Knight.
Sir Nicholas Calico, applying his person to my

mother, was the author of, sir, your humble servant.

Bell. So the letter says.

Cr. The letter contains verity.

Bell. Pox, I shall be teaz'd.

Cr. One thing more, sir. I am a person that as to understanding am under the circumstances of witchcraft. I lov'd in th' Indies a fair Christian curiosity, and a nauseous Indian baggage had a mind to apply to my person her tawny circumstances, and, I finding she could not obtain her ambition, applies herself to an Indian bawd, and bewitches me.

Bell. Pshaw! Bewitch'd! What stuff's here?
                                    [*Aside.*

Cr. Bewitches me, sir! what follow's thereupon? a loathing in me of females. I abhor women; fall into agonies when I see women. Pray let me see no women.

Bell. You shall not, sir.

Cr. Pray, my lord, no women.

Bell. I'll warrant you, sir.

Cr. But as much supper as you please, my lord.

Bell. You shall, sir.

Cr. You are highly civiliz'd.

Man. I told your honour he had such odd ways. Well, my lord, as soon as the ship is come up the river, which will be in few days, I'll bring the captain to wait upon your lordship, with the account of Sir Thomas his estate aboard, which will amount to forty thousand pound, besides ten thousand pound he has brought ashore in rough diamonds. So, my lord, your very humble servant! Sir Thomas, your servant! I leave you in good hands.

Cr. Your servant, sir!

Bell. I'll order things for you. I must dispose

this man quickly, for I'm horribly weary of him, and also impatient to go about my affairs.

Leo. 'Tis he ! I'm sure, 'tis he.   [*Leo. peeps.*

Bell. How now, sister ? What's your business here ?

Leo. Staring at this strange sort o' man.

Bell. You were no woman else.   Pray get from him speedily.

Leo. You are not jealous of a madman, sure ? He's mad, is he not ?

Bell. Yes, and impertinently brings me vexation too from the Indies, at a time when I've enough at home, as every man has that keeps a woman. Pray get from him—he hates to see women. [*Exit.*

Leo. Hates to see women ? ha ! ha !   Sir Thomas Calico, your humble servant ! you are welcome from the Indies ; but have a care of being discover'd, lest you be under the circumstances of a cudgel.

Cr. Truly, madam, I expect to have something stick by my ribs presently ; that is to say, a good supper, which I have order'd.   My lord and I will sup together, and you and Mr Farewel.

Leo. We sup together ? where ? in the grave ? A fatal accident has hap'ned will bring us both thither.   My brother has found Mr Farewel's picture in my chamber.

Cr. He shall not keep it.   He shall deliver both picture and jealousy.

Leo. Then thou art a master.   I told him my woman found it in Westminster Abbey.   Maybe thou may'st make something out o' that ?

Cr. Stay, let me consider—Westminster Abbey, or the Abbey of Westminster—um—um.   Let me alone—be gone ! he comes !   [*Exit Leo.*

Enter BELLGUARD.

Bell. Come, sir, let me wait on you to your chamber.

Cr. Hold, my lord, a word. I have business of great consequence. I must humbly apply to your understanding.

Bell. So, I must be hind'red with more non-sense?   *[Aside.*

Cr. I've in the Indies a delicate piece of my father's rib. I beg your lordship to advise me in the disposal.

Bell. Oh! dispose it how you please, sir.

Cr. 'Tis a sister I mean, sir.

Bell. Oh! that's something.

Cr. She's sweet and slender as a clove, and is worth two millions o' coxcombs. Three hundred of 'em comes to three farthings; 'tis a Chinese money. This money makes her much sought in marriage. The great hobbommoccoes o' the Indies come gallopping upon elephants, camels, rhinoceroses, and oxen to see her. Now, my father was under the circumstances of great obligation to a gentleman in England, and, out o' gratitude to him, ordered me, on his death-bed, to bestow my sister on his son and heir, if his actions have any sort o' simile in 'em to his incompatible father, which is the query. Pray, resolve it!

Bell. First, let me know the gentleman.

Cr. You shall. I'll give you a map of his face —a picture contain'd in my pocket—ha!—I ha' lost it! I ha' lost it!

Bell. Tell me his name, sir.

Cr. I ha' dropt it out o' my pocket.

Bell. Ay,—but his name.

Cr. I ha' dropt it out o' my pocket.

Bell. Ha' you dropt his name out o' your pocket? His name, sir!

Cr. Oh! his name?—I'll tell you both his name and cogname. His name is Andrew, his cogname Farewel.

Bell. Farewel ?—what comes into my head ?
Sir, can you guess where you might lose this
picture ?

Cr. A guess may be obtain'd—by the prayers of
mariners.

Bell. No other way ? Those I seldom hear of.

Cr. I was drawn down—stay, let me see—remembrance begins to be idle—has London no
place in the west ?

Bell. Ay, no doubt.

Cr. Ay, but something very west ? something
call'd West ?

Bell. Yes !—there's West Smithfield.

Cr. That's not th' appellative. Is there no
monster in the west called Westmonster ?

Bell. Westminster, I believe, you mean.

Cr. Y'ave nick'd it. To Westminster I rode, to
behold the glorious circumstances o' the dead ; and
diving into my pocket, to present the representer
with a gratification, I am fully confirm'd I then
lost it ; for my eyes and the picture had never any
rencounter since.

Bell. This exactly agrees with my sister's story.
What a prodigious thing is this ? a discovery o' my
sister's innocence sent to me from th' Indies, in a
heap o' nonsense ! and in so critical a minute ;
excellent Providence !

Cr. What's an excellent Providence, sir ? that I
ha' lost my picture ?

Bell. No sir, that I ha' found your picture.

Cr. Found my picture ?

Bell. Ay, sir, 'twas found by a friend o' mine, in
Westminster Abbey. There it is.——

Cr. O ! my picture ! my picture ! my picture !

Bell. O my eased heart.

Cr. O my picture ! my picture ! my pretty picture !

My Lord, I must requite this favour. Open that
casket, and give my lord a handful of diamonds.

Bell. A handful o' diamonds?

Cr. Ay, my lord, I beg your pardon for the inconsiderableness o' the present.

Bell. Inconsiderableness? What a market wou'd
some make o' this man!—Put up your diamonds.

Cr. By no means, my lord.

Bell. Put 'em up, sir, or you'll disoblige me.

Cr. You overwhelm me with favours. I wish I
had you at my house in Bantam.

Bell. I thank you, sir; we are better where we
are.

Cr. My lord, you put me under the circumstance o' blushing.

Bell. Pray let me put you into a chamber to
rest your self.

Cr. Rest is good——yours humbly!—

Bell. Yours as humbly!—What a fire did I
kindle in my house, to clear the air of a pestilence
was not in it! My sister and all my family are
innocent, but what a fantastic thing is women's
honour!

Whil'st she enjoys it, 'tis not seen or known,
And yet when lost she's utterly undone.

[*Exeunt omnes.*

ACT IV.

The Scene continues. Enter VIOLANTE *and* LEONORA,
laughing.

Vio. Ha! ha! ha! what an excellent fellow is
this! What engines he has in his head, not only
to wind himself into my lord's house, but the picture out of his hands!

Leo. He undertakes to bring Mr Farewel hither

to-night.   If he engag'd to bring him in a church
with a parson to marry us, I wou'd not doubt it.

Vio. Certainly my lord must be in a most mortified humour. Now is the time to scarify him, and
take out his worm.

Leo.. Here he comes ! Now will I carry myself
with all the insolence of a virtuous woman.

Enter LORD BELLGUARD.

So, my lord! have your slaves been gathering any
more scatter'd smiles o' mine ? What loads o' that
gold sand have your asses brought home ?

Bell. They have heard all. Now I'm asham'd to
shew my face.   [*Aside.*

Vio. Come, my lord, wou'd you confine a woman
of honour ? give her liberty. Would you corrupt
her ? confine her.

Leo. 'Tis true ! were I a wife to such a man I
should abuse him out o' pride, and think myself
not an ill but a great woman, since to punish is a
mark of Princely dignity.

Bell. This, I confess, is the English dialect ; and
when I talk of governing women, I talk of a thing
not understood by our nation. I admire how it
came about that we, who are of all nations the
most wise and free in other respects, shou'd be the
only slaves and fools to women.

Vio. Oh ! you are the wisest of all nations : you
know, let men do what they can, women will do
what they please ; and whereas other nations, by
their spies and governantes, are at great toil and
charges to be cuckolds, you have it for nothing.

Leo. Come, brother, do not dress me in a fool's
coat, nor hang spies about me, like so many gingling
bells, to give notice of all my motions. I can
count, and know that one and one, put shamefully
together, are two lewd fools, and not one happy

pair, as ill women reckon, and deceive themselves.

Bell. Sister, I believe you virtuous, but I wou'd have you not only be virtuous, but thought so. And truly a woman may be virtuous, but is seldom wise in men's company. Her vain honour will put her on new conquests, and women's conquests are pretty things ; they often end like those of highwaymen in a shameful execution on their own persons. And yet all the business of their lives is mustering up forces. To-day the beauty lyes ambush'd in undresses, the hair pin'd up in papers, like serpents coil'd to fly on you with greater force : the garments are loose and flowing as the sea, to shew a Venus is there. To-morrow she's as regularly fortified as a low-country town, and oft a party of charming looks are sent abroad to put all spectators under a contribution.

Vio. Your wife must not dress ?

Bell. Why should she ? I think women's points and embroideries but so many billet-doux in needle-work.

Vio. She must not go abroad or see a play ?

Bell. Yes, she may go to plays, provided she'll see plays and not fools ; it may be, enter into conversation with 'em, and instead of getting wit from the plays get folly from the fops ; and so her wit being spoil'd in her youth, and, like a clock set wrong in the morning, go false all the day after. In short, no wife or sister of mine shall dabble in conversation with any man ; I hate a slattern in her credit.

Enter SURLY, *peeping.*

Sur. I' my conscience I think I hear Bellguard and his mistress quarrel in good earnest. [*Aside.*

Vio. Let no woman marry a man o' your humour

but she that, for her crimes, is condemn'd to transportation.   The slave that in Virginia toils to
plant her lord tobacco is not more miserable than
she that in your bosom labours to plant a good
opinion; both drudge for smoke.   I scorn the
slavery, nor will marry a King to encrease his
dominions, but to share 'em.

Bell. I offer you the entire dominion o' myself;
only desire you not to aim at further conquests.

Vio. I shou'd be a fine Sovereign where jealousy,
pride, rage, and such a saucy committee shall give
me laws ; which they wou'd never do to a Prince
they lov'd.

Bell. I think I've given convincing proofs of
love.

Vio. When ?

Bell. When I offer'd, madam, to take you for
better and for worse ; those are heroical compliments.   The form of matrimony outdoes Ovid for
passionate expressions.

Vio. Ay, my lord, but that's none o' your wit,
and I wou'd not have a man o' your parts steal
other men's phrases ; so your lordship's humble
servant !—Come away, child ! [*Exeunt Vio. and Leo.*

Enter SURLY.

Sur. Rare ! they're parted ; once a woman spoke
truth.   My lord, your servant.   I've overheard your
quarrel, and I honour you, you are the only man
in the nation that understands himself.   Lock up
the women till they're musty ! better they shou'd
have a hogo than their reputations.   And their
honours are not, like their smocks, whitened by
lying abroad.

Bell. Nor have their ador'd faces the more esteem
for often appearing.

Sur. Pox on 'em, they varnish like copper, and

the women are sensible of it; that's the reason
they forge new faces every time they go abroad;
and all the arts of paint and dress are suborn'd to
give a bastard beauty title to reign, because the
legitimate face is fallen into contempt by familiarity.   No more to be said; keep your ground
like a man of honour, and lose your mistress
like a coxcomb.   (*Aside*.)   [*Exit*.

Enter a SERVANT.

Ser. An't please your honour, Mr Hothead and
Mr Testimony are return'd, as your honour gave
orders.

Enter TESTIMONY.

Bell. That's well! Come, Mr Testimony, here
has been a mistake gave me a harsh opinion of
you.   I'm sorry for't.
Test. Oh! my lord, have a care of censuring
Professors! for a Professor——
Bell. Nay, prithee, don't profess too much.   I
am satisfied with thee.
Test. Truly you would, if you knew what a
tender spirit I am of.   I was only deluded the
other day into a play-house, and truly it will be a
burden to my spirit whilst I live.
Bell. A lack a day! well I hope you'll be the more
tender of my sister; your trouble will not be long.
I have engag'd her to a gentleman, whom about
this time I expect.   What a clock is it?
Test. Truly I do believe it is about four, I cannot
say it positively; for I would not tell a lie for the
whole world.   [*Exit*.
Bell. This is an excellent fellow, if he be what
he pretends.   [*Knocking*.
Hark, some one at the door! maybe 'tis he—see!

Enter HOTHEAD.

Hot. Did you send for me, my lord?

Bell. Ay, cousin, to reconcile myself to thee. I was in a mistake.

Hot. I think you was, when you judged a rascally fanatick a better man than I.

Bell. The contrary, cousin.—I think thee so much the better man, I keep thee to have an eye over him, because I don't know if he be a knave.

Hot. Not know if a fanatick be a knave? You're fit to sit in the House o' Peers, i' faith.

Bell. Well, thou art a very honest fellow, cousin —·let me have thy company. But what are those patches on thy face? for ornament?

Hot. They are for plaisters, but they are ornaments. I have been in a fanatick coffee-house, and this is the beauty they gave me.

Bell. 'Twas to reward some honourable names thou gav'st 'em.

Hot. I gave 'em no wrong names. I call'd 'em rogues indeed, but that's their proper name; and they all set their hands to it immediately, and subscrib'd themselves rogues upon my chops,—the only true narrative they ever writ.

Bell. Thou art a mad fellow! prithee, go in!

[*Exit Hot at one door.*

Enter at another TESTIMONY.

Bell. Well—who's at the door?

Test. A lamentable soul.

Bell. A beggar?

Test. A more sad object; but I conceive he comes rather to rob than beg, for he comes arm'd with a strong bow and arrows.

Bell. A bow and arrows? what, is he a Tartar?

Test. A bow and arrows made of ribbons, laces,

and other idle vanities, wherewith he intends to wound your sister's heart.

Bell. Oh! the canting coxcomb.

Test. Nay, why canting coxcomb?

Bell. Begone, you senseless ass! and bring in the gentleman.

Test. Nay, why senseless ass? this is unseemly.

Bell. He won't stir.

Test. I am no senseless person—I ha' more senses than yourself; I have a sense o' vanity, and of the nothingness o' the things o' this world—and a sense o' sin, and a sense o' the insinuating nature o' sin—I dare not bring this wanton frothy young man to your sister—for she is frothy also—and sin will get in at a little cranny——and if sin once get in his head, he'll get in all his whole body. Now your honour has not that sense o' these things you ought to have. That your honour is a senseless person ——

Bell. How, sirrah?

Test. In a spiritual sense.—

Bell. There's no getting this preaching fellow away.—Cousin Hothead!

Enter HOTHEAD.

Hot. My Lord!

Bell. Why do you let this canting coxcomb plague me?

Hot. Why do you keep such a canting coxcomb? let him plague you, pox you, and damn you, I don't care.

Test. Oh! sad! oh! sad!

Hot. Oh! shad! oh! sot!

Bell. So, now I've brought 'em both upon me.

Hot. He's always tuning his nose, too high, too low, like a sowgelder's horn.

Bell. Well, sir, if you please, tell me who's at my door ?

Hot. Forty One is coming in ding dong.

Bell. Into my door ? who's at my door, I say ?

Hot. Old Forty One, i'faith.

Bell. I cannot have an answer ? Sirrah ! who's at my door ?

Test. Popery, I'm sure is coming in.

Bell. Into my door? I ask you, who's at my door ?

Test. Popery, I'm sure.

Hot. Roguery, I'm sure.

Test. Popery, I'm sure.

Hot. Roguery, I'm sure.

Bell. Confound you both !

Hot. And confound you both !

[Bell turns them both out.

Bell. You boy, is there any one at door?

[To a Page.

Pa. Yes, my lord !

Bell. So, this boy can answer. Who is it ?

Pa. Sir Courtly Nice, my lord.

Bell. Oh ! these rogues, have they made him wait all this while ? Introduce him quickly. He comes most seasonably to rid me of my plague, now I'm very sick of it.

Enter Sir COURTLY NICE *and the* PAGE, *bowing to one another.*

Dear Sir Courtly, my servants did not tell me who you were, that I have ignorantly made you wait. I am asham'd to see you.

Sir Co. Your lordship's most humble servant.

Bell. Your very humble servant ! Page, call my sister !

Enter AUNT *and* LEONORA.

Sir Co. Madam, your most—

[Goes to salute Leo., Aunt steps first.

Au. Sir Courtly, your very humble servant.

Sir Co. Oh! your ladyship's **very** humble servant—   [*Salutes Aunt.*

Au. Your most humble servant.

Sir Co. Now, madam, your most humble servant.   [*To Leo.*

Au. An incomparable fine gentleman !

Bell. Well, Sir Courtly, now I've brought you thus far o' your way to my sister's inclinations, I'll leave you to pursue the rest o' your journey by yourself; you need no guide to ladies' hearts.

Sir Co. Oh! your most humble servant.

Au. No, Sir Courtly commands all. If my niece does not receive you, Sir Courtly, in all the obliging manner in the world, 'tis for want of experience and understanding merit. I'll assure you, Sir Courtly, I, who have some little more judgment, have had a very particular value for you, sir, from the first minute I had the honour to see you, sir.

Sir Co. Oh! madam, your most humble servant.

Au. A very particular———

Sir Co. Oh! your most humble servant.

Au. And if my niece has not, it proceeds from her want of years to know desert. And indeed all youth is indiscreet ; I would by no means advise a gentleman of merit to marry any person that has not some years and experience upon her.

Bell. She's setting up for herself, I think. Aunt !

Au. Nephew !—

Bell. Pray leave the lovers together.

An. Sir Courtly, your most humble servant.

Sir Co. Madam, your most humble servant.

Au. Pray, niece, behave yourself so to Sir Courtly, as at least to do me right ; and, by all your expressions and behaviour, he may know how very particular an honour I have for him.

Bell. She has for him?   [*Aside.*

Au. Most particular.

Bell. Pray, Aunt in particular—come with me !

Au. Very particular.

Sir Co. Oh ! Madam—Madam—

Bell. Aunt !

Au. Yes, Nephew ! Sir Courtly, I am exceeding unwilling to leave you to the conversation of a young lady, whose years I'm afraid will not afford her wit enough to entertain so fine a gentleman.

Sir Co. Oh ! Madam ! Madam ! Madam !

Au. But I'll return with all speed possible.

Bell. But you shall not, if I can help it. [*Aside.*

Au. And so, your very humble servant.

Sir Co. Oh ! madam ! your most humble servant.
                    [*Exeunt Aunt and Bell.*

Leo. Now, will I manage him, humour him, pretend to admire him, to draw him into love ; laugh at him and revenge my self on him, for plaguing me.   [*Aside.*

Sir Co. Now, madam, is the glorious opportunity come which my soul has long wish'd to express how much I admire, adore—

Leo. Oh ! Sir Courtly——

Sir Co. Extravagantly adore !

Leo. Oh ! Sir Courtly, I cannot receive all this.

Sir Co. Oh ! madam, is there anything on the earth so charming ?   I never saw anything so fine as your ladyship, since I was born.

Leo. Fie, Sir Courtly !

Sir Co. Never since I was born.

Leo. You'll kill me with blushing.

Sir Co. I speak my soul.   Heavens ! what divine teeth there are.

Leo. Fie ! fie ! I shall never open my mouth more.

Sir Co. Then you'll undo all the world.   Oh ! there's nothing so charming as admirable teeth.

If a lady fastens upon my heart it must be with }
her teeth.

Leo. That's a pleasant raillery—ha ! ha ! ha !

[Feigns a foolish laugh.

Sir Co. Oh ! madam, I hope your ladyship has a
better opinion o' my good manners. Railly, a lady
o' your quality?

Leo. Oh, you wits turn all things into ridicule.

Sir Co. Madam, I never was so serious since I
was born ; therefore, I beseech your ladyship have
pity upon me.   I swear and vow if you do not, I
shall die.

Leo. Die ! ha ! ha ! you Wits will be raillying.

Sir Co. Heavens, madam ! how shall I convince
you I am serious ?

Leo. Really, Sir Courtly, I should be very sorry
if you be serious.

Sir Co. Oh ! heavens ! why so, Madam ?

Leo. Because 'tis pity so fine a gentleman shou'd
lose all his gallantry.

Sir Co. Now you frighten me, madam.   Is it
impossible for me to attain the glory of your inclinations ?

Leo. It will be impossible for me to keep the
glory of your inclinations, Sir Courtly ; so I dare
not venture on 'em.

Sir Co. Oh ! as to that, madam, I'll swear eternal
constancy, eternal services, and all those things.

Leo. You are not in your own power, Sir Courtly.
You fine gentlemen, like fine countries, are desir'd
and sought by all, and therefore in a perpetual
war.   If I should place my heart in you, it would
not have a minute's quiet.   A thousand potent
beauties would every day assault you, and you'd
yield out o' complaisance ; your good breeding
wou'd undo me.

Sir Co. Oh ! madam, this is extremity o' gallan-

try; your ladyship pushes things to a strange
height.

Leo. I speak my soul. Besides I've another
humour, but that's a *foiblesse* will ridicule me.

Sir Co. Oh! madam.

Leo. Nay, I'll confess it. I am strangely curious—extravagantly curious—I nauseate a perfume,
if it ever salute any nose but my one.

Sir Co. Oh! fortunate! my own humour.

Leo. Nothing must come near me, that was ever
once touch'd by another.

Sir Co. Is it possible?

Leo. Not if you'd give a hundred pound.

Sir Co. My own phrase too! I've observed it myself, I'm strangely fortunate; we shall be fond to
an infinite degree.   [*Aside.*

Leo. For that reason, your fine gentleman is my
aversion; he's so tempted by all ladies, so complaisant to all ladies, that to marry a fine gentleman is
to accept the leavings of a thousand ladies.

Sir Co. Oh! madam! you ha' met with the creature you desire. I never touch'd woman since I
was born.

Leo. That's pleasant! I believe you have ruin'd
a thousand.

Sir Co. Not one, upon my soul.

Leo. 'Tis impossible.

Sir Co. Oh, madam! there's not one lady in a
thousand I can salute. I can only touch the tip o'
their ear with my cheek.

Leo. Fie! fie!

Sir Co. Not one lady in a million, whose breath
I can endure. But I cou'd not go into their beds
if you'd give me a thousand pound. I could not
come into the air of any bed in England but my
own, or your ladyship's, if you'd give me all the
world.

Leo. This is all gallantry, Sir Courtly. You have been told this is my humour.

Sir Co. Is it really, madam?

Leo. Oh, above all things. I suffer nothing to come near my bed, but my gentlewoman.

Sir Co. Nor I, but my gentleman. He has a delicate hand at making a bed; he was my Page, I bred him up to it.

Leo. To making beds?

Sir Co. Ay, madam, and I believe, he'll make a bed with any gentleman in England.

Leo. And my woman has a great talent.

Sir Co. Is it possible? Ladies commonly employ ordinary chamber-maids, with filthy aprons on, made by sluttish women that spit as they—spin— foh!

Leo. Foh!

Sir Co. Your ladyship will pardon me—my linen is all made in Holland, by neat women that dip their fingers in rose-water, at my charge.

Leo. Delicate!

Sir Co. And all washed there.

Leo. And so is mine at Hearlem?

Sir Co. At Hearlem? I hold a constant correspondence with all the eminent washers there.

Leo. That's delicate! and agrees wonderfully with my humour.

Sir Co. Oh! happy! we shall be fond to an infinite degree.

Enter SURLY.

Leo. Oh! foh! here's that beastly rude clown, Mr Surly.

Sir Co. Oh! foh! what shall we do with him?

Sur. How now? how now? you two are intimate! Heark you, madam.

Leo. Oh! foh!

Sir Co. Foh!

Sur. Foh! what's this fohing at?

Sir Co. Nobody, Mr Surly; only at present we are accosted with an ungrateful smell.

Sur. Yes, I smell an ungrateful smell; your roguery. Madam, I employed this fellow to speak for me, and I'll be hang'd if he be not false to me.

Leo. To speak for him? ha! ha!

Sir Co. Ay, for him, madam? ha! ha!

Sur. Ay, for me, Nickumpoop.

Sir Co. Your humble servant, sir, y'are very civil.

Sur. So I am, that I do not execute thee for this theft upon the place; but thou plead'st thy face, as whores do their bellies; 'tis big with fool.

Sir Co. Very civil——sir!

Sur. Sure, madam, a woman o' your sense will not chuse him before me? He has more land; not more improv'd land. His acres run up to one great weed, I mean himself; and there it blossoms in periwigs and ribbons. Oh! but he has a finer person—that's a cheat; a false creed imposed on you, by a general council of tailors, milliners, and semstresses. Let my hat expound his face, and you'll see what a piece o' simple stuff it is.

Sir Co. Horrid! he has put his beastly hat upon my head. Pray, sir, do me the favour to remove it, or I shall grow very sick——   [*To a Ser.*

Sur. Sick? I hope thou wilt eat my hat. Now, madam, you see what a cheat he is, and whether he deserves any more favours than to be decently hang'd with the rest of his brothers.

Sir Co. My brothers hang'd, Mr Surly?

Sur. I mean the pictures in the hangings, for they and thou are all but needlework; and thou would'st serve for a piece o' tapestry; but for a husband, Lord ha' mercy on thee.

Sir Co. Your servant, Mr Surly. You are a very well bred gentleman, sir, and pay great veneration to a lady o' quality, and your mistress——ha ! ha !

Leo. His mistress ? ha ! ha !

Sir Co. Let's rally him to death, madam——ha ! ha !——

Sur. Rally ? does the ridiculous figure pretend to laugh at anything ?

Sir Co. De'e hear, madam ?

Leo. Sir Courtly, you are a martyr to good manners, and suffer out o' respect to me, more than is fit for a man to bear.

Sur. He a man ? I ha' seen a butler make a better thing out of a diaper napkin.

Sir Co. Your most obliged humble servant——sir !

Leo. Sir Courtly, I'll withdraw, that you may do yourself justice——and be kick'd—— [*Aside.*

Sir Co. Your ladyship's most humble servant.

Leo. I'll no longer protect such a coxcomb——as yourself. [*Aside.*

Sir Co. Your very humble servant, madam ! I'll push his soul out presently.

Leo. Oh ! don't do him that favour, sir ; only correct him.

Sir Co. Well, madam, what your ladyship pleases. Your ladyship's very humble servant.

[*Exit Leo.*

Mr Surly, I have receiv'd some favours from you, sir, and I desire the honour of your company, sir, to-morrow morning at Barn-Elms, sir,——please to name your weapon, sir.

Sur. A squirt.

Sir Co. A squirt ?

Sur. Ay, for that will go to thy heart, I'm sure.

Sir Co. Well, sir, I shall kiss your hands.

Sur. Kiss my breech !   [*Exit.*

Sir Co. Beast, clown, fool, rascal ! Pox take
him ! what shall I do with him ? It goes against
my stomach horribly to fight such a beast. If his
filthy sword shou'd touch me, 'twoud make me as
sick as a dog.   [*Exit.*

Scene, a GARDEN.

Enter CRACK and LEONORA.

Leo. Ha ! ha ! I'll secure the coxcomb——I'll
get him confin'd upon the guard, among tobacco
takers, and that will confine him to his bed and
bagnios for one month.

Cr. That will do rarely. About this time I expect Mr Farewel. I ha' sent for your brother to introduce him.

Leo. My brother ?

Cr. Your brother I say, to shew my skill. Retire, and stay conceal'd in the garden. Here your
brother comes !   [*Exit Leo.*

Enter BELLGUARD.

Now for lies and nonsense to entertain this
jealous brother till the lover comes.

Bell. Sir Thomas, your servant, what's your will
with me ?

Cr. Talk——I love talk ——begin.

Bell. Very pithy.

Cr. In what circumstance are we ?

Bell. Circumstance ?

Cr. Ay, what call you this, where we are ?

Bell. A garden.

Cr. A garden ? I have seen in the Indies a
melon as big.

Bell. As all this garden ?

Cr. Bigger.

Bell. Well lied of a madman. (*Aside.*) Are all your fruit so large ?

Cr. All !

Bell. Your nutmegs and pepper are not.

Cr. Your history is erroneous. We have nutmegs as big as small fly-boats. I have sail'd a hundred leagues in a nutmeg.

Bell. Well lied. [*Aside.*

Cr. Our oysters have wonderful conference.

Bell. Circumference, I suppose you mean.

Cr. Y'ave nick'd it. Three of 'em block up a harbour. 'Tis our way of mortification.

Bell. Fortification.

Cr. You are in the right——Pox on't, I have been so long abroad, I have almost forgot my mother-tongue.

Well——when will this lover come ? 'tis near the hour, and delicately dark. [*Aside.*

Farewel (*within*). Murder ! murder ! murder !

[*Clashing of swords.*

Cr. That's he ! he's come ! (*Aside.*) Murder cry'd out ?

Bell. And at my coach-house door ?

Farewel (*within*). Oh ! cowardly rogues ! four upon one ?

Bell. A gentleman assassinated ?

Cr. Open the door !

Bell. Who's there ?

Enter a SERVANT.

Ser. My lord ?

Bell. Call some o' the servants to assist a gentleman, set upon at my coach-house door.

Cr. Ay——quick——quick ! [*Draws.*

Bell. How, Sir Thomas ? will you venture among 'em ?

Cr. De'e think I wont ? a gentleman and not
fight ?

Bell. I must not suffer it, you may be hurt.

Cr. No, sir, I'll fight like a gentleman ; I'll come
by no hurt, I'll warrant you.——Come quick—
quick——open the door !

Enter SERVANTS.

Now sound a trumpet, tivy—tivy—tan tan—
tivy—tone,—pox on't 'tis a horn——I don't know
a horn, I ha' forgot, everything belongs to a gentleman. Among 'em, helter skelter !

> [*Exeunt Bel., Cr., and Ser., meanwhile
> Farewel steals into the Garden.*

Enter LEONORA and her Woman.

Leo. I' my conscience this is Crack's design to
let in Mr Farewel.

Fa. Dear madam, you are in the right.

Leo. Mr Farewel ? I know your voice——

Fa. Oh ! madam, I adore you for this bounty.

Leo. And I shou'd blush for it.

Fa. Why so, madam ?

Leo. Shou'd a woman admit a lover by night at
a back door into the same house where she lyes,
and converse privately with him before marriage ?

Fa. Your brother admitted me.

Leo. 'Tis true, indeed, you may thank him for
the favour. I thought your sufferings deserved
pity, and my brother wou'd let me shew it no
other way.

Fa. A thousand blessings on you !

Leo. I doubt not but my honour is very safe in
your keeping ; I wish your person were as secure
in mine.

Fa. I am glad o' the danger, since 'tis some
assurance o' my love.

Leo. Your friend, Mr Crack, plays his part very well, and I doubt not but he will secure us here, and convey us hence, but then other dangers will follow you.

Fa. What are those, madam ?

Leo. The danger of marrying without a fortune. My ten thousand pound is at my brother's dispose.

Fa. I am glad o' that too, madam ; 'twill shew my love is not mercenary.

Leo. The danger of being laughed at by the Wits, for marrying at all.

Fa. Oh ! let the Wits keep the jilting rotten wenches, and leave the sweet virtuous ladies to us marrying fools. I can be as well pleas'd to keep a fine wife to myself, as they can be to maintain fine wenches for all the town.

Leo. Nay, your keeping men, keepers like, have commonly but the offals for their slave. Well, the evening air will be unwholesome to you ; if you stay longer in it, you'll be in danger of thunder and lightning presently ; I mean my brother—— he comes——follow me ! [*Exeunt Leo., Fa., Woman.*

Enter BELLGUARD, CRACK, &c.

Cr. What cowardly rogues were these ? they ran upon our first sallying.

Bell. They had a reason ; you're a lion.

Cr. I us'd to kill lions and tigers in the Indies, as you do hares and conies here. I kept a tiger warren, I kill'd a brace every morning to get me a stomach.

Bell. It was a good one sure, you offer'd dear for it. Well I hope you ha' got no hurt ?

Cr. Yes, something very sharp went quite through my stomach.

Bell. How ? through your stomach ? then you cannot live.

Cr. Yes, if you 'noint it presently with a good dish o' jelly-broth, and tent it with a bone o' roast beef.

Bell. Is that the wound? it shall be heal'd presently.

Cr. Presently, for my stomach is captious.

Bell. It shall be done. Go to my aunt and desire her to order Sir Thomas his supper——

Ser. She's not very well, my lord, and gone to bed.

Bell. Then let the Steward do it. Sir Thomas, I am going out and shall stay late. Pray command my house——good night to you !   [*Exit.*

Cr. Your servant, sir——you keep a woman? ——now to the lovers——where are they?

Enter FAREWEL, LEONORA, *and her Woman.*

Fa. Here! here! thou divine fellow.

Cr. So, so : kiss! kiss! kiss!——

Leo. Before marriage?

Cr. Ay, for fear you shou'd not kiss after marriage. Well the house is our own, and the night our own——your aunt gone to bed, and your brother abroad, we'll tory-rory, and 'tis——a fine night, we'll revel in the garden——Slaves go bring my supper——quick——quick !

> [*Ex. Slaves—and enter with Dishes. Farewel, Leo, and Crack sit down.*

Enter SIAMITES *and* BANTAMMERS.

Now a song and dance o' your own fashion—— but shut the garden gates——and look to 'em well, for I'll be private in my pleasures.

> [*A Song and Indian dance.**

* The song which now follows, like that in the third Act, is printed at the end of the play in all former editions.

A Song.

*A Dialogue Sung between an Indian man and woman,
in the Fourth Act, to Farewel, Violante, Crack.
Being an imitation of a Song sung by some Natives
of India before the late King.*

Man. Thou lovely Indian sea of charms,
　　　　I'd envy no jaw-waw alive,
　　　　Might I be so blest to dive
　　In thy soft-yielding arms,
　　With Jimminy, gomminy, whee-whee,
　　　　whee,
　　With a gomminy, jimminy-whee.

Woman. I wou'd if you'd be true,
　　　　But when you've done
　　　　You'll be gone,
　　And throw me off with a shoo-shooh, shooh.
　　　　And a hush pooh,
　　　　And a fush whooh,
　　And a migotty, magotty, migotty, magotty,
　　　　Migotty, magotty, shooh.

Man. No, no, my other females all,
　　　　Yellow, fair, or black,
　　To thy charms shall prostrate fall,
　　　　As every kind of elephant does
　　　　To the white elephant, Buittenacke.
　　And thou alone shall have from me
　　　　Jimminy, gomminy, whee, whee, whee.
　　　　The gomminy jimminy whee.

Woman. The great jaw-waw that rules our land,
　　　　And pearly Indian sea,
　　Has not so absolute command
　　　　As thou hast over me.
　　With a jimminy gomminy, gomminy
　　Jimminy, jimminy gomminy, whee.

Both.   Thou alone shalt have from me
         Jimminy gomminy, gomminy
         Jimminy, jimminy, gomminy,
         Whee, whee, whee, whee, whee, whee.

Cr. So—now to my chamber ! well—there is no
public officer like your pimp.——
Pimps manage the great business o' the nation.
That is——the heavenly work o' propagation.

                              [*Exeunt Omnes.*

ACT. V.

Scene, CRACK'S CHAMBER.

Enter FAREWEL *and* CRACK.

Fa. Oh ! thou divine fellow ! what joys hast thou
procured me ?

Cr. What joys ?

Fa. All that innocence cou'd afford.

Cr. Innocence ? that's insipid stuff.

Fa. No, Mr Crack, there's difference between
the manna that came from Heaven, and that out
of 'pothecaries' shops ; a touch of Leonora's hand,
like manna from Heaven, has all that man can
fancy.   Here she comes !

Enter LEONORA.

This, madam, is bountiful, after an evening's conversation, to afford me a morning too.

Leo. We shou'd be charitable to prisoners.

Fa. I am a prisoner, but such a happy one, as a
King is when lodg'd in a Royal Tower, to prepare
for his Coronation.   My hour of Coronation draws
near, I want only the church ceremony and the oath.

Cr. Madam, how durst you venture hither by
daylight ?

Leo. My aunt and brother are both gone abroad, and won't come home till noon ; so all those hours are mine. And now, Mr Crack, to requite your music I ha' brought some o' mine to entertain you.

A Song—and enter WOMAN.

Wom. Oh ! madam, undone ! your brother——
Cr. How ? how ?
Wom. Just coming up stairs, to visit—you, Sir Thomas.
Cr. Pox of his civility. Hide, sir, Hide ! And do you women shriek !—shriek ! and cry out murder.

[*Cr. throws himself on the ground and scrambles in distracted postures after the Women. They shriek*—

Enter BELLGUARD.

Bell. So, here's my sister got into the madman's room ; and has put him into a frantic fit. Oh ! the insatiable curiosity o' women.

Cr. You whores !—you bewitching whores, do you come to bewitch me ? I'll fetch blood from you.

Bell. Why wou'd you offer to come hither, sister ?

Cr. What are you, sir,—the King of Bantam ?

Bell. No, sir, no.

Cr. Oh ! the Mogul ?

Bell. Nor the Mogul.

Cr. What do you then with all these concubines ? Oh ! I know you now ; you're a fine man ! you have put me into brave circumstances. Did not I desire you to let me see no woman ? and here, you keep a company of rambling whores in your house, that have put me into the circumstances o' distraction. I was a top o' the staircase taking a prospect o' the Cape of Good Hope, and these fly-boats came sailing under my nose. What do me I ? but leap down to break their necks, and ha' broke my own, I think. I am certain, I have broke something,

but what I don't know.   Pray take me up, and
look over my bones, see if none be missing! if they
be, bone for bone will be demanded.

Bell. Poor creature!   Who's there?

Cr. Who's there? will you trust me to your servants? So if a leg or an arm of mine be broke,
they'll leave it behind 'em, and I shall lose it.   I
expect all my limbs and bones from you, as you
received 'em.   So—come and take account of 'em.

Bell. I will—I will!   [*Takes him up.*

Cr. Oh! have a care—Oh!—

Bell. Alas! I fear he's hurt; your foolish curiosity has done this; did you not gape enough
upon him before?

Cr. Oh! gently! gently!—so—so—

                          [*Bell. leads him out.*

Fa. Oh! this pleasant rogue! ha! ha!

Leo. 'Tis an excellent fellow.   As soon as we
hear my brother is returning, slip into that passage!
'twill lead you to Crack's bed-chamber.

Enter AUNT.

Au. How, now, gentlewoman? a man wi' you?
Nephew—nephew—nephew!

Leo. Begone, begone, through that entry!

                [*Exit* FAREWEL *at one door, at another*

Enter BELLGUARD.

Bell. What's the matter?

Au. Our family's dishonour'd, dishonour'd—here
was a fellow, a handsome young fellow, wi' my
niece.   Oh! my flesh! my flesh!

Leo. Wi' me?

Au. Will you deny it, Confidence?

Bell. Who's there? Hothead, Testimony, all of
you, come hither!

Enter HOTHEAD, TESTIMONY.

Test. What's your honour's pleasure ?

Bell. To cut all your throats ! you are all bawds and villains.

Hot. Leave me out o' the number, you had best.

Bell. I will not, sir, for here was a young fellow wi' my sister.

Leo. My Aunt's whimsy and jealousy.

Au. I cou'd tread you under my feet.

Bell. Which way went he ?

Au. Into that passage : he cannot be got further then Sir Thomas Calico's bed-chamber.

Bell. Lock all the doors ! arm and beset Sir Thomas Calico's lodgings.

Leo. This will prove such another wise business as the picture.

Bell. Hold your peace ! get you into that room wi' my Aunt. Aunt, pray look to her.

[*Exeunt Bell., Hot., Test., &c.*

Au. I'll keep her, I warrant her. Come in, gentlewoman ! you are a fine gentlewoman.

Leo. Oh ! my heart trembles—Heaven inspire Crack.   (*Aside.*)   [*Exeunt Aunt and Leonora.*

Scene changes to another room.

Enter FAREWEL *and* CRACK.

Fa. Oh ! cursed fortune.

Cr. Well, don't trouble yourself. I'll bring you off safe.

Fa. Not trouble myself, when Leonora's honour is in danger ? she'll be the jest of every prating fop, and malicious beauty.

Cr. Her honour shall be safe too. This blust'ring —brother shall entertain you.

Fa. With a blunderbuss ?

Cr. Ay, full o' claret. Away, away—he comes !

[*Exit Fa. and*

Enter BELLGUARD, HOTHEAD, TESTIMONY, *and the*
SERVANTS *arm'd.*

Cr. How? the high and glorious Emperor o'
Siam with all his guards? Thou most invincible
Paducco, Farucco, melmocadin, bobbekin, bow,
wow—wow—why dost thou seek to destroy us
English, seated on thy dominions by thy own letters
patent?

Bell. Pish!—take him away.

Cr. Take away our privileges? Then this goes to
my heart.   [*Draws his dagger, and pre-*
                                                       tends to stab himself.

Bell. Hold, hold, Sir Thomas! Sir Thomas, no
hurt is meant to you.

Cr. Most great and glorious Emperor, I humbly
thank, and do humbly implore thee, that thou
would'st command thy invincible guards to lay
down their arms, and put us out of our frights,
and we'll submit our persons to thee. This is some
interloper's work.   [*Aside.*

Bell. Pox o' this impertinent, mad—coxcomb!
Lay down your weapons! May be if we humour
him, he may come to his senses, and give us
leave to search the rooms.
                              [*They lay down their weapons.*

Cr. My Lord Bellguard, your most humble servant!

Bell. He's come to himself; that's well. Sir
Thomas, your servant! how do you?

Cr. A little discomposed; something has frightned
me, and put me into the circumstance of a sweat.

Bell. I'm sorry for that. Shall I beg leave to
search your rooms for a thief that's got in?

Cr. Pardon's beg'd; search must not be made;
for I have a friend there you must not see.

Bell. Wou'd you and your friend were hang'd.
                                              [*Aside.*

Cr. A very honest gentleman, but very much addicted to marriage. 'Tis he that I told you is to marry my Indian Fubs of a sister—Mr Farewel.

Bell. Mr Farewel?

Cr. Ay, hearing of my arrival, and what circumstance I was in, hover'd all this morning about the house to get a sight o' me; but car'd not to come in, for it seems there is enmity between you.

Bell. 'Tis true, and I wonder how he got in without my knowledge.

Cr. I made him come in. I was throwing my legs about in the hall, and, the door being open, our eyes knock'd immediately, and gave remembrance such a bang, that we ran full speed into the circumstances of embracing.

Bell. And pray, who saw this?

Cr. Who saw? what care I who saw? I care not if the whole town saw; I'm not asham'd of owning Mr Farewel.

Bell. No, sir, but I mean which of my family saw? that I may thank 'em for their care.

Cr. What do I care for your family? If I may not bring a friend into your family, a fart for your family.

Bell. Nay, be not angry, Sir Thomas; your friend's welcome.

Cr. I doubt it not, for I have found you a very civil person. And now recollection is active, I fancy he's the man you take for a thief. 'Tis so— ha! ha!—excuse me—ha! ha!—leave is implor'd —ha! ha!—Brother Farewel!

Fa. (*within*) Brother!

Cr. Come out, and participate o' laughter.

Bell. So, now have I play'd the fool again, vex'd

myself, and wrong'd my sister with my impertinent jealousies.

Enter FAREWEL.

Cr. Come, brother—ha! ha! laugh—but first salute.

Fa. My lord, I believe you wonder to see me here, and you may. I call myself bastard, and renounce the blood of my family, by coming under your roof with any design, but to prejudice you, which at present I must acknowledge to my shame is not my intention. I visit my friend here for his own sake, and the sake of a great beauty, which you shall not hinder me of, my lord.

Bell. I will not, Mr Farewell; I scorn those effeminate revenges. If I hurt any man it shall be with my sword.

Fa. Your sword, my lord?

Cr. Hold! hold!

Bell. Ay, any where but here, Mr Farewel; my house is your sanctuary, and here to offer you violence wou'd prejudice myself.

Cr. What, a quarrelling's here? I'my conscience I believe, my lord, 'tis because you think he came to steal me, I being under whimsical circumstances, for I remember you call'd him a thief. Look you, my lord, don't fear me, I wont be stole—I know when I'm well. Brother, I'm very well provided for, I want nothing but my wits; and what do they signify? if a man lives like a gentleman, no matter whether he has wit or no.

Fa. Well, my lord, though I have the misfortune to be your enemy, I am none to good manners; I'm sorry to have given your house this trouble, and the more because my friend receives such generous usage in it.

Bell. Nor am I an enemy to love, and the fair sex. If the lady you come for loves you, for her sake I wish you success.

Fa. Now, my lord, you vanquish me.

Cr. He's a brave man, faith.

Fa. I fancy we shall live to be better friends ; at present I'll take my leave. My Lord, your servant.

Bell. Your servant, sir !

Cr. Brother, I must see you down stairs. This was a masterpiece—ha ! ha ! [*Exeunt Fa. and Cr.*

Bell. Now, I am cool again. What a flame had your negligence put me into ! Here, release my sister, I'm ashamed to see her. [*To a servant.*

Hot. Sirrah ! sirrah ! you did this to make me suspected.

Test. Ay—ay, I must be abus'd, because I'm a Protestant.

Hot. A Protestant ? a dog. But with such names the rogues divide the rabble, and make the nation go like the devil, upon cloven feet.

Bell. Hold your prating, and by your future care make amends for your past negligence. Your trouble shall not be long ; within this eight and forty hours I'll marry her, or send her into the country.

Hot. Well, well, I'll look to her, for the honour of my family, not your huffing. [*Exit.*

Test. I to discharge a conscience. [*Exit.*

Enter LEONORA.

Leo. So, sir ?

Bell. My sister——

Leo. Do you run from me ? is that the reparation you make for the intolerable wrongs you have done me ? [*Pretends to burst into tears.*

Bell. Well, I have wrong'd you ; I'm sorry for it, and beg your pardon. I must be gone about business, your business,—to fetch Sir Courtly Nice. Your servant, sister. [*Exit.*

Leo. Oh! your servant, sir—ha! ha!—he runs. I may chance, sir, to run as nimbly from you, if Crack's wit do not fail him. Here he comes.

Enter CRACK.

Thou admirable fellow, what hast thou done with Mr Farewel?

Cr. He's in the street staying for you.

Leo. Staying for me? and can'st thou convey me to him?

Cr. De'e question it? Put on a vizard and something over your cloaths.

Leo. Sweet rogue.

Cr. Nay, nay, begone!

Leo. Delicate rogue.

Cr. Nay, nay, he stays for you.

Leo. Incomparable rogue.

Cr. Pshaw! put on your vizard.

Leo. Most excellent rogue.

Cr. Oons! put on your vizard.

Leo. I will—I will—ha! ha! toll—loll—derol.

> [*Cr. goes out, and as Leo. is going out singing and dancing, she's met by Bellguard and Sir Courtly.*

Bell. Oh! sister, your tune's alter'd.

Sir Co. Oh, madam! I'm happy to find your ladyship in so gay a humour.

Leo. You'll not find it so. [*Aside.*

Bell. Sir Courtly, I'll betray her to you. I left her in tears upon an unhappy occasion, and at parting told her I wou'd bring you. Now you are come, I find her in joy. Nothing else cou'd cause the change.

Sir Co. Oh! fortunate.

Leo. Oh! fop. [*Aside.*

Bell. Now, improve your interest, and let us see

how great a master you are in courtship, by your dexterous dispatch. I leave you together. [*Exit.*

Sir Co. And upon my soul, I will. Oh, madam! am I so fortunate, so glorious, to be well in your fine inclinations?

Leo. Oh! fie, Sir Courtly—if I had any such guilt upon me, do you think I wou'd confess?

Sir Co. You do confess, madam—your fine eyes, and your languishing air, and your charming blushes, and all those things.

Leo. I hope I carry no such false things about me; for if they say any such thing they infinitely wrong me.

Sir Co. Oh! now you are cruel, madam; you kill me.

Leo. Can you hope for my heart, Sir Courtly, till I've some assurance o' yours?

Sir Co. What assurance wou'd your ladyship have?

Leo. All manner. He that pretends to my heart must sigh, and wait, and watch—and pant—and fight and write—and kill himself.

Sir Co. All this I ha' done, madam, and ten thousand things more. Drove by your windows a thousand times a day, sought you at the parks and the plays—was a constant faithful attendant at all tragedies—for I presum'd your ladyship nauseates comedies.

Leo. Oh! foh!

Sir Co. They are so ill-bred and saucy with quality, and always cram'd with our odious sex, that have not always the most inviting smell— Madam, you'll pardon me. Now, at tragedies the house is all lin'd with beauty, and then a gentleman may endure it. And I have gone, found not your ladyship there, drove home, kill'd myself with sighing, and then writ a song.

Leo. Oh, Heavens! Sir Courtly, did you ever write a song upon me?

Sir Co. Above a thousand.

Leo. Oh! there's nothing charms me like a song. For Heaven's sake—the song!—the song!

Sir Co. I've above forty here in a sweet bag. I'll show you the first I made upon your ladyship. 'Tis thought to be a pretty foolish soft song: most ladies are very kind to it.

> As I gaz'd unaware,
> On a face so fair,—

Leo. Oh! Sir Courtly—

Sir Co.
> Your cruel eye,
> Lay watching by
> To snap my heart,
> Which you did wi' such art,
> That away w'it you ran,
> Whilst I look'd on,
> To my ruin and grief—
> Stop thief!—stop thief!

Leo. Oh, fine! oh, fine!

Sir Co. That stop thief, madam, is pretty novel.

Leo. Oh, delicate! I'm charm'd! I'm lost!—fie, what have I said?

Sir Co. What makes me the happiest of creatures.

Leo. I only railly—I renounce all—

Sir Co. Not for the world—

Leo. Away!—the song again—the song; I'll hear nothing but the song. Is there no tune to it?

Sir Co. One of my own composing.

Leo. That accomplishment too? Heavens! how fine a gentleman is this!

Sir Co. Oh! madam, how proud you make me.

Leo. Oh! dear, how I betray myself! foolish creature—no more, no more—the tune, the tune.

Sir Co. I always humour my words with my air. So I make the voice shake at the last line in imitation of a man that runs after a thief. Sto— ho—ho—hop—thief!   [*Sings.*

Leo. Oh, delicate! cannot I learn it? sto—ho— ho—ha! ha! ha!

[*Imitates his foolish singing, and falls into a laugh.*

Sir Co. Dear madam, what makes your ladyship laugh?

Leo. At a coxcomb that thought to win me with a foolish song : this puts it into my head.

Sir Co. Oh, foolish! there are abundance of those foolish fellows. And does the song please your ladyship?

Leo. Infinitely. I did not think you had been so fine a poet.

Sir Co. Poetry, madam, is my great foible, and when I see a fine woman I cannot command my foible.   ·

Leo. How? De'e make songs upon other ladies? unfortunate—I've given my heart to an inconstant man.

Sir Co. Oh, madam!—only gallantry.

Leo. I'm abus'd—unfortunate! [*Pretends to weep.*

Sir Co. Oh, madam! you take it wrong.

Leo. I'm abus'd.

Sir Co. Oh, Heavens!

Leo. But the song's very fine!—sto—ho—ho— ha! ha!

Sir Co. Pleasant creature!   [*Sings and laughs.*

Leo. Coxcomb!   [*Aside.*

Sir Co. We shall be infinitely fond—a pretty glass this, madam.   [*Looks in a glass.*

Leo. So, he's making an assignation with his own foolish face. I'll leave him to court that and steal away.   [*Exit.*

Sir Co. Sto —ho—ho—hop !

Enter AUNT.

Au. Singing, Sir Courtly ?

Sir Co. At your service, madam. Well, madam, you have said so many fine things to me, that I assure myself of your heart, and now I am resolv'd to push this opportunity to an extremity o' happiness. . [*Sir Courtly looks in the glass while he speaks.*

Au. Oh ! fortunate ! this to me ? I did make him some advances to-day, I confess, and have they had this success ? My heart pants : I am surpriz'd with infinite joy, and am not able to answer.   [*Aside.*

Sir Co. Well, madam, I must be happy, and so upon my—the lady gone ?   [*Turns from the glass.*

Au. Sir Courtly, you put me in great confusion.

Sir Co. The lady's consent is very considerable— she governs her niece, and under her conduct may make me happy, with a reserve to modesty. (*Aside.*) Well, madam, shall I have your consent to my happiness—my glory ?

Au. Oh, dear sir ! is it possible to answer you so soon ?

Sir Co. So soon, madam ? You know my passion has been long.

Au. Is it possible ? I swear I never heard of it before.

Sir Co. That's strange ! Wou'd not my lord, your nephew, acquaint you ?

Au. He never said one word of it to me.

Sir Co. That's amazing !

Au. I find my nephew has been false to me. It seems 'tis me the gentleman loves, and my nephew wou'd defraud me of him for his sister. Here's fine doings !   [*Aside.*

Sir Co. I swear I thought your ladyship had

known, and granted your consent—you said so many fine things.

Au. I said no more, Sir Courtly, than what were the result o' my thoughts, upon the contemplation of your great desert.

Sir Co. Your ladyship's most humble servant! Then I hope, madam, since my passion has been long, though you knew not of it, you will not defer my happiness—'tis in your power, I'm certain : no person controls you.

Au. Controls me ?—that's pleasant. No, sir !

Sir Co. She says true—she can bring her niece. (*Aside.*) I beseech you, madam, take pity of a suffering lover !

Au. Oh, sir! shou'd I consent so soon, 'twou'd be against all forms.

Sir Co. I would not for the world offend against any forms. No man living more studies and adores all manner of forms, but my passion has been long.

Au. I know not what to say, sir; indeed, I must not.

Sir Co. Oh, pardon me !

Au. Oh, pardon me !

Sir Co. Oh, madam !

Au. You confound me, sir.

Sir Co. You distract me, madam. It must be !

Au. Well, sir, I yield ; but with an extremity o' blushing.

Sir Co. Your most obliged humble servant.

Au. My severe temper wou'd never ha' been wrought on so soon, but by so fine a gentleman.

Sir Co. Your most humble servant.

Au. And to revenge myself on my nephew for his false play.

Sir Co. Well, madam, we'll in my coach to the next church presently.

Au. 'Tis very hard to resist you, Sir Courtly. If you please, I will first put on a disguise ; for I desire it may be manag'd with all secrecy till the ceremony of marriage be over.

Sir Co. With all my soul ; for I infinitely love a secret intrigue, especially when everybody knows of it.

Au. Lest my nephew light on us and prevent it.

Sir Co. He's for the match !

Au. He's very false !

Sir Co. Is it possible ?

Au. Is it not apparent, when he conceal'd the whole matter from me, lest I should promote it ?

Sir Co. That's unanswerable—I'm amaz'd at it. Well, madam, I shall not fail of being happy ?

Au. Immediately, sir.

Sir Co. And you think you have power ?

Au. Power ?—that's pleasant.

Sir Co. So—so—she'll bring or send her. (*Aside.*) Well, madam, your most humble servant.

Au. Your very blushing servant.   [*Exit.*

Sir Co. Your humble—sto—ho—ho—hop—thief!
      [*Exit.*

Enter CRACK *and* LEONORA *laughing.*

Cr. An humble thief, indeed !—steal an old woman ?

Leo. This was a pleasure I cou'd not ha' thought of.   Now to our affair !

Cr. Come—on with your vizard !   [*Exeunt.*

Scene changes to the Hall.

Enter at one door HOTHEAD *and* TESTIMONY,
at another CRACK.

Cr. Barbarity ! falsehood ! treachery ! murder !

Hot. What's the matter ?

Cr. Did not I stipulate upon the surrend'ry of myself to this house, to be kept from women ? and I am devoured with 'em ; here comes into my chamber a hot burnt whore, with a black crust upon her face ; here she is ! avant !　　*[Exit.*

CRACK *pulls in* LEONORA, *vizarded.*

Hot. You damn'd whore, how came you into this house ? and what are you ? I'll see your face.

Cr. Then I'll see your brains, I swear by Gogmagog, and all the seven damnable sins.

Test. Oh, sad ! oh, sad !

Cr. Shew me the face of a woman ? I had rather see forty full moons.

Hot. Stand off impertinence! I will see her face.

Cr. Murder ! murder ! Call my lord——lord, lord——murder !—murder ! lord,—lord,—lord !

Hot. Hold your bawling ! I'll let her go—for, now I think on't, if my lord shou'd find this whore here when he gave such strict orders we shou'd let no body out, or in, he'll make more noise than this mad fool——so let us kick her out o' doors, and say nothing.

Test. Hold, let us not use violence to her !— she's a great temptation to me. (*Aside.*) I'll reprove the idle woman ; it may be I may gain upon her.

Hot. Gain a clap, sirrah ! for this is some of the footmen's whores, pick'd up in the dark. Get you out, you whore !

Test. No violence, pray ! She's a great snare to me. (*Aside.*) Woman, get you out ! woman—— and de'e hear ?——I'll follow you, and we'll drink a bottle.

Leo. Do, old Godly knave, and thou shalt be welcome.

Test. I come! I come! (*Aside.*) Get you out, woman.

Hot. Get you out——you whore!

[*They thrust Leo. out.*

Cr. Good morrow!—up so early?

Hot. What's the whimsy now?

Cr. Am not I i' bed?

Hot. In bed?

Test. Poor soul, poor soul——

Cr. I am not, i' faith? Then I walk in my sleep. I was fast asleep just now, and dream't I saw women, and vizards, and all that trash; and the fright put me in a fever. I burn! prithee give me a mouth full of sweet air. [*Exit Cr.*

Hot. Prithee, take a belly full and be damn'd! A fine time on't I have; with whores, and fools, and mad men, and *fanatiques.* [*Exit.*

Test. So now I'll steal after her, for I find in me a very great uproar. [*Exit.*

Scene changes to Violante's house.

Enter FAREWEL, LEONORA, *vizarded,* TESTIMONY.

Fa. Come in, come in honest old fornicator! though the girl be mine, when I have had my collation, if she'll consent, faith, thou shalt have a bit; I love a wenching rogue i' my heart.

Test. Oh! dear sir, your very humble servant, and truly I am a kind of a wag. I love a pretty bit sometimes.

Fa. And I love thee the better for it, and this is a pretty bit! thou shalt see her.

[*Leo. pulls off her vizard.*

Test. Oh! dear! undone! undone!

Leo. Nay, nay, Mr Testimony, won't you be as good as your word? Shan't we have a bottle?

Test. Oh! madam, don't discover me to my lord, and you shall not only have my prayers, but the prayers of all the sober party for you all days o' my life.

Leo. So, he runs from whoring to praying.

Fa. Are not you o' rogue, sirrah?

Test. I know I shall be call'd rogue by the Popish party——they will rejoice at my fall, but I hope my fall will be sanctified unto me for my better upstanding——

Fa. Among the wenches——Sirrah——come, sirrah, you shall stay till my lord comes, for his mortification as well as yours.

Test. Oh! my flesh, it has undone me.

Enter VIOLANTE, *and* CRACK.

Vio. My dear!

Leo. My dear!

Vio. Excellent Crack; for this great piece o' service, I'll ha' thee knighted under a petticoat. Well, we must send for my lord, to laugh at him.

Test. Oh! dear! I tremble!

Vio. Who's there? Tell my lord I desire to speak with him.

Leo. Pray let him bring Sir Courtly Nice, and his bride with him; be sure you say nothing o' me.——   [*Exit Footman.*

Vio. Are you a bride yet?

Leo. Not yet.

Vio. Get in, and let my chaplain make you one!

Leo. Come, Mr Testimony. Mr Crack, bring him!

Cr. How now, you rogue? what's your business?

Test. Oh! my reproach will be great.

                          [*Exeunt Fa., Leo., Cr., Test.*

Vio. Mr Surly!

Enter SURLY.

Sur. Well, what now ?

Vio. Now, you shall be my husband.

Sur. Your Jack ? to turn and roast you for another, whilst I ha' no share in you.

Vio. According to the share I have in you. You men wou'd feign engross all manner o' sins, by the pretended prerogative o' your sex ; well, if iniquity be your estate, when you ha' married me I'll put in for my thirds.

Sur. I doubt it not. Within this week I shall see in a fop's hand a billet doux, that is a ticket to let him into your play-house.

Vio. Pr'ythee leave off this dogged humour.

Sur. I ha' none ; fawning is a dog's humour.

Vio. Nay, but sullenness ! it taxes thy estate, that thou art never the better for it ; 'tis a French estate.

Sur. Ay, but to lick a fool's shoe is a spaniel's estate.

Vio. Pr'ythee, dress like a gentleman.

Sur. So I do ; but I wou'd not dress like a gentleboy, lag at my years among those children, to play with their toys ; be always folded up like a love letter, with a superscription, these to the next pretty girl.

Vio. There's no altering thee——go in a while !
[*Exit Surly.*

Enter Lord BELGUARD, Sir COURTLY, AUNT,
vizarded.

Vio. My lord, your humble servant ! I invited you hither, to reconcile you to your sister. She's weary of your government, and has dispos'd of her self.

Bell. Ay, madam ! but according to my own

desires, that now I suppose you will acknowledge the good effects of my government. Sister, salute your friend.

Vio. Do you take that for your sister ? then I'll shew you the good effects of your government. Open the door.

The Scene is drawn, and FAREWEL, LEONORA, *a Parson,* CRACK, TESTIMONY, *appear.*

Bell. My sister there ? call my servants !

Cr. Nay, then call mine ! the great Mogul, and the King o' Bantam. I'll pepper you.

Bell. Then you were the pimp were you ?—sirrah ! I may chance begin with you.

Vio. How ? i' my house and presence ? Touch him if you dare.

Bell. I'm made an ass on.

Cr. Not far from that circumstance.

Bell. You rascal !

Vio. Again ?

Sir Co. But what the devil am I made ? what have I got ?

Leo. Even my stale Aunt.

Au. Saucy huzzy.

Sir Co. The Aunt ? What, have you put upon me, madam ?

Au. What have I put upon you, sir, more than yourself desired ? Did not you declare you have long had a passion for me ?

Sir Co. A passion for you ? Comical ! that's probable ! Rot me if ever I had a passion for you in my life. I meant all to your niece ; a passion for an old woman ?

Au. Ill-bred fop !

Sir Co. Very fine——

Vio. Now, my lord what say you of your fine

cotquean art of conserving woman ? Will she keep
if not candied with virtue ? here is a piece o' dried
sweet-meat you see cou'd not keep; and proves by
her example, that the huffs of either sex, when
they are boldly attacked in private, soonest deliver
their weapons.

Au. This is all ill manners.

Vio. Ay, but here's an old cat will suffer no
vermin to come into the house ; but then he has a
liquorish tooth, and loves to have a sweet bit for
himself; he wou'd fain ha' pick'd up your sister for
a wench.

Bell. How ?

Test. 'Tis true, indeed, my lord ; I will not tell a
lie for the whole world.

Bell. Oh ! villain——Well, sirrah——I'll leave
you to my cousin Hothead's correction.

Vio. But your faults, my lord, I'll take into my
correction, and give myself to Mr Surly.——Mr
Surly !

Enter SURLY.

Sur. Well ?—

Bell. To Surly ?

Sur. Ay, now, Nice thy quarrel and mine is at
an end, I'll let thee be an ass forty years longer.

Sir Co. You are a rude fellow, and you are ill-
bred—— and I'll revenge myself on you all, as far
as my sword and my wit can go——

Leo. Wit ?—ha ! ha——   [*All laugh.*

Sir Co. Very fine manners this !—my coach !
——Madam, you may follow your own occasions
——I have none with an old woman. [*To the Aunt.*

Au. You are a coxcomb !

Sir Co. Your servant——my coach !

Leo. Must I lose you, Sir Courtly ?——stop
thief——stop thief !

Sir Co. Oh! your servant——my coach, you dogs!   [*Exit.*

Vio. Come, my lord, I see patience in your face; all may be well yet.

Sur. How! jilting already?

Vio. Promise I shall enjoy all and singular the privileges, liberties, and immunities of an English wife.

Bell. All!

Vio. That is to say, ramble, rant, game, dress, visit, prate, ogle, kiss——and——

Bell. Hold——hold——whither the devil is she running? Kiss, kiss — and——stop for Heaven's sake.

Vio. Kiss, and before your face? is it not the prerogative of an English wife? Surly, I owe thee a reward for service; kiss me!

Bell. That's not to be borne.

Vio. Surly, I am thy wife.

Bell. Hold——hold——for Heaven's sake—— do not use me thus?

Vio. Then do not rebel, but practise obediently the postures of an English husband, before you are listed; poise your hat, draw your left leg backward, bow with your body, and look like an ass, whilst I kiss like a wife. Surly, kiss me!

Bell. If he does—— [*Lays his hand on his sword.*

Sur. With all my heart. If I kiss thee, let the devil marry thee.

[*He offers to kiss her, and she gives him a box o' th' ear.*

Vio. And the devil kiss thee. Cou'dst thou think any woman wou'd suffer thy face to come near her, but some dairy maid, to curdle her milk?

All. Ha! ha! ha!   [*All laugh.*

Sur. Hoh! hoh! what a society o' Gotam's are here, to laugh at a man for missing a woman? Had

I married her, as my lord Wiseacre intends to do, I had deserv'd to ha' been laught at, for a cox-comb and a cuckold, as he will be in a few days.

Vio. How?

Sur. Ay, you are all whores, pox on you! all whores. [*Exit.*

Enter HOTHEAD *and all the Servants.*

Hot. Did you send for us?

Bell. Yes, do you see where my sister is?

Hot. By what witchcraft was this?

Vio. Do not you remember a vizard you turn'd out o' doors?

Hot. Was it you?

Leo. Even the same.

Hot. Then you deserve to be turn'd out o' doors again.

Bell. But what do you deserve, sir? that not only turn'd my sister out o' doors——but let Mr Testimony——pick her up for a wench.

Hot. Oh! dog——oh! rogue——

Test. I am no rogue——a man may fall, and be Godly in the main——I am satisfied in my spirit, I am a Godly man——

Hot. Here's a rogue——sirrah——sirrah!
[*Beats and kicks Test.*

Test. Persecution — persecution——Papist—— do——kick the Godly, kick the Protestants out o' th' kingdom——do Papist—I see what you would be at. [*Exit.*

Bell. So cousin, now I have done with spies—— you may follow your own business, if you have any——

Hot. Business? yes I have business, and will have business as long as there is a fanatick in the Kingdom! and so, farewell. [*Exit.*

Bel. I am now convinced, virtue is a woman's

only guard. If she be base metal, to think by
chemystry to turn her into gold

Is a vain dream of what we never see,
And I'll proclaim to all——It cannot be.

[*Exeunt Omnes.*

EPILOGUE.

'Tis a hard case an audience now to please,
For every palate's spoil'd with some disease.
Poor plays as fast as women now decay,
They're seldom car'd for after the first day.;
How often have I heard true wit call'd stuff,
By men with nothing in their brains but snuff?
Each shante* spark, that can the fashion hit,
Place his hat thus, role full, forsooth's a Wit;
And thinks his clothes allow him judge of it.
The city gallant, the exchange being done,
Takes sword at Temple-Bar which Nice stuck on.
Comes here and passes for a Beaugarzoon.
Audacious vizards too so fast do grow,
You hardly can the virtuous from 'em know.
Nay, parents now not likely can endure
Their children's faults, but what is worse procure.
Of old the mother, full of parent sway,
Kept Miss a vassal to her work all day;
And to the wooing spark Miss was not brought,
But some fine golden thing her wheedle wrought:
Now you shall meet young lady and her mother,
Rambling in hackney-coaches masqu't together;
Yes, and to say the truth, to work they go,
Fine work, but——such as they will never shew,
Unless some nott † to draw a fool to wed,
And then he finds Miss rare at work a bed,
But the grand rendezvous is kept of late,
Exact at nine, hard by, o'er Chocolate.
Sad fate, that all the Christian youth o'th' nation,
Should be oblig'd to Jews for procreation.

* Smart, gay, showy.
† Device ?—To nott; to fleece.

Nay, what is worse, that's if reports be true,
Many a Christian gallant there turns Jew ;
That is, so oft some rotten strumpet plies him,
The chirurgion's forc't at last to circumcise him.
Our Bridges Street is grown a strumpet fair,
Where higgling bawds do palm their rotten ware.
There fowler-like the watching gallant pores
Behind his glove, to get a shot at whores,
And from his tongue lets fly such charming words,
That strait he carries off the wounded birds.
Another waits above in the great room,
Till a new cargozoon* of strumpets come.
There, by three glasses plac't, the affected dunce
Acts you four Courtly-Nices all at once ;
Our galleries too were finely us'd of late,
Where roosting masques sat cackling for a mate.
They came not to see plays but act their own,
And had throng'd audiences when we had none.
Our plays it was impossible to hear,
The honest country-men were forc't to swear :
" Confound you ! give your bawdy prating o'er,
Or zounds, I'll fling you i' the pit, you bawling
    whore."
This comedy throws all that lewdness down,
For virtuous liberty is pleas'd alone :
Promotes the stage to th' ends at first design'd,
As well to profit, as delight the mind.

---

* " My body is a cargason of ill humours."—*Howel.*

DARIUS.

Darius, King of Persia. A Tragedy as it is acted by their Majesties Servants. Written by Mr Crowne. London: Printed for Jos. Knight and Fr. Saunders at the Blew Anchor, in the Lower Walk of the New Exchange, in the Strand. 1688. 4to.

Ib. London: Printed for R. Bentley, at the Post-house in Russel Street, Covent Garden. 1688. 4to.

SURELY Crowne must have been born under the influence of an unlucky star. Charles the Second patronized him, and had acceded to his request for a permanent appointment but on condition that he adapted for the English stage a Spanish play which the King recommended to his consideration. No sooner had the dramatist completed the task, than the unexpected death of Charles deprived him of his reward; and although Sir Courtly Nice, the play in question, was deservedly received with applause by the public, and for many succeeding years was retained on the stock of acting dramas, he failed in obtaining from James what had been promised by Charles.

The fortunes of the dramatist did not improve in the reign of James, whose morals were not much better than those of his predecessor, but whose vices were more quietly practised. The genial habits of Charles made him, manifold as were his faults, a favourite with the people, whilst the unmistakeable resolution of James to restore Popery put him in an antagonistic position to his subjects, who, although inclined to look leniently on the frailties of the one brother, regarded with the deepest disgust the intolerant religious fanaticism of the other.

In the commencement of the eventful year of 1688 Crowne ventured to place his tragedy of Darius on the stage of the Theatre Royal. He had taken much time in its preparation, during which he had suffered greatly from indisposition. He had with much ingenuity composed an underplot, which would enable Mrs Barry, as the heroine, to charm the audience by her inimitable delineation of character. James promised to attend on the author's night, and Crowne informs the public in his dedication that the King redeemed his promise.

In the dedication of Darius to Sir George Hewytt, Bart., one of the lieutenants of his Majesty's Horse Guards—afterwards created by William III., 1690, an Irish Peer, by the titles of Baron of Jamestown in the county of Longford, and Viscount Hewit of Gowran in the county of Kilkenny,—Crowne gives the following account of how his hopes were blighted.

Upon its first representation "a misfortune fell upon the play," that "might well dizzy the judgment of the audience. Just before the commencement Mrs Barry was struck with a very violent fever that took all spirit from her, by consequence from the play. The scenes she acted fell dead from her, and in the fourth act her distemper grew so much upon her, she could go on no further; but all her part in that act was wholly cut out, and neither spoken nor read; so that the people went away without knowing the contexture of the play, yet thought they knew all."

What serious consequences resulted from this unhappy illness of the actress may well be imagined, when we read what Cibber says of her:—"Mrs Barry, in characters of greatness, had a presence of elevated dignity, her mien and motion superb and gracefully majestic, her voice full, clear, and strong, so that no violence of passion could be too much for her; and when distress or tenderness possessed her, she subsided into the most affecting melody and softness. In the art of exciting pity she had a power beyond all the actresses I have yet seen, or what your imagination can conceive."* The character of Barzana was peculiarly suited to such an actress as the lady so well described by the Laureate. Barzana, a young and beautiful Princess of the blood-royal, is married to Bessus, Viceroy of Bactria, who has a son called Memnon, by a Queen of the Amazons. Memnon having been engaged in the wars, where he has distinguished himself, is not aware that he has a stepmother. They meet, and Memnon falls in love with her, altogether ignorant of the relationship. She, on the other hand, becomes cognizant of his being her husband's son, and there is an excellent scene, in which she endeavours to control the incipient feeling which is increasing in her bosom towards her stepson. In the fourth act, where Barzana parts with Memnon without disclosing the secret of her being the wife of Bessus,—a scene in which the

* An Apology for the Life of Colley Cibber. 3d edition. London, 1750, 8vo, p. 132 See also Memoir of Sir William D'avenant, Vol. I. p. lxxxiii. in this series.

acting of Mrs Barry would have carried the audience with her,—she became so ill that she could exert herself no longer, and yielded to the overpowering force of the disease. The tragedy was doomed from that moment, and has never recovered the place it might otherwise have taken among the acting tragedies of the day.

" By the advice of some I much regard," observes Crowne, " the Queen of Darius and his family were omitted from the play, and the episode of Barzana and Memnon introduced, to the obvious benefit of the drama, which otherwise would have been somewhat tedious in representation." Darius, being a genuine Persian, is naturally inclined to praise himself and boast of his own exploits, which makes him occasionally very tiresome. The tragedy commences after the defeat of the Persian monarch at the battle near Issus, when his mother, Queen, and children, are captured by Alexander, who treated his prisoners with every respect and kindness, and took subsequently as his wife his daughter Statira, the heroine of Lees' celebrated tragedy of the Rival Queens, or Alexander the Great. Personally brave, Darius had the misfortune to head an army enervated by luxury, and unable to resist the hardy Macedonians, and who, deeming the better part of valour to be discretion, usually ran away as soon as the fight commenced.

The camp of the Persian King, on the occasion of the first battle between him and Alexander, had an attendance of two hundred and seventy-seven cooks, twenty-nine waiters, eighty-seven cup-bearers, forty servants to perfume the King, and sixty-six servants to prepare garlands and flowers to deck the dishes and meats for the Royal table.*

After his last defeat, the death of Darius speedily followed, and his false friend Bessus became his murderer. Whether Nabarzanes was directly implicated in the atrocious act is uncertain, for although the former traitor was subsequently caught, and delivered by Alexander, upon his capture, to the tender mercies of Oxarthes, the brother of Darius, the latter was pardoned, which would hardly have been the case had he been directly

* Athenæus, as quoted by Lempriere.

concerned in the murder. The conqueror was wedded
to Statira, the murdered Monarch's daughter, and to
Roxana, her cousin, in this way becoming so nearly connected with the late ruler of Persia. That Alexander
lamented his fate, and showed every kindness to his
family, may be assumed from the fact that the mother
of Darius became so deeply attached to him that she
died of grief at his premature death.

As it was impossible to rally the effeminate Persians—
who ran away, terrified, as Curtius observes, at the mere
name of Alexander—Darius resolved to surrender to his
opponent. What followed will be best given in the
words of the author just referred to:*—"Bessus et
ceteri facinoris ejus participes, vehiculum Darii assequuti,
cœperunt hortari eum, ut conscenderet equum, et se
hosti fuga eriperet. Ille deos ultores adesse testatur,
et Alexandri fidem implorans, negat se parricidas velle
comitari. Tum vero ira quoque accensi, tela injiciunt
in regem; multisque confossum vulneribus relinquunt.
Jumenta quoque, ne longius prosequi possent, convul-
nerantur; duobus servis, qui regem comitabantur,
occisis."

Darius, according to Justin, was not quite dead when
he was found by a Macedonian, called Polystratus, in
the waggon or vehicle into which his assassin had thrown
him, and which had stopped at a fountain, having
deviated from the proper road from want of a driver.
The kind Macedonian, finding the unfortunate man still
living, brought him in his helmet some water, which so
far refreshed him as to enable him to plight his troth to
Alexander; and in token thereof, placing his right hand
in that of Polystratus, he expired.

Of this incident the reader will find Crowne has availed
himself in the last act of the tragedy. His dying words
are worthy of note :—

" How vainly do we pity poverty !
The gods sit at the table of the poor,
And turn their water to delicious wine.
Never had I in pompous luxury
Such pleasure as this draught of water yields.

* Lib 5, cap. xxxv.

But Fortune does pursue me to the last ;
I'm forc'd to beg even water for my thirst,
And though a King, I cannot pay for it
But Alexander will ;—give me thy hand,
The sole remaining pledge I have to give
For all my grateful love to that brave Prince. [*Dies.*"

Bessus assumed the title of King, but was subsequently seized and delivered to Alexander, who gave him up to the brother of King Darius and the rest of his kindred. According to Diodorus Siculus, "after they had put him to all manner of torments, and us'd with all the despite and disgrace imaginable, they cut his body into small pieces, and hurl'd every part here and there away out of their slings."*

Curtius gives a different version from that of Diodorus as to the punishment of Bessus. He was given to Oxarthes, the brother of Darius, "ut cruci affixum mutilatis auribus naribusque, sagittis configerent barbari, asservarentque corpus ut ne aves quidem contingerent."† Crowne has preferred Curtius; the concluding scene represents Bessus and Nabarzanes hung in chains. Soft music precedes the drawing of the scene. At another part of the stage is seen the ghost of Darius, brightly habited. Patron exclaims—

" Oh ! now I see the cause of these Divine,
Miraculous sounds—I see the King !—the King
More lively than he ever was in's life ;
    *   *   *   *
The royal shadow *smiles* and points to them."

The idea of the ghost of Darius appearing to soft music, to smile and point at his murderers, is assuredly original, but as Alexander pardoned Nabarzanes, his appearance as a ghost on that occasion was rather out of place. Perhaps it was the absurdity of the thing that induced the apparition of Darius to *smile*—a very unusual circumstance with spectres.

In " Charles the Eighth of France," acted in 1672 at the Duke's Theatre, Crowne introduces the ghost of young Galeazzo, Duke of Milan, " with a cup of Poyson in his hand. The ghost passes over the stage." Then

---

* Booth's " Diodorus, the Sicilian." London, 1700. P. 537.
† *Ib.*, Lib. 6, cap. xxii.

re-enters, and, after giving his wife some excellent advice, informs her he will give her one more summons before she dies. He redeems his promise, waits till she expires, and then vanishes.

There was during this period a taste among playgoers for the appearance of ghosts on the stage. Otway, in his " Venice Preserved," acted at the Duke's Theatre in 1682, after treating the audience with some amorous passages between the venerable old Senator and a not particularly virtuous lady, and killing off Jaffeir and Pierrè, places Belvidera in the palace of her cruel father, Priuli, which neither of these worthies when alive would have been permitted to enter, but who, after their death, without leave asked, do so in their spiritual capacity, but for what purpose other than to terrify the poor lady it is impossible to imagine. Modern taste has not admired either the Senator's follies or the spectral illusions, so that those passages have been excised.

Previously, in "The Rival Queens; or, the Death of Alexander the Great," a tragedy by Nathaniel Lee, acted at the Theatre Royal in 1677, whilst the conspirators against Alexander are in consultation, the ghost of King Philip, his father, " walks over the stage, shaking a truncheon at them," which, although it frightened, did not prevent them from persisting in their villany. The tragedy was successful, and kept the stage for a long period, notwithstanding its extravagance and bombast. A ghost "shaking a truncheon" is not unlike the ghost of Hamlet's father appearing with " a pair of green spectacles," a circumstance which actually did once occur, the performer having forgotten he had them on until he was reminded by a roar of laughter from the audience, in which Hamlet could not help joining.

With Queen Anne the taste for these unearthly appearances gradually disappeared. Her Hanoverian successors delighted more in comedy than in tragedy, which was for awhile banished the stage, until Shakespere's name could again command an audience for Macbeth, Hamlet, Julius Cæsar, or Cymbeline.

Geneste * commends the last scene of the second act of

* Vol. I. p. 462.

Darius, and observes, "it is well written, and borrowed in great measure from the Hippolitus of Euripides, in which Phædra at first endeavours to conceal her passion for her husband's son, and afterwards discloses it." He nevertheless characterises the play as only "tolerable." It assuredly does not merit the epithet. If judiciously curtailed—a portion of the egotistical declamation of Darius omitted,—the ghostly abomination removed,—the tragedy terminating with the death of Darius,—with a Barzana and Memnon who could do justice to their respective parts, it would assume a different aspect, and have a fair chance of becoming popular. But at present there is as little hope of procuring performers qualified to represent the unfortunate lovers, as of obtaining audiences capable of enjoying their acting.

To the notice relative to Sir George Hewytt * may be added a few additions from Luttrell's notes, which were for the first time printed at Oxford from the original MSS. in the Bodleian Library.† He was made an Irish Baron and Viscount by King William on 10th April 1689. The entry is as follows :—" His Majestic has been pleased to create Sir George Hewyt baron of Jamestown and Viscount Hewyt of Gowran in the Kingdom of Ireland." As this was the day before the coronation of William and Mary, the new Peer would be enabled to attend the ceremony in that character.

King James was then in Ireland, and Londonderry was under the siege, which was raised in the month of August. From Luttrell's Notes it appears that most of the Horse had been landed in Ireland by the 6th of September; and, as Viscount Gowran was a cavalry officer, he would naturally accompany them.

That he was not long there is proved by Luttrell,‡ " The letters from Chester say that Sir John Davis, since his arrival there, was dead of the distemper he brought from Ireland ; that the Lord Hewyt and Lord Roscommon were also very sick there." Upon the 6th December 1690, Colonel John Cutts was created " Baron Cutts of Gowran, in consideration of his faithful services."

---

* See Introduction to the Country Wit—*ante*, p. 3.
† Oxford, 1857, 6 volumes. Vol. I. p. 520. The book has this title, " A Brief Relation of State Affairs."
‡ 15th November, Luttrell, vol. I. p. 608.

Upon the 14th Dec. following, Luttrel says, "The Lord Hewyt's corpse is brought from Chester, and was carried thro' London with great state, in order to its interment."

The first Lord Gowran was an admirer of the drama, and patronised Crowne; the second was a poet,* and patronised Steele—to whom he gave his first military commission. Steele dedicated to his lordship his excellent manual, entitled the "Christian Hero,"—a work which, at the present time, seems to be forgotten.

Having procured a title, his next step was to get a partner suitable to share his honours; and he was so successful as in twelve days to accomplish his wishes. That is to say, on the 18th of December "the Lord Cutts was married to the lady Trevor, a widow of a great fortune," his patent of creation being dated the 6th of the same month.

This lady was probably the widow of Sir Thomas Trevor, Bart., the heir-male of the ancient family of Trevor, and who was made a Knight of the Bath at the coronation of Charles II. He married Anne, daughter and heir of Robert Jennor of London, Esq. But, dying without issue, the title became extinct in the same reign, and the representation of the Trevors in the male line passed to Sir John Trevor of Trevallen in the county of Flint, Knight. Lord Cutts of Gowran died without issue in Dublin, January 1706, and was buried in the Cathedral of Christ Church.

The first drama on the subject of Darius was by William Alexander of Menstrie, afterwards better known as Earl of Stirling and Viscount of Canada, who, says Lord Orford, "was a very celebrated poet, and greatly superior to the style of his age. His works are printed in folio, the chief of which are four tragedies in alternate rhyme."† His Lordship, it is presumed, refers to a volume in folio entitled "Recreations with the Muses," Lond. 1637, which contains his tragedies, and other works, but not his "Aurora," considered by many persons to be his best performance.

---

* He was author of "Poetical Exercises written upon several occasions." London, 1687. 8vo.

† Orford's "Royal and Noble Authors," Park's Edition, London, 1806, 8vo, vol. V. p. 73.

It is only of his Darius that it is requisite to take notice here.

In 1603, William Alexander of Menstrie printed at Edinburgh " The Tragedie of Darius," his first dramatic essay which, according to the Biographia Dramatica, was " written in a mixture of the Scotch and English dialects." This edition, which is of great rarity, is in the British Museum, and upon collation with the edition of 1604, " London, Printed by G. Elde for Edward Blount," appears to differ very little from this English one. In another edition dated at London 1616, " by Sir William Alexander, Knight," the text is to a certain extent altered but not improved.

Poetically considered Darius has great merit, and abounds in beautiful passages. The language is forcible, and the versification usually harmonious; but as a drama, it is not at all calculated for representation. The length of the speeches and the want of action are sufficient to exclude it from the stage. The time occupied in the representation would, before it was a third part through, tire the spectators, whilst the long sonorous lines falling monotonously upon the ear could not fail to beget an inclination to sleep. This is said from no wish to detract from the merits of Darius and the other three Monarchic tragedies, but as showing that they are more fitted for the closet than the theatre.

Lord Stirling introduced the mother, wife, and family of Darius into his drama, as well as Alexander and his Generals. These characters are very properly omitted by Crowne, who, acting on the judicious advice of his friends, has based his plot on the conspiracy against the Persian Monarch and the loves of Barzana and Memnon. Throughout Lord Stirling's tragedy the second vowel in Darius is short, in place of being long as we have it. Can this really have been the accent in which the word was pronounced in the days of King James, to whom the author dedicated his first edition ? The King was a good Latin scholar,* so much so, that he used personally to instruct his great favourite, Robert Car, in that language.

* George Buchanan was his tutor, and educated his pupil thoroughly.

The following sonnet, corrected in the well-known hand of James VI., is preserved amongst the Balfour MSS. in the library of the Faculty of Advocates :—

"The complainte of the Muses to Alexander vpon himselfe for his ingratitude towardes them by hurting them with his hard hammered wordes, fitter to be vsed vpon his mineralles*—

" O holde your hande, holde! Mercie, mercie, spare
   Those sacred Nine that nurst you many a yeare,
Full ofte, alace, with comforte and with care
   Wee bath'd you in Castalia's Founteyns cleare,
Then on your winges aloft wee did you beare
   And set you on our statelie forked hille,
Where you your heavenlie harmonies did heare ;
   The rockes resounding with their echos stille
Although your neighbours haue conspir'd to kille
That arte that did the laurell croune obteyne ;
   Who borrowing from the rauen theyr ragged quille,
Bewray their hard, harsh, trotting, tumbling veyne.
   Such hammering hard, youre metles hard require,
   Our songes are fill'd with smooth and floueing fire."

A tragedy under the name of Darius is, in the Biographia Dramatica, attributed to the Rev. Dr Stratford ; but whether it is referable to the first, second, or third Persian Monarch of the name is not mentioned, it never having been acted or printed.

* The grant of the silver mines of Hilderston in West Lothian.

TO

SIR GEO. HEWYTT, Baronet,

One of the Lieutenants of his Majesty's Horse Guard.

Sir,—Poor Darius is decreed to be unfortunate everywhere. His stars pursue him two thousand years after his death, tear his image, and employ his friends against him; for I am one of 'em. I find him in Curtius, a Prince of valour, clemency, justice, and great moral virtues, suffering under the heaviest calamities that ever befel man. And I have much pity for him; and more abhorrence for the villains that murder'd him, than those that cut off Alexander. Darius has no success, the greater still the pity. If Alexander moves my pity, 'tis he has success, because 'tis the ruin of his great virtues. Darius never parted with his; nor good nor ill fortune vanquish'd his virtue, that Darius, of the two, seems the greater conqueror, and, in a common waggon gor'd in his blood, appears a more glorious prince, than Alexander in his chariot triumphing over the Indians. For Darius in all misery triumphs over fortune. Fortune most insolently triumphs over Alexander. The description Curtius gives of him and his army, when they came from the conquest of the Indies, is a perfect picture of our lewd debauchees of quality, coming in the head of drunken ruffians from beating a watch. Curtius says, a thousand sober men might have taken 'em all prisoners. And no doubt, cou'd a lusty whiggish London watch have met with 'em, Alexander the

VOL. 3. 24

Great had been carried to the counter, notwithstanding his Royal dignity, or perhaps the sooner
for it. Therefore, if Darius moves no pity, I am
afraid it is not his fault, but mine ;. and he is once
more fallen into ill hands. I am apt to think I
committed a fault, in not taking the whole story ;
but leaving out Queen Statira and her two daughters, highborn Princesses, well-known to the world,
whose misfortunes wou'd have probably mov'd
more compassion than those of a strange lady, ob-
scurely descended from my fancy, which I have
introduc'd in their stead. But when I first contriv'd and writ this play, my judgment was over-
borne by some I much regard; who told me, those
Princesses had been already seen very often, their
beauties wou'd now seem stale, and a new face be
more agreeable. My judgment at that time might
be easily borne down, for it was weak, as I myself
was, by a tedious sickness, else I had not meddled
with tragedy ; for there is nothing more plain than
that the humour of the present age runs quite to
another extreme, too far. Nor do the present
company of actors abound with tragedians enow,
to master that humour. And they have no reason
to contend with it, since they can please at a much
cheaper rate, by farce and comedy ; and truly so
can I, they cost me less pains than tragedy does.
But when I first meddled with this play, and long
after, I was not in humour for comedy. A poet,
like a fiddle, will never sound merrily in wet
weather. The trebles, which are the strings for
jigs, will not endure stretching. So I was forc'd
on grumbling tragedy : and having done something
in it, was loth to lose my labour. Thus much I am
willing to say against myself, because it is truth.
But as I will not be arrogant, so not over-fawning,
because there is foppery and affectation in both.

A misfortune fell upon this play, that might very well dizzy the judgments of my audience. Just before the play began, Mrs Barry was struck with a very violent fever, that took all spirit from her, by consequence from the play; the scenes she acted fell dead from her; and in the fourth act her distemper grew so much upon her, she cou'd go on no farther, but all her part in that act was wholly cut out, and neither spoke nor read; that the people went away without knowing the contexture of the play, yet thought they knew all. Now we know, how hard it is to recover the reputation of one that's executed; it is almost as hard as it is to recover his life. The circulation of blood is stopt in the strangled, and the circulation of reason in the living, by violent prepossessions. And when the multitude are possest of anything, it is not easy to get it from 'em. They have great strength and authority too. And not alone in these trifles, but in things of the highest consequence even in matters of religion. As in these toys, people dare not be pleas'd, but as they find others are; so in religion, they dare not be sav'd, but in the way they find others go. Now though in matters of religion, where truth is of great concernment, and to suffer for it, honourable and advantageous, a man may boldly contend with the whole world, but in so foolish a cause, as whether the fall of Darius be a good story of a play, and whether I have manag'd it well or no, to hector the world, if it dares differs from me, wou'd be notorious arrogance and folly; nay, injustice too : for let men have what opinions they will of this play, they have paid me for 'em, and paid me handsomely, why shou'd I seek to take it from 'em? I will then say no more concerning the play; if that be faulty, I must take care to have the fewer faults in myself. But certainly I shall not be endur'd by any good man, nay, even by myself, if I shou'd not here take occasion to render, with all possible humility and dutifulness, my thanks to his Majesty for the honour of his presence on the day which was to be for my advantage; which he was pleased to grant me, out of a most gracious and Royal regard to what had formerly appeared well in me, both as a poet and a subject. I know not how the minds of others are wrought upon; but such a piece of Royal justice and favour is to me more strong than a law to bind me for ever to my good behaviour. I cannot also forbear to mention the many special favours I have receiv'd from the present Lord Chamberlain. Obligations are chains, but when they come from princes, and men of worth, they are badges of honour, and a man is tempted to show 'em when he goes abroad. I confess, not only my gratitude, but my vanity, makes me name him. Past dispute, his excellent understanding, and many other great qualities, are an ornament to his high office; then well may his favours be a grace to me.

Now, sir, I shall come to you, I have receiv'd several kindnesses from you, have found in you at all times an inclination and readiness to do me any friendly office; all which have extremely won upon me; and I am very uneasy under obligations, till I have made some return. But I can make no other than of this kind, which I therefore beg you to accept. It is true, common dedicators have brought this sort of addresses into as much contempt, as common evidences have done swearing. The true and first intent of 'em was sacred. A dedication ought to be a little chapel, consecrated to the memory of some friend of worth; and a repository of holy relics. Now, 'tis become like

the Temple Church, a place where knights of the
post ply; that are ready to say anything for any
one. But I have kept a better reputation in the
world, you will come amongst good company.
There are few names fixt before my writings, but
may serve like the phœnix's, on the front of our
new buildings, for marks of insurance; and might
insure 'em, were it possible. But I come to you
with no such foolish design. For how ridiculous,
and unreasonable is it, to desire another to defend
my impertinence? An office no wise man will
undertake, and the greatest man that is cannot
perform. My writings, when they are out of my
hand, are no longer mine; the world pays for
'em, and will manage 'em as they please. All
care of 'em is vain, therefore I take none. My
honesty no man shall dispose of but myself. 'Tis
to preserve that, and not my writings, I beg your
leave for this address; and I wou'd not accept
your leave, if it wou'd cost me any flattery. You
have liv'd in the last court, and this, with great
reputation. Have approv'd yourself to be a man
of honour, loyalty, courage, generosity, good sense,
good nature, and good morals; which ought to
be celebrated for the public good, which too
much wants such examples. I know how ill the
sick and corrupt world digests the least praise
of any but themselves. How tir'd even good men
are, if you lead 'em far into the commendation of
any man; and the bad will not go along with
you, but on some ill design. Therefore I shall
keep where I am safe, where every man will be o'
my side. No man that knows you, but confesses
you to be one of the worthiest gentlemen they
know. I shou'd therefore shew very little worth
in myself, if I shou'd slight both your favour and
desert. And, sir, I hope you, who have forgiven

writings of mine, that shew my follies; will not be displeas'd with this dedication, where I shew the few virtues I have, my justice, and integrity, which are the best claims I have to the title of

Sir,
Your most humble
And obliged servant,
JOHN CROWN.

DRAMATIS PERSONÆ.

DARIUS, . . *King of Persia.*

ARTABASUS, { *A nobleman of great quality, loyalty, years. General of all the king's armies.*

BESSUS, . . *Viceroy of Bactria.*

NABARZANES, *Viceroy of Hircania.*

MEMNON, . . { *A beautiful, valiant, loyal young man, son of Bessus, by an Amazon Queen.*

PATRON, . . { *A valiant faithful Greek ; General of the Greek auxiliaries, that serve in the Persian army.*

DATAPHERNES, { *A Bactrian officer that serves under Bessus.*

TYRIOTES,

BARZANA, . { *A beautiful Princess of the Royal blood, married to Bessus.*

ORONTE, . *Her confidante.*

Guards, Eunuchs, Bactrians, Greeks, &c.

SCENE : *The Plains, and Town of Arbela in Persia.*

When a young writer poetry first woos,
Oh ! how he's charm'd with a fond flatt'ring muse ;
Scorns physic, law, divinity ; he climbs
To heaven, by ladders made o' ropes o' rhymes.
Finds heaven, and gold in verse, and, while he
     pores,
He pities judges, bishops, chancellors ;
They ne'er attain his joys, they're rich and great,
But he's above 'em all, for he's a Wit ;
A Prince in verse, and Princes titles give,
His pen at will makes honour die, or live ;
He dubs this man a knave, a coxcomb that,
Gives any brow a horny coronet.
Orders some famous beauty every hour
His letters patents to be call'd a whore,
Deserv'd, or not, he does it all by power.
Thus like a beau, and bully o' the town,
He by debauching beauties gets renown :
That is, their names, for he enjoys not one.
Thus was our poet, by his muse drawn in ;
'Tis true, she always innocent has been,
Kept shop, like a good creditable cit,
But traded in damn'd never thriving wit.
Lawyers have fees, howe'er their causes go,
And parsons with lean sermons fat can grow,
Of lawyers your undoing you must buy,
And doctors will not cheaply let you die ;
The vilest quack by ignorance can get
More than the best of poets by his wit.
Then you may ask, why will the poet write ?
He says, his genius bids, and hours invite ;

No lumb'ring business in his way is laid,
His life's a private and a vacant shade ;
And with design, both to instruct and please,
He plants the walks with various images,
And humbly prays you, if with art he writes,
You'll not take pains to damn your own delights.
Nay, do not damn him much, if he writes ill ;
For then he writes like you, that is gentile.

ACT I.

SCENE, *The field.* *Trumpets sound.*

Enter ARTABASUS, BESSUS, NABARZANES, MEMNON,
PATRON, DATAPHERNES. *Persians, Bactrians,
Greeks.*

Ar. So now, my lords, the dreadful day is near
That will for ever ruin, or confirm
The greatest throne, that ever the sun saw.
To-morrow, oh! to-morrow, thou art big
With vast events; time ne'er produc'd the like.
At Granicus we had not half our strength,
But in this army is all Persia.

Be. I think, my lord, we are effective men
Seven hundred thousand.

Ar. Ay, and more, my lord.

Na. Yet, of all these, my lord, you and I lead
Scarce fifteen thousand.   [*Aside to Be.*

Be. Silence!

Ar. We have left
Our cities, towns, and fields, all desolate,
That one wou'd think the Conqueror had been
    there;
The valleys bend beneath us, the hills groan,
The fields, nay, all the Heavens seem to stretch,
And give us room; and we have room to fight.
We are not here at the Cilician streights,
Where we were pris'ners ere the fight began;

Penn'd in with mountains that clipp'd both our
    wings,
And squeez'd our bodies close, till they became
As weak and slender as the enemy.
The King has done his duty, furnish'd all
This multitude with arms, and ground to fight,
And his own glorious example too.
Let us do ours, but dare be Conquerors,
We shall be so, we must be so, or ghosts,
Or worse,—poor wretched slaves ! our liberties,
Our fortunes, wives and children, are all here.
Lord Bessus, is not your fair Princess here,
The King's late beauteous gift ?
    Be. She is, my lord !
    Ar. Wou'd you not rather see that beauty dead,
Than given up to Macedonian lust ?
    Be. She shall be rather by my sword enjoy'd.
    Ar. And here I see your son, a noble youth.
    Me. Oh ! my good lord.
    Ar. Lord Memnon, give me leave.
I think, Lord Bessus, I have heard you say
An Amazonian Queen's warlike embrace
Presented you this gift.
    Be. 'Tis true, my lord !
    Ar. Believe it, 'twas a bounty to the world.
    Me. Nay, now my lord.
    Ar. Nay, pray, let me be just.
Who wou'd not grieve to see this worth in chains ?
And yet, now I reflect, more worth than his,
Ay, or than half our Kingdom, is in chains.
Even half our King is there ; and almost all
The Royal blood, but what is in his veins.
His mother, brother, daughters, little son,
Nay more, his beauteous Queen are slaves to those,
To whom they once scorn'd to be Sovereigns.
Two Royal virgins in their early spring
Lye, like fallen blossoms, at their mother's feet.

At her fair bosom hangs her infant son
A withering branch, torn from his once great
    hopes;
He, who was lately heir of half the world,
Is now, not lord of his poor little self,
His greatest happiness is ignorance;
He does not know the glory he has lost,
But hugs the enemy that ruins him.
The·conqueror cannot see this, without tears,
And cursing his unfortunate success.
And then, oh! can it be endur'd by us?
But I may spare all this, to men so brave,
So tried, as you have to your glory been,
Lord Bessus, Nabarzanes, and your troops.
    Na. We may one day be tried upon yourselves.
                                    [*Aside.*
    Be. Silence, Lord Nabarzanes! have a care.
                                    [*Aside.*
    Ar. Fortune, Lord Bessus, seems afraid of you.
She's Alexander's mistress, but your slave;
She gives him favours, but you ravish 'em.
At our great blow, at the Cilician streights
All came off safe, as privileg'd from fate,
That kept within the precincts of your sword.
    Be. Indeed, my lord, my Bactrians did well.
    Ar. And you, Lord Patron, and your valiant
    Greeks
Must give me leave to give you your due praise:
These gallant men are to our fortune tied
By indispensable allegiance,
But you are strangers, loose from any bonds.
    Pa. My lord, we are for ever bound to you
By gratitude, and honour; Greece indeed
Gave us our birth, but you our happiest hours,
That our best blood is yours.
    Ar. Most noble lord!
Well, if we fail to-morrow, 'twill be strange,

We have the strength of this vast monarchy,
The justice of our cause, necessity,
Ay, and th' inconstancy of fortune too.
That mutability which ruin'd us,
In the last field, may be our friend the next.
Now to your tents, and take a brief repose,
That so prepar'd, you may not be surpriz'd !
The King suspects these Macedonian thieves
Will act like thieves, and steal on us by night,
They will not dare to look on us by day ;
And therefore he has wisely given command,
Great part o'th' army be in arms all night ;
And all be ready at the trumpet's sound.

   Be. 'Tis wisely order'd.

   Ar. Now, my lords, good night !

   Be. My lord, we wish your excellence good
     night.

Heaven give us all to-morrow a good day !
                           [Ex. Ar.

   Pa. I'll to my charge ; my lords, good-night to
     you !   *[Ex. Pa.*

   Be. Good-night, Lord Patron ! this is a brave
     Greek.

   Na. And our old General a brave Persian.

   Be. He's like the sun, a largesse to the world ;
And not to be consum'd by age or toil.

   Na. The King, and he, are th' only gallant men
In this whole nation.

   Be. Memnon, to your tent !

   Mem. Good-night, my lord !   *[Ex. Mem.*

   Be. He's honest, but he's young.
Our talk has too much weight for his green youth.

   Na. And our affairs I think have so much weight,
We shall not sleep beneath 'em much to-night.

   Be. 'Tis true, my lord ; come let us to my tent !
Come with us, Dataphernes.

   Da. Ay, my lord !   *[Exit.*

All go out, and re-enter immediately.

SCENE, *Bessus's tent.*

Be. Our fortune places us in a strange post ;
For we are bound to fight against ourselves.
Let who will conquer, we shall be subdued.
For, say the Persian army gets the day,
We know they cannot do it without us ;
The noble fruits of our own gallantry
Will all be set in this luxurious soil.
Our swords will be as barren as our lands.
These cowards must rule the brave, by whom they
    rule.

Dat. They govern us ? they have not power to
    rule
Men, wine, or women ; or their own silk-worms.
The men are all devour'd by luxury,
And Alexander only has the orts.

Na. Therefore they're nauseous both to heaven
    and earth,
And it is insolence in mortal man,
To force upon the gods what they disgust.
Cram nations down the throat of Providence,
Which it throws up again in every field.

Dat. I do declare, I'd no more fight, to guard
The King's dominions over heartless cowards,
Than I wou'd fight for eagles, to defend
Their principality over other birds.

Be. Nay, I have ever thought, a Persian King
Was at the most but master of a mint.
Persia has gold and jewels, but no men ;
It has been long depopulated, all
By slavery, and·vice·; by women too.
Women shou'd fill, and they unman, their towns,
War lays 'em not so waste, war mars and makes.
This war has made more men than it has kill'd ;
The slaughter'd heaps were only loads of clay,

Where there was the image of a man.

Na. My lord, they are all images of whores.
They march into the field, rather equipp'd
Like ladies for a ball than troops for war.
Like women too, with weapons weaponless,
They die unwounded by the sight of wounds ;
And serve the ravens up in massy plate.
The Persian crows are fed in greater pomp
Than Kings of Macedon.

  Dat. Oh ! never cowards
Were at more cost, nobly to hide themselves.
The men cannot be seen for plumes and gold.
Nor can the gold for diamonds be seen.
The Royal mettle is oppressed by jewels.
Their modest swords, which abhor nakedness,—
Though heaven knows in state of innocence,—
Sleep in their scabbards, as in velvet beds,
Under rich coverlids of cluster'd pearl.

  Na. And to what end is this ? they only prove
Fine sumpter horses to the enemy,
To carry baggage for 'em to the field.

  Be. Yet they must lord it o'er brave nations;
Who can subdue both men and elements.
How does our naked flesh vanquish the cold ?
How oft is snow our only winter shirt ?

  Na. Yet does our gallantry far exceed theirs.
We have no ladies' favours on our swords,
But victories, the favours of the gods,
Are always there.

  Be. No thanks to Persians,
Who do not only quit us in the field,
And so most cowardly expose our lives,
But stint our troops, that they may starve our
  fame.
I have five thousand horse, and only fight
To be a slave to cowards.

  Na. Nay, to brutes.

Europeans are men, for they enjoy
Their reason, wisely gather'd into laws.
Here they are brutes, for only strength commands.
Our only law is, that there is no law :
All things are lawful here, to power, but laws,
The only rule of justice, here, is might,
The strong devour the weak, and no wrong done.
The wolf is not unjust that eats the lamb,
The lamb is in the wrong to be a lamb.
  Be. In short, the nature of the King is mild,
But cruel is the nature of his crown.
Then to whose lot soever it befals,
If I survive, they shall not keep it long.
Not that I mean to fix it on my head,
But to crown nature, freedom, and sense,
In which all men have equal shares with me.
  Na. My lord, you'll have a crown in those great
    thoughts ;
Not what's without, but what's within the brow,
Shou'd be the mark of sovereign dignity.
  Be. How goes the night away ?
  Na. The morning star
Long since gave darkness warning to be gone.
  Dat. See, see, 'tis gone ! the day possesses
    heaven.
  Be. Nay, then 'tis time we wait upon the King.
  Na. 'Tis more than time, no doubt he's come
    abroad,
I see his golden chariot gild that hill.
  Be. Then he is there viewing the enemy,
  Dat. Now all the shining crowd descend this way.
Let us go pay our adorations.
  Na. Our adorations to a mortal man ? ha ! ha !
  Be. Now gods aid us, whoever you destroy !
These Kings but for one man their swords employ.
Each for himself has all his force design'd,
We fight for you, and for all your mankind.
  VOL. 3.   25

They wou'd be sovereign lords, but I contend
Only to be your creatures' sovereign friend. [*Exit.*

*All sorts of martial musique. Enter priests bearing
fire on silver altars; then a train of officers in
golden robes and collars; then* DARIUS, *followed
by* ARTRABASUS, BESSUS, NABARZANES, MEM-
NON, PATRON. *The King surveys them ; and all
prostrate themselves, and kiss the ground ;
Patron excepted, who only bows.*

Da. I gave command the ground where I expect
The enemies' horse to charge, shou'd be struck full
Of sharp and bearded irons, but with marks
For us to know and shun 'em.——Is it done ?
 Ar. 'Tis, mighty sir !
 Dat. 'Tis well ! I am inform'd
Our rash, fierce enemies are become wise.
The sight of this vast dreadful multitude
Has cool'd their boiling blood.
 Be. Sir, so we hear.
 Mem. Sir, 'tis no more than truth and what I
  saw,
I was commanded, with a thousand horse,
To make discovery how the enemy lay.
Fear was to them a multiplying glass :
They believ'd all our army was come down ;
And cried Darius—arm !—Darius here !
Your Royal name alone half routed them,
Nay, I was told even Alexander fear'd.
The dreadful shouts of your vast multitudes
Shook forests, mountains, and the conqueror's
  heart,
And gave us time to make a good retreat.
 Pa. Nay, if that Prince has fear, it comes from
  Heaven,
For terror is not natural to him.
 Da. 'Tis true ! the omen appears promising.

Enter DATAPHERNES.

Da. The eunuch Tyriotes, Royal sir,
That lately did attend upon the Queen,
Has made escape out of the enemies' camp,
And brings some mournful news.
    Da Ha! from my Queen?
    Dat. His eyes are drown'd in tears, and garments
    torn.
    Da. Nay, then it is my turn to tremble now ;
If ill but threatens her, it destroys me.
Bring hitherto Tyriotes,——bring my death.
    Be. Were it not better, sir, defer the news,
And not begin the day ?——
    Da. Dispute my will ?

Enter TYRIOTES.

Come hither! speak, while I have sense to hear.
Silence is vain, thy garments and thy eyes
Plunge me into a thousand tort'ring fears.
Speak—do not spare me, 'cause thou see'st me
    grieve,
For I have learnt to be unfortunate,
And to the wretched 'tis a little ease
To know how far their misery will extend,
—Oh ! I distrust one thing, I hate to think
Much more to speak.—Thou com'st to let me know
She, whom I prize above my crown and life,
Has, in her miserable vassalage,
Receiv'd indignities I cannot name.
Say—ease my torments—stab me with the truth!
    Ty. Oh ! let not, sir, vain fears afflict your heart,
Your real cause of sorrow is too much.
But oh ! the generous conqueror paid your Queen
All honours that a slave cou'd give his Prince ;
He rather did appear a slave to her.
But now she is no more——your Queen is dead.

Ar. How? the Queen dead?

Da.——Martyr'd for chastity——
'Tis so—'tis so—She did oppose his lust,
And he has murther'd her,——barbarian !——
What injuries have I done to thee, and thine,
That thou shou'dst take this infamous revenge?
There's no just reason for thy war on me,
But say, 'tis glorious to subdue a King,
Can it be so to violate a Queen?
Cou'dst thou not spare her beauty, and her sex?

Ty. Oh! sir, he did,—again y' afflict yourself
With visions, shadows,—she receiv'd from him
All kind and honourable usage, sir.

Da. Ha! kind?

Ty. Yes, sir,-- for when she died, he wept;
You cannot more lament.

Da. Ha! this is worse——
There was a friendship grown between them then.
And he had favours from her—it was so——
Men lament not the death of enemies.
I cannot bear the thought.

Ty. Oh! hear me, sir.

Da. I would have privacy.   Away! be gone!
                              [*Ex. all but Da. and Ty.*
This is not fit for any ears but mine,
No, nor for mine—for it will make me mad.

Ty. Oh! sir, indeed—

Da. Preparing to deceive?

Ty. No—sir—

Da. It will be folly—have a care!
For now my grief is height'ned into rage—
My tears are turn'd to fire, then do not lie!
By lying thou wilt fool thyself, not me.
For if I find thou dost conceal the truth,
The rack shall force it from thee.

Ty. I'll speak truth.

Da. Do! thrust me not upon extremities,

For cruelty and I never agreed.
In sparing thy own self, thou wilt spare me.
I do conjure thee, by the love thou bear'st
Thyself, or me, deliver me the truth!
Tell me—oh! whither am I going now?
But must go on, though the way lead to Hell.
Tell me if Alexander —fortunate—
Victorious—young and brave—did not attain—
What I'm asham'd to ask, and dread to know.—

   Ty. No, sir, indeed.
   Da. Lie not!
   Ty. I will not, sir—
What should I gain by telling you untruth?
   Da. Hopes of my favour by soft flattery.
   Ty. Sir, here I freely offer up these limbs
To any torment that can be endur'd.
There's strength enough in truth to bear 'em all,
And then I hope you will believe me, sir.
   Da. This is all cunning to avoid the rack,
But that thou shalt not do— ho! bring the rack,
   Ty. With all my heart.
   Da. So bold? I like it well.
He cannot love my ease more than his flesh:
Bring torments on himself to soften mine.
Thou hast half won me to thee—speak! I'm calm.
   Ty. Then I appeal to all the powers divine.—
Oh! now attest my truth, attest yourselves——
If I deliver fictions to the King,
You are all fictions if you spare my head.
The virtuous conqueror did treat the Queen
With all the honour, virtue, and the pure
Religion due, to one so much divine.
He never saw her beauteous face but once,
And then, to give her comfort for her loss,
Her divine beauties only tempted him
To greater virtue; and he did not serve
His pleasure, but his glory, by her charms.

He serv'd her honourably in her life ;
And when she died, he mourn'd the public loss,
And gave her Royal pompous funerals.
   Da. Oh ! Alexander, thou hast vanquished me:
Till now, thy fortune only conquer'd mine,
But now thy virtues have subdued my soul ;
Have thrown me down, into a weeping slave.
I blush to shew my face.—But all these tears
Must not be thine; my Queen must share with
    thee,
Whose honour I have wrong'd. Oh ! thou bright
    shade
Of my chaste Queen, forgive my jealousy,
It was th'excess, and frenzy of my love.
Now, you great gods, protectors of my throne,
I first implore your favour to my right !
Restore the throne to me the lawful lord,
But, if your powerful mysterious wills
Forever have excluded me and mine,
Oh ! give this great and glorious monarchy
To this so brave, so just, and glorious Prince.
I humbly beg it for my peoples' sake.
How happy will they be, under a Prince
Whose virtues make captivity a joy !
Now call the General to me, and the rest.

   Enter ARTABASUS, BESSUS, NABARZANES, MEM-
    NON, PATRON, DATAPHERNES.

I like not the beginning o' this day,
'Tis a dark morning, for my light's eclips'd,
—Gone down—and I shall never see her more !
I wou'd redeem my children, save their right,
And give renown and victory to my friends,
To all my people peace and happiness.
I care not then how soon I'm with my Queen.
   Ar. The King is sad and pensive.
   Pa. Yes, I see't,

With no small trouble, for it bodes no good.

Da. Come, to our work ! the enemy draws on,
And 'tis a shame so few shou'd challenge us.

Be. Nay, he is rash, and puts great confidence
In light, uncertain fortune, who is soon
Tir'd with her favourites ; soonest of all
With prodigals like him.   She has no fund
Of bottomless successes to maintain
A mad eternity of rash attempts.

Da. Forbear ! and do not rudely touch his name
Who with such gentleness treats all my friends.
Revile him not, subdue him if you can ;
Let's fight him well, for that he'll give us thanks.
Now by our Persian tutelary gods,
By the eternal fire before us born,
By the sun's splendour rising in my realms,
And even a sacred, glorious native here,
By Cyrus's immortal memory,
By your own honours, I conjure you all,
Transmit the Persian glory, you receiv'd
From your brave ancestors, to your own race !
Do—as you see me do, I'll ask no more.
If I be mounted on a chariot
Above you all, 'tis to be seen of all ;
By my example to instruct you all.
Seek not one danger you see me decline ;
Nor let one bosom have more wounds than mine.

[*Exit.*

All go off. A noise of a battle.

Enter BESSUS *and* DATAPHERNES.

Be. Pursue, pursue, improve our good success !
The day's our own ! the great Parmenio,
Greatest of Macedonians, gives ground.
Pursue, and we are masters of their camp
And then their baggage ! and their souls are ours,
For in their baggage lies the greedy souls

Of these poor thieves, they only fight for gold.
But we for glory and dominion.

    Da. My lord, when we are masters of their camp
We'll free our pris'ners—we have thousands there,
Who, free, and arm'd, will fall on th' enemy,
With fury whetted on their iron chains,
Sharp for revenge.——

    Be. 'Tis well advis'd—fall on !   [*Exit.*

A noise of fighting—Pris'ners run over the stage shaking off their chains, and shouting.

    Enter BESSUS *and* NABARZANES, *at several doors.*

    Be. The news, the news, my lord ?
    Na. Undone, undone !
    Be. What say you ?   Undone ?
    Na. By the King's gallantry.
    Be. His gallantry's no news,—we know him
      brave.
Where did you leave him ?
    Na. Fighting hand to hand
With Alexander.
    Be. Ha ! a glory indeed,
And to be coveted above a crown.
Oh ! Gods, shou'd Alexander fall by him—
    Na. I fear'd it, and drew off upon pretence,
To wheel, and charge the enemy i'th' rear,
Indeed, to leave him to his Persian cowards.
A howl—   [*A great howl and cry is heard.*

    Enter ARTABASUS.

    Ar. All's lost, my lords ! the King is kill'd !
    Na. Ha ! the King kill'd, my lord ?
    Be. Nay, then all's won—   [*Aside.*
The kingdom's ours——Ha ! I forget myself,—
The gods forbid. How do you know, my lord ?
    Ar. I was inform'd by those that saw him fall.

Did you not hear an universal howl ?
Na. We did, and thought it came from dying
men.
Ar. Nay, I believe by this time, they are dead ;
For, with the King, the hearts of thousands sunk,
And our despairing men no longer fought
For victory, but death : and had their wish,
For thousands die, and by a thousand ways.
Na. Then by survivorship, the world's our own.
                                                    [*Aside.*
Ar. Away, and carry off, if possible,
The Royal body, for our honour's sake,
For our dear fallen King, and country's sake.
'Tis all the service we can do 'em now.
Na. Here's brave Lord Patron!

Enter PATRON.

Ar. We will beg his aid.
My lord, my lord, our gallant King is kill'd !
Pa. 'Tis false !
Be. How, false ?
Na. I'm sorry to hear that.—   [*Aside.*
Pa. 'Twas nothing but his charioteer that fell.
Ar. Oh ! then that fatal error ruin'd us.
Pa. No, your men's cowardice has ruin'd you.
Ar. Methinks I have some hopes if the King
lives.
Pa. Of what ? for, though the gallant King's
alive,
He's almost the sole Persian that has life,
Or has had any since the day begun.
Before a stroke was struck, the cowards died ;
Stabb'd by the glittering of th' enemies' steel.
The Macedonians had no more to do
But to inter the dead ; throw dirt to dirt,
I mean heap carcasses on carcasses,
A very pious work.   And, for my part,

I think 'tis sacrilege to hinder 'em.
So I am going, for I find we come
Not to a battle, but a funeral.

    Ar. You'll not desert the King whilst he's i'th'
field.

    Pa. He's fled! I forc'd him to't. I was inform'd
He rush'd with too much bravery into th' heart
Of the enemies, to tear away the life—
I mean the valiant Macedonian King;
I, fearing much his danger, not alone
From his brave enemies but his base friends,
March'd to his aid. And found him, as I fear'd,
Left by his men; and fighting not alone
With Alexander, but all Macedon.
All the King's fire warm'd not his heartless men,
But scar'd 'em, for they fled like ghosts from day.
The enemies' trumpets blew 'em all away.
No doubt they wou'd have fled, had the cocks
    crowed;
As, they say, guilty timorous spirits do.
I interpos'd between the two brave Kings,
And made the Macedonian retreat,
Then shew'd the King his frightful solitude;
How all his Persian guards lay in himself,
And his sole safety in a quick retreat;
Else he wou'd fall into the enemies' hands.
Then in despair, and rage, he bent his sword
Against his own brave life. I held his hand,
And with kind violence forc'd him to fly.
And I am told, he's towards Arbela gone.
I'll follow him, I will not kill brave men
To defend cowards, who deserve not life.   *[Exit.*

    Ar. Persia, thy glory's lost!   *[Exit.*

    Na. But ours begins.

    Be. It does, and Patron lied, the King's not
fled,
Darius is indeed; but the King's dead.

Here fallen lye his Empire, and our chains,
Now a fresh stronger hand shall take the reins.

[*Exeunt.*

ACT II.

SCENE, *A room in the palace at Arbela.*

Enter ARTABASUS, DATAPHERNES.

Ar. Lord Bessus with his Bactrian horse in
town ?

Dat. Just come, my lord. Lord Nabarzanes
too,
With his bold Scythians are not far behind.

Ar. This is reviving news ! the King has now
Considerable strength.   See, my lords here !

Enter BESSUS, BARZANA, ORONTE.

Oh ! my lord Bessus, welcome from the grave,
For the devouring fields you left behind
Are but one grave of many miles extent.

Be. 'Tis true ! where half the Kingdom lies in-
terr'd.
Where is the king, my lord ?

Ar. I do not know.
I mean the glorious King you saw to-day
March to the field, with pomp that made the
day ;
It had more light from him, than from the sun.
Here's a despairing, and deserted Prince,
That came to town a private charioteer,
And has not only lost dominion
Over great nations, but his Royal self,
His passions rule, which they ne'er did before ;
And rule so ill, the gallant enemy
Wou'd, I'm sure, treat him with more gentleness.

Be. No wonder, he has had a heavy blow.

Ar. What lady have you there ?
Be. My wife, my lord.
Ar. Oh ! madam, I'm in doubt, if I may say
I'm glad your life is safe, for I believe
'Tis better to be dead than as we are.
Be. Not so, my lord, we may recover all.
I find great numbers of brave men in town.
The King has yet great provinces entire,
And chiefly Bactria, where I command.
There are a thousand towns well fortified,
Where the proud conqueror's fortune may be lost,
As in a labyrinth with a thousand doors,
And the King 'scape, and re-ascend his throne ;
Therefore he need not much submit to grief.
Ar. Alas ! he grieves not only for himself,
But all his suffering friends ; for you, and me.
The griefs and losses of his faithful slaves,
Are all of ours, that he wou'd ever share.
Other proprieties he'd never touch,
Though he be lord of all ; but wou'd neglect
All right, but what he has in his friends' tears.
Those he too carefully collects himself.
Now, in the midst of his great monarchy,
He's all alone, as in a wilderness.
I'll go to him, and, when I can have leave
To speak to him, I'll tell him you are come.
'Twill greatly comfort him ; he loves you much.
Be. The Gods preserve him !
Ar. Madam, your sweet youth
May live to better days ; heaven grant you may.
                             [Exit.

Be. Madam, your beauty may make better days ;
At least with me, let fortune do her worst,
Wou'd it please you.   But sorrow pleases you
More than my love ; and ever has done so,
Since first you saw my face.   How ! Saw my
    face ?

I do not know you ever look'd on me,
Your eyes are turn'd away, or veil'd in tears.
Madam, this cannot easily be borne :
I am less safe with you than among all
The Macedonian swords, I've 'scap'd from them,
Yet die with torments in Barzana's arms.
I am resolv'd I will find out the cause.

  Ba. Alas ! I fear he will discover me. [*Aside.*
           [*One whispers Dat.*

  Dat. My lord, my lord, I've joyful news for you !
Your belov'd son, Lord Memnon, is come safe.
           [*Barzana starts.*

  Ba. Lord Memnon ! ha ! (*aside*). My lord, I
  beg your leave
I may retire ; I'm weary and not well.

  Be. Madam, I wish you may have more repose
Than you can find in me.

  Ba. Nay, why, my lord,
Will you be cruel to yourself and me ?
I pray, forbear, if you desire my life !

  Be. More than my own ; I've done ! all health
  to you. [*Ex. Ba., Oron., at one door. At another,*

Enter MEMNON.

Well, I will trace her sorrows to their spring.
So ! Here's another joy. Welcome, young man,
Come to my arms, for you deserve my love !
Y'ave done me, in the field, no little grace,
It wou'd be strange, if thou should'st not be brave,
Thy mother had more manhood than our men.
Well, thou art come into a ruin'd world,
Where thy great virtue will have no reward.

  Me. My lord, I am rewarded in your love,
Our honour, and our friends, is wealth enough.

  Be. 'Tis true, indeed ! there is great wealth in
  love.
Oh ! son, I've married so much excellence.

Me. So I am told, my lord.

Be. Do not admire,
I never brought thee yet into her sight,
I durst not do it; for, to produce thee,
Had been too bold a boast of my past love
To thy fair mother, to affront my wife.
And I would not offend her for the world.

Me. My lord, you need not make excuse for
 this,
You but observe the custom o' the place.
'Tis thought a horrid profanation
To Persian beauties to be visible:
They are conceal'd, like divine mysteries;
A sister does not see a brother here.

Be. True! and, I prithee, come not in her sight!
I brought her from the battle. She's in town.

Me. How shall I shun her? for I know her not.

Be. Do not approach this palace! here she's
 lodg'd
With other beauties that escap'd the fight.

Me. I shall observe your pleasure carefully.

Be. Now, go thy ways! here is another friend.
        [*Exit Memnon, and*

Enter NABARZANES.

Na. Lord Bessus? I am glad to see you safe.

Be. I doubt we are not safe; the King is strong.

Na. In what?

Be. In Persians.

Na. Strong in Persians?
They can be strong in nothing but perfumes;
They have no spirits, but from essences.

Be. They're above thirty thousand.

Na. Say, they be.

Be. Danger breeds valour. They who poorly
 fell
Were embrios, and miscarriages of war,

But danger has gone out her time with these.
Then, he has Patron, and four thousand Greeks.
    Na. They, I confess, give the King's sword an
      edge.
    Be. And I have scarce four thousand Bactrian
      horse.
    Na. True! and my Scythian archers are no more.
    Be. And then he has a guard, which all slaves
      fear;
Religious awe of Kingly majesty.
    Na. When other forces fly, that never stays.
That Kings have the militia, on earth,
Is fit; should they have that of heaven too?
Vain panic fears, and superstitions!
I'll suffer none to list among my troops.
    Be. He has one guard, I fear, that's misery.
It something touches me, but that's not all,
I've an insatiable and burning love
For glory; and to fall on a fallen King,
Will much deface the beauty of my fame.
    Na. We'll serve the King, save him from misery.
Fortune declares herself his enemy;
And we will lay him safe out of her way.
He shall enjoy the ease and pomp of power,
And we'll endure the danger and the toil.
    Be. Ha! 'tis well thought. The King will
      yield to this.
    Na. We'll make it our request.
    Be. Do! I agree.
    Na. Where is he now?
    Be. He is shut in with grief,
And Artabasus, the old General.
    Na. Let us prepare our friends, and watch our
      time.
    Be. Do! 'tis a brave design, to save one King
And beat another; save a ruin'd King
And beat his conqueror, then save the world

From both, by liberty.   It will be great,
It will be glorious! we shall be ador'd.
   Na. There will be cause, while glorious mur-
    derers
Destroy mankind to form a tyranny,
We'll destroy tyranny to form mankind.
   Be. 'Tis true ! how cruel is it and unjust
Whole nations should in sorrow live and die,
That one great lion may his lust enjoy.   [*Exeunt.*

SCENE is drawn.

DARIUS *is set musing and sad,* ARTABASUS *attending.*

   Da. Oh ! why was Alexander born for me,
To make my crown a misery to me,
Which I have made a happiness to all ?
Tyrants, who spar'd not heaven and earth, were
    spar'd :
How can man find what way it is to walk,
If fortune will thus blindly plough up all.
   Ar. Come, sir, I pray, do not afflict yourself!
You gave your pleasure bounds, limit your grief,
And you, who ne'er broke law nor injur'd man,
Do not break reason's law in your own wrong.
   Da. I'd know my crimes, that have deserv'd all
    this.
   Ar. I know of none.
   Da. Nay, prithee, flatter not !
   Ar. Oh, sir ! was ever I a flatterer ?
   Da. Never, till now.
   Ar. And this is an ill time,
In your calamity and my great age,
For what can you bestow or I receive ?
I've reach'd a hundred years, now wanting five.
My love to honour, conscience, and my king,
Are all the appetites I have to please.
   Da. Oh ! Why have I all sorts of miseries ?

Ar. Those happen to you, as you are a man.
For what is a man ? a congregation
Of disagreeing things ; his place of birth ?
A confus'd crowd of fighting elements,
To nothing fixt, but to eternal change ;
They wou'd all lose their natures, shou'd they fix.
    Da. Why, say they did, were they not better
    lost
Than kept at such expense ? what does poor man
Pay for vain life ?
    Ar. What's matter what he pays ?
Gods did not make this world only for man ?
He's but a parcel o' the universe ;
A fellow-servant with the meanest thing,
To carry on the service o' the whole,
And pleasure o' the gods, the lords of all.
    Da. Can human sorrows be delights to Gods ?
    Ar. Our sorrows are not, but our troubles may.
A great man, vanquishing his destiny,
Is a great spectacle worthy of Gods.
    Da. Give me thy hand ! years have not gone by
    thee,
Like empty idle vagrants, but like Kings,
And given thee riches to relieve a King.

            Enter an Eunuch.

    Eu. Lord Bessus, Nabarzanes—
    Da. Are they here ?
    Eu. They have been waiting for access some
    time,
Lord Memnon, Patron too.
    Da. Bring 'em all in !

Enter BESSUS, NABARZANES, MEMNON, PATRON,
    DATAPHERNES, *several* BACTRIANS.

    Da. Oh ! welcome, my brave friends, come to
    my arms,

I'm joy'd to see your safety and your love
Follow me now !   You are true friends indeed.
I will complain of misery no more,
For I perceive it is the great art of heaven
To give us better taste of what we have :
A friend was ne'er so sweet to me before.
'Tis hard in prosp'rous fortune to know friends :
Now I am certain you attend on me,
This is to me my first apparent Court.
Though I've not fought, I've lov'd with great
    success.
There is no state, in which the bounteous gods
Have not plac'd joy, if men wou'd seek it out.
Well, sirs, what news ? How many have we lost ?

    Be. Above four hundred thousand, sir, 'tis said.

    Da. Oh ! my amazing merciless destiny.

    Be. 'Twas not a battle, but a massacre.

    Na. Oh ! sir, I wish your sorrows might end
    here,
But though they're heavy as the heart of man
Has strength to bear, I must enlarge 'em yet.
Your great Lieutenants, sir, and Governors,
Have flung up all their towns and provinces.
Mithrenes has resign'd Armenia,
False Mazeus, the once glorious Babylon,
The governor of Damas with the town
Betray'd the Kingdom.   For, sir, in that town
You had lodg'd wealth enough, to regain all.

    Da. Two hundred thousand talents in coin'd
    gold.
In silver twice the sum ; with diamonds
And jewels of inestimable price.

    Be. Alas ! this was not all the riches, sir.
Your Princes, and great Lords, had, as they thought,
There secur'd all the beauty o' the East,
I mean their lovely wives and daughters, sir.
And this inhuman coward betray'd 'em all.

That wives of Princes serv'd the lusts of slaves,
And poorest wretches shone in robes of Kings ;
Such scorn did fortune throw on this world's
    pride.
Da. Oh ! my immense boundless calamities.
Though I've so many thousands lost in fight,
I must lament that I have lost no more,
Better my cities mount to Heaven in fire
Than sink by cowardly villany to Hell.
And they're prefer'd, who meet with noble death,
Above the villains, who by treason reign.
Me. A little joy were seasonable now,
And I've a little for you, sir.
Da. Ha ! joy?
Me. The coward of Damas fled to Babylon,
And, with his brother villain Mazeus, went
To meet the enemy, with triumphant pomp,
As if the conquest of their honesties
Had been most honourable victories.
I heard it wou'd be so, took some brave friends,
And slew 'em both before the Conqueror's face,
Then brought their heads away, and there they are.
    Da. Oh ! brave young man ! Now I'm subdu'd
        by thee,
I've nothing to reward thy gallantry,
So thou hast made a vassal of thy King.
I'm overcome by enemies and friends.
Good Gods, for all my losses, suff'rings, wrongs,
Favour my gallant friends ! I'll ask no more.
    Ar. Oh ! exc'llent Prince ! will the Gods leave
        a Prince,
To whom they give such pledges of their love,
I mean such god-like virtues and brave friends ?
    Da. 'Tis true ; can I despair, and have such
        friends ?
By you, I'm still a great and glorious King,
Able to fight with Alexander yet :

And, by the Gods, I'll do't.   I thought on flight,
The vile decree with horror I revoke.
Shall I fear anything while I have you ?
And, I am sure, there is not in the world,
A danger you wou'd shun like shameful flight.
And shall I lead you on to infamy ?
No, I will shew I deserve men so brave,
I will march back, and fight the enemy,
One blow may scatter all his victories ;
They're lumber pil'd disorderly in haste.

 Pa. Oh! Fortune, in this Monarch, see thy faults,
            [aside.
And frailties; he'll be great in spite o' thee.

 Da. What means this silence in you all, my
  Lords ?
If you have fear, I'm sure it is for me.

 Be. Ay, so it is, great Sir !

 Da. So I believe.
But is there anything to fear, like shame ?
And shall I shamefully desert myself ?
In my own Empire be a banish'd man ?
Or, like my traitors to the Conqueror, creep,
 1o be a petty Lord of some poor town,
And there in safety lock my little heart ?
I charge you, kill me, when I e'er devise
Such infamous destruction for your King.
No I will be a King, or not at all.
My life and reign shall have one period.
But if your resolutions be like mine,
We will yet give our sorrows a brave end.
Justice is for us, so may Fortune be ;
I'm a bright proof of her inconstancy,
But if no God will lend us any aid,
Let us be Gods, and Fortune to ourselves,
And signalize ourselves by such a fight,
May shew, at least, we deserve better fates.
—All silent still ?

Ar. Sir, you exceed us all,
As much in spirit, as in dignity.
What soul but yours is not with horror seiz'd,
Viewing the danger that approaches us ?
Sir, you deserve the Empire o' the world,
And we'll endeavour, sir, to deserve you.
Great Sir, go on, and we will follow you !
You have prepar'd us all with glorious arms,
With hopes of victory, and scorn of death.
    Pa. Sir, we are strangers, owe our birth to
      Greece,
So are free troops, and may march where we please ;
But yet to shew we fight for fame, not pay,
And did not serve your money but yourself,
We are all ready to lay down our lives,
And on our sepulchres erect your throne.
For what a glory will it be to us,
To make the Persian king our monument ?
    Da. I look'd, brave Patron, for no less from thee.
Now it will be a shame if Persian Lords
Let a poor stranger, in their King's own Court,
Outshine them all, in love and loyalty.
    Me. The Gods forbid. Lead on, most Royal Sir!
I have some wounds require my present care,
But, Sir, they will not indispose me long.   [*Exit.*
    Be. Now speak our thoughts to him, we are
      prepar'd.
    Na. You show a courage, sir, that shames your
      fate,
Which gives your Crown from your descent and
      right.
But what has made heaven blush, shall make you
      bleed :
Fate plots your ruin by your gallantry.
Alas ! we are not now, as we have been,
A sea of men, that delug'd the whole earth,
Swallowed the rivers, devour'd nature's store,

Emptied the spacious vessel o' the world,
More than the grasp o' Providence cou'd hold ;
That down we fell in heaps: now 'tis not so.
We may be numbered now ; all we can do
Is but to gain some pity for ourselves,
And honourably throw away our King.
Brave men scorn death, but yet they value life,
Because their lives are useful to the world.
It is enough—too much,—danger and death
Follow us fast, let us not follow them.
Sir, I most humbly move,—Heaven knows my soul,
In tenderness to you, not to ourselves ;—
Retreat with us, to neighb'ring Bactria!
Sir, there are endless forests of brave youth,
Whence in few days we will have rods enow,
To scourge the Macedonian pride to death.
But then we beg you'll make one more retreat.
    Da. Whither ?
    Na. Sir, out of the dominion
Of your ill planets.—
    Da. Ha !—What dost thou mean !
    Na. Sir, we dare fight with men, but not with
      Heaven :
And all the Gods appear your enemies.
What if you hid in privacy and ease ?
It wou'd be pious reverence to Heaven,
And a brave conquest over your own mind.
Let none subdue Darius but himself.
Fling up awhile to th'importuning storm
Some of our dignity to save the rest,
And make your court to Heaven, and all brave
    men,
By honouring the favourite of both,
Lord Bessus, with the Sovereign power.
    Da. How now ?———
    Na. Nay, Sir, but for a while, till he has lur'd
Gods, and revolting nations to your aid.

He is ador'd by men, obey'd by Gods.
They all observe his will, they'll not deny
Your Crown to him, and, when 'tis in his hand,
He'll faithfully return it to your self.

 Da. Oh ! villain ! most amazing, impudent,
And cowardly villain ! hast thou watch'd thy time
When treason may be insolent and safe,
And to my face abuse me, unchastis'd ?
No, traitor !—

 Dataphernes draws—Bessus and his men interpose
   and hold the King.

 Be. Hold, sir, do not hurt yourself !

 Da. Ha ! I am seiz'd and threatened—are you all
In this conspiracy ?

 Pa. No, I am not [*Patron and the Greeks draw.*

 Be. Hold, Patron, hold ! hold all, that love the
 King,
He will receive no hurt, except from you ;
Our blood is his, perhaps his vital blood.
In me you'll cut whole nations from his aid.

 Na. Before we spoke, we did consider well
The strength, both of our reason, and our swords.
     [*Exeunt Bessus, Nabarzanes.*

 Da. Ha ! Was this Bessus ?

 Pa. Sir, will you bear this ?
By Heavens, I would rather endure the swords
Of these bold villains, than their impudence.

 Da. It stunn'd me, but I now recover sense.
Brave Patron, follow me ; follow me all !
Though my hard fortune will not suffer me
To conquer Kings, I'll be more like a God.
I will defend all Kings, even those unborn !
By the reward these villains shall receive,
Their dire confusion shall be the defence
Of Kings and Kingdoms, forty ages hence.

 Ar. Oh ! he is running to his certain death.

Oh! sir,—   [*Artabasus falls at the King's feet.*
Da. What dost thou mean?
Ar. Pity yourself,
Your friends, your children! you will ruin all
Da. Will none stand by me then?
Pa. Yes, Sir, we will!
Da. De'e see? Oh! shame! More love, more
    loyalty,
In this brave stranger, than in all my friends,
Whom I have made more rich, than all his
    Greece!
Come, Patron, bring thy Greeks, they're strength
    enough.
Ar. Oh! If you'll go to ruin, pass through me!
My life has long been useless to myself.
I shall abhor it, when 'tis so to you,
And, nor my sword, nor counsel can prevail.
Da. Oh! How am I beset? the enemy
Is at my back, my friends fly in my face.
Ar. Oh! sir, I speak my loyal care of you,
The enemy is near, your army small;
The Macedonian was too great a weight
For us to bear, when we had millions.
Alas! what shall this little body do,
When you have maim'd it too, and have cut off
Its strongest limbs? for so these great men are.
Da. They are cut off from all their love to me.
Ar. Indeed, Sir, I believe their meaning good.
They have stood bravely by you, Sir, till now,
Stood stronger than the walls of Babylon:
For they have fallen in shame by base revolt.
If they meant well, pardon their erring love:
Do not destroy 'em for some kind mistakes.
If they be bad, Mercy may change their hearts.
Da. Do what you will; for all must reign
    but I.
Oh! my misfortunes.

Ar. Pray, Sir, do not grieve.

Da. Nay, prithee, if I may not be a King,
Yet let me be the mourner of a King,
I am all the mourners that my death shall have.

Ar. Then am I false?

Da. No! pardon me, good man.

Pa. Who can pretend to honour, or a soul,
And not be touch'd with such a Prince's wrong?

    Da. 'Tis true, then can the men he has
      oblig'd
Conspire to wrong him? if they had the thought,
I doubt not but they will abhor themselves;
And I shall fling them at his feet in tears.

    Pa. Or, by the Gods, I'll fling them there in
      blood.

Da. Oh! how shall I reward thee, noble Greek?
Well, it is possible they may mean well.
Then, on submission I will pardon them,
And take them to my favour yet; for I
Fear more to do injustice than to die.   [*Exit.*

    Pa. Come, my brave countrymen, stand to your
      arms;
And let us show what a true soldier is!
He's no mechanique slave, that sells his breath,
But a just generous Lord of life and death.
Not a wild beast, that knows no law, but lust;
He destroys bestial men, or makes them just.
The cut-throat does a Soldier's name profane,
Pretending to be more, he's less a man;
The worse for reason, by that artful tool,
More hurtful than a beast, he kills by rule.
But the true Soldier does mankind create,
By forcing reason on a brutal state:
    When oaths are wind, and laws but childish
      rods,
The Soldier comes, like Thunder, from the Gods.

                        [*Exeunt.*

SCENE, *A Room in the Palace.*

BARZANA *sate melancholy, attending to a song—sometimes weeping.* ORONTE *waits.*

Ba. Oh miserable me!

Or. Astonishment!
In everlasting sighs, complaints, and tears?
This must not be, it leads her from her sense.
Madam! She minds me not—madam, I beg?—
You will not always listen to your griefs,
But to your friends sometimes.

Ba. Trouble me not.

Or. Madam, you are a trouble to yourself.

Ba. Be gone! I'd be alone.

Or. I wou'd you were.
But you associate with a cruel grief,
That does return your kindness very ill.
You grace a melancholy that devours
The beauties, whence it has its wondrous grace.
Nay, madam, it is dangerous to your life:
You neither eat nor drink nor take repose;
You go to bed for liberty to weep,
And the night leaves you, as she found you, in
    tears;
Day dries not up that dew, you only breathe
To sigh, and not to live. Your reason wastes,
You see not, hear not, mind not any thing.
Sometimes your fancy hunts a thousand things,
But ere they're found, alas, your fancy's lost!

Be. Thou wilt be troublesome, but thou mean'st
    well;
Therefore I pardon thee. How tir'd am I
With sitting, and till now, I knew it not.
Come, let us walk!

Or. Where will you please to walk?

Ba. I know not where.

Or. Abroad in the fresh air?

Ba. No, I shall be disturb'd with company.

Or. Then in the gallery ?

Ba. No, it wants air.

Or. Then in the grove ?

Ba. I will not walk at all.

Fetch me a book, I'll read,—let it alone,—

Go call the musique back again !—no, stay,—

It was too noisy ; a soft gentle lute

Wou'd please me better.   But another time,—

How ill you dress me, sir ? *

Or. Dear madam, why ?

Ba.   I'm cumber'd with a thousand needless
things.

Art need not study vanity for us ;

We have too much from nature.

Or. Will you please

To change your dress ?

Ba. Then you will be a toil.

Wou'd I cou'd change myself

For any thing besides.

Or. She weeps again.

Ba. I'll to my closet,—no, I will abroad !

Release me quickly from the slavery

Of all this formal and superfluous dress.

The world's in war,—I'll be an Amazon,—

Tie back my hair, but not with any art.

Come, – a short robe,—lay naked my right arm !—

A javelin there shou'd be the only grace.

My horse ! my horse ! Oh ! I am prest to death

Under your earthly sloth.   Oh ! you good Gods !

That I were now among the warriors,

Gaining eternal honours to myself.

Eternal honours ? no—eternal shame,—

Shewing my follies, as I madly do.

—Oh ! I am curs'd—curs'd by some angry power,

* "Sirrah. In old plays this term is frequently addressed
to women."—*Halliwell.*

That makes a foolish and vile thing o' me,
And then exposes that to shame for me.
Gods, if you'll take my reason, take my life !
Leave me not sense, only to feel my grief.

   Or. Oh, madam, madam, in all reverence
To your command and will, I've borne your griefs
Till they have torn your reason, and my heart.
I must assault them now,—and on my knees
I humbly beg you will discover them.

   Ba. Away, away !

   Or. No, madam, pardon me,
I will pay all obedience to yourself,
But, oh ! no more to your distractions.

   Ba. Begone, I say !

   Or. I will not, cannot, go.

   Ba. Thou dost not know how troublesome thou
      art,
And to what little purpose; shou'd I tell
My griefs to thee, it wou'd increase 'em more.

   Or. You know not that, you have a noble mind,
But at the present 'tis not in your power.
My little counsels now may aid you more.
Be not so faithful to your misery ;
Betray it to me.

   Ba. 'Tis impossible !
Oh ! I could easier rip my bosom up,
And shew the sun my naked heart, than thee.

   Or. I do not think the dangers o' your Lord—

   Ba. Ay, there it is—

   Or. No, you are cold to him.
Oh ! there is something more, and I must know.

   Ba. Well, I will tell thee.

   Or. Do !

   Ba. Another time.

   Or. When 'tis too late,—consider what you do.
I know you've so much kindness for your lord,
You wou'd be loth wholly to lose his heart ;

And there's a beauteous Amazonian queen
By whom Lord Bessus has a noble son.
   Ba. Undone ! undone ! Thou hast discover'd me.
   Or. Discover'd what ?
   Ba. As if you did not find.—
   Or. Madam, I swear I know not what you mean.
   Ba. You know too much. Had I a dagger here,
I'd lock thy bosom to eternity.
   Or. I wish you had, and it were in my breast,
If any ill has hap'ned to yourself.
   Ba. She takes a pleasure to repeat my shame.
   Or. Your shame ?—Your shame, de'e say ?
   Ba. My Hell—nay, worse—
Shame is a torment which the damn'd know not :
The damn'd have darkness to conceal their shame.
But mine will suddenly break out to light,
I cannot bear the torment of my love.
   Or. Oh! now your sorrows shew their mournful
     face.
You love—your husband's son.
   Ba. No more—no more!
I tremble at the thought—I'm sick to death,
If the word love but touch my tongue, or ear.
'Tis sin to talk of sin.
   Or. Your love's no sin.
It is your glory, now you vanquish it.
   Ba. I do not, do not, cannot vanquish it,
I dare not trust myself, with love or life,
I'll seek out death by all the ways I can.
   Or. Hold, madam, hold—
   Ba. Why ? am I fit to live?
   Or. If you be not, you are less fit to die.
   Ba. Death ends my sin.
   Or. Murther increases it.
   Ba. It will be justice or an impious wretch.
I'll thrust all Hell into one painful hour,
And then, Good heaven, I hope, will claim no more.
                        [*Exit.*

ACT III.

· SCENE, *The Palace.*

Enter DARIUS, ARTABAZUS, *Guards.*

Ar. Oh! Sir! the men are good and penitent;
And brave as good; and I shall see you yet
As happy, great, and glorious as ever.
    Da. No, Artabazus, no! my Queen is dead.
I never can be happy in this world,
But I wou'd give my Kingdom happiness.
Go, call 'em in—

Enter BESSUS *and* NABARZANES, *who prostrate them-*
    selves before the King, and weep.

Be. Oh! great and gracious King,
Oh! infinite is our confusion,
We humbly beg you will regard our tears—
We can express our grief no other way.
    Da. Indeed, I do not know what to regard,
Nor what you are—you seem so strange to me;
I think you are my subjects, are you not?
    Na. Yes, sir, and faithful ones, whate'er we
        seem.
    Da. A subject without terror of his King
Is an unnatural thing in Persia.
You are portentous omens of my death.
    Be. Oh! narrow world! a virtue that exceeds
The common size appears portentous here.
The world is fallen on your sacred head,
And now we cannot stand on forms of State,
But we must get you out what way we can.
And, Sir, indeed we thought this was the best.
But now, because 'twas bold, it appears bad.
    Da. What cou'd befal me worse, than what
        you sought,
Tamely to yield my crown, at your demand,

And serve my slaves? nothing can throw me down,
So low as that, but my own cowardice.
I will not yield the Conqueror my Crown,
I'll rather singly fight with all his troops;
For by them all I can be kill'd but once.
But yield my Crown I suffer many deaths,
In my own shame, and my dear children's tears,
Who then no more are children of a King.
And wou'd you wish me cowardly, infamous,
And cruel to my children? Oh! Is this
Your kindness to me? You ingrateful men.
Oh! who wou'd not ha' thought you were my
    friends?
Who wou'd ha' thought you cou'd be otherwise?
For I beset you with my favours so,
No hearts, but yours, cou'd scape from loving me.
And now for you to hurt your King, and friend?
And at this time when I am prest to death
Under a fallen throne, a ruin'd house,
My mother, brother, little only son,
Both my sweet daughters in captivity,
And my Queen dead?
    Na. Oh! Sir—no more—no more—
    Be. Yes, Sir, go on, go on, and break our hearts!
For we desire to die, since we grieve you.
    Da. You [do] deserve it for your cruelty.
Had you by private treasons stolen my life,
You had shewn more humanity than now;
For then I had not felt the barb'rous blow;
That had shewn Reverence, call'd me a Dread King;
This calls me fool and coward to my face.
I shew'd no fear o' the brave enemy,
Why shou'd you think I wou'd be seiz'd by you?
    Na. We did not hope to work upon your fear,
We know you have no fear—but on your love.
We know you have a truly Royal soul,
That love your people with paternal love,

And we petition'd, Sir, for all our lives
Which hourly perish by your destiny.

Be. Yes, Sir, 'tis plain; while you are in the
    field
We fall in heaps; you are no sooner gone,
But, as your chariot wheels turn'd Heaven round,
Success is ours, and the whole day is chang'd.
And we wou'd fix our Fortune to your Crown,
Your dangers to our heads; in off'ring this
We have discharg'd our duties, and can die.

Na. Nay, wish to die, to ease you of your fears!
Better we die, than you shou'd want repose:
We pray not for our lives, Sir, but your love.

Da. Oh! now you vanquish me, come to my
    arms!

Be. Oh! excellent King.

Na. Too good—too gracious.

Da. Great things to vile men I'll not sacrifice,
Nor good and gallant to revenge and fear.
No, do your duty, sirs, and I'll do mine.
Leave the dispose of Crowns to Kings and Gods,
Preserve your honours, that's enough for you.
Conquer a Conqueror, not a fallen King,
And your own King, you want no enemies;
Oh! make not any for yourselves by crimes.
The Macedonian King pursues us fast,
And I perhaps shall perish by his sword,
That you may spare the guilt of murd'ring me.

Be. Oh! horror! do you think we have the
    thought?

Na. Oh! you suspect us! that is worse than death.

Da. No—no— I only counsel you in love,
For you possess my heart, though I've lost yours.

Be. Oh! say not so.

Da. I hope 'tis otherwise.

Na. But you believe it not.

Da. Well, I have done.

Be what you seem, and all shall be forgot;
And what we do, let's do like gallant men.
Who bravely fall have this one happiness
Above the Conqueror, they share his fame,
And have more love, and an unenvied name.
[*Ex. Darius, Artabasus, Guards.*
Na. This was the only way to vanquish him.
I found we cou'd not gain the Persians:
I often talked to 'em of liberty,
Alas! they understood not what I meant,
For in the Persian tongue is no such word.
They answer'd nothing, but the King, the King!
His sacred Majesty, long live the King!
That mighty comprehensive word, the King,
Had all the sense a Persian thought cou'd hold.
So I thought this our only secure way;
We cou'd not fight the Greeks and Persians.
Be. Now I cou'd easier have fought 'em both,
Than stoop'd to all this base hypocrisy;
I think 'tis harder to subdue him now,
Than if he had his millions at his heels:
For Sovereign power springs out o' the sword.
If I had conquer'd him in a fair fight,
I had both gain'd his Kingdom and his Right.
Now on ourselves, and our brave friends we fall,
And turn them into fools and villains all.
Glory I court, and I wou'd have my Love
Fair and complete, as she's enjoy'd by Jove.
Na. And so you will! Jove did for Empire frame
A world of fools and knaves, we do the same.
Were there no knaves, what use of Sovereign sway?
And if there were no fools, who wou'd obey? [*Exeunt.*

SCENE, *Another Apartment in the Palace.*

Enter BARZANA, *and* ORONTE.

Ba. Now I have told the secrets of my heart

I have much eas'd my heart ; it is more cool,
My reason does begin to come in play ;
Though I find great misfortune in my love,
I have this comfort, there is no great guilt.
I lov'd the son, ere I the father saw.
It pleas'd the Gods—I know not for what sin—
In the great field, at the Cilician straights,
First to begin the dreadful day on me.
Darted into my eyes, into my soul,
The shining, the confounding killing charms
Of the most noble youth, they ever form'd.
At the first sight of him my soul dissolv'd :
It was some time ere I had breath to speak.
At length I hid my face, and, whisp'ring you,
Bid you inquire, who that Commander was.

    Or. You did ; I thought 'twas curiosity,
And gave you information.

    Ba. To my joy!
He quickly rode away out o' my sight,
But left such strong impressions on my soul,
Though many thousands fell before my face,
The day was lost ; nay, my own liberty—
I saw it not, Memnon was in my eye.
But oh ! my misery soon waken'd me ;
And then I shriek'd, more out of fear
For Memnon than myself ; for I despair'd
To see him more, except amongst the dead.
As we were led over our slaughter'd friends,
Envying their gory mangled carcasses,
The same brave youth, whom I had in my heart,
Came shining once again into my eye
With new, and brighter splendours than before ;
For he brought Honour, Conquest, Liberty,
Dispers'd the enemy, as winds do sand,
And quickly made free passage for my flight.
You must remember it, for you were there
In the same chariot with me.

Or. Yes, I was,
And so was he, I think.
    Ba. What do you mean ?
    Or. I'm sure his eye was, and I think, his heart.
    Ba. Away! but if it was, so much the worse,
For then his misery wou'd be like mine.
    Or. Would it afflict you to be lov'd by him ?
    Ba. Yes, to his grief ; else, 'twould extremely
    please.
    Or. I know not if he loves; this I am sure,
He was your guard, your beauty was his guide : .
For, all the way he by your chariot rode,
His eye did never fail to follow yours,
His tongue said little, but his looks said much.
Indeed that was no time or place for talk,
Our ears were with a thousand noises fill'd,
Ay, and our hearts too with a thousand fears.
Alas ! This short success was only lent,
Fortune did soon demand her favours back :
The enemy pursued ; the gallant youth
Was forc'd to turn on them, and you to fly.
    Ba. Oh ! I fled slowly, with a heavy heart.
A thousand times did I turn back my eye,
Ay, and I think as oft my chariot,
Wishing to see him come a Conqueror.
But 'twas in vain to stay, the night came on,
So I went forwards, and let Fortune drive ;
Who led me to eternal misery,
In the first place, where I my safety sought.
There, with the King, Lord Bessus lay conceal'd,
Who at first sight of me, flam'd out with love,
And beg'd in me his ruin of the King.
    Or. Why did you not inform the King your
    love ?
    Ba. I did, in what I cou'd, blushes and tears,
But the word love I had not power to speak.
    Or. Oh! fatal modesty ! But see, my Lord !

Ba. Oh! my disorders will discover me.
What can I say, why I, as yet a bride,
Have all the sorrows of a captive slave?

Enter BESSUS.

Be. Madam, may I approach?
Ba. My Lord, you know
You are a Sovereign here.
Be. I have some right,
But grief usurps my room; I cannot bear
A rival in my bed.
Ba. Rival, my lord?
Be. That is my rival sure that shares with me,
And I methinks have the least part in you.
What favours I receive, you rather give
To marriage vows than me.   Those cherubims
Are not for idols, but for ornaments,
To grace Love's altars, not to be ador'd.
Madam, you may believe it troubled me,
To be excluded thus my joy and right.
I wou'd not very tamely yield it up;
I have been searching for my enemy,
And I believe I have th' offender found.
Ba. What does he say?   [*Aside.*
Be. Madam, I call to mind
When we last parted, news was brought to me,
My son was come; his name disorder'd you.
Ba. Undone!—undone!—I am betrayed—
                                          [*Aside.*
Be. 'Tis so.
My son! my son—
Ba. Your son? what of your son?
Be. Undoes me; your confusion shews it plain.
Ba. In what confusion am I?
Be. All your face
Flames with a blush; your breath goes thick and
     short.

Your speech cou'd scarcely falter more in death.
Ba. Fetch me a dagger !   [*Aside.*
Be. I'll remove this grief.
I'll send for him and stab him in your sight.
Ba. Oh! horror, horror, hold! You shall know
    all.
Be. Oh ! I know all, and will remove it all.
Madam, you very highly injure me.
Ba. I do not—do not.
Be. Oh, you do!
Ba. In what ?
Be. I here invoke the Gods.
Ba. And so do I.
Be. Tear out my heart, if it be false to you !
Ba. Have you suspicion I am false to you ?
Be. No, madam, no, but you have entertain'd
Causeless suspicion of my truth to you.
Not that my humble heart is worth your care,
But your own merit is : you are enrag'd
Your Royal birth, and divine excellence,
Which may deserve to have more Heavens than
    one,
Gain not the entire heart of one poor slave.
But you are triumph'd over by the Queen,
Because I show some fondness of her son.
Ba. Oh! I am scap'd ! Shame and death
    threat'ned me,   [*Aside.*
And then rode by far, far out of their way.
He thinks my grief is jealousy of him.
Be. Come, madam, throw the Queen out of your
    thoughts,
For I'll assure you she is far from mine :
I never lov'd her in her softest youth.
Nature indeed had given her charms for love ;
But the embraces of the wanton wind,
And sun's hot kisses had debauch'd them all.
And they were all the kisses she endur'd :

She must perform the office of her sex,
Or have no heirs to her renown and throne,
So our embrace was but a bed cabal,
More for a State, than amorous intrigue.
Love did but little in the whole affair,
The Gods did all; therefore the gallant youth
Is like a God, and therefore lov'd by me.
I know you'd love him, if you saw him once,
Which you shall do, and let him kiss your hands.
Run for my son—   [*To Oronte.*
  Ba. I will not see his face.
He's setting his own house all in a flame—
                                    [*Aside.*
When it already burns in smothering fire.
  Be. Oh, how disturb'd she is!   Cou'd I believe
A trouble to thy heart shou'd delight mine?
This is a mark of love, but the only one
I do not wish to have,—lay it aside,
And let [us] all three love.   I must confess
My son is a record of my past love,
But he's so fair a one—
I'm very sure if you beheld him once
You wou'd be loth he shou'd be blotted out.
  Ba. With what a pleasing dream he is deceiv'd!
                                    [*Aside.*
'Tis cruelty to waken a sick friend,
Whose sleep is all his ease; let him dream on!
Nay, I am told your son,—your son's a gallant man,
And I am troubled that I cannot give
His merit the reception it deserves.
  Be. Why not, my love? you may if I consent.
  Ba. I'll not consent to an undecent thing,
And so it is t' encourage vicious love.
Such was your kindness for the Amazon Queen.
  Be. Thy virtue is too nice.
  Ba. Nay, I'm content
You love and favour him.

Be. A thousand thanks!

Ba. But do not let him come into my sight.

Be. Well, dearest, you shall see the Divine power
You have o'er me, that the least sigh of yours
Can shake the universe from under me.
My Memnon is to me a world of joy;
He offends you, and vanishes for ever.

Ba. Oh! now I grieve.—   [*Aside.*

Be. What say you, do you grieve?

Ba. O'er-heard?—   [*Aside.*

Be. Oh! this is kind, now he shall go.

Enter MEMNON.

Ba. I see him. Oh! I tremble, burn and faint!
I cannot stay or go—   [*Aside.*

Be. See, see! I swear.
The very sight of him distempers her.
You shall not see him, love, away, away!
A thousand thanks for all this tender love.

     [*Exeunt Barzana, Oronte.*

Come hither, Memnon, thou wert once my all,
And still thou art a most dear part of me.
I tell thee this, 'cause I'm to lose thee soon,
And I wou'd make our parting soft to thee
Whate'er it is to me. I am compell'd
To banish thee for ever from my sight.

Me. Compell'd to banish me?—Alas, my Lord,
I fear my loyalty displeases you.
I have heard dreadful news about the King.
Oh! I have wept, and rav'd, and torn my hair,
And cursed my birth, now doubly infamous,
First by my mother's sin, and now by yours.

Be. You know not what you say, I had great aims.
I saw the Kingdom fall.

Me. Had Heaven fallen,

And you had done your duty, you had stood.

Be. 'Tis true I sallied out beyond my bounds,
But 'twas to serve the King.

Me. He serves him best
Who keeps his post.   Obedience was yours.

Be. No more of this ; if the King pardons me,
Sure you may do't.

Me. Oh! is the King so good?
And after that, can you forgive yourself?

Be. Have done!

Me. I shall—but let me do you first
What services I can ; and set you free
From all temptations you may have from me.
Perhaps you think a Crown may delight me?
Oh ! I wou'd rather have my head be cleft
In my King's service, than by treason crown'd.
Let but my sword command the spots of earth,
On which I fight to guard his Crown and life,
And nobler Fortune I will ne'er desire.
The Gods be prais'd, there I have lordships yet ;
And let us all preserve our loyalty,
Then our true glory lives, though our pomp dies,
For that is vanity ; now I have done.
I'll make but one request, then take my leave.

Be. What's that?

Me. To chuse the place of my exile.

Be. Where's that?

Me. In the fair arms of one I love.

Be. And who is she?

Me. I know not, wou'd I did.
It was my fate at the Cilician streights,
To give her liberty and lose my own.

Be. Didst thou make no enquiry of her name?

Me. I found her grac'd with all perfections,
And these I think are names enow for one.
They took up all my thoughts, and all my time ;
Which was not much, for soon we were pursu'd.

I was compell'd to face the enemy,
I had the honour of the victory,
But lost the best reward, the sight of her ;
For she was fled away ; and from that hour
I saw her not till now.

    Be. Where saw you her?
    Me. Here, in this Palace.
    Be. Here? My wife lives here—   [*Aside.*
When did you see her?
    Me. Not a minute past.
    Be. Oh ! how I tremble ! This must be my wife.
                            [*Aside.*
Was no one with her?
    Me. Yes, yourself, my Lord.
    Be. Infernal horrors!   [*Aside.*
    Me. Ha ! he is disturb'd.
    Be. Oh ! he has stab'd me, sleeping in my
      bed,
And waken'd me in Hell. Past all dispute
Her secret sorrow is a love for him.
I've been soliciting for my own shame.
'Tis so !—'tis so !— my son has whor'd my wife,
Has whor'd her in her soul, and that's enough.
I'll rip him up, and carry her his heart!
Hold ! he is innocent, and she may be.
Shall I skin o'er my wound, with that may be,
And probe no farther? No, 'twill fester then.
Oh ! better see her once in the foul act,
And so conclude my torment, and her sin,
Than see her hourly sinning in my thoughts.
    Me. My Lord, I fear I love not as I shou'd,
For I perceive it discomposes you,
Though you in tenderness conceal my fault.
Pray let me know it, I will freely part
With all the joys I have, to pleasure you.
    Be. Oh ! noble youth ! sure I am safe from him,
                            [*Aside.*

But not from my own thoughts; I cannot bear
Thorns in my bed,—if I have torment there
Where shall I rest? No, I must search it well.
No, son, I only doubt your good success.
Had you any encouragement?
    Me. I thought I had.
    Be. 'Tis done!—th' adultery's finish'd o' her
    part.   *[Aside.*
So is her life.—Memnon—you have my leave
To make this beauty yours be who she will.
    Me. My Lord, I never can requite this love,
Because you fight against yourself for me,
For I see great contention in your thoughts.
    Be. 'Tis over now; go in! you'll find her there.
                        [Exit Memnon.
Oh! Memnon, now I wish thy virtue strong.
For if you mingle smiles, you mingle blood.

As BESSUS *is stealing after* MEMNON, NABARZANES
                    enters.

    Na. My Lord, my Lord—
    Be. Who's that? I'm employ'd.
    Na. I've business for you that concerns your life.
    Be. I'm busied in concerns above my life.
    Na. Well, let 'em be of more concern than
    Heaven,
You shall abandon them, and go with me.
Patron, the Greek, has been among our troops,
Discovered our designs, and told the King.
    Be. Wou'd Patron were in Hell!
    Na. He shall be worse.
For, head your troops, he shall be in our power.
    Be. I'll come immediately.
    Na. Immediately?
What business have you here, but with your wife?
Do you prefer a kiss above a Crown,
And all the lives and fortunes of your friends?

Then I believe Patron had this from you,
And you have sold us all.
  Be. Who, I ?
  Na. Yes, you.
Your wife, and you ! the cause and the world sink,
I'll save myself.   Farewell !
  Be. Hold—hold—I go !
Oh ! you have wrong'd me.
  Na. Shew it in the field.
  Be. I will, but I shall perish—go or stay.
Stay, and the hangman's sword falls on my head.
Go, my wife's whor'd—[*aside*]—oh ! cursed, troubled
    world,
Where nothing without sorrow can be had,
And 'tis not easy to be good or bad.
For horror attends evil—sorrow good,
Vice plagues the mind, and virtue flesh and blood.
                                        [*Exeunt.*

ACT IV.

SCENE, *The Field.*

Enter DARIUS, ARTABASUS, PATRON, GUARDS.

  Ar. Oh ! have I sav'd villains to kill my King.
  Da. No more, no more, I know thy honest
    thoughts.
Oh ! my dear children, now a long farewell !
To all my glory now a long farewell !
Nay, oh ! my fate, I must for ruin fight ;
Cyrus and Alexander did not shew
More courage, to be lords o' the whole world,
Than I must do to have no share in it.
For if these villains perish by my sword,
I cut off all the army that I have.
And I, the once great Monarch of the world,

Shall want a cave, where I may hide my head.
But justice will be best for all mankind :
I'll shew that I deserve the world I lose.

Pa. I must entreat your leave for one word
    more.
Alas ! I sooner shall have leave from you
Than from myself ; for every word I speak,
That grieves your heart, stabs mine, yet I must
    speak ;
There's scarce a faithful man in all your camp.

Da. What dost thou say ? Are all the Persians
    false ?

Pa. They are as true to you as to themselves.
But as in danger they have always done,
So they do now, forsake you and themselves.

Da. Ha ! Do they join the traitors ?

Pa. Oh ! sir, no.
They join with nothing but confounding fear ;
And that they meet with wheresoe'er they go,—
Terrors beset them : Alexander comes,
And here the traitors boldly threaten them.
They who had any life in them are fled,
And they that stay are held by cowardice ;
They have not soul enough, even for flight.

Ar. He has told truth which I was loth to
    speak.
We may as well force men into a camp,
From sick and dying as from wanton beds:
From plagues as luxury, a flattering pest.

Da. Oh ! Alexander, where wou'd be thy fame,
Hadst thou my army ? Well may'st thou subdue
Kingdoms, by men who merit to be Kings ;
For mine do not deserve the name of men.

Pa. Sir, one word more, and then I shall have
    done.
Not far from hence, I have four thousand Greeks.
We march'd to Persia, fifty thousand men ;

Did ever Greek forsake you, but by death ?
Alas ! sir, now we cannot if we wou'd,
For in your service we have fought ourselves
Out of our blood, our country, and our friends.
There is no Bactria, no Greece for us,
Your Royal self is now our sole retreat;
We humbly beg, for all our services,
No greater honour than to be your guard.
 Ar. Sir, he desires an honour he deserves,
And what may be of mighty use to you.
His Greeks will be a bulwark to yourself
And all your men, give them new courage.
Sir, grant him his request.
 Da. Not for the world !
A glorious King shou'd ever more regard
The honourable counsels than the safe.
In my own camp be a poor fugitive ?
To my own nation a foreigner ?
To foreigners a little pensioner ?
Have no authority, but what they give ?
And so descend from being a Persian King,
To be a petty lord of a few Greeks.
The traitors then will·say they fight a Greek,
And I shall give them colour for their crimes.
No, I'll not fall by any fault of mine,
I'll not forsake my friends : if they quit me,
The fault's not mine ; and I had rather fall
By Royal charity to my own slaves,
Than reign, by stranger's charity to me.
Patron, a thousand thanks ! I will accept
The service of thy sword, but not this way.
Go to thy noble Greeks, and serve me there,
And Heaven reward thy love and gallantry.
 Pa. Heaven be your guard, I fear y'ave little else,
Besides what you shall ever find in me.
 Da. Thou honour of thy nation, shame to mine !
              [*Exit Pa.*

Now put my men in readiness to fight,
And then command the traitors to my feet.
If they dare disobey—fall on—   [*An alarm*.
How now ?
   Ar. What shou'd this mean ?   [*Exit Ar.*
   Da. They make the first assault.
Mychariot speedily !—the news—the news ?

Enter ARTABAZUS.

   Ar. Sir, the vanguard of Alexander's troops
Is in your camp.
   Da. Two enemies at once!
Thou fight the rebels, and I'll fight the King.
   [*Exeunt Darius, Artabasus: a great cry, alarm and
      disorder within, and*

Enter DARIUS *stopping the flying Persians.*

   Da. For shame! for shame, you cowards! quit
     your King,
And fly from sound ? this is a false alarm
The traitors made, by Alexander's name,
To frighten you from me.   Fly from his name!
How will you meet his sword ? but, by my life,
You shall encounter with his sword or mine.

Enter ARTABAZUS.

   Ar. Oh ! sir, a cheat ! a cheat !
   Da. I know it well.
How many of our men may be disperst ?
   Ar. Sir, almost all ; y'ave not a hundred left.
And now the traitors have surrounded you,
Have interpos'd between the Greeks and you,
And are in a great body drawing down.
   Da. Then it is time !
   [*The King offers to kill himself, but is held by Ar.*
   Ar. Hold, sir !
   Da. Now I reflect,

This crime belongs only to Regicides,
Why shou'd I take their guilt upon myself?
I ne'er yet stain'd my sword with innocent blood,
Why shou'd I do it in my dying hour?
    Ar. Oh! mournful hour! oh! wou'd you had
      receiv'd
The gallant offer of the noble Greek,
You had been safe as in a tower of steel.
    Da. Not from myself; it wou'd have stab'd my
      heart
To beg poor life from a few wand'ring Greeks.
Alas! from them I cou'd have had no more.
    Ar. No doubt the Persians wou'd have followed
      you.
    Da. I'm better follow'd now, and more secure.
I'm safe from the dishonour and the crime
Of quitting them, or doing anything
That may deserve my miserable fall.
The thought brings many comforts to my soul.
    Ar. A dreadful fall, indeed! how have I seen
A hundred nations follow you to wars!
Follow! adore you. Now your only guards
Are a few Eunuchs, and a weak old man.
And you, who oft have rode on golden Gods,
Are trod on now, by every little slave.
    Da. Oh! these are many darts, and they're all
      keen.
Yet did they only light upon myself,
My pain wou'd be no more, than if they fell
On a dead part; for in my Queen I'm dead!
But in my children and my friends I live:
Oh! there my sense is quick, my torments sharp.
Prithee, dear Artabasus, when I'm dead,
Go to my mother, children, all my friends,
And tell them how I fought, and how I mourn'd;
My courage, honour, and my love to them
Stuck to me [to] the last; but nothing else.

I give them cause to mourn, but not to blush.

Ar. Oh! sir, you rather give them cause of pride;
Men are admir'd, not prais'd for happiness.
Virtue's the lustre, pomp is but a shew:
That pleases Gods, This women, fools, and boys.
You conquer'd power, where Alexander falls,
And now in misery y'are glorious still;
But, Sir, wou'd you wou'd try if you cou'd 'scape.

Da. Ah! whither can I 'scape? to scornful life?
I wou'd not have it, were it in my power.
Then sure I wou'd not steal so poor a thing
And if I wou'd, now the attempt is vain
I shall be catch'd in the disgraceful theft.
No, here I will attend my destiny!
And now, good Artabasus, take thy leave.

Aa. How! leave you, Sir, in all this great distress?

Da. Alas! thy stay can do me little good:
'Twill rather hurt me much; encrease my grief.
If thou hast any pleasure in my sighs,
Continue with me; I have none in thine.
No, we afflict each other; prithee, go!
I love to have my friends share in my joys,
But wou'd have all my sorrows to myself,
And I can best contend with them alone.
For sorrow I perceive's love's solitude:
I prithee take not from me solitude.

Ar. I am not us'd, sir, to dispute your will,
But I shall never never see you more,
Or at least never till we meet in Heaven.
There is a Heaven, or there are no Gods.
Gods wou'd not suffer so much misery
In their poor creatures, but for some great end;
And all this world can never recompense
The sorrows of the least poor honest man.
What shall be done then for a martyr'd King?

Da. Nay, I confess I look, and long for death.

Come Artabasus, take my last embrace,
'Tis all I have to give thee for thy love.
  Ar. My King! my King!
  Da. My ever faithful friend.
Oh! thou art rooting deeper in my heart,
Tear thyself from me, or we cannot part.
  Ar. I have not strength to do't,
  Da. I cannot part—
Or see thee go—first let me veil my face,
And then betake to my last friend, the earth,
In whose cold bosom I shall rest secure;
No traitors will have plots upon me there.
Now, go!—

> [*The King flings his robe over his face, then falls on
> the ground.*

  Ar. Farewell for ever, Sir!   [*Exit.*
  Da. Farewell!
Go all—and as you go, plunder my tents!

> [*To the Eunuchs.*

Let not my bloody murderers be my heirs.
Better my gold pay your fidelity,
Than their base villany. Go—'tis enough.
Your faith and love have liv'd as long as I.

> [*As the Eunuchs go off, they set up a mournful
> cry, at which
>   BESSUS, NABARZANES, and DATAPHERNES, and
>   their GUARDS, rush in upon the King with
>   drawn swords.*

  Be. What means this cry?
  Na. Has the King kill'd himself?

> [*Darius rises.*

  Da. No, villains! I yet live to punish you,
And lash your crimes with crimes, your cowardly
Dissimulation, Hellish cruelty,
Ingratitude more horrid than them both,
By the most barbarous murder of your King.
  Be. Sir, in this noise and storm of passion,

It is in vain to utter peaceful sounds.
But time, that removes mountains, calms the sea,
Will calm and clear up all ; and you, who think
You have receiv'd unpardonable wrong,
Will ask us pardon for the wrong done us.

Da. Oh! insolence!

Na. Sir, you will find this truth.
Mean while we must go on in this foul way,
To find the fair.   There! Guards secure the King.

Da. D'e say secure me ; and yet call me King?
Oh ! rise in my revenge and aid, all Kings!
This is your common cause, I am a King.
Rise all mankind ! for all humanity
Is by these villains scorn'd, disgrac'd, and curst,
By what they do to me their most kind friend.
Nay, rise all Gods ! your power suffers in me
Your Minister, and a deputed God !
Your Justice suffers, I am innocent.

Be. Well, sir, we pray then spare the innocent !
Beat not yourself against the loyal force,
Which we have built to fortify your life.

Na. Yes, Sir, we mean your service, and we
     pray
Force us on no indecent violence.
We'll treat you honourably, if you please.

Da. Monsters of treachery and ingratitude !

             [*The King is led out by a Guard.*

Be. Ho ! Dataphernes !

Dat. I am here, my Lord.

Be. I trust the King to you—upon your life,
Keep a strong Guard !

Na. That will not be enough,
Let him be chain'd !

Be. It is not ill advis'd.
But, for the honour that we bear ourselves,
Let's honourably treat his dignity,
Since we ourselves design to be both Kings.

Then let us beat gold ingots into chains,
'Twill give a lustre to our black attempt.
                        [*Aside to Nabarzanes.*
Na. Th' attempt may appear black; our ends
    are fair.   .
Be. 'Tis true ; Sirs, you shall have an inheritance
In manly freedom ; your posterity
Shall all be born with titles to themselves.
Now, my brave friends, plunder the Royal tents !
                        [*Guards shout.*
Then let us face the Greeks and Persians,
And see what they will do.
Na. What dare they do ?
Destroy the King ? for if they stir, he dies.
Be. 'Tis true, but if they will our power obey,
We'll do such things shall give us right to sway :
The right, that only does from birth proceed,
In my esteem, springs from a bastard breed.
But virtue is the offspring of a God,
Virtue alone legitimates the blood.   [*Exeunt.*

SCENE, *The Palace.*

Enter BARZANA *and* ORONTE.

Ba. How ! chain his King ? Oh ! execrable
    wretch !
Now I perceive whence springs my horrid love.
'Tis an unnatural fire rain'd down from Heaven,
To burn a bloody traitor in his bed.
I wonder not it never cou'd be quench'd ;
I fasted, wept, and pray'd, yet found no cure ;
No safety even at the altars of the Gods ;
Love seiz'd me there, and very well it might :
It has, it seems, commission from the Gods.
    Or. Madam, no doubt you have conjectur'd
        right.

A dreadful storm hangs over your Lord's head !
So you, the part most tender, feel it first ;
For else I know you cou'd control your love.
But, oh ! it is no more within your power
Than the day is ; for the same reason too
'Tis hurried on by Heaven.

    Ba. I'm apt to think
All love is fate, the will and choice of Heaven
Compelling ours.   But fate, to conquer me,
Has in brave Memnon gather'd, for its aid,
All the perfections that can be in man.
Now, who can stand under so great a force ?
'Tis true, I know my temper is so firm,
Not all the love and excellence on earth
Can ever melt me down to one loose thought.
But yet the pain and sorrow of my love
Will throw me into the grave.

    Or. No, madam, no :
Your love will wear away by length of time.

    Ba. Oh, never ! Memnon's charms are powers
      Divine,
To punish the ill father by the son ;
And I must love whilst Heaven's anger lasts :
For ought I know, to all eternity.   [*Knocking.*
Knocking ? I'm overheard.   [*Oronte runs to the door.*

    Or. Lord Memnon's here.

    Ba. Undone ! undone !
Thou hast betray'd—betray'd me.

    Or. No, indeed.

    Ba. Thou hast, thou false, thou wicked, cruel
      wretch :
Not Heaven itself can make me happy now,
Except by falling on my cursed head.
Fall on me, Heaven ! sink beneath me, earth !
Anything swallow me, but infamy.
But I will stop its course, cost what it will.
Who is there ?

Enter a Woman.

Wo. Madam?

Ba. Run, and call your Lord.

Or. Hold, madam, hold,—oh! do not take our
lives,
Before you know our guilt.

Ba. Is it not plain?
Can he have innocent affairs with me?
Th' address alone is highly criminal:
It wou'd undo my honour, were it known.
Do Persian ladies that regard their fame,
Hold any secret intercourse with men?
No, no,—he comes to do his father wrong;
And has, it seems, a secret hope I'll yield.
Whence cou'd he have this hope, but from thyself?
Thou hast half cur'd my heart, I hate you both!
And I'm resolv'd, his father shall know all.

Or. Oh! madam, hold—indeed, I'm innocent.

Ba. What brings him hither then?

Or. I do not know.
Yet now I call to mind, perhaps my Lord
Has cast him off in compliment to you.
He said he wou'd, and now Lord Memnon's come
To beg your intercession.

Ba. That may be.
It is well thought; I'm griev'd I've censur'd him.
Now I will see him; but I am afraid
I shall be all confusion, and let fall
That port of honour I wou'd fain maintain.
Reach me a veil to guard my eyes and heart,
And cover my disorders what I can.
Now, call him in!,   [*She veils and seats her.*

ORONTE *brings in* MEMNON.

Or. Madam, my lord is here.

Ba. My Lord, I'm to your valour so oblig'd,

I'm in confusion with the sense of it.
I am now discompos'd ; and cannot give
Your visit the reception it deserves :
Pray, if you have any commands for me,
Express your will, that I may know my own.
For I shall serve myself, by serving you.

    Me. Here's more encouragement ! Good Gods
        be prais'd !   [*Aside.*
Madam, when fortune—Heavens ! how I shake—
                              [*Aside.*
When fortune gave me,—pray be not displeas'd—
The glory Kings wou'd purchase with their Crowns,
To save your honour, liberty, and life ;
She blest the universe, but ruin'd me,
By hopeless love for you.

    Ba. Oh ! thou false wretch !
        [*Ba. rises in anger, and flings off her veil.*
Nay, stir not ! trust my mercy you had best.
                              [*To Or.*
My Lord, I thought not to hear this from you,
So fam'd for every virtue as you are,
I sooner shou'd have fear'd the fall of Heaven ;
That I shall look for now,—nothing is strange !
And better Heaven fall, than innocence.
Therefore be gone ! and think of me no more,
Or else I will acquaint your father all.

    Me. Madam, 'tis done already ; ere I came
I told him all, and had his free consent.

    Ba. Oh ! horror ! now 'tis worse than I be-
        liev'd !   [*Aside.*
This traitress has inform'd my husband all,
And he, in rage, has flung me off to Hell.
Did he consent you shou'd address to me ?

    Me. No, madam, not to your fair self by name.
I do not know your name.

    Ba. Not know my name ?

    Me. No, madam, when I met you in the field,

Love and amazement took up all my sense,
Had I been told your name, I had not known.
The enemy and night then parted us ;
And a long night it was ; I saw no day
'Till here, this happy morning, I saw you.
I found my father, told him what befel.
He gave me a full grant to make you mine,
Be what you wou'd.
    Or. Now, madam, was I false ?
                    [*Aside to Barzana.*
    Ba. I am more wretched than I was before :
I have found treasure which I cannot keep.
The love of him I love is now my grief,
For I am forc'd to cast it all away.
I must discover to him who I am.
Alas ! my Lord, this love is but a dream,
Your heart receiv'd my image as it past ;
Remove the face, the shadow vanishes ;
Leave me, your love is gone !
Be't as it will,
All heaven and earth is plac'd between us two,
For, to be plain with you, I am a wife.
    Me. Madam, I will acknowledge a bold truth :
I sought you much, but guide I cou'd have none,
For you are far above description.
Chance brought me hither, when the wanton
    winds
Open'd the folding doors, and shew'd me you,
My soul retir'd in a religious awe,
But your enchanting words soon brought her
    back.
I heard your own inspiring love for me.
Madam, wou'd you do that, were you a wife ?
    Ba. Oh, I shall blush to death. [*Aside to Oronte.*
    Or. Good madam, why ?
He knows not who you are ; you did not say
You are his father's wife—   [*Aside.*

Ba. 'Tis very true—   [*Aside.*
What held my tongue ?   But, oh ! he knows too
    much,
He knows my love, more he shall never know.
I'd rather burn in any fire than shame.
I will get free, then like a vision,
I'll vanish hence, and never be heard of more.
        Me. Oh ! madam, I perceive you are disturb'd.
        Ba. Indeed, my Lord, y'ave given me great
    offence.
        Me. Alas ! I fear myself am the offence.
Why shou'd you be asham'd of innocent love
Unless you be asham'd of him you love ?
Oh ! is it so with me ?
        Ba. Y'ave made it now
Indecent to consider what you are ;
And if you have not, your ill father has.
Your wicked father has destroy'd your hopes.
        Me. Oh ! must I suffer for my father's faults ?
        Ba. And must I suffer for your father's faults ?
I am a Princess o' the Royal blood,
And, if I league with you, I cast away
My fortune, conscience, honour, nay, my life,
Nay, both shall die,—and by your father's hand.
        Me. Oh ! madam, I am sure that fear is vain.
Pray send for him ! I know he'll give consent.
        Ba. Oh ! horror—horror!
        Me. Madam, do not fear.
Run for my father!
        Ba. Will you murder me ?
All of the Royal race will seek my life,
If I be known to love your father's son.
        Me. Madam, we'll fly to the brave enemy.
        Ba. I fly away in secret with a man,
And with the son of the King's enemy ?
Shou'd my friends pardon me, yet I shou'd die
With shame, and horror.   And I'm much displeas'd

You shou'd embrace such shameful thoughts o' me,
And I even scorn you, for your loving me,
Since you believe I have no more desert.
  Me. Madam, your merit seems so great to me,
As gives a grace to everything you do.
You can do nothing will appear a fault.
Madam, I'll do such things to serve the King,
As will conceal the faults of my ill birth.
  Ba. You can do nothing ;   Nature binds your
  hands.
Will you destroy your father ? horrid thought !
Yet if you do not, he destroys the King.
That Hell surrounds you ; 'tis impossible
To come at you, but through all misery.
And why should you desire such ill to me ?
Then go ! if you'd preserve my love or life,
Your stay will but incur my mortal hate,
Nay, perhaps bring my blood upon your head.
  Me. The Gods forbid, I'll rather sink to Hell.
  Ba. Then go ! whilst I have one kind thought of
  you,
And my kind thoughts are all you shall enjoy.
  Me. All this I fear'd, expected, almost wish'd,
So much I tender you above myself,
For my ill father's son must look for plagues ;
They are my birthright, and inheritance,
And I shou'd be most cruel and unjust,
If I shou'd seek to fix them upon you.
No, madam, fly our cursed house, and me !
Your generous loyalty I praise and love,
Though 'tis the sword of Heaven to cut me off.
Well, madam, I will take myself away :
Nay, more, I beg you'll throw me from your
  thoughts,
That I may ne'er be trouble to you more.
  Ba. Now he goes nearer to my heart than ever.
                                              [*Aside.*

'Tis dangerous to see or hear him more ;
And cruelty to send him bleeding hence,
Without some balm.—My lord, I were unjust
To love you least when you deserve it most.
No, no, you ever shall possess my thoughts ;
And Heaven that made me has no more of me.

    Me. Oh ! madam, many thousand thousand
      thanks
For this compassion ; though 'twill be no more
Than a fair monument o'er a dead wretch.

    Ba. Oh ! I have held my violent grief till now,
To make our parting easy as I cou'd.
But now I've lost all power o'er myself,
And if you longer stay I shall fall dead.
Go, if y'ave pity for yourself, or me.

    Me. I go—I go—and now can easier go.
Your kind tears comfort me—oh ! wretched me !
The grief of her I love is all my joy.
And now a long farewell !—my love was born
In a most fatal field, in death's dark shades,
And it will ne'er have health till it repair
To death again ; its mournful native air.—   [*Exit.*

    Ba. He's gone ! And I shall never see him
      more.
I must not, will not, dare not see him more.
I'll fly if possible all thoughts of him ;
All knowledge of myself—poor womankind—
Heaven, for our ruin, gifts on us bestows,
Charms to allure, no power to oppose.
In passion we are strong, in reason weak,
Constant alone to error and mistake.
In virtue feign'd, in vanity sincere ;
Witty in sin, and for damnation fair.

                  [*Exeunt omnes.*

ACT V.

SCENE, *A Garden.*

Enter MEMNON.

Me. Oh ! I am blasted in my bloom of youth !
I am more miserable for my youth.
For the more years and life I have to come,
The larger fields of misery and shame,
Has my unhappy father sowed for me.
Well—I will trouble nothing but myself.
I'll wander from my friends, my fortunes, hopes—
Then, like a plummet parted from the line,
I will sink down in deep obscurity,
Where never more shall trace be found o' me.
Ha !—oh! my heart ! the Princess comes this
    way,

Enter BARZANA *and* ORONTE.

Comes like a sudden spring on my dead hopes,
And forces them, methinks, into new life.
Something, methinks, from Heaven stops my
    way,
And tells me, she and I must never part.
· *Ba.* Where is the chariot ?
Or. At the garden gate.
Ba. Come then away—Oh ! heavens ! Memnon
    here ?
Turn from him quickly.
Me. Hold, dear madam, hold.
Ba. My Lord, what mean you ?   Thirst you for
    my blood ?
Me. Oh ! madam, do not entertain those fears.
Ba. Do not you entertain false dangerous hopes.
Your father has this minute left the field.

Me. But not his love to me.

Ba. You'll find him quit
His love to you, and all humanity,
If he shou'd catch you seeking leagues with me.
I fear he's at the Palace window now;
Oh! if he be, this minute is our last.

Me. These are vain terrors; oh! wou'd he were
here
This minute were the last of all our griefs,
But oh! the first of our immortal joys.
And something in me says, it will be so;
Methinks I have a sight of paradise.

Ba. Oh! you speak oracles,—methinks in you
A voice from Heaven has prophesied our death.
The pangs of death already seize my heart,
I tremble, sweat, and I've scarce breath to speak.
Know there is yet another stronger cause,
Than any I have nam'd, why we must part.

Me. Another cause?

Ba. Oh! do not enquire what,
If you take any joy in loving me.
For when I've told you, you must love no more,
If you have any tenderness for me;
When I have told you, I shall speak no more,
The secret will tear out my heart—Oh! fly,
If you wou'd love, or live, or have me live.

Me. Y'ave stunn'd me so, I have no strength to
stir.

Ba. Oh! he will loiter till his father comes,
The Gods will bate my passion no disgrace.
Know, I'm a wife! nay, more, your father's wife.
He faints, he faints!—now shou'd his father come,
And find him in my arms?—
　　　　[*Me. faints, Ba. runs to him and supports him.*
Or. Madam, he's come!

Ba. Oh! horror! we are lost!—my Lord, my
Lord!

Enter BESSUS, *who seeing Memnon in Barzana's arms,
draws. Memnon recovers, Barzana runs to hold
Bessus.*

Be. Oh ! Villain.

Ba. Oh ! my lord,

Be. Oh ! impudent

And foolish whore ! wilt thou proclaim thy
shame,

And murder him, thou hast a mind to save ?

Had he a thousand lives, now he shou'd die.

Ba. Oh ! hear me first.

Be. Hear thee encrease thy sins,

By falsehood ? Is not incest crime enough ?

I saw you from the Palace, meet, caress.

And is not this your second meeting ? ha !

I will provide for you a third meeting place,

In death and Hell,—thou frightful monster,—die !

     [Wounds Me., who falls.

Ba. Unnatural parricide ! dire Regicide !

Be. The fitter match for an incestuous wife.

Me. My Lord, you wrong us ; we are innocent.

I lov'd,—but knew her not,—she banish'd me,—

I was now going to obey her doom,

When Heaven contriv'd this meeting for our death ;

We sought it not,—for ever to prevent

All future meetings, she reveal'd herself.

Then did I sink to death, under surprise,

And horror, for my faulty unfortunate love ;

Which is more trouble to me, than this death.

Oh ! I had rather have a thousand deaths

Got by misfortune, than your ill-got Crown. *[Dies.*

Ba. Oh ! he has told the truth,—thou murderer.

He was too excellent ! for all the Gods

Thought him a God, and took him to themselves.

And I will follow him ; yes I will do't,

And we will revel to eternity ;

And it shall be chiefest of our joys
To be the chief of thy eternal plagues.
    Be. A damp goes to my heart! I am afraid
I've been too rash : I wish this were undone.
Come, take her to my chariot!
    Ba. Touch me not!
The Gods be prais'd I've found my dagger now.
I'll go another way.
    Be. Sh'as stab'd herself.
Call help—I'll have her live if possible.
    Ba. I have help here.
    Be. Horror! she tears her wound.
Hold—hold—her hands.
    Ba. Then I will hold my breath.
    Be. Is this thy virtue? Thou, who canst commit
This most unnatural sin against thyself
Wou'dst not refuse thyself a sweeter crime?
    Ba. Indeed, I'm sorry for this sinful death;
I wou'd shun Hell, if only to shun thee.
Hell, purg'd by fire, has less offence than thou.
    Be. Oh! thou art most ungrateful to my love,
I have more love for thee than words can speak.
    Ba. I am glad of it! then 'twill be thy plague,
And to encrease it, know I'm innocent,
So was thy noble son ; he sought my love,
But knew me not, for I conceal'd myself,
'Cause he had found my secret love for him,
And then I cou'd not show my blushing face.
    Be. You lov'd him then it seems?—
    Ba. That I confess,
I lov'd him, but it was ere I was thine ;
Since that I did subdue myself for thee,
Reveal'd myself, and banish'd him for ever.
And he was taking his eternal leave,
When thou, oh! murderer! took'st his innocent
    life.
    Be. If this be true.—

Ba. 'Tis true ; they're my last words.
All my past life is evidence enough,
And so is that of thy most excellent son,
For had he any other fault but thee,
And I had less, my birth was glorious.
Yet has my life honour'd my Royal birth,
And now I hope my death will crown my life.
It has some sin which you, good Gods, forgive !
Your justice has had honour by my fall.
Oh ! honour now the virtuous part of me,—
My soul—you know I never sin'd in will ;
Only in blood, and that foul blood I spill. [*Dies.*
Be. Oh ! horror ! horror ;

Enter NABARZANES.

Na. How now ? why this rage ?
Be. Look there !
Na. Your belov'd son and wife in blood ?
Amazing ! how came this ?
Be. No matter how.
They're dead, and I am curs'd, nay, I am forc'd
To curse the virtues of my son and wife :
The world's great blessings were my miseries.
Na. I'm glad o' this ; they did divide your
      soul,
And cut the stream into small rivulets,
It cou'd not bear the burdens o' the State.
Now 'twill be all united in the Crown.

Enter DATAPHERNES.

Dat. My Lord, the enemy, the enemy !
Be. What enemy ?
Dat. The Macedonians,
And Alexander.
Be. Alexander ? ha !
Na. How do you know ?
Dat. We had it from our scouts.

But go upon the mountains, you may see
The spirit of that Monarch in his march.
He wings along the air in clouds of dust,
And does not march, but fly.

Be. Bring out the King!

Na. Ha! what to do?

Be. What else, but take his life?
I will not die in compliment to him;
Spare him a Guard, when we want men ourselves?
I've bath'd my sinews in my son's hot blood;
Now they are strong enough for any thing.

Na. Hold—hold—you are too hot! let him alone.
If we shou'd barbarously butcher him,
The crime will have such a grim ghastly face,
The basest Persian cowards will be scar'd
Out of their natures into something brave.
Cowards oft by flying, into valour fly.
Our friends will leave us, and our enemies
Fly in our faces.

Be. True, what shall we do?

Na. Tempt him to yield.

Be. I know he scorns to do't.

Na. We will deceive him by feign'd penitence.

Be. I do not find him easily deceiv'd.

Na. Let's make a trial! if he'll not be gain'd,
We'll murder him unknown to any one,
Besides ourselves, and then give out he yields,
And what we do is by his own command.

Be. 'Tis well advis'd,—draw up our troops with
  speed! .   [*To Data.*
And then give out the King and we are friends.
                              [*Exeunt.*

SCENE, *A Prison.*

Enter King in chains of gold.

Da. A King! a Persian King, chain'd by his
  slaves?

The slaves he once so favour'd and so lov'd ?
Oh ! the amazing villanies of men,
And stupifying patience of the Gods !
The gracious Gods seem only infinite,
In suffering ill, and man [in] doing it.
Man therefore is most fear'd, and most obey'd.
My murderers come ! my griefs are near their
    end.

    Enter BESSUS *and* NABARZANES.

   Na. Now if these chains weigh the King's spirit
    down
To our desires, we shall be legal rogues.   [*Aside.*
   Be. What is it spirits me away to fear ?
He's in my chains, yet I am in his power.
   Na. I find it so with me ; I've fought my way
Through bravest men, why am I fear'd by dreams ?
Let's kneel, and speak to him !
   Be. Well, do you speak :
I am an ill dissembler.
   Na. Royal sir—   [*Kneels.*
We humbly beg you, lend a gracious ear
To your poor slaves, by your hard fortune thrown
On th' only things we fear ; on infamy,
Your anger, and a seeming horrid crime ;
Though what we did was all in loyalty.
   Be. 'Tis true ! we saw Fate quarrel with you,
    Sir,
And so we came between to part the fray.
   Da. Oh ! you poor wretches, how I pity you !
Cou'd you have fallen thus miserably in fight,
There you had been the envy of the brave.
Now y'are the scorn of all. As to myself,
Y'ave given me endless rest. The greatest weight
Hangs on these chains is your ingratitude.
Oh ! how have I deserv'd all this from you ?
   Be. You have deserv'd no ill, and shall have none.

Ba. Indeed I do not know the man I've
    wrong'd;
Bring him, I'll give him power to take my life.
If I've offended, 'twas against myself:
In all my kingdom, I was the sole slave.
I toil'd the most, and most observ'd the laws.
The great prerogative, I most desir'd,
Was to be uncontrol'd in doing good.
If I gave fear, it was to potent Kings.
I was in danger most, in pleasure least.
My luxury lay all in my fair Queen:
My sole intemperance was my love to her —
My love and grief for her admit no bounds.
And oh! how have I lov'd and favour'd you?
I gave you Kingdoms, and with greater joy
Than you receiv'd them—oh! methoughts, I gain'd
What I gave you, and these are my rewards:
You murder me, who wou'd have died for you.
Alas! It is your fault I am not dead.

Na. Indeed we mean you good; and do no more
Than what priests in devotion do to Gods,
Who fasten them from falling, or [from] flight.
We fear'd your flight to mercenary Greeks,
Or falling into Macedonian power.
And, Sir, to shew how much we honour you,
We have given shining pomp to misery,
Since 'tis become a waiter on our King.

Be. And if you'll pardon us, and favour us,
We'll make you greater than you ever were.

Da. I favour treason? I assume your guilt?
I'll rather bravely die than basely reign.
Indeed my children are most dear to me,
But, for that cause, I will not taint their blood,
And make the children of a King become
The children of a traitor to a King.
I can, and will be great without your help.
Yes, in these chains, I'll triumph over you;

I will reign o'er you when y'ave murder'd me ;
In my grave punish you.   All Kings and Gods
Will be the ministers of my revenge,
And execute whate'er my blood commands.
   Na. We lose our time—come, strike !
   Be. I will, and home.
                    [They wound Darius, who falls.
   Na. So, this is a great work ; but common spirits
Have not reception for things great and high.
Let us not trust them with this spectacle.
Ho ! guard !

Enter a GUARD.

   Gu. My lord ?
   Na. The King has kill'd himself.
We fear false tongues will lay his blood to us,
Therefore conceal his death, till the fight's past,
As you regard your lives.   In the meanwhile,
Cover the body in a waggon close,
That it may pass for baggage ; drive it then
Into some private place, out of all roads,
And kill the horses, lest they wander thence.
              [Guard carry out Darius.
   Be. Now, let us to the field ! for there's our
      doom,
Our innocence, or treason is to come.
It is success makes innocence a sin ;
And there is nothing but a sword between.
If th' end be glorious, glorious is the way ;
They always have the Cause, who have the day.

SCENE, *A field.*

A noise of a battle.   After shouts, Enter ARTABA-
   ZUS, PATRON *and* GREEKS, *dragging* BESSUS
   and NABARZANES.

   Pa. Oh ! thank you, for this justice, you good
      Gods.

Ar. Go to King Alexander ; let him know
The Gods have given the traitors to our swords.
Let us enjoy revenge for our King's blood,
And then he shall command our swords and lives.
  Pa. Oh ! that the King enjoy'd it ! where have
    you
Conceal'd his body, you damn'd regicides ?

Enter PERSIANS.

  Per. My Lord, my Lord ! the King—
  Ar. What of the King ?
  Per. He's found ! a Macedonian officer,
By help of Persian guides, searching a spring
To quench his thirst, after the heat of fight ;
He in the woods saw a poor waggon stray,
Drawn by faint dying horses stuck with darts,
And looking in it, found a dying man
Gor'd in his blood ; which prov'd to be our King.
  Ar. Horror ! he lives !—let us away, away !
That he may see revenge before he dies.
  Pa. And we will weigh him out exact revenge.
Here chain, and cut them as they did their King !
[*Exeunt.*

The Scene is drawn, a Waggon appears. The horses
    bloody, and full of darts, some falling, others
    fallen. POLYSTRATUS *and* PERSIANS *support*
    DARIUS, *who is bloody and faint.*

  Pol. Run, run for help, while we will bind his
    wounds.
  Da. Ha ! who art thou ?
  Pol. A Macedonian, Sir.
  Da. My enemy so kind ?
  Pol. A gallant man
Fights out of love to duty and renown ;
And loves and honours a brave enemy.
  Da. What is thy name ?
  Pol. 'Tis Polystratus, Sir.

Da. Brave man! more kind to me than my
friends are.
These were the presents of my once dear friends,
Bessus and Nabarzanes.
Pol. Hellish dogs.
Da. 'Tis no small comfort in my wretched state,
My grateful dying thoughts will not be lost.
Tell thy brave King I die deep in his debt :
I never once oblig'd him in the least, ·
And he has nobly treated all my friends,
My mother, brother, children, my fair Queen. ·
Granted their lives, and Royal splendour too,
They scarce cou'd tell they were unfortunate,
When my near kindred, and once bosom friends,
On whom I life and Kingdoms have bestow'd,
Have plunder'd me of all. Oh ! tell thy King,
I beg the Gods, for universal good,
To make him Monarch o' the universe.
And for the common cause of all crown'd heads,
I challenge the revenge due to my blood.
Pol. Sir, it will be reveng'd ; your murderers
Are in the hands of your most faithful slaves.
Da. I'm glad on't ; for the sake of all mankind.
Pity the sea has bounds, if sin has none,
Better men sunk in sea, than villany.
I'm faint, and thirsty ; I but lately saw
Some drinking at a spring, not far from hence.
A little water wou'd refresh me much.
Pol. Sir, it was I ! you shall have some with
speed.
[*Pol. fetches the King water in his helmet, the
King drinks.*
Da. How vainly do we pity poverty !
The Gods sit at the table o' the poor,
And turn their water to delicious wine.
Never had I, in pompous luxury,
Such pleasure as this draught o' water yields.

But fortune does pursue me to the last :
I'm forc'd to beg even water for my thirst,
And, though a King, I cannot pay for it.
But Alexander will ;—give me thy hand !
Prithee for me touch Alexander's hand :
The sole remaining pledge I have to give
For all my grateful love to that brave Prince.

          [*Dies.*

Pol. He's gone ! he's gone ! and it is well he's so.
Oh ! wretchèd Prince, whose happiness is death.
Let's bear the sacred body to our King ;
For he will give it Royal funerals.

      [*Exit Poly. and Persians with the body.*

Enter another way, ARTABAZUS, PATRON, PERSIANS,
  GREEKS ; *with* BESSUS *and* NABARZANES
  chain'd and wounded.

 Per. Here is the spring ! the King's not far from
  hence.
 Ar. Oh ! no—for see the ground all stain'd
  with blood !
And no doubt Royal blood. Let us pursue
The dreadful track, 'twill bring us to the King,
 Pa. 'Twill bring these villains to damnation.

     Enter a PERSIAN.

 2 *Per.* My lord, I met the Macedonians
With the King's body, and the King is dead.
 Ar. Oh ! Prince, the best, and yet most wrong'd
  of men.
What joy and glory did he not deserve,
And yet what misery did he not endure ?
And now denied the comfort of revenge.
 Pa. Perhaps he may enjoy it after death.
Oh Royal shade ! if yet thou be'st not fled
To blest abodes, bear this detested place
But while we entertain thee with Revenge.

Drink sweet Revenge, till thy great sorrows sleep,
Then thou, and all good things, fly hence for ever.
Here take these monsters, torture 'em to death.
Ha! pleasing harmony! hear you it not?
[Soft music.
Ar. Yes, with great admiration; for methinks
This is no time or place for such delight.
Pa. A sense of the King's murder seems imprest
On beasts and plants, and everything but those
Who threw at once their King and nature off.
Lions came roaring from their caves, then died.
The cedars groan'd, then fell. Th' earth deeply tore
Her bowels, and then wept a bloody spring.
Straight all the plants and flowers droop'd, and died,
They must be most unnatural villains then,
That now find pleasure, but none such are near.

Enter a PERSIAN.

Per. My lord, the traitors are in torments dead.

> [*The Scene is drawn, and the carcases of* BESSUS
> *and* NABARZANES *are seen, hung in chains,
> and stuck with darts, a Guard attending.
> At another part o' the stage, is seen the Ghost
> of* DARIUS *brightly habited.*

Pa. Oh! now I see the cause of these Divine
Miraculous sounds; I see the King! the King
More lively than he ever was in's life,
More pompous than in all his Royal pomp.
Ar. I see him,—and my spirit, rais'd with joy,
Ascends to meet him,—happy vision!
Virtue triumphing over villany.
Pa. The Royal shadow smiles and points to them.
Ar. This is the difference 'tween the good and
bad.
Death shews it truly, Life is a false light,
But the true diamond appears by night. [*Exeunt.*

EPILOGUE.

Spoke by her that acts Barzana.

Our poet fears he too much blood has shed,
So I am come to shew I am not dead.
My part will all the wanton Masks displease ;
That's half the pit, and all the galleries.
Rather than take into my breast a fair,
And brave young lover, thrust a dagger there !
You put your bosoms to another use,
'Tis a vile Pagan custom I produce ;
Pagans may rather die, than be debauch'd,
Good Christians sin, to be well kept and coach'd.
Besides, to kill myself for love, I fear
Will to you sparks improbable appear,
Who in side boxes daily crowd, and there
Plant all your murdering shot against the fair,
Four tier of beaux, o'er one another plac'd,
And each one hopes to kill a box at least.
And yet with all this terrible design,
Sink not one heart, only the playhouse coin.
How you look down with scorn on a pit beau !
The wretch into his grave does living go.
The Lord may have some mercy on his ghost,
But as for his poor body, that's quite lost.
Now our side boxes are a Smithfield grown,
Where town and country nags for sale are shown :
Where any lady may her humour fit,
With a tall palfry, or a little tit.
And yet I do not hear the ladies buy ;
Nay, sirs, they towards you hardly cast an eye.
The ladies nobly pay the house their due,
Why shou'd they give four shillings to see you ?
Not all your faces are worth half the sum,

Get flags and trumpets, and try who will come.
The images of virtue, we have shewn,
We know will please you heroes o' the town,
And heroines, because they are your own.
In gallant faithful Patron, and my dear
Lov'd Memnon, you brave men of arms appear.
The ladies in Barzana, see your face,
Of their fair minds, but in no flattering glass.
All love to see themselves ; the foul will stare
In glasses, though they meet with goblings there.
But all the little hopping fluttering sparks,
You catch with glasses, as you do the larks.
Place a fair glass directly in the eye
Of a young beau, he never can pass by.
Young soldiers discipline their graces there,
Face to the right ! the left ! then, as you were !
   [*She combs first o'er the right shoulder, then o'er
      the left, then sets her cravat strings.*
We pray all daily to this glass repair.

TURNBULL AND SPEARS, PRINTERS, EDINBURGH.